NINE LOVE LETTERS

NINE LOVE LETTERS

GERALD JACOBS

QUARTET

First published in 2016 by Quartet Books Limited
A member of the Namara Group
27 Goodge Street, London W1T 2LD
Copyright © Gerald Jacobs 2016
The right of Gerald Jacobs
to be identified as the author of this work
has been asserted by him in accordance with the
Copyright, Designs and Patents Act, 1988.

ISBN 978 0 7043 7 4225

Typeset by Josh Bryson
Printed and bound in Great Britain by
T J International Ltd, Padstow, Cornwall

Who would not sing for Lycidas? he knew
Himself to sing, and build the lofty rhyme

John Milton

1

3 June 1941
Baghdad, Iraq
Rivke Haroun to Yusuf Haroun

Yusuf, my precious son,

These past days have brought home to me what a priceless gift it is to have a son—to have you, always my devoted, loving and clever child. I thank the Almighty that you are far away from the hatred and devastation we have seen so recently in this city in which our family has lived for generations. It is impossible to measure my sadness.

Today is the funeral of cousin Sarai, such a poor, quiet and helpless girl who had the misfortune to be in the street when the horror began. The family, especially her parents and brothers (including of course Izaak, your dear friend), are reeling from grief.

Everyone is agreed we must make plans to leave. But your father, who as you know has been unwell, cannot bring himself to stir from this house, where he and his brothers and his sister grew up and where all their memories belong. And our Muslim neighbours—the Al Mukhtar family, Mrs Habash and others—have been begging us not to go. I hug these kind ladies and we weep together.

Yet after such violence and destruction around us (many homes were destroyed though ours suffered only a small amount of damage, thank God) you and I must persuade your father to come away, even with a heavy heart. They say that hundreds of Jews were killed and many more attacked and wounded over the last two or three days.

Even your uncle Fouad is urging us to go to Palestine. But your father will not listen. He says that would be to 'surrender' and that things are even worse there. Your aunt Yocheved is also reluctant to leave. With the world so threatened by the forces of

1

war, of evil, nowhere is safe she says. She thinks it will be easiest to manage here in Iraq.

But I dearly long to be near you my son and, the Almighty willing, see you and your lovely bride Farah have children and bring them up in a happier time and place. And that cannot be in Baghdad the way it is now. You must stay where you are in London. I know that our cousins Azi and Miriam are so happy to have you both with them. Please send them my love. We hear they have become very British, very polite and knowing how to use all their knives and forks properly. It is even said that Azi is joining the British army. Can this be true?

We also hear of difficult times for people in London. But the British are brave and united against the Germans. They do not fight each other as they are doing now in Baghdad. I do worry about you, though I know that you are staying on the outskirts of London, away from the bombing in the centre that we have heard about. Please be careful and look after Farah. Keep away from the areas of danger. This will pass. The British are honest and strong people. They will not let Adolf Hitler win.

Whatever happens, you must not come back here. You must not bring Farah back here. It is no longer safe, no longer home. Please, let my future grandchildren grow with the view of a fresh horizon. I have always dreamed of England. I pray we can be together there one day. I pray to God its soldiers will win their war against Germany and you will do well in Uncle Azi's business and not have to struggle like your sisters' husbands have had to in America. As it happens, a message came from Rachel yesterday to check that we were unharmed. She is trying to persuade us to join them in New York. Your father, your beloved, stubborn Baba—he who had such grand ideas of America—barely even shrugged at the idea. It is too difficult to travel now, he says.

Somehow you must help me get Baba to move. He has become an old man overnight. All he does is sit in his chair eating dates and drinking coffee. He hates to see me weeping and turns his head away. The only thing that makes his eyes light up is the mention of your name. The only word he responds to is 'Yusuf'. You are the hope for our family now.

All the time, I pray to God. This helps to stop my heart from breaking. And I can close my eyes and think of your wedding, still so fresh, how you smiled and how you looked at your bride and danced and made me so happy. My little Yusuf, the boy I had to carry to other children's parties because you were so timid. Standing tall and handsome beside your beautiful cousin Farah in the same synagogue where you were bar mitzvah. It all seems like yesterday.

May the Almighty One bring us all together soon and shine His light upon you. I send you my deepest love my wonderful son.

Your adoring Ummi

It was in 1878 that Moss Haroun, a newly-married Jewish carpet trader, opened a small shop in Baghdad, the city of his birth and of his ancestors. Having inherited a large, solid and secure house built by his father, Moss took advantage of the growing commercial opportunities under Ottoman rule to set up a textile business in an old, damp-walled building within sight of the hallowed River Tigris.

Two years later, Moss Haroun's first child, a son named Sami Ben-Moshe Haroun, was born, and so the succession was established to the ownership of what was already a thriving business. Sami proved to be a quiet, serious and intelligent child, attentive to his school lessons, respectful to his parents and especially devoted to his father. The fact that, as the eldest son, he would take over the family business in the fullness of time was never questioned. Sami accepted it as part of the natural order of things. Indeed, from a very young age, he was eager to help his father in the shop and took every opportunity to do so. He worked diligently and, by the age of nineteen, was devoting himself to working alongside his father to the exclusion of all else, including marriage.

Almost alone among the local Jewish boys of his age, Sami Haroun appeared uninterested in looking for a bride. If he thought about the possibility, he would become anxious and immediately put it out of his mind and throw himself into his work. By contrast, Sami's two younger brothers, Reuben and Fouad, would frequently claim to have lost their hearts under the spell of even the faintest of female smiles.

This was, however, one of the few similarities between the two younger brothers. In most other ways, they were very different. Fouad, the youngest, was shy and withdrawn, Reuben was outgoing and irrepressibly dramatic. At seventeen, he struck the mournful pose of a romantic lover worshipping his cruel, imaginary mistress from afar. He dressed in extravagant, flowing robes and liked to cover his head with a red felt fez. He composed long, idealistic verses about perfect, unattainable love—'that teasing hint of heaven', as he called it.

The contrast in character and temperament was even greater between Reuben and Sami. Nevertheless, before showing or reading his verses to anyone else, Reuben would first seek Sami's opinion. Reuben regarded his older brother as a shrewd and guiding influence. And Sami was indeed shrewd; he realised that Reuben's emphasis on the unattainable nature of love indicated that he dreamed not of the earthy, fleshly and fragrant maidens of Baghdad but of something more elusive, and possibly forbidden.

Sami himself took silent pleasure in the dark, expressive eyes and soft, olive skin of the Baghdadi-Jewish girls, in the warmth of their laughter, and in the determinedly fashionable way they dressed, in contrast to their mothers, whose wardrobe was much like that of the local Muslim women.

Unlike Reuben, and despite his anxious nature, Sami had confidence in the attainability of love and was happy to be patient. His family would gently mock him for his diffidence but also express concern, especially during Moss Haroun's last illness, when Sami was first called upon to take charge of the shop, a responsibility he assumed both dutifully and effectively.

His mother Rachel's concern was the most vocal. 'Sami, what's the matter with you,' she would regularly demand in her rapid, high-pitched way of speaking. 'Are you never going to show an interest in becoming a husband?' One evening, she asked him pointedly: 'You don't like girls?' And then, in an unusually nervous tone: 'You are not telling me you are one of those boys who… you know…' and she shrugged before continuing in a lower register, 'look at other boys' faces, smile at boys instead of girls?'

Sami laughed quietly and shook his head.

'You laugh,' his mother said, her voice resuming its higher, forthright tone, her manner remonstrative. 'You don't care if you break my heart? How do you think I would feel if my big firstborn son turns out to be a boy fairy? Against the commandments! A sin! Nobody would talk to us. So tell me I have nothing to worry about.'

'Ummi, you have nothing to worry about,' Sami echoed, smiling, and, after a pause to allow his smile to fade, added: 'From me at least.'

Rachel rejoined without a pause: 'Nothing to worry about, he tells me. Look at you. You're wearing yourself out. You are a fine one to advise about not worrying. Of all the Jewish boys in Baghdad, you must be the one who has taken on the duty of chief worrier. You spend all day and night worrying. You take on too much. There's no need. You should not let that shop take over your life completely. Your little brothers—two fine boys—are helping you now that your poor father is not well. You don't have to take it all on yourself and get into such a state that you forget about finding yourself a nice bride. I'm not the only one; Baba is also worried.'

Having reminded Sami of the shame he could bring upon his family if he persisted in his single-minded, celibate existence, his mother tried a more mollifying approach. 'There are many Baghdadi-Jewish girls you could marry,' she said. 'Many parents I know would grab the chance of marrying off their daughters to a young Jewish man like you, in charge of a good business, doing well when others are not.'

But whenever Rachel uttered these sentiments a note of impatience would always break in: 'What's the point of making money,' she would ask, throwing up her hands in an expressive shrug, 'if you don't also make a family to spend it on?'

'Ummi, I understand and value what you are saying but there is plenty of time to think about marrying,' Sami gently protested. 'I need to get the business running properly before anything else, especially now that it is my responsibility. If there are so many nice Baghdadi-Jewish girls now, there will be more in a few years' time.'

'Ah,' his mother—who had a warm heart but little perception when it came to her sons—responded with a nod and a sigh: 'Let us hope so.' And then, in a tone and gesture at once both conciliatory and self-pitying: 'You always were the quiet one.'

Moss Haroun fell ill in the summer of 1901, which was when his eldest son Sami took on full responsibility for the shop that bore the simple sign 'Haroun' above its entrance. Sami was then not yet twenty-one. After a few weeks, it became clear that his father was suffering from consumption and would never be able to return to the business.

Sami had tried to convince his father, and especially himself, that Moss's absence was temporary, that he would recover. Sami either refused to admit the seriousness of his father's illness, or pretended to himself and his family that Moss could be persuaded to accompany him to the shop occasionally, as a prelude to a permanent return.

And then, one evening at home, when Sami offered his hand to help Moss rise from his favourite armchair—which had formerly belonged to Moss's own father—Sami suddenly realised how thin his father had become. He found that he was able, with just one hand, to encircle his father's upper arm, and feel bone rather than flesh.

Having always felt able to depend on Moss, whose wisdom and love had shaped him, Sami was now frightened by the implications of his father's descent into weakness. He reacted by dealing industriously with his expanded workload at the shop and this became a solitary yet powerful distraction from his mounting sadness.

Every day, when Sami returned home exhausted, and hoping that he hadn't made any harmful mistakes during his hard day's work, he would sit with Moss and, over a glass of tea, tell him how the day had gone. They would talk about whether or not the supplies were being delivered on time, how many people had come in, how many had bought something—and about any unusual or unfamiliar customers.

'Today, we had two American visitors,' he was able to report one evening. This was when Moss could still sit up in his armchair. 'A husband and wife, from New York,' Sami explained.

'Did they buy anything?'

'No, sadly.'

'You couldn't sell something to rich Americans?'

'I don't know if they were rich,' Sami said.

'Of course they were rich. They were Americans. And you had them in the shop.'

'We had a very interesting discussion about the new moving picture industry in America.'

'And what do you know about such things?'

'I have read about it. It is a very big new business in America.'

'So big that these grand Americans cannot buy one item from the shop?' And then, lest his beloved son should think that he was angry with him, Moss Haroun smiled and put forward a lean, bony hand to touch Sami's cheek.

Less than two weeks after this exchange, and one week after his fiftieth birthday, Moss Haroun—husband of Rachel and father of Sami, Reuben, Fouad and their young sister Yocheved—was dead.

This being a patriarchal, Haroun death, hundreds attended the funeral. It was held on a hot and humid day at the Jewish cemetery in the east of Baghdad. Sami led his brothers in reciting the Kaddish funeral prayer seeking 'abundant and lasting peace' for all present, in addition to such other benefits as 'healing, solace, liberation, rescue and deliverance'. An uncle delivered a short tribute, praising Moss's 'God-given' business sense.

Later, after a rabbi intoned prayers, Sami crouched silently at the graveside, his hands covering his eyes, seemingly oblivious to the sound of women loudly and contagiously wailing. Fouad and Reuben stood some way apart from their elder brother, Fouad's expression serious, Reuben's strained. Rachel, the new widow, rocked back and forth, softly weeping as she was comforted by Yocheved.

On the same morning that the funeral took place, a young aunt of Sami's went into labour; the loss of one Baghdadi Haroun was about to be balanced by the gain of another, a baby girl named Rivke. Sami's mother took this happy event as a sign from heaven.

With his father gone, Sami threw himself ever more energetically into the business. His youthful brothers, Reuben and Fouad, helped him but neither had his heart fully in it. Reuben preferred to spend time chattering with one or more of the many pretty young girls who lived in the neighbourhood. He seemed most at home in their company, particularly when they talked about clothes and jewellery.

Fouad was more interested in books than business. Sami usually gave him menial tasks because he felt that Fouad's bored face would discourage the customers. The youngest in the family, the boys' sister, Yocheved, who occasionally came in to help keep the shop tidy and assist with the accounting, was of considerably more use to Sami than his two brothers.

In the days immediately following Moss Haroun's death, as the house swelled with visitors comforting the mourning family, Moss's widow and three of his children spoke of him together in sad remembrance, extolling his kindness and generosity. But the other child, Reuben, seemed unable to do so.

Reuben's conversation was largely taken up with the marriage that had been arranged for him with a distant cousin, a marriage about which he told Sami: 'I was unable to talk to Baba about my doubts—more than doubts. I felt that he would be too strict, even though I believe he

8

would have understood. But now he is no longer there to talk to. And I must go to my bride with buried feelings, overcome my confusion and learn to live up to what is expected of me... and not bring shame upon the family.'

Sami was reluctant to ask Reuben about his doubts and tried instead to reassure his younger brother. 'You could never bring shame to the Harouns,' he told him. 'You are a fine boy, Reuben, a man now, Ummi's favourite, and the first of us to take a bride. Baba would be proud of you. You should be happy.'

'What about you?' Reuben asked. 'Are you happy that Ummi keeps pressing you about taking a bride? How have you got out of having a marriage arranged? After all, you are the big prize.'

'I am not the big prize, just the big brother who has to manage the business. I have to make my own decisions.'

At the end of the year of mourning for his father, in which he had played only a peripheral part, Reuben, still just nineteen, had a quiet wedding. It was without music or dancing, much to the disappointment of his lively young bride.

'The end of mourning is the time to celebrate life,' she had insisted. 'And what about my happiness? Your father is gone now, it will make no difference to him.'

At which point, Reuben found himself trying, and failing, to hold back a sudden stream of tears. A dam had been breached.

But the bride-to-be's parents (who not only were saved the expense of extravagant Iraqi-Jewish wedding-style celebrations but were delighted at the prospect of having their 'unruly' fifteen-year-old daughter taken off their hands) were happy to fall in with the wishes of Reuben and his family.

One month after Reuben's suitably subdued wedding ceremony, he resumed working with Sami in the shop. Around the same time, their brother Fouad left for Jerusalem, where he studied day and night to become an engineer.

Reuben was now very different from the flamboyant young man of his bachelor days. He no longer brought poems for Sami to read and, in between frequent sighs, mostly spoke in a low voice without enthusiasm. He seemed to have no interests outside the routine of work, which he carried out with unfussy competence.

9

Then, suddenly, after seven childless years of marriage, Reuben suffered what was described by a doctor—and subsequently within the Haroun fold—as 'an unexplained mental collapse' and died, a mystery that was never probed and rarely spoken of thereafter within Haroun family circles.

Sami quickly found a resourceful seventeen-year-old boy called Habib to replace Reuben as his assistant in the shop, and the boy's vigorous involvement helped Sami to expand the business significantly. A mere few weeks later, Reuben's widow left Baghdad to marry a Persian businessman in Tehran. She never returned.

Sami's mother Rachel, having recently and joyfully married off her only daughter Yocheved, was devastated by the loss of Reuben, the gentlest and most affectionate of her three boys. She was further saddened by the rarity of Fouad's visits from Jerusalem—but delighted at his engagement to an Iraqi-Jewish girl who had left for Palestine a month or two before Fouad's own departure.

Even though Sami's unobtrusive presence at home prevented his mother from being alone, this, too, displeased her because she continued to worry that he would remain forever a bachelor, like one of her uncles who had been the subject of much whispered disapproval. Accordingly, she brought to bear her natural persuasive powers—and her purse— upon the parents of Rivke, the young cousin born on the day of her husband's funeral.

Thus was Rivke secretly promised to Sami. Five years later, when Rivke was fourteen and Sami was thirty-four, they were married and living with Sami's mother Rachel in the house that Moss Haroun's father had built in the early 1840s. When Rachel died, a mere month after the wedding, it was said that she had a smile on her face.

'What is happening?' Sami began to panic.

It was 1917. A few weeks had passed since Baghdad's streets were thronged with people welcoming the British conquerors of the ruling Turks. But the atmosphere still felt dangerous and unsettled. When Sami, just as he was reaching home from the Haroun shop, saw a crowd of women beneath the palm trees in the courtyard of his family house screeching loudly and surrounding his young wife Rivke, some of them holding her hands and stroking her face, he was filled with apprehension.

As he drew closer, Sami recognised several of his wife's friends as well as his sister Yocheved and some neighbours. In their midst was Rivke, her hands now covering her face, seemingly crying and laughing at the same time. Sami quickly went to her.

Rivke held him tight and called out his name—'Sami, oh Sami'— and Yocheved and some of the other women wished him luck and many blessings. Now, his mood changed. He was no longer fearful but baffled. Again, but in a softer tone, he asked: 'What is happening?'

'Sami,' Rivke told him. 'It's true. Aunty Alfassa predicted it and now the doctor has told me for certain.'

Aunty Alfassa was the woman who served as the community's matchmaker, soothsayer and purveyor of herbal remedies. Women across the wider Haroun family had gone to her for advice for years. It was said that she was possessed of ancient wisdom and could foresee the future. Aunty Alfassa had been at Rivke's mother's house the previous week when Rivke was visiting and, as she had entered the room where her mother and Aunty Alfassa were sitting at the table, the two older women inclined their heads together and fell into what Rivke called 'Arabic whispers'. Rivke greeted the two women with a smile behind which lay youthful amusement and scepticism. As Rivke began to cut open an orange for herself, Aunty Alfassa nodded at her and, patting her own abdomen, began grinning knowingly and chanting: 'Soon… soon…'

And now the doctor had confirmed it. Sami's wife, herself still a young girl, was pregnant.

'I am having a child,' Rivke announced to her bemused husband. 'We are going to be parents!'

Rivke Haroun was sixteen when she gave birth to her first child, a daughter named Rachel after Sami's mother; seventeen when she had a second girl, Nura; and nineteen when Yusuf, her son, was born, in 1920. An intelligent young woman with firm opinions who liked to read books and newspapers, Rivke was far from the typical young Baghdadi wife. Not that she was wild or disobedient; she was devoted to her husband and to her family's traditions and way of life.

As the years passed, the three children developed into fully committed members of the many-branched Haroun clan. Rachel and Nura were close companions throughout childhood and Yusuf made friends easily. He was a very active child; at school, he took part in wrestling contests and his summer evenings were mostly spent among an excitable pack of boys kicking a football for hour upon hour.

As he grew into adolescence, Yusuf passed increasing amounts of time with his cousin Izaak. He was attracted to Izaak's rebellious attitude. But this always gave expression within more-or-less acceptable limits and Sami and Rivke took a benign view of the boys' friendship. They were more protective towards Rachel and Nura who, notwithstanding that they were both spirited individuals, were happily content with their parents' boundaries. That's the way it was for young Iraqi women.

Sami worked hard to provide for his family and build a profitable business. He bought the two small shops adjoining the original Haroun premises on either side, creating one large area—now called 'Haroun Silks'—into which he introduced more exotic textiles, a few select garments and various traditional Baghdadi household items.

The street outside the shop was constantly noisy and crowded, the pavement thronged with shoppers and various merchants who would carry their wares in a basket balanced upon the head. Haroun Silks often attracted casual customers passing the door on their way home with baskets or large handkerchiefs full of such delights as spices, bottled orange-blossom water, oranges or watermelon.

Occasionally, a neighbour, relative, or a friend from the synagogue would come into the cool of Sami's shop to sit down and talk after a session at the hammam or a visit to the open-air barber's stall that offered not only haircuts and shaves but also tooth extractions, massages and boil lancings.

For several weeks, a loud, colourful purveyor of sweets and watermelons occupied a space directly across the street from Haroun Silks. He was a large, slightly stooped man with an exotic turban worn above a scarred and pimpled face. By contrast with his unsavoury appearance, he appeared to have clear and healthy vocal chords and powerful lungs. His name was Emre and, from morning to night, he mercilessly advertised his wares in loud, sing-song fashion—*Halkoon-a, halkoon-a! Gargaree, gargaree!*—inviting potential customers to sample his Turkish delight or candy, and Sami would arrive home in the evenings with the man's voice ringing in his ears.

The strangest cry employed by Emre the watermelon man was: '*Ala al-satchiin! Ala al-satchiin!*'—'By the knife! By the knife!' This was to demonstrate that he was so confident of the high quality of his melons that he would be prepared to cut a piece from one for free tasting before purchase.

But not everyone would buy the melon after accepting the free sample. In these cases, Emre would react aggressively, waving his knife in the air. This often led to disturbances that deterred potential customers from entering the surrounding shops. Eventually, Sami and some other local merchants gathered together to insist that Emre the watermelon man go somewhere else to chant about his sweets and his melons—which he did, somewhat resentfully, costing Rivke several sleepless nights as she worried for Sami's safety in case this knife-wielding watermelon merchant came to exact revenge.

Rivke had good reason to be anxious. For, although Emre was almost certainly harmless, others did brandish knives with more deliberate menace in the Baghdad of those days. Moreover, Rivke's fears had been fanned a couple of weeks before Emre's departure when, out shopping in Shorjah market on Rashid Street, she saw the wizened Aunty Alfassa emerge from an alleyway across the road. When Aunty Alfassa had caught sight of Rivke, she beckoned her with a bent and shrivelled finger.

Rivke was more sceptical than most of the Harouns about Aunty Alfassa's mystical powers but nobody, whether a Haroun or any other member of the Baghdadi-Jewish community, would have defied the commanding power of Aunty Alfassa's index finger. And, on this occasion, Aunty Alfassa held Rivke's attention for fifteen minutes or so, standing at the mouth of the alleyway.

Her purpose was to tell Rivke about a Jew called Eliyahu, who, said Aunty Alfassa, had been attacked a few days earlier in one of the market's alleys. Alfassa was a renowned storyteller and Rivke wondered how much the mystical matchmaker had embellished the story. Even so, it was still plausible enough to put fear into Rivke's head.

It seemed that Eliyahu had been stopped in the alleyway by a pair of young Muslim men with knives who demanded that he hand over all the money and valuables he was carrying. Terrified, he emptied his pockets and his purse and handed over their contents. 'Now, give us your ring,' the rougher of the two men growled into Eliyahu's face, pointing at the gold and ruby ring on the second finger of his left hand.

'I can't,' Eliyahu protested. 'It's too tight. I can't get it off.'

13

'Hmm,' the thief mused, rubbing his chin (just as Aunty Alfassa rubbed hers when telling the story), before pointing the knife's blade at Eliyahu's chest, and replying: 'Count your blessings. If we did not fear Allah, we would cut off your finger with the ring on it.'

'Blessed be Allah that you fear him,' said Eliyahu. 'That money you have taken from me was my month's wages for me to feed my family. If you truly feared Allah, you would give it back.'

Amazingly, and quite spontaneously it seemed, the two men handed everything back and then Eliyahu, fearing another possible attack, asked the robbers to escort him out of the dark alleyway into the brightness of Rashid Street, 'in case I meet a thug who does not fear Allah…'

After the departure of Emre the watermelon man, the atmosphere was calmer, which pleased Sami, but the shop's takings were down, which did not, of course. Perhaps this was simple coincidence; after all, his profits did dip from time to time and Haroun Silks was not always prosperous. There were difficult spells, which Sami had to negotiate on his own, notably in the uneasy, bellicose atmosphere of the late 1930s.

It was at such times that Sami would smile to himself and recall his mother's stricture in the days when he was starting to find his feet in the intricate ways of commerce in Baghdad: 'What's the point of making money if you don't also make a family to spend it on?'

After almost four decades, during which he had secured a sure business footing—unaffected by the departure, after seven years, of his young assistant Habib to start his own business in competition with Haroun Silks—Sami still had not succeeded in shedding his habitual anxiety.

This was partly fuelled by Rivke's increasing expressions of concern about events beyond Baghdad's boundaries. She was disturbed by scraps of information from the radio about the difficulties people were experiencing in Europe, and by snatches of conversation among Jewish women at the market telling what they had heard about Arab men admiring the Duce in Italy and the Führer in Germany.

Closer to home, she worried that Sami was working too hard and urged him to slow down. A couple of times, in the early evening sunshine, seated at a table shaded by one of the great trees in the courtyard in front of their house, Sami smoking and Rivke preparing food or sewing, she asked: 'Sami, do you think we will always live here, in this house? In Baghdad?'

14

'Where else? This is our home,' was as much as he would say, his eyes half closed and his hands outstretched. And then Rivke would begin her entreaties for him to lighten his load and Sami would shake his head and smile.

One cool February evening in 1938, Sami and Rivke were drinking tea at their courtyard table, upon which was a plateful of overripe fruit. Rivke's eyes were directed at the fruit, not at her husband, as she urged him yet again to take life more easily, her voice—and sentiment—an echo of his mother's from years earlier. 'You have given so much to that business. Devoted your life to it. It's time to rest, to enjoy yourself, let others do the work.'

'Others? What others?' Sami asked.

'Your son, Yusuf, of course. He is intelligent, capable. He wants to work hard, marry and have his own family.'

'Maybe he wants to work hard but he doesn't show me that. I can't leave the business in his care, as my father did with me. But you are right about him wanting to get married. He's a good boy but a dreamer.'

'He can take responsibility,' Rivke responded stiffly as she sliced a pomegranate into quarters. 'You should give him more to do.'

'I remember when I tried that with his uncles, Fouad and Reuben, all those years ago,' Sami said, with a sigh. 'I still found myself having to do most of the work.'

'You were younger and stronger then. You can't carry on doing all the important stuff. You are squeezing out Yusuf's interest in the business.'

'He has no interest in the business.'

'Well then, encourage him. He'll be more eager to learn.'

Sami sighed again, picking off a handful of pomegranate seeds and swallowing them before speaking. 'I remember encouraging Reuben,' he said, and shrugged. 'That didn't work. He was so clever. But too sensitive. Impractical. Always seemed to have his mind on other things.'

'How was he too sensitive? What other things?'

'I don't know… Other young boys used to call him names. And he worried that he would never become… tough, or manly enough. For hard work in the shop. He deeply wanted to please our father.'

'What really happened to Reuben?'

'Well, you know what happened. He died… Though he didn't have to.'

'So why did he?'

15

'People said he went mad. Lost his mind. An illness of the brain.'

'Is that what you think?'

Sami paused, picking distractedly at another pomegranate segment: 'Not really.'

'So what do you think killed him?'

'He was unhappy.'

'You cannot die from unhappiness.'

'You can if you want to.'

Soon after that conversation, Sami did at last, after closing the shop a little earlier in the evenings, start learning to enjoy sitting with his friends in the cool night air, drinking coffee, smoking, talking and arguing. And, gradually, he did introduce Yusuf into the business and looked forward to giving him greater responsibilities with a view to his eventually taking it over.

Unfortunately, Yusuf could not match his father's enthusiasm for Haroun Silks. On the other hand, he did inherit the family disposition to anxiety—for no good reason that he could think of other than that both of his parents, most notably his father, always seemed to convey a sense of unspecified concern.

'At home, as a child,' Yusuf would later recall, 'I felt that my mother and father had spun a kind of protective thread around me—one through which the outside world could be viewed only as a dim and vaguely threatening place.'

Even when he became engaged to marry his beautiful young cousin Farah, with whom he was completely and unabashedly in love, he still felt concerned that his father was concealing some deep problem or fear. He began to study Sami's face for clues.

Yusuf Haroun had always been fascinated by the lines on his father's face. He endowed them with great significance, throughout his childhood and beyond. His mother Rivke's face was round and soft, her cheeks like apricots, but his father Sami's, in its colour and texture, reminded Yusuf of the dates that Sami was forever eating—plump and yellow in the sunshine, dark and wrinkled in shadow.

Sami, at sixty, had a large nose that projected nobly above a moustache that was darker and thicker than the accompanying silvery mess of stubble that invariably coated his jaw. Yusuf could never imagine his father as a young man, despite the impressive photographs of him—as a boy, a bridegroom, and a pleased-with-himself young proprietor standing in front of the family shop—contained in the Harouns' lovingly preserved family album.

Rivke and most of the other strikingly hazel-eyed members of the extended Haroun clan physically resembled one another to a remarkable degree. But, in Yusuf's eyes at least, Sami looked much more like the preceding generations whose expressionless faces haunted the photograph album.

In contrast to his restlessly energetic younger self, Sami the responsible and sedate family head would sit for long periods in the patriarchal armchair, smoking as he gently stroked his moustache, his stillness disturbed only by a slight crinkling around the eyes as he inhaled the aromatic fumes of his Turkish cigarette.

For Yusuf, this tranquil image of his father's deeply-lined face would invariably invoke the sepia-tinted pictures of his forebears, particularly the portrait of his grandfather, Sami's father Moss Haroun, seated in the very same armchair. But while Yusuf always thought of his father as the perennial elderly gentleman, he believed too, that, in happy times, the creases that gave Sami's face such a venerable air would soften and his skin become smoother and younger-looking—although they would once more deepen and darken when sadness threatened.

So, when dark furrows appeared across Sami's forehead in the weeks preceding Yusuf's wedding to Farah, in early April 1941, it was as though a cloud had blown across the young bridegroom's previously serene mental landscape. For although Yusuf, now twenty-one, was no longer a child, some of his childish superstitions clung on and, because they were childish and would have been humiliating for him to admit to, they stuck all the more tenaciously and secretly in his mind—along with his propensity to worry.

Although Yusuf loved accompanying Sami to synagogue, he could not, in his own mind, claim to be genuinely religious—unlike his father, mother, his mother's father and his father's recently widowed sister, Yocheved, who were united in a seemingly unassailable faith in a divine creator. Yet, despite being unable to share the devotion of his parents, aunt and others of their generation, Yusuf still prayed earnestly at night in his bed and kept to all the religious laws.

One day, however, out with his more reckless cousin Izaak, at the Rose Café in Rashid Street—a former haunt of British soldiers—Yusuf ate some meat that was not kosher. Later that evening, almost paralysed with guilt, he prayed for forgiveness to the God in whose existence he did not believe.

There was nothing religiously forbidding about Baghdad's Shaf Ve-Yativ Synagogue, where Sami took Yusuf nearly every Sabbath. Though a grand building in the Persian style, the synagogue's atmosphere was informal and relaxed, and most of the men in their enclosure, and the women in theirs, gossiped as much as they prayed. And the men also wandered freely throughout the service across the open, carpeted floor in front of the raised *bimah*, from where the rabbi looked down upon them.

By contrast, the more elderly congregants, including Yusuf's widowed maternal grandfather Eli (known to all the family as '*Bobbe*', a term he himself chose in preference to the usual word for 'grandpa'—'*seeda*'), kept themselves apart and tended to concentrate on the service, and chant the prayers with as fervent a devotion as their physical frailty would permit.

Once a week, on the Sabbath, *Bobbe* Eli, stooped, arthritic and ninety, would abandon his habitual seat at the open door of his house—as well as his notional one at the open door of death—and summon up the strength to sway and chant at the back of Shaf Ve-Yativ for three hours or more. He would then shuffle home to a meal of stuffed chicken and baked eggs prepared for him by his devoted Muslim housekeeper, Leyla Jaffari, a round-bodied and permanently aproned widow of eighty. 'Eat up,' Mrs Jaffari would urge. 'Will make you strong. Live to one hundred and twenty.'

As was the custom, in the weeks leading up to his wedding, Yusuf found himself more frequently than usual alongside Sami—and, on Sabbaths, *Bobbe* Eli—among the worshippers at Shaf Ve-Yativ Synagogue. While standing next to his father, Yusuf would frequently and furtively glance at those deepening lines across Sami's forehead. Especially on mornings following nights when Yusuf had been kept awake by the sound of his father's cough echoing through the house.

Yusuf's concern was reinforced by the fact Sami sometimes appeared to find it a considerable task to walk home from synagogue. His shoulders were hunched and his breaths were like sighs.

At home one day, Yusuf asked him: 'Baba, are you looking forward to my wedding?'

Sami took his son by the shoulders and, looking into his face, told him how proud he was and how excited at the prospect of seeing Yusuf and Farah together under the marriage canopy. 'She is a fine girl,' Sami often said of his future daughter-in-law. 'As beautiful as the lily and as sweet as the pomegranate.'

Even though Sami smiled as he said this, Yusuf imagined he could see a frown squeezed beneath the smile. 'But, Baba, you look worried,' he told his father.

'Worry is man's lot,' Sami answered, and then with a laugh: 'So don't worry about it!'

Yusuf's method of pushing this nagging concern to the back of his mind was to concentrate on some physical aspect of his beloved Farah— her unblemished skin, the exciting curve of her breast, the way she opened her mouth when she smiled, and how she would sometimes draw the tip of her tongue along her upper lip.

The one area of certainty in Yusuf's life was his love for Farah—even though it had not been completely certain that Farah's parents would accept Yusuf as a bridegroom for the eldest and most beautiful of their four daughters. His cousin Izaak's father—who, like Farah's father, was a diamond merchant—had tried, in many conversations in the souk over glasses of sweet coffee flavoured with rosewater, to persuade Farah's father that Izaak would make the perfect husband for Farah, frequently employing fanciful, flowery language. 'My precious, first-born boy and your precious first-born girl,' he would proclaim. 'Together they will shine like the most precious of jewels.'

Meanwhile, the close friendship between Yusuf and Izaak was never really undermined by their rivalry for Farah's hand. If they spoke of her at all, it would be in scrupulously respectful tones. And, for all of Izaak's father's urgings, Yusuf knew, and Izaak realised, that it was Yusuf whom Farah favoured. She and he had shared secret embraces and made a mutual, whispered declaration of love to each other.

Together, they certainly presented an arresting sight. With the same, ebony-black hair, similarly dark eyes—Farah's glittering and Yusuf's tranquil—and an easy, natural way of talking to each other, they seemed to radiate happiness.

Moreover, Farah's family preferred Yusuf. They believed him to be the more responsible young man. They could see that Izaak was resistant to convention, whereas it was obvious that Yusuf was a dutiful son to

19

Rivke and Sami—who, if they could not be described as truly wealthy, were unquestionably sound and respectable. And, when Farah turned eighteen, although her father promised Izaak's father that he would give every consideration to Izaak's prospects before coming to a decision about his first-born daughter's destiny, the matter was already settled in his own mind and certainly in the mind of his wife Haya—Rivke's sister.

Farah instinctively understood this and, when her parents announced one day that, on the following Sabbath, they would like to talk to her about her future, she felt confident that she would soon be able to wed the man she already loved dearly.

That Sabbath eve, Yusuf took her aside and suggested that if, as expected, her parents should name him as the desired son-in-law, she should accept firmly but a little reluctantly. 'That way,' Yusuf said, 'they will know that you are a devoted daughter who wishes above all to overcome any of her personal doubts and do her parents' bidding—and they may offer you more of a dowry for accepting.'

'Oh, *Yusuf*,' Farah retorted, pushing him away with a playfully shocked gesture. 'How *could* you?'

The old Jewish quarter of Baghdad had not for several years seen such an expansively joyous celebration as the wedding of Yusuf and Farah Haroun that spring of 1941. 'This,' *Bobbe* Eli had declared grandly, 'will be a true *simcha*!'

Bobbe Eli, who had grown up in an Arabic-speaking family whose members had for generations described themselves as 'Babylonian-Sephardi', liked to recall his younger days as a merchant travelling across the Middle East and Europe by using Farsi, Hebrew, Ladino and sometimes even Yiddish words when, to his mind, the occasion merited it. And, he decided, the wedding of Yusuf and Farah certainly merited it. This outstanding event was remembered, and not just in *Bobbe* Eli's mind, as a Hebrew and Yiddish *simcha*, rather than the more commonplace Arabic term, *hafla*.

Seven dark-eyed young bridesmaids decorated Farah's palms and fingers with henna as her lustrous black hair was gently brushed by her silently concentrating cousin Sarai—the youngest of Izaak's three sisters. A honey-voiced cantor chanted ancient prayers and an ancient-looking rabbi pronounced the union of the two young people facing him.

20

Standing in the open air of Sami and Rivke Haroun's courtyard, beneath the wedding canopy—upon which four Haroun aunts had weaved an intricate design depicting rain, corn and grapes, echoing the verse in Genesis: 'And God give thee of the dew from heaven, and the fatness of the earth and plenty of corn and wine'—Farah paced a circle seven times around her groom.

The cantor positioned a wine glass, wrapped in cloth, beneath Yusuf's raised foot, and he stamped down decisively upon the glass, the splintering impact bringing forth roaring wishes of good luck from all around the canopy, and releasing Yusuf into the whirling embrace of Izaak and several other young men prepared to abandon themselves to the dance.

Tables were set up across the courtyard, around its two handsome palm trees, in front of the house where the bridegroom lived with his parents. Crowds of young children stood enthralled as photographs were taken and women in traditional dress carried platters heavy with chicken and rice baked with saffron, almonds, aubergines and raisins. Bands of musicians—including the illustrious al-Kuwaiti brothers—played from the sunset of one day until the sunrise of the next.

Rivke and her sisters and cousins ululated into the night air while Sami and his friends happily succumbed to the effects of glass after glass of arak. Sami did, however, experience one moment of sadness after emptying his second or third glass. As he stood up from the table and turned away to search for a new bottle of arak, he saw his sister Yocheved standing alone, a little apart from the music and hubbub of celebration.

'All by yourself,' he remarked. 'And you look sad.'

'Well, I do feel a little sad,' she said. 'Weddings always give me that feeling. And it's not just because I remember my own and my later loss. It's that two people are becoming reduced to one—which forms a kind of barrier to everyone else. I am very happy for Yusuf, and for Farah, and yet...'

'That is how I am, too,' said Sami. 'Very happy and just a little sad. I am so pleased that Yusuf and Farah are now man and wife. Our two families are pleased to have made such a fine arrangement. And it is easy to see that the two young people are also pleased—they are truly in love. But it is indeed because it is such a happy occasion that I can't help feeling so sorry for poor Reuben.'

21

'Yes, I know. His wedding took place when we were mourning Baba.'

'It's not just that. He never found happiness and his wedding seemed to confirm that he never would.'

'You mean he didn't love his bride?'

'No,' said Sami with unintended abruptness. 'No,' he repeated more quietly, looking down at the empty wine glass he was holding. 'He didn't. Not in the way a man should love his wife. But, come, this day is a truly happy day. I am going to raise more glasses to my son.' And Sami and his sister both went back, smiling, into the throng.

More than three hundred guests were dancing and clapping hands to send the bride and groom on their way. Sami hugged Rivke and they both joined in the singing. Yocheved, usually so staid, stood and clapped and swayed to the rhythms of the musicians. Muslim neighbours and passers-by also joined in, lured by the sounds wailing over the rooftops.

In those days, Jews and music went together in the popular consciousness. Almost all of Iraq's musicians, especially the virtuoso instrumentalists, were Jews and, on Yom Kippur, the holiest day in the Jewish calendar, radios would fall silent across the land owing to the lack of Jewish players to perform live on air.

But there was no silence on the night of the Haroun *simcha*. Musicians kept up a high volume for hours. Singers moved among the celebrating family and friends, improvising songs dedicated to individual guests in praise of their fine qualities.

Bobbe Eli sat at the head of a table of seven ageing Haroun relatives loudly sharing memories of Iraqi-Jewish weddings of the past, including one where the groom died on his wedding night; another where the bride ran screaming from the house of her new in-laws who had prepared for her a bridal bed with black sheets; and of many 'nights of entry' where a stained sheet would be thrown over the bridal balcony to prove to the still-dancing family and friends outside that the bride had been a virgin.

Almost as soon as Yusuf and Farah's engagement had been announced, a decision was taken about their honeymoon. 'America!' Sami had told everyone surrounding him after the service beneath the canopy in the Haroun courtyard. 'America?' Aunt Yocheved had echoed in interrogative delight, her voice rising on the word.

A similar declaration had taken place in earlier years at the betrothals and weddings of both of Yusuf's sisters, also to cousins, one of whom,

David—the husband of Yusuf's elder sister Rachel—lived in New York and was beginning to build a reputation as a lawyer.

Despite the obvious implication of Sami's overjoyed urging of Rachel to take this once in a lifetime chance to see the 'Golden Land'—and indeed of the very fact of her engagement to a promising, New York-based lawyer—Sami had felt a little deflated by the couple's announcement at their wedding that New York was now to be Rachel's new home, just as it was already David's.

But when his second daughter, Nura, married the son of Sami's American cousin Efraim and went to live near her sister Rachel in New York, Sami took a liberal slice of the money he had made—and saved—out of the business, and accompanied the young couple across the Atlantic. He was as excited as they were. America had always been a magical concept for him. As a young man, he had read as much as he could about the emergent American silent-film industry and had also looked longingly at magazine pictures showing the bustling glamour around the new skyscrapers of New York and other cities.

Throughout the four years since then, Sami had dreamed of the possibility that he and Rivke would themselves eventually settle in the land of Hollywood and high buildings. But Rivke did not share her husband's enthusiasm for America. She felt upset and frustrated at how he would simply wave away her arguments. 'Your golden land is not so golden,' she told him. 'Rachel's David had to struggle to get through college and make something of himself.'

'And now he's a lawyer!' Sami's rejoinder was delivered, hands outstretched, in the manner of a scientist stating a conclusive proof. 'It's the land of the free. A place where you succeed as a result of your own hard work.'

'It's a place where Jews are not so welcome.' Rivke's reply was made with a solemn nodding of the head, a gesture warning her husband against complacency.

'Ah, the biblical prophetess once again warning of doom!' During such conversations, Sami's dismissive words were always softened by his affectionate tone.

'You may laugh,' Rivke remonstrated, 'but they have priests on the radio in America who poison the minds of people and turn them against the Jews. And what about that motor car man, that Henry Ford. A great American hero—and a friend of the Nazis in Germany.'

'We all have our madmen,' Sami said, indicating with both hands that the discussion was closed.

In his heart, Sami wished that things had been different. For all his dreams of America, he could not imagine feeling at home in any country other than Iraq, or any place other than Baghdad, where Jews made up a quarter of the population and, for generations, had mingled freely and amicably with the Baghdadi Arabs. And he would have liked his family, friends and neighbours to feel the same way.

Iraq was the land of his forebears and, although he was not as rich as some—such as Farah's father, who had paid for the lavish wedding party for his daughter and Sami's son—his family had nevertheless achieved both material comfort and social standing. And, though he considered himself a devout Jew, he found it impossible to identify with his brother Fouad's attachment to Jerusalem, or with certain of his friends who had in more recent months emigrated to Palestine, declaring it to be their spiritual home and expressing sentiments of longing, need or lifelong ambition.

Sami was sceptical of such utterances. He contended that these emigrants were acting in the belief that, with the world in a state of upheaval, they were saving their own skins, reckoning that the Jews' ancient homeland was the best refuge. Sami regarded them as mistaken and had frequently told them so. 'This is a Jewish homeland,' he would say. 'Jews have lived here since it was Mesopotamia, thousands of years ago, long before it became Iraq. It is the home of our history, the nation of Babylon.'

In his own mind, he was simply unable to contemplate the possibility of anything crossing his threshold that might disrupt the settled rhythm of his existence.

Yet, for all Rivke's railing against America, she was far from content with life in her homeland. She constantly pointed out what she saw as ominous portents for Baghdadi Jews. Mutterings of discontent—about business, government, or the British—grew louder and spread wider. Groups of youths had begun to roam the streets chanting pro-German slogans. She had heard a rumour about two Jewish boys being attacked with knives, and another story about German army officers landing in Iraq and building an Arab fighting force.

What was more than rumour was the fact that Haj Amin al-Husseini, the Nazi-supporting possessor of the orotund title Grand Mufti of Jerusalem, had fled Jerusalem and was now in Baghdad stirring up local Arabs against the British and Jews alike. With the whole region and much of the world in the shadow of war, Rivke felt that her family and her friends would no longer be safe, that a scapegoat would be sought, and that the days of Baghdad as a 'Jewish city' were numbered.

Sami tried not to think about Rivke's dark warnings and carried on with his regular routine. Haroun Silks was prospering. The premises were four or five times larger, and considerably lighter and dryer, than they had been in his father's time. He still enjoyed the company of friends in the evenings, sitting outside in the cooling air, drinking coffee and playing cards and *shesh besh*—the local version of backgammon, also known as *tawla*.

Sami was a sociable man and always attended with a feeling of warmth the frequent family *haflas* to celebrate a wedding, betrothal or bar mitzvah, or the worldly success of a scion of the Haroun clan in a far-flung part of Europe or America, or to mourn the death of another, closer to home. And, although he didn't always attend the daily morning prayers at the synagogue, he seldom missed a Sabbath service.

Despite the misgivings of his wife, the growing pessimism of many of his business associates, and the vast geographical separation from his children, behind his ever-deepening frown Sami Haroun convinced himself that he was a happy man. He certainly believed himself to be a fortunate one.

Should conditions ever become intolerable—truly intolerable—well, he argued, there was still the possibility of retiring to America. 'One day, maybe,' he would say, with a shrug, to his coffee companions at one of the tables set outside the neighbourhood houses and cafés, or under palm trees in domestic courtyards.

Inwardly, however, he doubted whether the evening air of an American city street could provide him with the sense of ease he enjoyed in the distinctively fragrant evening air of Baghdad. This was a question he tried hard to suppress along with worries brought on by Rivke's and his cousin Efraim's comments about American discrimination against Jews. And, in planning the projected visit of his son to the distant city of his daughters, Sami was, in his own mind, also exploring the possibility of the family as a whole settling—one day—among New York's busy streets and imperious buildings. 'It's time to think about such things,' he told himself. After all, he had been working too hard lately and this had brought on his cough.

But, Yusuf—like his mother—was not completely of the same mind as his father. He was pleased to have the chance to cross the ocean to see America and his sisters and their families but, in the same way that his father's imagination had been captured by early Hollywood stories, his own escapist obsession had been directed at the other side of the Atlantic, and the tales of Sherlock Holmes by Arthur Conan Doyle.

Thus it was England, and in particular London—Sherlock Holmes's London—that attracted Yusuf. And Farah was happy to support the act of gentle defiance by which Yusuf persuaded his parents to bless the idea of the young couple beginning their honeymoon with a visit to London (and, by extending the length of their trip, putting off the day when he would be expected to take a more active role in his father's business).

Even though Britain, long-time ruler of Iraq, was now at war, it was not difficult for Sami and Rivke to accede to Yusuf's request. A couple of families from the scattered Haroun tribe had already settled successfully in London. Two brothers, Azi and Ben, were frequently mentioned at Haroun dinner tables, variously and vaguely as cousins or uncles but always with a kind of reverence on account of their having built up a thriving textile and oriental carpet business in London. 'They have their own warehouse,' Sami would tell visitors. 'As big as a *field*! Can you imagine?'

And so it was decided: Yusuf and Farah's long honeymoon journey would start in Britain, where they would enjoy the hospitality of Uncle Azi. Then, after a month or so, if war conditions would allow and they could obtain official permission, it would culminate in New York. They were both looking forward to practising the English they had learned at school, and Yusuf was keen to show his sisters, Rachel and Nura—who had been unable to come over for his wedding—how their long-teased, little-boy brother had become a man, and a married one at that.

It was an emotional send-off. The day after the wedding there was a party in the courtyard outside Sami and Rivke's home, with many of the previous day's guests back again. And, again, a considerable amount of arak was drunk by the men as they ate fat dates stuffed with marzipan or halva, and sticky slices of baklava.

As the guests surrendered to weariness and the evening yielded to the night, Sami urged the company to drink one last farewell toast to the young married couple. His eyes filled with tears as, after kissing his new daughter-in-law's cheek, he held his son in a strong, paternal embrace. He would have said these were tears of unmitigated joy even though fleeting thoughts had passed through his mind of his late, childless brother and his living, barren and widowed sister. Marriage, he knew—but could not say—did not always follow the intended path.

After a few seconds, Yusuf pulled away, held his father by the shoulders, kissed his forehead and asked him: 'Baba, why do you wear such a frown? It is a happy occasion and yet your face is so creased.'

'Of course it is a happy occasion,' said Sami, wiping away a tear and putting his arm around Rivke, who was standing nearby. 'And of course I have creases in my face. I am getting old! You must know that I am so proud of you and Farah. Ummi and I will find it too quiet without you. And, as for the lines here,' he said, tapping his forehead, 'I cannot help my face.'

'I know,' said Yusuf. 'And it shows what you are thinking, happy or sad. It is like a barometer, which is why I am nervous of the future, even at moments of great happiness.'

Yusuf could not have realised how warranted his nervousness was and that his and Farah's memorable wedding would be the last, grand *simcha* to take place in Jewish Baghdad.

After two unseasonably hot nights spent under the silken canopy of a bridal bed on the roof of Sami and Rivke's house, overlooking the courtyard's celebrated pair of palm trees, Yusuf and Farah began their travels soon after dawn on a warm spring morning.

The sun was already casting its light and heat upon the city when their cousin Izaak arrived in his latest prized possession—a shining black English Wolseley motor car—to drive them the fifty or so miles to Habbaniya lake. From there, thanks to Sami's friendship with a British Royal Air Force officer to whom he had once sold some Ottoman silk cushions at a big discount, they would travel on a BOAC flying boat to England.

'Izaak!' Farah's spontaneous cry could have woken residents on all sides of the Haroun courtyard. 'How did you manage to keep this a secret? Is it really yours?'

'Of course,' said Isaak. 'I bought it yesterday. It is a Wolseley 18/85, not brand new of course but it came from the factory only three or four years ago. I bought it from one of my father's clients. In three years, this man had hardly driven it—but he had looked after it. See how clean and polished it is. Look, you can see the sun reflected in it. I drove it around all day yesterday after I bought it.'

At this point, Rivke and Sami appeared on the street, loudly mingling their farewells with admiration for Izaak's Wolseley.

'I'll take you for a ride, Uncle Sami, maybe tomorrow,' said Izaak as Sami patted the gleaming black bonnet. 'It is beautiful to drive,' he added, his face aching with pride, before turning to Yusuf: 'You will see. Plenty of room for your luggage. Come on, get in.'

As Farah and Yusuf climbed into the car, Farah on the back seat, Yusuf in front next to his friend and cousin, Izaak continued: 'My father has taken over the old car. He is going to have it patched up, he says. Can you imagine, my father behind the wheel of that old boneshaker?'

The three of them laughed as Sami and Rivke stood pointing and waving. Izaak released the brake and drove off, enjoying the impression his surprise had made. 'Listen to that engine,' he urged his passengers loudly.

'It is hard not to listen,' Farah shouted from behind the two young men.

'It is truly wonderful,' added Yusuf, patting Izaak on the back.

'I will never forget your wedding,' the exuberant Izaak yelled as the car picked up speed and the engine soothed into a constant purring sound. 'I think your father was drunk. I've never seen him that way before.'

They seemed to arrive at Habbaniya very quickly. After animated farewells and renewed congratulations to Izaak for his acquisition of the Wolseley—'you have given us an early taste of England'—Yusuf and Farah were ushered into the airline office and shortly afterwards on to the flying boat.

They were among no more than twenty passengers, the majority of whom were uniformed British service personnel. The exceptions were three local merchants who were seated well apart from Yusuf and Farah—which was fortunate, as the three men kept up a loud, garrulous dialogue in Arabic more or less from take-off to landing.

While Farah remained excited throughout the flight, Yusuf was taut and nervous, gripping his wife's hand a little too tightly. This was not on account of the fact that this was his first time in an aircraft—he had no fear of flying—but because he was still prey to that vague sense of unease expressed to his father at the post-wedding farewell party.

When Farah asked why he was so quiet, Yusuf replied: 'I am struggling to cope with so much happiness.'

Neither Yusuf nor Farah felt any anxiety over the fact that they were being taken to a country at war, in a seaplane bearing that country's colours. Like Rivke, who had waved them off emotionally but enthusiastically just a few hours earlier, they had too much confidence in Britain and the British for that. And within their inward-looking, Baghdadi-Jewish society, the war outside lacked reality.

They could not have explained whether it was despite, or on account of, being surrounded by men in military uniform that neither of them spoke a single word about the conflict, into the heart of which they were heading.

Before the end of the month, that conflict would encroach upon their homeland, around the very airfield and lake from which they had just departed. Had they attempted to fly from Habbaniya a mere three weeks later, it would have been impossible. A bitter battle would then be raging between the British forces and troops under the command of the Axis-supporting new leader of Iraq, Rashid Ali al-Gaylani, the latter having surrounded Britain's Habbaniya base.

In the event, the young Haroun couple's flight, on 8 April, was calm and comfortable—Farah even managed an hour's sleep—and though they arrived to a somewhat grey and bleak prospect of the port city of Bristol, they disembarked with a feeling of exhilaration at being in Britain.

'Farah, what a pleasure to see you! Yusuf, I haven't seen you since you were this high! Welcome to Great Britain! How marvellous you look! Not even tired from the journey! What a splendid and handsome young couple you make, *bel ayn el raa'a.*'

Uncle Azi ended his effusive greeting sotto voce with the traditional imprecation to ward off the evil eye. Though he had been living in London for several years, Azi Haroun continued to uphold the super-stitions that were common currency in Iraq. His English vocabulary was laced with many phrases with which his new visitors would be familiar—especially '*bel ayn el raa'a*', since all Iraqi Jews learnt from their mothers to remain alert to the threat of the evil eye.

Azi, his wife Miriam, and their eldest son, fourteen-year-old Joseph—who at that moment was standing shyly behind his father in the arrivals area where Azi had brought him to meet his relatives—lived in a respectable suburban house, along with their other children Daniel and Violette, aged twelve and ten, in Stamford Hill, north London. In a similar house around the corner from Azi and Miriam, lived Azi's younger brother Ben and his family.

'Everybody is excited that you are coming to our home,' Azi told his young visitors. 'My wife cannot wait. My brother will come with all his family to see you. This is a very special visit. You must feel free to treat my home as your own.'

Azi and Ben had emigrated from Baghdad six years before Iraq was granted nominal independence by the British in 1932. They quickly established a supply route of carpets and other goods from the Middle East to London. The shipments had continued after the outbreak of war, if less regularly and more expensively. And, though business had receded since late 1939, there was still a pool of British aristocrats and others willing to pay for fine hand-woven carpets and rugs.

Moreover, while Azi concentrated on the trade in Iraqi, Turkish, Persian and Afghan carpets and rugs, Ben increased the stock of European items, and goods other than carpets, such as tapestries, furniture, lanterns, candlesticks and exotic nargila bubble pipes. So much so that, by the time of Farah and Yusuf's arrival in the spring of 1941, the two brothers were operating from different office premises, though they continued to share a combined warehouse and showroom.

Azi was a small, round man of forty with a ring of dark hair around a shining, bald dome. He had thick, curly eyebrows and a bushy, black moustache. His eyes were small, dark buttons, his nose a large strawberry. He talked rapidly, without pause, making points with a shrug, a frown, a wave of the hand or any number of other facial and manual gestures.

Yusuf had expected to take Farah by train from Bristol to London but Uncle Azi had surprised them by meeting them from the flying boat. He was keen, just as Izaak had been back in Baghdad, to show off a recently acquired motor car. In Azi's case it was a black and green Riley Kestrel, its long, sleek bonnet tapering forward between the headlamps like a nose between two eyes. Farah and Yusuf squeezed on to the back seat while young Joseph sat in front alongside his father.

Joseph looked subdued and barely spoke during the drive from Bristol to London (which took almost the same amount of time as the flight from Habbaniya to Bristol) but then, he didn't need to—Azi kept his young relatives awake by pointing out various landmarks along the route;

asking questions about the flight, the family, the wedding, Baghdad's traffic, its businesses and its Jews; and imparting information about his own business and his family's attachment to the Sephardi and Oriental community of Jews centred on the Lauderdale Road Spanish and Portuguese Synagogue in Maida Vale.

'It's in a wonderful part of west London,' Azi told his passengers. 'One day we will move closer to it but it suits us for business reasons not to be in the heart of the Iraqi Jews. And Maida Vale is not where my religious young brother Ben takes his family to pray. Instead, he goes to a little synagogue—*shul* he calls it in honour of its Lithuanian Ashkenazi rabbi—with lots of Persians, Turks and families from Aden, and even India, in Stamford Hill. You will see lots of Persians in Stamford Hill. Ben's *shul* is in walking distance—because he doesn't drive on Shabbat, or *Shabbes*, as he now calls it.'

When Yusuf interrupted this monologue with a question about the war, Azi briefly turned off his smile and waved away the interruption. 'Oh, don't let's worry about that now,' he said. 'We have plenty of time to discuss everything. We'll talk tomorrow. Now let's get some refreshment.'

They stopped approximately half-way, at a café where Yusuf had his first taste of English tea—a strong and, to him, strange brown brew in a large white cup, into which a laughing Azi stirred sugar and milk. Farah confined herself to one small sip from her husband's teaspoon. Yusuf, on the other hand, liked the way the sweet liquid settled warmly in his stomach.

When they arrived in Stamford Hill, Miriam Haroun's greeting was almost as overpowering as her husband's had been. 'This is your home for as long as you want,' she told her guests, having managed simultaneously to hug Yusuf, kiss Farah, ruffle Joseph's hair, introduce young Daniel and Violette to their Baghdadi cousins and urge her husband quickly over the doorstep.

Miriam was a year or two younger than Azi and at least as plump. She may have been pregnant but it was difficult to tell. As her husband went to park his car under shelter in the yard of a nearby clothes factory run by a family friend, Miriam fussed cheerfully and insistently over Yusuf and Farah.

She brought them drinks and cakes (repeatedly apologising for their quality and sparseness on account of 'the rations') and proudly showed them the meticulously prepared guest room. This contained a heavy,

31

dark wooden wardrobe and two single beds that had headboards made from the same dark wood as the wardrobe. The beds were covered by floral-patterned eiderdowns.

It was evident from Miriam's words and her overall manner that she was pleased and excited at having two young members of the Haroun tribe stay under her roof. 'You bring a little bit of Baghdad with you,' she told them. 'To warm us in our cold, grey times.'

The morning after Yusuf and Farah's arrival, Azi drove them in the Riley Kestrel to his office, a mile away. This was a bright room on the ground floor of a 1930s commercial building, into which, alongside the expected desk and filing cabinets, Azi had incongruously squeezed a pair of maroon and gold ottomans. In a smaller adjacent room with two identical small tables, a typewriter on one, a kettle on the other, sat Azi's secretary, Mrs Gibson, a local Hackney-born widow.

Having introduced his guests to Mrs Gibson and asked her to bring coffee, Azi led Yusuf and Farah back into his office and invited them to sit down on one of the ottomans while he took his place on the other. Once Mrs Gibson had placed a pot containing coffee—'brought by sea from Iraq'—along with three cups and a dish of ration-defying baklava on a long, low, glass-topped table between the two ottomans, there followed a conversation of mutual revelation and astonishment.

Although the honeymooners' stay had been arranged in an exchange of letters facilitated by Sami's RAF contact, very little hard information had passed between Sami and Azi. Sami had expressed gratitude to Azi for making his home available, written about the impending wedding, and about business, and told Azi about 'this fine, trustworthy British airman' who would take care of everything. And, despite the fact that Azi was based in a city devastated by war, neither he nor Sami had expressed any concern about the possible dangers to Farah and Yusuf during their proposed journey or about the general situation in London.

Both men preferred not to contemplate difficulty or disappointment. For his part, Azi longed to play host and knew that Miriam would be delighted not to be left alone in the house when he was out at work, while Sami simply closed his mind to the possibility of anything interfering with his son's wishes.

So, when Azi calmly explained to Yusuf and Farah, over coffee and baklava, that four months earlier, in December 1940, the basement of his brother Ben's home had collapsed when a nearby house was destroyed by an incendiary bomb—and that it was sheer chance that no one had been in the basement at the time, as this was where the family normally sheltered from German air raids—Yusuf and Farah were both visibly shaken.

Farah and Yusuf were also shocked to hear from Azi that, when he had met them in Bristol, he had driven there having first collected his son Joseph from a small mining village near Cardiff, where he had been staying for several weeks with a Welsh couple and their son, who was the same age as Joseph. But that wasn't all—Azi would be taking him back there in a couple of days, while his other two children would be returning by train to another 'billet' on the edge of Bath, in the west of England, close to Bristol.

'They're all in the same region, really. Not far from each other but by law I have to confine my driving to daylight hours and therefore to the one destination,' Azi explained, his genial, optimistic manner appearing to falter for the first time.

'They are all at home this week to collect school books—and to see you, of course. It's good if 'evacuees'—which is what they are called—can see their family from time to time. It's not easy. Miriam wants them to avoid… well she gets very upset when they're away and is so glad that you will be in the house… but she wants the children to be safe, to avoid the… you know, the risk. Not that there is a great risk just now. The Blitz is almost over. Everyone is saying so.'

Neither Yusuf nor Farah had heard the word 'Blitz' before. All of this news came as an overwhelming surprise. Their parents and others back home did listen to the radio but they did so with cynical ears. The news reports were generally regarded as parochial and biased. It seemed the extent of the German bombing of London had not filtered through to the Iraqi-Jewish community.

'We have heard about the fighting, of course, but not the detail,' Yusuf said, embarrassed at his failure to appreciate the conditions in the British capital. 'We thought—we assumed—that you were all far from any bombs, that this was happening just in the centre of town and only occasionally.' In truth, even that was an exaggeration of his knowledge.

'I hope we haven't upset things by coming,' Farah said, expressing her concern. 'And prevented you and Miriam from leaving London.'

'Oh no,' replied Azi, with a reassuring smile. 'There's no question of that. We are going nowhere—unless I am conscripted by the British army,' he said, his smile widening.

33

'Is that possible?' Farah asked.

'It's possible,' said Azi. 'My brother Ben, also. But at the moment it looks unlikely. And, as you can see, we are carrying on with our business. But is there no talk of the war back home?'

'The family has been occupied so much with the wedding,' Yusuf said apologetically. 'But the talk at home, among the Jews, does seem to be getting more anxious. Many of the Arabs have taken the side of the Nazis. There have been incidents. Ummi says we could be in danger.'

'I knew nothing of this,' said Azi. 'We are ignorant on both sides. We should all keep our ears open. It is very worrying. It's a terrible shame that we are not more in touch, especially in these difficult times. But listen. We must not allow gloomy talk to spoil the happiness of such a lovely young couple,' he added, brightening. 'I cannot show you London at its best while things are as they are, but it will be easier to move around town during the daytime. And I will take you to other towns in my new car!

'We will visit Oxford and Cambridge, where, please God, one day, at least one of my children will go to study,' Azi said, smiling and wagging his index finger in a mark-my-words gesture. 'You will be safe with me. Perfectly safe. You will have a good time. Please God, we Iraqis—the great Haroun family—will all be together again. Maybe in London. I know your mother loves the British, Yusuf.

'And we ourselves feel British more and more. The children are much more British than they are Iraqi. Just listen to Joseph's accent!' Azi laughed as he added: 'He loves football. He is a supporter of a local football team, Tottenham Hotspur. Can you imagine?'

Azi was true to his word. He escorted his two young visitors by bus, underground train and, sometimes, car to see, among other places, Buckingham Palace, the Tower of London and the National Gallery, and took them to a service at the Lauderdale Road Synagogue—whose Hebrew name, *Sha'ar Hashamayim*, Azi pointed out, meant 'Gate to Heaven'. On one exceptionally sunny day, a more ambitious outing in the Riley was undertaken to Cambridge, where Azi gazed longingly at college buildings and Farah and Yusuf had their photograph taken by 'a very English lady' called Lettice Ramsey in her studio in St Andrew's Street.

'My brother Ben says he loves the prayers in his *shul* in Stamford Hill,' said Azi as they drove away from Cambridge on to the A10 back

34

to London. 'He says they feel more meaningful. If that's true I think I am going to go with him next week and pray for no bombs to drop on Cambridge.'

'Or Oxford,' Yusuf prompted.

'Or Oxford,' Azi took his cue. 'Or on London or Wales or Bath or on any of us. Those bastards.' He had started by offering the sentiment lightly, with a smile. Now, suddenly, in the space of a minute, he was emotional, sniffing and wiping his eyes, trying to control his voice as he said: 'You young lovers are going to fall in love again—with England. You'll see.'

On the morning that Miriam accompanied the two younger children, David and Violette, to Bath on the train, Farah and Yusuf took their places in the back of the Riley as Azi drove a silent and palpably distressed Joseph back to Cardiff. For much of the return journey, Azi, too, was quiet and subdued. In the evening, Azi, Miriam, Yusuf and Farah went to the Regent cinema in Stamford Hill to see the film, *Citizen Kane*. The next day, while Farah stayed at home with Miriam, Azi took Yusuf to observe the family business.

Yusuf could not put into words how or why he quickly became so fascinated by Azi and Ben's business operation but the moment he walked into their company showroom, a short walk away from Azi's office, he was enchanted.

'So, this is our emporium,' Azi announced as, with one hand, he held open the door for his young visitor and, with his opposite arm, traced a wide semi-circle in the air. The vast, high-ceilinged 'emporium'—the term that everyone used to describe it—took up the equivalent of two floors at the foot of a four-storey building with flats above the showroom.

Everything about the place charmed Yusuf—the slightly spicy, faintly musty smell; the colourful piles of carpets and rugs, their rich patterns and delicate, tufted fringes redolent of traditionally garbed old women in villages and workshops back home; the loud, flamboyant conversations between staff and customers, staff and staff, and even customers and customers; the ancient shared desk of the fraternal owners, adorned with framed photographs of their families and small heaps of exotic trinkets alongside account books, scattered letters and receipts and tiny, decorated cups that were constantly being filled with sweet, steaming liquids and then gratefully emptied though moustachioed lips.

Farah, who had already been instructed in the ways of the Iraqi-Jewish kitchen by her mother, was fascinated to see how Miriam adapted her cooking to the restrictions of rationing, and the translation of traditional Baghdadi recipes into a north London setting. Miriam, in turn, took Farah under her wing and gradually broke down her young guest's demure, reserved way of looking at the world.

Farah was very impressed by this bustling woman who was so much more than a housewife, who spoke knowledgeably of her husband's business and helped her children with their Hebrew, English and other lessons. Miriam had grown up in a moderately traditional household in Ramadi, seventy miles from Baghdad, and was introduced to Azi at the age of twenty—when her parents were worried that she was becoming too old to be a bride. By the time Farah and Yusuf arrived in London, their hosts had been devotedly married for eighteen years.

In later years, Farah would describe Miriam as her teacher, the person who had helped her find her feet in Britain and instil in her the revolutionary idea that strength and independence are as valuable to a woman as they are to a man.

A week or so after their arrival, while Miriam took Farah shopping to introduce her to the intricacies of rationing, Yusuf offered to help Azi and Ben at the showroom. They allowed him to roll and carry a few carpets, deliver a couple of local letters and even clean the windows. The following morning, Yusuf went with Azi to his ottoman-adorned office and eagerly learned some of the basic elements of trading in oriental carpets.

This was to be a lesson of greater, and more immediate significance than either man could have imagined. A couple of weeks later, Azi received his call-up papers, ordering him to report to his local army recruitment office in Hackney. His brother Ben received his papers two days later. The salient nature of this command was mitigated by the ending of the Blitz.

The brothers' business would now be in the charge of their manager, Mr Miller, a neat, silver-haired, dapper little man of sixty, who walked with a limp. Yusuf's willing presence was about to prove invaluable.

In Stamford Hill, Azi was the first to learn of it. In a short news item in June 1941, under the heading 'MOB RIOT: HUNDREDS FEARED KILLED', the *News Chronicle* carried three paragraphs reporting that people, businesses and homes had been attacked in Baghdad. Although the victims were described as Muslims, Jews and Christians, it was clear to Azi from the location of the rioting that it had taken place in the area where most of the Harouns lived. Many, if not all, of the victims would almost certainly have been Jewish.

In Baghdad, both Rivke and Sami in their different ways had anticipated it. Most Jews had simply shrugged their shoulders and uttered curses when the Nazi-sympathiser Rashid Ali al-Gaylani seized power in Iraq at the beginning of April. Both Yusuf's and Farah's families had eagerly continued with the wedding preparations but Rivke's previously joyful sense of anticipation was undermined by the installation of Rashid Ali's military clique, the Golden Square.

While others seemed to be able to ignore it, remaining cheerful even in the face of inflammatory public speeches by members of the new government supporting the Germans and vilifying the British and the Jews, Rivke found it a struggle to maintain a brave face and push the new political situation to the back of her mind. But that is what she did.

Once the wedding was over and Yusuf had left Baghdad, Rivke became less inclined towards concealment and increasingly vocal in her warnings of calamitous change. She continually tried to rouse the Harouns—and not just her husband—from what she called their 'blind indifference'.

As for Sami, it had been clear throughout this entire period that all was not right with him, though he would never talk about it. Even as his son's big day drew near, he would retreat to his armchair for hours at a time, smoking more and coughing more, staring into the distance as if at an approaching spectre. And, in the wake of Yusuf's departure, his moods grew darker by the day.

When disaster did strike, not only did it do so at a most unlikely moment, but it was on a scale that neither Sami nor Rivke could have imagined.

Azi, at home in London on weekend leave from the army, had been reading his newspaper in the kitchen when he saw the item about his family's homeland. He called Miriam, Farah and Yusuf. Neither of the women were able to speak. Farah wept. Yusuf, his hands over his eyes, sighed heavily. Miriam put her arms around them both.

Information emerged in fragments. Azi managed to make telephone contact with associates in Iraq and discovered that the *News Chronicle* report was published several days after the events it described. A report on the radio spoke of a heroic battle by members of the RAF and other British forces against a large band of renegade Iraqis equipped with German weapons, culminating in a decisive victory on the edge of Baghdad, where the authorities had now restored order after limited disturbances.

Some days after the violent rioting, a note that had been hastily written on 2 June arrived in Stamford Hill from Rivke to say that she and Sami were safe but several friends and some relatives had been killed or injured and their property looted or destroyed.

This was followed by a longer, much more reflective letter, which reached Yusuf in London in mid-June although it was dated 3 June. In it, Rivke informed Yusuf of the violent death of his young cousin Sarai and expressed her deepest love for her son, urging him to keep away from the now defiled land of his birth.

Yusuf was so overcome by this longer letter that he could not immediately show it to the others, even Farah. It felt so personal; it conveyed a sense of his mother's warming presence, her understanding, her profundity, her sheer goodness. And, as if for the first time, he felt the deep power of her love for him. His father, sisters and Farah were momentarily irrelevant. His determination to stand firm against these new and tragic circumstances, to be strong and not to break, collapsed with Rivke's evocation, towards the end of the letter, of his childhood, when he had felt so safe in her care, and he had to inhale deeply into his throat to keep down the rising sobs.

'She wants us to stay here, in London,' were his first words once he felt able to communicate the contents of the letter to Farah, Azi and Miriam.

'You have to,' said Azi.

'You can stay with us as long as you like,' said Miriam.

'You are so kind to us,' responded Farah.

'Our beautiful homeland; our Iraq; our Baghdad,' sighed Yusuf, putting an arm around Farah.

'How could this have happened,' said Farah. 'And poor little Sarai. She was so happy at our wedding. I can still see her dancing. I can still smell the sweetness of Baghdad.'

'Even after all the years we have been here,' said Miriam. 'I still sometimes long for the colours and the sounds of the market, the sunlight on the Tigris.'

'We must bring them out of there,' said Yusuf.

Like Azi, Rivke too had been in her kitchen when the first hint of the catastrophic events entered her consciousness. She was listening at her window for the cry of the *abul 'am bah*—the pickle merchant—but instead she heard the first screams.

It was the beginning of the Jewish festival of Shavuot, coinciding that year with the first day of June. After a tense and fearful May, the signs for the new month had seemed good. The smiles on the faces of people outside in the courtyard and on the street indicated genuine happiness as well as relief. Two days earlier, Rashid Ali had fled in the face of the advance on the city by the British army. The malevolent Grand Mufti had also departed. Yet the malevolence had not. The screams were followed by gunshots.

A delegation from the Baghdadi-Jewish community had set off that morning for the airport to welcome back the Regent, Emir Abdul Allah, ruling on behalf of the infant King Faisal II, who had been deposed by Rashid Ali.

The Regent's return had been engineered by the British, who had overcome an Axis-supporting Iraqi force. Other Jews were out on the streets, dressed in their holiday best for Shavuot. Many were in synagogue, celebrating the collapse of the Golden Square at least as fervently as they celebrated the festival itself. Everywhere, however, the British were a notable absence.

As the Jewish welcoming party crossed the Al Khurr bridge, it was intercepted by a group of followers of Yunis al-Sabawi, an Iraqi politician whose devotion to Hitler was such that he had translated *Mein Kampf* into Arabic. After the flight of Rashid Ali al-Gaylani, Yunis al-Sabawi had declared himself governor of central southern Iraq and called upon Baghdadi Jews to remain in their homes during the forthcoming weekend of 31 May and 1 June while he took care of the volatile situation.

But al-Sabawi's way of dealing with the situation was to organise gangs to carry out violent assaults upon Jews in their own homes. On the Saturday, the plans took shape. On Sunday 1 June, the early visibility of the Regent-supporting Jewish delegation at the Al Khurr bridge provided the touch-paper.

Over two days, an armed mob, comprising young men and boys, students and even policemen, looted and rampaged unchecked, while the victorious British soldiers remained outside the city on the orders of the British ambassador, Kinahan Cornwallis.

Inside the city, more than nine hundred homes and five hundred shops and businesses were attacked. Hundreds died—the exact number never officially established—and many more were injured. The dead were buried in a mass grave—the sacrificial victims of Ambassador Cornwallis's decision to keep back the men of the British Army on those first two dark days of June.

The British eventually marched into the city and restored order on the evening of 2 June. Al-Sabawi was deported over the border to Iran. Sami and Rivke ventured into the street, as soon as it was safe to do so, to count the cost. Their home, a sturdy building facing inwards into its walled courtyard, had withstood the attacks. There was some damage and daubings on the outer wall and debris had been hurled into the courtyard. Nothing more.

Several of their neighbours were not so fortunate. Many houses had been destroyed. And, while Rivke and Sami had been able to shelter from the mob, others had not. Yusuf's cousin and closest friend Izaak had had his nose and teeth broken, and his new Wolseley car was reduced to burnt, skeletal ash, but his distress at this was as nothing compared to his discovering the body of his adored, sweet and shy sister, Sarai.

The events of those two days in June came to be known as the *Farhud*, the Arabic equivalent of the Russian word, 'pogrom'. It deepened Sami Haroun's depression and caused Rivke to abandon her wish to take a holiday in London. Instead, she would stay to care for her declining husband and see if some sort of family and Jewish life could be restored.

But such was the extent of the violence, rape, destruction and theft from shops and homes that the same sentiment swept over the entire community: in the space of two days, two thousand years of rich and fruitful Jewish life in Mesopotamia had come to a sudden, savage end.

2

15 March 1944
Budapest, Hungary
Dr Chaim Weisz to Anna Weisz

Dearest Anna,

If this reaches you, then the one who delivers it is truly a hero. I am sitting in a clearing with a number of other Jewish male prisoners—yes, prisoners—many of whom are familiar to me. There are other doctors here, and teachers and lawyers. We are being taken somewhere to work but we have not been told where. I cannot be sure how things will turn out. I don't know when or even if I will be back home. I have no other way of communicating with you. Our freedom has been taken away. You can see from the way I was so suddenly taken from home that things are going from bad to worse in our country. You and Mama must get out! She refuses to see how serious the threat is. Please, take her away, by force if necessary. Go to my cousin Istvan in London. Mama has his address. Do not hesitate. I don't know when we will see each other again so let me tell you and Mama that I love you both with all my heart and think of you constantly. I only had time to write this one letter and thought it might have more effect to send it to you, my darling girl. Your mother is so stubborn. I must go now.

Your devoted, loving and concerned father

Anna Weisz was an unusual girl. Among her group of friends, she was the only one who had no brothers or sisters. She was also marked out by the fact that she and her parents lived in a large apartment at the end of Budapest's Dembinszky Street, a long distance from her friends' homes near the Dohanyi Street Synagogue.

From an early age, Anna found serious subjects such as literature and classical music much more interesting than dresses and cosmetics, which was what her friends liked to talk about. And, while they dreamed about getting married and having children, Anna longed to have a career in medicine like her father, Dr Chaim Weisz. She was never happier than when he came home in the evenings with stories about Mr A's imaginary headaches, Mrs B's enormous stomach, or Miss C's sixth finger.

One day at school when the teacher had to leave the room for a few minutes, Anna astonished her classmates by going to the old and battered piano in the corner and playing Chopin's *Heroic Polonaise*. Nobody knew she could even play the piano.

'Who taught you that?' her best friend Eva Kaller asked her, Eva's face a picture of amazement.

'My mother,' Anna replied. 'She plays it all the time.'

This, too, puzzled Eva. She had visited Anna's home many times after school and had been taken there by her mother on two separate Sunday afternoons. But she could not recall seeing a piano on any of these occasions.

Anna possessed a simple beauty—clear, smooth skin; long, chestnut-coloured hair, smiling eyes and a confident mouth. Some found Anna too secretive and superior but most loved and admired her. And nobody could have loved her more than her parents, especially her father, who would hug his only daughter close and tell her that she was a lucky girl because hers was a home full of love. This gave Anna an inner happiness and an optimistic attitude to life.

Anna's mother Sarah's family had come to Hungary from Poland and settled in Budapest in the early 1900s. Sarah was the youngest of five sisters and the only one to be born in Hungary, in 1906. She was also the only one not to have her husband chosen for her by her family. Having met Chaim outside a Budapest musical instrument shop on Lánchíd Street when she was seventeen, Sarah announced to her family: 'I will marry for love, and only for love.' And that is what she did, less than a year later. Less than a year after that, her only child, Anna, was born.

As a young girl of three or four, Anna contracted diphtheria and for several weeks was in and out of the Jewish hospital in Szabolcs Street, where her father Chaim was then working as a newly-qualified graduate. It was from that period that Anna's love of anything connected to medicine began to grow.

Not that she closed her mind to other subjects; Sarah and Chaim both encouraged her to learn about physiology and biology but also always to pursue her curiosity generally. Both of her parents ensured that, in addition to the language teaching she received at school, she learnt German and English to a level high enough to read serious literature. They bought second-hand books for her from the market, Sarah taught her piano, and Chaim frequently took her to the Museum of Fine Arts and the National Gallery.

At the same time, they imbued her with a love of Judaism. Sarah could number several rabbis among her Polish ancestors and Chaim, though not a man of deep religious faith, loved the traditional Jewish reverence for learning and was familiar with the writings of Moses Mendelssohn and Samson Raphael Hirsch. And though Sarah was not a reader in the same way that Chaim was, she prized her small collection of Jewish religious books that had been passed down through her family.

On most Friday evenings, the Dembinszky Street apartment was full of family members who had come to welcome in *Shabbes*—the Sabbath. These included Chaim's and Sarah's widowed mothers, Eva and Hana, always given pride of place at the table. Chaim's brother David, a lawyer, would be there with his wife Rachel and their sons Sandor and Miklos. As would Sarah's sister Ruth and her husband Mordy, who owned a shoe store, and their two daughters Ibolya and Judit.

Sarah, and sometimes Sarah's mother, would light two thick, plain candles placed in a pair of silver candlesticks that were decidedly not plain but looked like miniature Corinthian columns.

Once the candles (of which the prudent Sarah Weisz always kept an abundant stock) were lit and the women had together uttered a short prayer, Chaim would chant the traditional blessings while holding a silver goblet of sweet red ceremonial wine and two plaited *challah* loaves covered with a special cloth. He would then break one of the loaves into hunks, which he would sprinkle with salt and hand to all the adults and children pressed together around the table.

Anna loved Friday nights. Chaim carried out the ritual with an enthusiasm that was unfettered, despite his lack of religious belief. He loved the sense of tradition and the comfortable routine, culminating as it always did with Sarah playing the piano. And he derived enormous pleasure from being surrounded by his family. At such times, he rarely missed the opportunity to pour scorn on those he described as bloodless, cold and rigid, religious hair-splitters.

Chaim Weisz considered Jews of unquestioning faith to be sheepish and gullible. His deepest contempt was reserved for the Budapest clan of Satmar Chasidim. To Anna, these men with thick beards and sidelocks who wore strange, black coats and huge circular fur hats, were alien and slightly frightening creatures, who averted their eyes whenever she passed them in the street, whether she was alone, with her friends, or out walking with Sarah. To Chaim, they were hypocrites and philistines.

Leaning back in his chair, the *koppel* that he wore on Friday nights balanced on his thick, black curls, he took delight in loudly and expansively dismissing the fanatically observant.

'All these nonsensical, casuistic black-coated holy ones,' Chaim would cry, waving a hand from side to side. 'Blessing this and blessing that— when they are not cursing and prohibiting, that is, or deciding on the minutiae of how to sit, how to stand, how to pass wind and in what direction! *This* is a blessing! *This evening*, all of us together. I don't need a divine rulebook to tell me what is blessed. Here, with the children, our sisters and brothers and our two dear mamas to keep an eye on us. Family is a blessing!'

Anna always looked forward to being with her cousins on Friday evenings. Throughout the meal, they would chatter, laugh and tease one another and, after it was finished, beg Sarah to allow them to play on her beloved upright piano. This was kept in the music room—a small antechamber with little space left for anything but the piano itself, a stool, and a single bookshelf.

This was all by way of prelude to the moment when Sarah, having feigned reluctance, allowed herself to be persuaded to play for the assembled company—Anna's two grandmothers, Eva and Hana, seated on chairs gathered from the dining room, sucking lumps of sugar as they drank from glasses of tea, the others scattered behind them in the hall outside the open music-room door, sitting, leaning or standing expectantly.

When Sarah played light and jolly folk tunes or contemporary music she had learned from the radio, the children cheered and danced. When she aimed at the heartstrings, with sentimental Yiddish, Polish or Gypsy songs, the two older mothers, Hana and Eva, would sigh and sing, closing their eyes and shaking their heads as they relished the words:

Oyfn pripetshik brent a fayerl,
Un in shtub iz heys...
('In the hearth, a fire is burning,
and in the house it is warm...')

But when Sarah played something by Beethoven or her beloved Frederic Chopin, they all listened in respectful silence, digesting their roasted goose or chicken, the men quietly sipping their wine, as the atmosphere took on a peaceful quality.

Anna enjoyed the polonaises, especially the 'Heroic', the one with which she surprised her classmates at school, but there was a nocturne—*Opus 9 Number 1*—which she loved above all else because it was her father's favourite and his eyes would be filled with love as he looked at Sarah for he knew she was playing it for him.

The music room was Sarah's haven. As a young girl, her promise was such that her father had somehow found the money to pay for her to have lessons with the piano teacher Marta Frigyes, who had studied under Nikolai Rubenstein at the Moscow Imperial Conservatory. But, after a relatively short time, the lessons ended, partly on account of Sarah's refusal to play in public.

Her family made no objection to this. For one thing, the strain on her father's finances was eased but, most importantly, Sarah retained her love of the piano and, years later, the very first purchase that she and Chaim made in Budapest was the upright that so neatly fitted into what would become her music room. Here, she would retreat for hours, and only on Friday nights would she leave the door open.

Sometimes, Sarah went to the piano to get away from the loud and exuberant discussions between her husband and her daughter that began after Anna entered Budapest's Jewish high school at the age of eleven. While both of her parents took an active interest in Anna's lessons in general and participated in her homework, Chaim would get very exercised about any flaws he believed he could detect in her education—especially her religious studies.

Continually throughout Anna's first two years at the high school, he complained about the 'idiotic prejudices, fears and superstitions' that her religious studies teachers were putting into the heads of 'my daughter and her classmates' and wrote out questions about Jewish ethics and the existence of God for Anna to put to Mrs Revesz, the pious, bewigged and drably-dressed woman who taught Judaism to her class.

One day at home, when Anna was twelve, she began the usual after-dinner inquest into what she had done that day at school by laughing.

'Sounds like a good day,' Chaim said, smiling.

'Well, no,' Anna corrected. 'It was just that the religion teacher said something so stupid.'

This was the signal for Sarah—whose Judaism, though never rigorously examined, was nevertheless central to her life—to escape to the piano. 'Oh, no,' she said firmly, holding up the palms of her hands in a gesture of refusal. 'I don't want to hear this.' And she promptly stood up and left the table.

'Our lesson was on the Ten Commandments,' Anna told her father once the soft, sweet sounds of her mother's piano began to flow out from behind the closed door. 'Mrs Revesz was talking about not coveting your neighbour's possessions. She said this meant we should not be jealous of rich people because God had decided who should be rich and who should be poor. It was just the way she said it. Eva and I looked at each other and laughed. Mrs Revesz was angry,' Anna continued, mimicking poor Mrs Revesz's voice: '"Don't you believe the word of God? You think Moses"—she called him *Moshe Rabbeinu*—"is a *liar*?"'

Anna and her father both laughed as he threw up his arms and said, in a mock-puzzled voice: 'Of course! Commandment number ten-and-a-half: thou shalt not envy rich people because I have decided that they should be rich.' And they turned their attention to the more stimulating biology lesson.

46

But, the next day, Chaim continued to be irked by the teacher's interpretation of the Decalogue and made an appointment to see the headmaster at the end of school hours.

'Thank you for seeing me,' Chaim said as the headmaster, a corpulent man who permanently wore a black *koppel* on his head and a tight waistcoat around his resistant midriff, ushered Chaim into his study and waved an arm at an empty seat facing his own across a large, heavy desk that looked at least a hundred years old.

'Not at all,' the head replied. 'We are very pleased with Anna. You should be proud. She is an excellent student.'

'Thank you,' said Chaim once more. 'We are indeed proud of Anna. Our only child and she is a gem. But I wanted to inform you of the kind of instruction the pupils are receiving from their religion teacher. Yesterday, she told my daughter's class that everyone who is rich—and everyone who is poor—deserves to be that way because that is what God has decided.'

The headmaster stroked his neatly-trimmed beard and moustache as he listened to Chaim. He thought for a moment and then said: 'And so?'

That evening, Chaim told his daughter that the school she was attending was generally a good place to build up her knowledge but that she should always question everything she was told, not necessarily directly to the teachers but at least in her own head, and to read more than just the prescribed text books.

As for the religion class and Mrs Revesz, this, Chaim argued, was like a diseased branch of the tree of knowledge, or a simple relative in an otherwise sound family who should be treated politely, with kindness, but whose words should not be taken seriously.

In the months that followed, Chaim became increasingly earnest in the discussions at home and Sarah became increasingly disinclined to participate, or even listen. The polonaises would resound louder and louder in the background as Chaim spoke much more quietly and seriously with Anna about her longing for the medical life. During this time he shared with her his concerns about the Hungarian Regent, Miklos Horthy, who appeared to be growing closer to Nazi Germany by the day.

Hungary's relations with Nazi Germany were the subject of the only serious quarrel that Anna could remember her parents having. Close to midnight, the day after her thirteenth birthday, she was awoken by her father's voice, sounding loud and impatient through the wall between her parents' bedroom and her own.

'Open your eyes, Sarah! Open your *eyes!*' he shouted with great emphasis.

At first, Anna was frightened and climbed out of bed to run to her parents' bedroom. But then she heard her mother's reaction and decided not to intervene.

'You think all Jews in Budapest are threatened?' Sarah responded, her voice firm though not as loud as Chaim's. 'Don't be ridiculous! A quarter of the city's population is Jewish. Jewish life is threaded into Hungarian life—commerce, politics, books, music, law, *medicine!*' Anna could picture her mother counting off the professions on her fingers. 'If Jews are threatened, then so is Budapest. Hungary itself is threatened!'

'What do you mean by "Hungarian life"?' Chaim spoke more in despair than anger. 'The Germans are our neighbours now. There is no Austria any more. Not that the Austrians are so well-disposed to the Jews. But after this Anschluss it is a hundred times worse. Germany—Nazi Germany—has taken over Austria. And, among the Austrians, the ordinary, ignorant and foolish citizens are thrilled. Can't you see, Sarah?' And then, after a pause, more softly: 'Don't you understand, my darling?'

Anna told herself that this dispute had nothing to do with her and covered her head with a pillow to try to shut it out of her hearing. This failed to work and she found it hard to sleep until, overcome with anxiety and sadness, her unexpected, rhythmic sobs exhausted her.

But Anna was wrong. The substance of the dispute between her parents did indeed have to do with her, and with all Jews living in Hungary. At around the time of that overheard quarrel, in April 1938, the Hungarian government had let it be known that previously dormant legislation limiting the involvement of Jews in the nation's professional and educational bodies would be reactivated.

A bill was introduced into parliament stating that activities in certain fields, such as law, engineering, theatre, newspapers and—in an ironic echo of Sarah Weisz's enumerative protest to her husband—medicine could be practised only by members of the relevant professional chamber. The percentage of Jews in any chamber should not be allowed to exceed twenty.

In an article written in a Hungarian journal on 14 April 1938, the democratic politician Janos Vazsonyi—who, seven years later, would perish in Dachau concentration camp—used a football analogy to criti-cise the bill. He described the legislation as a kick that indicates no goal, is not directed at a ball and causes pain to many people. Referring to the quota to be attached to Jewish professional people, he wrote: 'Eighty and twenty… two very telling numbers, which will soon be the cause of many complaints. Complaints of starving, of people who have lost their jobs. Bitterness and tears.'

A few days after the publication of Vazsonyi's article, the first of a series of visits to the Szabolcs Street Jewish hospital by a black-hatted government official took place. Chaim saw him through the glass win-dow on the office door of Dr Laszlo Farkas, the hospital supervisor. The official, a large, moon-faced man with spectacles and a thick moustache, was sitting across the desk from Farkas and reading something to him from a printed document.

Once the official had left, Chaim took the first opportunity he had—which happened to be as he was walking along a corridor—to stop Laszlo Farkas and ask him what the visit had been about.

Farkas's voice seemed to break as he answered: 'I am not allowed to say.'

'Laszlo, what do you mean?' Chaim asked, agitated. 'Is this the new law coming home to us?'

'I am truly, sorry, Chaim. I cannot tell you yet. If I did, things would get much worse.'

When Chaim came home that evening describing these events, Sarah, as usual, played them down. 'It could be nothing, Chaim. You know how these officials cherish secrecy. It gives them a feeling of importance.'

And, when the official returned three or four more times over the following fortnight and left shaking hands with Laszlo Farkas, who was smiling, Chaim did feel a little reassured. Dr Farkas still would not explain the purpose of the official's visits, however, though he seemed to be much more at ease than he had been after his first encounter with that moustachioed moon face.

Farkas took particular pains to placate Chaim, knowing him to be the most politically aware of the hospital staff. 'Do not worry, Chaim,' he urged. 'The secrecy is just some government formality. Be patient. You will have no cause to be upset.'

This was a sentiment echoed, a week later, by Sarah after Laszlo Far-kas was able to reveal that he had managed to secure a ruling from the

National Social Insurance Institution that the hospital's four senior doctors, including Chaim, would fall within the twenty per cent quota, should the proposed legislation take effect.

Chaim's anxiety, by contrast, was, if anything, slightly deepened by this news. But he resolved not to shake Sarah out of her optimism, knowing how important it was for at least one of them to remain confident.

'You must stop this worrying, my dear,' she told him. 'Things are normal and comfortable in the city. Your job is safe. And all of our neighbours, the Jewish and the non-Jewish, are as friendly as they have ever been.'

'I love you,' Chaim answered.

At the beginning of May, the eminent composer Bela Bartok was among fifty-nine distinguished, non-Jewish Hungarians who signed a declaration against the 80:20 bill. The declaration issued a strong moral challenge charging that, 'all our contemporaries should consider their responsibility if, despite the protests of our conscience, a bill is enacted which some day all Hungarians will have to remember with shame.'

When the bill had its final reading, it was endorsed by Hungary's leading Christians and, despite the protests of conscience by Bartok and his fellow signatories, the so-called Act of Balance was passed on 28 May 1938. In neighbouring Austria at that time, Jews were being forced to clean pavements and, to Chaim Weisz, the Act of Balance was only a beginning. To others, like Sarah Weisz, it was little more than an irritant designed to placate the domineering Germans.

Despite these contrasting reactions, Sarah and Chaim emotionally and steadfastly supported each other through the subsequent years, during which the state's suppression of Jewish freedom in Budapest and other parts of the country gained momentum. The 'Hungarian life' that Sarah held so dear, and about which she had argued with Chaim in that nocturnal disagreement that had so shocked the thirteen-year-old Anna, was unravelling its Jewish threads. It was also falling under the shadow of Germany and the exponents of National Socialism.

In 1941, an estimated 18,000 Jews were deported to Galicia, an eastern European territory nominally given over to Hungary by the Germans who had recently captured it from Soviet Russia. The deportees had fallen foul of a new law preventing Jews becoming Hungarian citizens through marriage or naturalisation. Within Galicia, in the town of Kamenetsk-

Podolsk, they also fell under the control of an SS commander by the name of Friedrich Jeckeln.

Jeckeln's middle name was August, which as it turned out was all too hideously appropriate. For, towards the end of the month of August, in 1941, Höhere SS und Polizeiführer Jeckeln ordered his troops, with the assistance of the local police battalion, to massacre the Jewish deportees together with many hundreds of Ukrainian Jews. Around 23,500 Jews were killed over two or three days.

This act of slaughter formed a template for the Nazis' Final Solution to the Jewish Question. Columns of naked human beings were herded into large, readily dug, open graves into which they would fall, one cluster of bodies on top of another, as they were all shot in the back of the head. This method of mass execution, devised by Friedrich August Jeckeln, became known as 'Sardinenpackung'—sardine packing—or, coldly and simply, 'The Jeckeln System'.

The established Jews of Budapest were not directly touched by these matters, and remained largely ignorant of them, but for those such as Dr Chaim Weisz, who were sensitive to the prevailing winds, it became imperative to make plans to escape the coming storm. To Sarah, however, this still seemed too drastic. For all the petty restrictions and the occasional hostile outburst by young thugs or individual rabble rousers, it had to be remembered, Sarah reminded her family, that, 'we are living through a war, in decent accommodation, and the city is still our home.'

'But people—our people—have been *killed*, Sarah,' was Chaim's forceful retort to this line of thinking. 'And not just by German soldiers,' he added. 'I have heard at the hospital reliable information about a mass murder of Jews by Ukrainians. You think our friendly Hungarian fascists aren't eager to join in the Nazis' game? I am sorry, my darling, but I am making plans for us to leave Budapest, including both of our families, not just you, me and Anna. I have already written to my cousin Istvan.'

It took three months for Istvan's reply to arrive, and it had been posted from a Royal Artillery camp in Whitby, Yorkshire, where Istvan—now known as Ivor—was serving as a Lance Corporal. He wrote only two lines, informing Chaim that he, Ivor, would try to help when he was next on leave from the army but he didn't say when that would be.

Chaim asked people at the hospital, patients, staff and visitors, if they knew of any promising routes out of Hungary but nobody expressed any

51

wish to go. Those who wanted to leave had already gone—'except me,' said Chaim, as cheerfully as he could, to the nurse who told him this.

In any event, Chaim was constantly busy at the hospital and at home, and this, together with Sarah's reluctance to leave and the general sheen of normality across the city, kept the Weisz family continuing their lives from day to day in the Dembinszky Street apartment.

Over the course of these years, their daughter Anna developed into a young woman of strong will and subtle elegance. She thought, talked and even walked with confidence. As she entered her eighteenth year, she became more aware of her powers of attraction. She seemed to possess a rich, intelligent aura, evident in the inviting depth of her eyes and the steadiness of her gaze. Not only men, but her young women friends, too, consistently sought her company.

She had grown closer to—and, at the same time, further apart from—her childhood friend Eva Kaller. Closer, because the two girls remained fond of each other and, given a freer rein by their parents, spent more time together, visiting cafés, parks and the cinema. But further apart, too, because, while Anna desired independence and a career, Eva thought only of finding a husband. Anna wanted to travel to other countries while Eva loved Budapest and never wanted to leave. Anna read Imre Madach and Sandor Marai; Eva read magazines.

Anna still wanted very much to follow in her father's medical footsteps. By now, Chaim was making extra money by seeing patients at the Dembinszky Street apartment, having cornered off a section of the family sitting room with a screen, a desk and shelves—considerably reducing domestic living space—while still working shifts at the Szabolcs Street Jewish hospital.

However, even though her father was a registered, practising doctor, it was clear that Anna would find it almost impossible, as a Jewish woman, to pursue a medical career in the ostracising, quota-enforcing society that was Hungary in the 1940s. But she and her father were both of determined calibre and Chaim took the unusual step of teaching Anna himself, taking her as often as possible into the wards and laboratories of the Szabolcs Street hospital, where she was made very welcome by the staff—and where she met Imre Handler.

Imre was a young trainee doctor from Bonyhad, in south-western Hungary. On first seeing Anna, he could hardly draw breath. Chaim sometimes included him in the personal tutorials he was giving Anna

52

and a close friendship inevitably arose between them. Imre was invited to Dembinszky Street for meals and entered easily into the noisy, open atmosphere that Sarah and Chaim had cultivated throughout their married life, an atmosphere in which Anna had never been patronised or ignored but instead, from an early age, credited with the rights and reasoning ability of an adult.

Imre and Anna were rarely alone together but when they did find time to go to the cinema or a café, for a stroll alongside the Danube, or a picnic on Margaret Island, Sarah and Chaim would be quite unconcerned about it. They were both fond of Imre, who was a respectful and intelligent young man with an engaging manner. They were also sure that their beloved Anna was a perfectly responsible young woman.

Anna herself was attracted by Imre's natural, humorous manner. She thought him handsome in his own fashion and liked the way his wild, black curls—like her father's—flopped over his forehead when he laughed, which he did often. He was neither embarrassed nor embarrassing. Though warm and witty, like Anna he had little time for empty frivolity but loved books and music.

It was after a visit to the State Opera House that Imre first kissed her. Her recollection, in her diary that evening, was typically analytical. 'So, is this what Eva and the others are so obsessed about? Is this love?' she wrote. 'Imre is lovely, I like to be with him and listen to him speaking—I love his voice and the way he laughs. But I am not feeling "enslaved", "overcome", or any of the other terms of total surrender that Eva uses. I will never place myself under the control of another. I will only allow love to happen when it is the right time and the right person. As it did with Mama and Papa. Will it be Imre? We shall have to see.'

They had known each other for four months or so when, in the autumn of 1943, Imre went to spend a weekend with his family in Bonyhad, something he did from time to time. But, on this occasion, he did not come back. At the hospital, Chaim was told that the whole family had left their home town, indeed had left Hungary, and Imre would 'not be continuing his studies in Budapest', as the short note received from Imre's father had put it. But Anna heard nothing.

She was upset and puzzled at the abrupt nature of his departure and she missed his company, but the experience strengthened her resolve to live her own life, creatively and responsibly. She certainly did not believe that Imre's leaving was on account of anything she had said or done. 'If he cannot write to me,' she wrote in her diary, 'I cannot weep for him.'

Some months later, in the early evening of 9 March 1944, Chaim and Anna were sitting together at Chaim's desk. They were in a cheerful mood. The daughter of a patient had just left having brought gifts of a watch for Chaim and flowers for Anna as a mark of gratitude for their seeing her elderly mother through a long illness at the Jewish hospital. Siggy, a friend of Anna's on leave from the Jewish Labour Battalion—the *Arbeitsdienst*—was due in an hour to take her to the opera. Sarah was at the piano, vigorously pounding out Rachmaninov—whose death she had mourned two weeks short of a year earlier.

'Is that Siggy?' asked Chaim, hearing an unexpected knock at the door.

'It can't be,' said Anna. 'He would never be here so early.'

In Sarah's music room, the Rachmaninov went on apparently uninterrupted.

'Sarah, it's somebody knocking,' Chaim called out to his wife, as he stood up and moved towards the door. 'Probably a neighbour to complain about your playing. It's too loud.'

Sarah reduced the volume to *pianissimo possibile* but continued playing.

As he opened the door to the apartment, Dr Chaim Weisz framed his mouth into an apology. 'I'm sorry,' he was about to say. 'My wife is such a music lover, she gets carried away—and she is still in mourning for Rachmaninov!' Or some such phrase.

But, faced with two serious-faced men in dark suits—one short and stocky, wearing a trilby hat, the other larger, his suit stretched across a thick, muscular body, his expression a mixture of resentment and disdain—Chaim hesitated. Curious and anxious, he left the apology hanging in the air, getting only as far as a quiet, distracted, 'I'm...' before the smaller of the two men, the one wearing the trilby, addressed him.

'Dr Chaim Weisz?'

'Yes, that is me. How can I help you?'

'I am from the central municipal department,' the man announced, reaching up as if to touch his trilby but then drawing back from doing so. 'This is Captain Budai of the police bureau,' he added, indicating his gruff companion by a slight backward twisting of the neck, but not offering his own name.

'I see,' said Chaim warily.

Sarah stopped playing and came out of the music room.

Anna crossed the room to stand next to her father.

'I am instructed to inform you that you are needed for some urgent government work,' said the trilby-hatted official. 'We require you to come with us straight away.'

'But what kind of work? I presume it is medical. Can you not give me a few details?'

'You may bring some personal belongings in a small bag,' the official said, tightening his lips.

At this point, Sarah came forward. 'Won't you gentlemen come in for a moment? Perhaps a coffee?'

'That is very kind of you, Mrs Weisz, but I am afraid we are in a hurry. We will wait here at the door while your husband gathers together a few things.'

'But what is this about? Why the police?' Sarah felt panic rising through her body.

'Don't worry, my darling,' said Chaim. 'I will quickly go and pack some clothes. There has probably been a traffic accident with casualties that need attending to urgently.'

'That's right, Mrs Weisz, don't worry,' said the official. 'I'm sure your husband's work won't last long.'

Less than fifteen minutes later, Chaim reappeared with his bag, which he put down so that he could hug his wife and daughter.

'This way please, Dr Weisz,' said the man, pulling his trilby down more tightly on his head as he stepped back to let Chaim pass and walk away with the policeman. 'Goodnight, Mrs Weisz,' he said to Sarah. He turned to leave but then stopped and stared at Anna. 'Goodnight,' he said softly, holding his stare, his face portentous.

It was a face, and a moment, that Anna would never forget. Nor would she forget her father putting down his bag of belongings and hugging her and her mother.

Nor would she forget the face of the boy on the bicycle who, two days later, called her name as she walked out of the apartment into Dembinszky Street and, as she turned, thrust into her hand an old envelope containing a single sheet of paper.

'My father gave it to me to give to you,' the boy cried out as he rode away. 'He says it's from your father.'

'My father?' Anna called after the boy. 'Who are you? Where did you get this? Who gave it to you?'

But he was gone.

The envelope was creased. A name—'Dr Balogh'—was written across the front above what seemed to be an address scribbled over by a heavy hand. As she pulled out the sheet of paper and recognised her father's handwriting, she felt her heart beating and a sudden gasping in her throat.

For a moment, she could not read the letter; the words blurred before her eyes. She had to lean against the wall of her apartment building and take a deep breath before taking in the message that she held in her shaking right hand.

She read it through twice, the second time hovering helplessly over the phrase, 'I don't know when or even if I will be back home,' and then whispering, with her dampened eyes closed: 'Oh God. Please bring him home. Papa, come home. Please.'

All of this, and the long, visceral sound that issued from her mother when Anna showed her the letter—to which Anna responded: 'We must find him'—she would never forget.

Nor would she ever forget the last time that she and her mother would leave the Dembinszky Street apartment and Sarah, who for several days would barely have touched the piano's keyboard, would take a hammer to the instrument while the gendarme stood waiting at the door and Anna herself concealed her father's hastily written note in her underwear.

She would never forget any of it.

Though Anna Weisz acknowledged that there were things that she would never be able to forget, there were, nonetheless, many that she tried very hard to forget. Most of these belonged to a period of a year or so that followed the night that her father was taken away from the Dembinszky Street flat.

For several days, her mother held on to the possibility that Chaim would return, even after Anna had shown her his scribbled note. Every time Sarah heard the sound of footsteps outside the apartment, she would rush to open the door, and silently curse those passing by for not calling at her door, for not bringing her news, encouraging news, of her husband—or for not being her husband. In between, she tried to keep her life as normal as possible, going to the shops, meeting her family, sewing, reading and, above all, playing the piano.

Anna was rarely at home during that time. She frantically tried to find out what had happened to her father, at the municipal department, the central police station, the Jewish hospital and the Jewish community offices. Sarah went with her to the hospital and the police. Nowhere could they obtain any genuine information.

At the central police station, they saw the captain, Budai, who had accompanied the man in the trilby who had come to collect Chaim, but he affected not to recognise them or to know anything about a Dr Weisz. His only sign of recognition was to look at them as though examining a piece of evidence in a criminal investigation.

'You're Jews, aren't you?' he said, narrowing his eyes. His question did not require an answer and he continued without waiting for one. 'You people are a burden, and you make trouble. Hungary is now in a mess and it would not be if it weren't for you. And I can tell you that, if any male in your family has been taken from you, it is because he is a traitor and he will not be coming back to you.'

'You pig!' As Anna shouted a fierce, instinctive response to Budai, she was immediately restrained by her mother. At first, she struggled forcefully as Sarah tried to hold her. And then, suddenly, Sarah felt her daughter go limp in her arms. She had stopped struggling and her facial expression altered from defiant to downcast. Her mood seemed to change just as quickly from angry to resigned. But she held up her head again as Budai stepped towards her.

'If it were not for the fact that you have a mother who possesses some sense, who at least understands the situation,' he said, bending down to look closely into Anna's face, 'you would be in a lot of trouble.' As he turned away, muttering 'stupid Jewish bitch', Sarah clamped her hand over Anna's mouth and dragged her out of the police station.

Reluctantly yet fervently, Anna began, after the encounter with Budai, to concentrate her energy on trying to persuade her mother to leave with her. She heard of Jewish families who were fleeing Budapest, joining relatives in the countryside or, if they could, getting out of Hungary. Several of her friends' families and some members of the staff at the Jewish hospital departed, leaving others to speculate about their destinations.

Rumours abounded. Anna was told that some had gone to Switzerland, others to Bulgaria. Even Australia and America were mentioned. Wherever Jews gathered together, rumours were repeated and analysed over and over.

But Anna could not persuade her mother to leave the flat. Sarah continued to believe that the situation was a temporary one, that order would be restored. In a sense, her belief was correct. Around two weeks after Chaim's apparent arrest, there was order in Budapest. But this was not a reinstatement of pre-war calm by the Hungarian parliament. Certainly not for the city's Jews.

Adolf Eichmann of the German SS had arrived in Budapest on 19 March 1944, his thirty-eighth birthday. By then, the Nazis had ceased to tolerate the Hungarian regime, having discovered that it had conducted exploratory peace negotiations with Britain and the United States. Consequently, the Germans had marched into Budapest, ejected the sitting government and placed Eichmann on the trail of the Hungarian-Jewish population, operating from his base in Budapest's Majestic Hotel.

German order—Nazi order—had been brought to bear upon the capital. In late March, at the direction of Hitler's Germany, a new government was installed in Budapest, with the support of the country's fascist Arrow Cross Party. In April, Jews were ordered to wear the stigmatically identifying yellow star.

Sarah and Anna seldom left the apartment except to visit Anna's two grandmothers. The Jewish hospital was closed and Anna tried to collate and study the medical books and papers that Chaim had accumulated. Sarah, inevitably, sought consolation at her piano keyboard. After a while, she found she could not complete longer pieces without being overcome by sighs and tears. When Anna heard her mother crying, she too began to weep under a growing burden of sadness that had started to erode her formerly powerful spirit.

Sarah's and Chaim's mothers, Hana and Eva, together with David, Rachel, Ruth, Mordy and the children, still came on Friday nights as often as possible but the atmosphere was now solemn and no longer celebratory. Food was scarce and some *Shabbes* ceremonies were held without bread or wine—though there were always candles in Sarah's plentiful stock. Sarah herself no longer felt able to give her *Shabbes* recitals to the family, however, and if young Sandor, Miklos, Ibolya or

Judit persisted in urging her to play, their parents would warn them off—sometimes, it seemed to Anna, a little too sharply.

Then, when David, Rachel, their sons, and David and Chaim's mother Eva, were moved from their flat into a yellow star building where, like the rest of the Jewish families resident there, they were crammed together into one squalid room, Sarah became so dispirited that she virtually ceased to play the piano altogether, although she would still sit for hours at the keyboard and sometimes try to play the Chopin *Opus 9* nocturne and pray that Chaim was safe.

May 1944 was a bitter month. At its beginning, Chaim and David's mother, Eva Weisz, all her life an intelligent, resourceful, sociable and well-read woman who loved nothing more than to engage in lively argument or gossip, suddenly stopped reading books and listening to the radio. David and Rachel and their boys all tried to coax their beloved mother, mother-in-law and grandmother out of this uncharacteristic torpor, but she resisted. And then she stopped speaking.

She became mute, unable, or refusing, to utter a word and stayed that way for about three weeks, until one night she fell to her knees wailing with such baleful force that David turned his face from her, closing his eyes, covering his ears and screaming inwardly, in silence. His face pale and his throat dry, he turned shakily back to his mother as her eerie sounds gradually became transformed into a rhythmic repetition of his brother's name: 'Chaim, Chaim, Chaim…'

This reiteration of a single cry to her absent, first-born son was the last word that Eva spoke. That night, she collapsed and died in her daughter-in-law Rachel's arms. The city authorities denied the family a Jewish burial and removed her body to dispose of it in their own way.

The authorities also closed down Mordy's shoe shop around this time and conscripted him, and David, into the service of the Hungarian army, where they faced a posting to the battlefront. Within a day of her husband losing his business and his freedom, Ruth and her daughters were sent to the same yellow star building in which Rachel and her sons were trying to continue their lives.

Immediately after her mother-in-law's death, Sarah brought her own mother, Hana, to the Dembinszky Street apartment to live with her and Anna. But the month of May came to its sombre conclusion with notice being given to Sarah that she, Hana and Anna were to be transferred to a room in a yellow star building some distance from that in which her sister Ruth and sister-in-law Rachel now lived.

On their last night in the old apartment, in July 1944, once the elderly Hana had gone to bed, Sarah surprised Anna by sitting at the piano and, in a newly-defiant mood, playing Chopin's *Heroic Polonaise*.

Hearing the old familiar notes, Anna went into the music room and sat on a chair alongside her mother's piano stool.

'Mama,' she said with feeling as she placed her arm around her mother's shoulders and kissed her cheek. 'It's going to be a long time before you will be able to play Chopin again. If you had only said goodbye to him and your piano, where you have sat and worshipped him for so many years, the day that we returned from the police station... If only. We might have been able to get out of this hell.

'Daddy was right. You are so stubborn. My friend Eva and her parents left weeks ago, and so did other friends from the hospital. Even Imre did the right thing, however much he upset me at the time. I understand his family's motives now. You can't afford to be sentimental any more.'

'Maybe Imre did try to get in touch with you. These days, you can't rely on the postal system... or anything.'

Sarah's defiant stance was wilting.

'Maybe he did, Mama. Maybe he did. Or maybe he knew that any letter sent to me from abroad could land me in trouble. But I don't know if we will have another chance to escape. You know what it is like in these yellow star buildings. There is no way out!' Anna almost yelled this last sentence.

'There is no escape from the streets either, wearing these yellow stars. We are sitting targets. People have been shot and dumped in the Danube.' Sarah's voice was rising too.

'Yes, Mama. I know. Another friend of mine—do you remember Frida? She and her mother were in a round-up. Frida was clever enough to realise what was happening. It sounds like it was complete chaos—a hopeless, confused crowd being steered towards the Danube. Frida ripped off her yellow star and made her mother do the same. She pulled her mother away from those poor, doomed Jews flowing like a flood along the street with just a handful of gendarmes urging them forward. None of Eichmann's thugs; only Hungarians. Frida and her mother managed to mingle with the crowds in the streets and make their way back to their home.'

60

'You think that's so easy to do? With more and more Arrow Cross *mamzers* running around?' For Sarah to swear was extremely unusual. After a pause, she added: 'Well, maybe it is. If your friend Frida and her mother can run away, so can we.'

'But, Mama, it's too late. I'm certainly not saying it's easy to do. We're going into a *ghetto*.' Anna was standing up now.

'I've only ever tried to do what is right!' Sarah turned resolutely to look her daughter in the eyes. 'Do you think I'm going around carelessly, without feelings? Do you think I don't want to know what has happened to Daddy? I cry for him every night and morning!'

Both women were crying now. Anna became fearful and could barely look into her mother's face, crumpled as it was by such distress. They had reached a peak of anger, frustration and sadness. They hugged each other and wept together—for Chaim, for themselves, for the Jews, for Hungary, and for the morrow upon which the gendarmes would come and order them peremptorily out of the apartment, telling them that they must leave all their possessions behind, except for one suitcase of belongings between the three generations, Anna, Sarah and Hana.

Anna would still have time to hide her father's note. And Sarah would still have time to open up her piano stool, take out the hammer she had put there the night before and deliver a last, shattering crescendo.

After the dislocation of the move from the flat on Dembinszky Street to the room, with its rusty pipes and rat-droppings, which would be their home for the next three months, they rallied somewhat.

The atmosphere in the streets was quieter, daily life somehow steadier. Anna's grandmother Hana was a calming force. Anna herself managed to get out and meet her cousins. This uneasy security, in a country at the heart of a continent riven by war, could not last.

Shortly after the Arrow Cross's growing strength took the party into power in October 1944, on a day when Grandma Hana was at her daughter Ruth's flat at the other end of the area that was being converted into a ghetto, Anna and her mother were scooped up by Hungarian gendarmes—'Not a German in sight,' said Sarah, at the time—allowed to quickly pack one small suitcase each, and sent off by cattle-train to Auschwitz-Birkenau, a place unknown to either of them.

The last demoralising indignity forced upon them in their native city came when Sarah's attempt to pack into her case her inherited and cherished religious books was thwarted by a sneering gendarme, barely out of his teens, who roughly took them from her and threw them into the gutter.

Auschwitz was—they were told upon arrival almost twenty-four hours after they had been bundled into an overcrowded, sweltering, fetid wagon—a work camp in Poland, or, rather, a network of camps. They remained there together, in the women's section, for a week or two, long enough to have consecutive serial numbers tattooed on to their forearms, until Sarah fell ill and was taken to the camp hospital.

'We will find out what is wrong with her,' said the SS guard who escorted Sarah away. 'I hear that she plays the piano,' she continued, knowing that Anna understood German. 'When she recovers, perhaps she will be put in our orchestra. She can play for the girls in the officers' block.'

This at first seemed to Anna an isolated moment of woman-to-woman compassion but, as captive and captor walked slowly away and the image of the guard's carefully rolled blonde hair, tiny nose, mean mouth and obscenely well-fed face stuck in Anna's mind, she reflected that the SS guard's comment, delivered as it was with a leering wink, might have been deliberately ambiguous.

This feeling was reinforced when, the following day, the same guard made a dismissive gesture and merely shook her head in response to Anna's enquiry about her mother's condition. Then, as Anna turned to return to her block, the guard called her back.

'Is your father *Doctor* Weisz, Chaim Weisz?' she asked.

'Yes,' Anna answered guardedly.

'He was here, you know, in Auschwitz camp.'

'*Was?*'

To this frantic question of Anna's, the guard compressed her lips and turned her eyes skywards, in a contemptuous show of not knowing the answer. When Anna attempted to enquire further, the guard repelled her with a fierce expression and by holding up a single, silencing hand.

Two days later, Anna herself was under escort, along with several other prisoners. She was leaving her mother in Auschwitz, in the land of her rabbinical forebears, while her own destination was in northern Germany, just south of the towns of Bergen and Belsen.

Anna's friend Frida had indeed rescued her mother and herself from what turned out to be a mass killing carried out by the Arrow Cross on the banks of the Danube. Just as Anna had told Sarah in their last night in Dembinszky Street, Frida had torn the yellow star from her coat and helped her mother to do the same before slipping away from the ragged cluster of women being marched towards the river near Budapest's historic Chain Bridge.

Frida's action saved them from almost certain death. The rest of the women, arbitrarily plucked from the yellow star area that was then being reconstituted into a ghetto, were gunned down and tossed into the water. For hours it flowed with their blood. The freedom gained, however, was limited. Frida and her mother had nowhere else to go but the nascent Budapest ghetto, where they continued to live in constant fear of another round-up.

Even though many ghetto-dwellers were left alone and the Nazis and the Hungarian fascists themselves became anxious as Russian forces advanced towards the city, the fear that Rosa Goldberg and her daughter Frida felt was justified. They did once more get caught, this time in Eichmann's net, and suffered a similar fate to that of Anna and her mother.

Nevertheless, they both felt something like relief when, on an unusually warm but otherwise unremarkable day in October 1944, they were removed from the daily privations and anxieties of their life in the yellow star building off Kazinczy Street to be taken, as part of a small group of women, to 'carry out work for the Reich in the east'.

They arrived in Auschwitz a few days after Anna and Sarah were installed. In due course, Frida would follow Anna in being moved on to the Bergen-Belsen concentration camp, a former prisoner-of-war institution in Lower Saxony. By the time of Frida's arrival in Bergen-Belsen, in January 1945, Anna would be an established inmate. But Frida's mother, unlike Anna's, did not last even for a few days in Auschwitz. Rosa never even entered Auschwitz I, where Sarah had been taken ill. Rosa and Frida Goldberg were parted on the platform at Birkenau, the arrival point for the Auschwitz camp complex.

While Frida was ushered towards a snaking column of people hurried along by gaunt-looking figures in striped uniforms, her mother found herself walking in a different direction among a mass of mostly older or infirm people coughing and groaning, limping and shivering.

In the subsequent three months working in a quarry under the supervision of some of Auschwitz's most brutal female SS guards, equipped with whips and accompanied by Alsatian dogs, Frida learned nothing of her mother's fate but, as she would tell Anna when they met in Bergen-Belsen, she had no illusions.

Though they had been at school together, Frida had never been an especially close friend of Anna's but the two girls had always admired each other. And when Anna saw Frida on that January day among a group of newly-arrived prisoners, after registering shock and dismay at the realisation that Frida had not, after all, escaped from the cruel forces within Budapest, it somehow gave her a feeling of reassurance, of home.

Frida arrived at a time of upheaval in Bergen-Belsen. The Nazis were flooding the camp with captives from other camps in the east, left empty or partially destroyed as the Russian army moved inexorably closer. Bergen-Belsen's population rapidly increased tenfold and, with the growth in numbers came a growth in typhus, dysentery and starvation.

In Anna's hut, the overcrowding changed the atmosphere dramatically. She had hitherto occupied a single bunk and been on tolerably good terms with her neighbours, young women from Budapest, rural Hungary and Poland, all of whom had been in Auschwitz.

She had made herself popular by helping people overcome minor illnesses and injuries but had not allied herself to any intimate extent with any individual prisoner. As more prisoners were admitted into the hut daily throughout January and the existing occupants were made to share bunks and rations with the newcomers, Anna began to crave the friendship of somebody of her own age and background. She was now sharing her bunk with a studious-looking, grey-haired teacher from Warsaw, who reminded Anna of her mother—a reminder she did not need.

When Frida arrived, Anna profoundly hoped that here at last was a ready-made confidante with whom she could share her secret fears and dreams. Physically, she felt very protective towards Frida. As Anna hugged her old friend tightly for the first time on meeting in Bergen-Belsen, she was alarmed at how fragile Frida felt. She had always been thin but now the skin across her back felt like the most delicate gossamer through which the shoulder bones were on the point of protruding. Her chest was not so much flat as corrugated. Her limbs betrayed little sign of flesh.

Mentally, by contrast, Anna felt she needed Frida's protection. Frida calmly accepted that her mother was dead, while Anna could not let go of the hope that Sarah would have recovered in the Auschwitz hospital and would eventually emerge after the war and that they would both be reunited with Chaim.

'This is a hard reality, Anna,' Frida told her. 'If you don't make yourself understand that, it will be much harder for you to survive. You can do nothing about your mother and father's survival. You have to concentrate upon yourself.'

'But it's so difficult,' Anna said. 'I cannot stop thinking about them. It's bad enough that they are not together. That in itself is such a wrench for two people who are so deeply in love. But to be apart and alone, in such a world as we are living in…'

Frida comforted her, placing a scrawny arm around Anna's shoulder. 'Whether or not either or both of them survives,' Frida continued, 'it will not have been on account of anything you will have done here in Belsen. You must act with as much determination as you can muster. I know it sounds cruel but you have to behave as though your parents are dead. If my mother is alive, in spite of what I think, it will be a wonderful surprise. But it will be a terrible surprise for her if she survives and discovers that I have wasted away and died through pining for her.'

Over the next few weeks, the two young women were inseparable, supporting each other through ever-deteriorating conditions. The standard rations of bread, water, a thin and tasteless liquid made from turnips and called 'soup', and a bitter-tasting brown drink described as 'coffee', diminished in size and regularity and on some days did not appear at all.

At dawn, on a day towards the end of February 1945, after Anna and Frida had not received rations for two days, they were called out by an SS guard to help with a 'special task' for which they would receive extra rations.

Along with about twenty other prisoners, also sorted into pairs, from their part of the Bergen-Belsen complex, they were taken to a part of the camp with which they were unfamiliar and where, a few yards from a barbed-wire fence, they were directed towards a pile of female corpses—hundreds of women whom life had abandoned or who had abandoned life.

The pairs of prisoners were then deputed to wait until empty wagons, drawn along by other inmates, were brought to them. Each pair then had to collect one dead body at a time, one holding the feet, the other the arms, and toss it into a collecting wagon. And then repeat the process with another corpse. And another…

Anna and Frida alternated who would take the arms and who the feet with each body they were forced to dispose of in this way.

'Don't look at their faces,' Frida told Anna—a piece of advice that helped them work their way through scores of the remains of poor, wretched souls, stacked up like pieces of firewood, without themselves passing out.

As they slowly consumed their extra ration that evening—a piece of bread and a bowl of ersatz coffee—neither of them uttered a word.

While some of the new female arrivals were put into tents, some prisoners began sleeping outside the huts to avoid the scramble for space inside, not just in the bunks but also on the floors; to avoid, too, the lice and the cholera, and the cries of fellow human beings afflicted by pain, hunger and despair.

At first, the guards would beat the people lying outside in the open and remove the blankets and shoes of those that had them, before shoving them back inside the huts. Or they would shoot them. Eventually, as winter passed, they simply ignored them.

Delirious inmates began to beg on the pathways of the camp as though these were the streets of a thriving city. Others simply dropped to the ground, where they would be left, dead or dying. The spread of disease, from tuberculosis to dysentery and various kinds of fever, could not be contained. Veterans from Auschwitz and other camps were almost unanimous in claiming that conditions in Bergen-Belsen were by far the worst that they had endured.

A turning point for Anna and Frida came when they were walking one morning behind a line of huts and saw a woman hobbling towards them, awkwardly carrying a small package from which a long, soiled cloth was hanging. As they came nearer to the woman, they were both shaken by her appearance. Even among the many stick-like creatures they had become accustomed to seeing around them, this insubstantial speck of humanity was exceptional.

Her eyes were almost closed, the lids as dark as charcoal in contrast to the ghostly pallor of her face. Her cheeks were no more than folds of bruised skin sucked into her jaw. It was impossible to estimate her age. She could have been seventeen; she could have been seventy.

She was moaning to herself as she stumbled along unable to keep upright or straight, all the time struggling to maintain her precarious grip on her package. Only when Anna and Frida came within a few feet of her could they make out the shape and nature of the package.

Frida managed a desperate cry: 'Oh, Anna. How can this poor creature, this thing, be a mother? What life can such a poor child have?'

'Oh, God,' was all that Anna could say, shaking her head, her eyes too dry for tears.

Upon hearing Anna's voice, the woman lifted her head slightly and slowly as though the weight of it was too much for her. And, with a surprisingly quick, jerky movement, handed the bundled-up infant to Anna, uttering a muffled, single syllable as she did so. This could have been 'help' or 'take' or almost anything, so indistinct was the sound. It could have been just that—a sound yet unformed into language. But it could not have been more expressive. It was elemental. It was the sound of death. Having let her baby go, the woman slumped to the ground, directly behind and in the shadow of a hut.

From the grey appearance of the child's face and the combined lightness and stiffness of its body, Anna guessed that it been dead for at least two days. There was no help to be called, no help to be had, not for mother or child and not for the two young women who not so long ago had thought themselves to have a future in the inspiring city of Budapest. Now, they were in a place where the unthinkable had become unremarkable.

Anna placed the baby in the now completely still arms of its mother, upon whose face were signs of something like serenity. Her immobile body was curled, one arm crooked as if she had intended to take her doomed offspring finally and peacefully to her. The two friends stood and stared at the pitiful sight until Anna turned Frida away.

'Come on,' she urged. 'We must live, Frida. We must live. One day, somewhere, we will talk about this. But now, here, we must just keep going.'

In the ensuing days, Anna, her own strength failing, desperately tried to ensure that Frida would eat whatever scraps of food were around. Thousands of prisoners had been dragged to Bergen-Belsen and huge numbers of them had died, their corpses left to lie on the ground next to the living and the scarcely living who could not move.

Anna frequently had to pull Frida's failing body across the unmoving bodies of others, to forage for food or water or just to keep moving.

'Hold on,' Anna pleaded with her. 'Just like you have told me so many times. Hold on, Frida. Please.'

Having curtailed their honeymoon and converted it into a voluntary British exile, Yusuf and Farah Haroun would not get to visit Yusuf's sisters in the United States until 1950, by which time profound changes would have taken place in so many people's lives. The Harouns were not exempt.

In between various unsuccessful attempts to travel to Iraq to see his parents, Yusuf put most of his energy into helping to steer Azi and Ben's business through bleak times in the early 1940s—particularly after their manager, Mr Miller, had fallen on an icy pavement and broken his hip in December 1942.

The two brothers were stationed in army camps at opposite ends of England—Azi in Hampshire and Ben in Yorkshire—but they enjoyed regular periods of leave and, when they came home, never failed to check on shipments of goods from the Middle East, peruse the accounts or inspect the stock in the warehouse.

After several rounds of often-hostile interrogation by unsympathetic officials, Yusuf was eventually allowed to stay in the United Kingdom on a permanent basis. He and Farah became naturalised British citizens in 1943, a process made easier by an Act of Parliament passed that year relaxing the nationality rules and by the fact that Yusuf's birth in 1920, and Farah's a year later, had both taken place in a country under British rule—as it still was, albeit somewhat more loosely, at the time of their naturalisation application. Immediately after his citizenship was granted, Yusuf was placed on the British forces reserve list, but he was never called upon.

Rivke continued to write letters, constantly asking questions about life in wartime London while painting a demoralising picture of the fading Jewish life in Baghdad. Only the elderly Jews were likely to stay beyond the end of the war, she predicted, and it was only Sami's fragile condition that was keeping her there while others were planning to leave, the majority of them going to Palestine.

In September 1943, Sami's brother Fouad came to help him with the family business and within a short time arranged for it to be sold to the owner of a local firm called H. Aziz Textiles. The 'H' stood for Habib—the same Habib who years before had been Sami's teenage assistant. Fouad conducted all the negotiations and Sami merely signed the documents. When he met Habib, he failed to recognise him. When it was explained who the buyer was, Sami hugged him and told Fouad: 'He will pay a fair price. He is an honest boy.'

Later that year, Sami died. 'The official cause was emphysema and pneumonia,' Rivke wrote to Yusuf. 'But the truth is he had long ago given up on life. He came to see himself repeating his father's last days, seated for hours in the same armchair. He often spoke your name.'

Yusuf had tried desperately to see his father in those last weeks but the obstacles to civilian travel between the two countries proved insuperable, and he was overcome with grief when Sami finally succumbed and he still could not get into Baghdad for the funeral.

For Yusuf, this, even more than the *Farhud*, marked the end of an era. His father, the third-generation patriarch, seated in his armchair smoking and eating dates, represented permanence. Whatever change and uncertainty life brought, however far from Baghdad Yusuf might travel, so long as Sami sat in the Haroun house with a paternal presiding eye beneath his furrowed brow, there was always a place of origin and return, a deep familiarity, a home.

As he took in the news of Sami's death, Yusuf's brain overflowed with a rush of memories, of his childhood; of standing alongside his father in the Shaf Ve-Yativ Synagogue; his wedding; Sami hugging him at the farewell honeymoon party and again as Izaak waited for Yusuf and Farah to get into his Wolseley. And then the guilt and regrets—for not sharing or understanding Sami's dedication to Haroun Silks; for selfishly trying to coax him out of his apparently anxious moods; and, above all, for not being with him in his last days, or at his burial.

Although Yusuf's never-strong attachment to his religion had further weakened over the period he had been in London, he went to Lauderdale Road Synagogue each day for a month following his father's death to recite the mourner's Kaddish prayer. For the first week he was accompanied by Azi. After a month, Yusuf ceased to go and mourned his father in his heart.

Farah consoled her husband as best she could, reminding him that Sami's legacy was in Yusuf's hands—and hers. At the moment when the news of Sami's death had reached them, she had good cause to look ahead. But, a week later, a new sadness was conjoined with Yusuf's mourning for Sami when Farah experienced her second miscarriage.

She and Yusuf had moved to a small, rented flat in Cricklewood, a few miles west of Stamford Hill. This was partly in order to be nearer to the synagogue in Lauderdale Road, which they now attended regularly, Farah more eagerly than Yusuf. She was growing in confidence and had joined the Lauderdale Road ladies' guild. She was an enthusiastic cook and, following Miriam's example, had become skilled at creating imaginative Iraqi kosher dishes out of meagre resources—a talent that made her one of Lauderdale Road's more valuable assets.

Ashamed of how ignorant she had been about the war on her arrival in London, Farah had followed developments much more closely during her stay in Stamford Hill than either Yusuf or Miriam. And, with the one spending long hours at the family emporium, and the other not allowing her to perform any housework, she'd had a considerable amount of time on her own to devour the news on the radio and in the newspapers. Though this was reduced after the move to Cricklewood, she still resolutely kept her eyes and ears open.

But what drove Farah most of all was her desire to become a mother. Based on her reading and hearing about America stepping up its presence in Europe under General Eisenhower as 1944 wore on, Farah believed that an Allied victory was imminent and that this was now a safe time in which to bring a child into the world. With Yusuf having clearly found his feet in business—customers were already coming back and Azi and Ben were due to be discharged from the army in the spring—she was more than ready to take on maternal duties.

But her body wasn't. She and Yusuf were almost disbelieving when it happened the first time. Once they had discovered that she was pregnant, they simply assumed that things would proceed along a normal, uninterruptible course and were reduced to utter helplessness when, after eight weeks, Farah was taken to hospital after doubling up in pain and bleeding in Miriam's bathroom.

Miriam accompanied Farah in the ambulance and devoted herself to her recovery, urging the young couple to stay in the Stamford Hill house for as long they wished. But Yusuf, and even more so Farah, believed that it was time to be more independent and forge their own path in Britain. When Farah lost the second baby, Miriam was the first to visit her in hospital. Several ladies from Lauderdale Road also came, bringing home-made soups, cakes and soothing reassurance.

Now, in addition to the telephone at the carpet showroom, Yusuf and Farah had the use of one at their Cricklewood flat, on a shared line. This spurred Yusuf to try to persuade Rivke to have a telephone fitted in the house in Baghdad, now that she was alone there. Farah's parents had one and Yusuf suggested it would be good if they could all talk to each other instead of always relying on the postal service.

But Rivke wasn't interested. The telephone was a true luxury in Baghdad; only a few people had a connection. 'It would be too expensive,' she said, even though she could easily afford it with Sami's money.

In the longer term, Yusuf was trying to arrange for his mother to come to London and this now became an urgent priority. There was not enough room for Rivke in their flat, however. Azi and Miriam certainly had space but Yusuf was reluctant to ask them as they had already shown great generosity in allowing himself and Farah to stay for so long without paying rent.

In any event, Yusuf reasoned, Rivke was too accustomed to running a household. However kind and understanding Miriam might be, these two Iraqi-Jewish matriarchs would certainly clash in the kitchen.

As 1944 dissolved into 1945, Rivke still cherished her hope of seeing London. 'I will stand beside you in front of Big Ben,' she wrote to Yusuf. 'Soon, this war will be over and you will be in the land of victory, which is where we shall be reunited, my dearest son.'

Yet, notwithstanding the altered atmosphere in Baghdad, especially after Sami's death, and her generally negative view of the prospects for Baghdadi Jews, she was some way from being ready to leave her home permanently. Although the bustling, confident Jewish life that had permeated Baghdadi society for centuries was over, the impact of the *Farhud* had faded. Jewish-owned shops were trading again and the community was doing its best to look to the future.

Rivke's relations with her Muslim neighbours had not been affected. Indeed, the non-Jewish residents in the district surrounding the house that she had lived in with Sami for so many years had all been at pains to show sympathy and kindness to the local Jews. Moreover, two innocent members of one of these families—the Al-Mukhtars—had themselves been singled out and beaten by thugs back in those first two days of June 1941.

Rivke frequently mentioned one or other of her Muslim neighbours when she wrote to Yusuf. A page of her first letter to him after Sami's funeral had been devoted to her oldest Muslim acquaintance. 'Mrs Habash, who bravely stood up to the mob during the *Farhud*, came to see me today to offer her condolences,' Rivke wrote. 'She brought me a gift—a box of fruit. She is a fine woman. I consider her a friend.

'We both observe our different religions and speak to each other without any disagreement or rancour. It is so easy when you think of it. Conflict over religion is stupid. We all have parallels, with similar rules and similar festivals at the same times of the year. And though we pray in different ways, we all pray to the same God.

'It is a blessing to be part of a community but it should always be remembered that other communities are made up of individuals too. And it is individuals of whom we must think and speak. The individual and not the crowd. If I ever leave this house and this city I shall be sorry not to see Mrs Habash again. She is more thoughtful and kind than many of our own people.'

Rivke's sister-in-law Yocheved sometimes stayed with her for a few days at a time but, although Rivke also employed a sweet-natured servant-girl, Khalida, whose duties kept her overnight in the house four times a week, she often felt lonely without Sami and she was nervous sleeping on her own in an empty room.

She missed her children, Yusuf most of all. The two girls, Rachel and Nura, had been playmates throughout their childhood while Yusuf was often on his own. He was the shyest of the three and Rivke had always felt very protective towards him. Now, she felt she needed his protection.

If such reflections on absence induced a melancholy mood as Rivke moved about her home, sitting perhaps in Sami's armchair or coming across one of Yusuf's old toys, she nevertheless loved the house. Even with Sami gone, she still felt that she belonged there.

It had, after all, been built for the family by Sami's grandfather a hundred years earlier and she could not imagine relinquishing its familiar spaces, exquisitely decorated walls and doors, or the comforting view from her bedroom window across the courtyard, the two steadfast palm trees standing as if on guard, her ever-reliable, twin protectors.

It was not only the house to which Rivke was emotionally attached. Baghdad itself had shaped her identity. The sounds and smells of the Shorjah market. The *tannoor* bread ovens, the coffee and baklava, dates and apricots. The merchants in the souk and the hustlers in the alley-ways. The sunlight at dawn and the nights when the men would play *tawla* in the streets and families would sleep outside on the rooftops. The Rashid Street cinema, Shaf Ve-Yativ Synagogue. The gossiping Jewish women.

Now Rivke herself had become one of those gossiping Jewish women, exchanging memories, recipes and gentle words of pride, commendation or disapproval depending on who was the subject of conversation. Most evenings she would sit in the courtyard with two widowed friends, or a cousin or two, the local doctor's wife, or the schoolmistress from across the street, sipping tea while eating date-filled *kleicha* biscuits, halva, or kosher *lokum* delight, carping, complaining, and enjoying every moment.

In the mornings, Rivke would sometimes take a walk to the riverbank and gaze at the old family shop from across the street. She was glad that Habib, the new owner, had retained the shop name and sign, 'Haroun Silks', which Sami had painted with delicacy and patience. Rivke constantly missed her husband and such shafts of unbidden recollection made her miss him deeply.

Each day brought pessimistic news or rumours: the British were about to abandon Iraq to anarchy, a second *Farhud* was being plotted, another Jewish family or individual was leaving for India, America, England or Palestine.

Zionist emissaries were occasionally to be seen in or around synagogues or Jewish shops, stoking the fires of doom and promising help for anyone deciding to 'make *aliyah*' ('go up') to the Holy Land. Younger people in particular were receptive to such offers.

But it wasn't only because of emigration that the Jewish population was dwindling. One Sabbath morning in June 1945, Leyla Jaffari, the widow who cooked and cleaned for Rivke's father, *Bobbe* Eli, came shrieking to Rivke's front door, breathing pneumatically and weeping at the same time. She was barely able to speak.

Rivke suddenly experienced a sinking sense of everything she loved slipping away from her. 'What is it?' she pleaded with Leyla, steadying herself by holding the old woman's hands. 'My *baba*? *Bobbe* Eli? What has happened?'

'Oh Mrs Rivke, Mrs Rivke!' Leyla kept repeating, until she was at last able to get the words out: 'I cannot wake him. He is still in his bed. He is not... he is not,' and she fell, sobbing, against Rivke, who held her gently as her own cheeks moistened.

A month short of his ninety-fifth birthday, *Bobbe* Eli had prayed his last prayer. Sung his last psalm. Attended his last Sabbath service. Shaf Ve-Yativ would be poorer without him, the distraught Mrs Jaffari would have nobody to cook stuffed chicken and baked eggs for, and Rivke Haroun would experience the beginnings of a new and stronger feeling of isolation.

Before that June was out, with her brother-in-law Fouad's assistance, Rivke set in motion plans to sell the family house along with some of her furniture and arrange for the rest of it to be shipped to London, where it would be stored. Once forms were signed and hands shaken, she composed a short note to her son and daughter-in-law. It ended with a flourish, a bold announcement: 'Tell Mr Churchill. I am coming to England!'

3

23 April 1945
Bergen-Belsen, Hanover Province, Germany
Captain Roderick Vane to Anna Weisz

Anna! I love the sound of your name. Anna! I even sing it. My beautiful little wounded bird. I do not know if I will have the courage to give you this letter or if you will even understand my English handwriting but because of those two things I feel able to spell out my true feelings for you without hiding them behind a mask of British politeness.

I have never felt this way before. And please don't think it is pity that makes me want to devote myself to you, to lift you into my arms and care for you. Of course I understand the horrific things you have experienced and that you need to recover your health and that this will take some time. And who could not be sympathetic to the broken and destroyed bodies that we have found here in Bergen-Belsen?

There is so much death around and yet my heart feels lifted, there is brightness in my darkness. Brightness that comes from your amazing brown eyes, the most beautiful I have ever seen.

I don't want to shock you or to destroy any chances that I have with you. I know almost nothing of your past, your family, your religion. And so I may not give you this letter because I need to say things that may overwhelm you. Things that you may reject, and I could not bear that. But it helps to write them down.

I love you, my little bird. I love you Anna! This must sound ridiculous but I want to take care of you and be with you forever. Take you away from this foul place and make you happy and free in England with me. Am I dreaming? I suppose I am but I will do all I can to make this dream come true. After all, the war is now over. The people who put you in that slaughterhouse are facing defeat.

Already I feel my courage slipping but I can compensate by pouring my inner, secret thoughts into this letter. Secret thoughts that will come out at some stage.

Why can't I just speak my mind and tell you that I am in love with you? I want to marry you. I want you to have my children. Those wonderful eyes of yours, that smile, can melt away all the pain.

And in case I haven't made it clear, I LOVE YOU!
Roderick

On her twentieth birthday, Anna Weisz awoke in a hospital bed. She didn't know where she was or why she was there. The first person she saw was a woman in the next bed to hers, but she was asleep with her back to Anna, her lungs wheezing as she breathed.

'Frida,' Anna whispered. 'Is that you?'

But there was no response. She turned the other way. The bed on that side was empty. Anna held up her hand. It looked and felt clean; both hands did—and had a chemical smell.

'What is this place,' she wondered to herself. 'With *sheets*. Where have all the emaciated people gone? The dirty wooden bunks? The bodies, mixed up dead and alive—half alive. What's happened? Where am I? Did I dream all that screaming? No! Such screaming... and *praying*. How could those poor ridiculous wretches pray? Chanting Hebrew blessings. Wish I could pray.'

She lifted her head, astounded that it had been resting on a pillow. She tried to smile as she struggled to say the word out loud, to exclaim it—'a pi, a pil... a pillow!'

She looked up and, beyond the sleeping woman, she saw that there were another ten or more beds. All with women lying in them, inert. And then, approaching her, a woman for all the world dressed like a nurse. A woman not much older than Anna herself, with a soft, round, compassionate face, increasing her pace, almost rushing now, towards her.

Anna's voice had very little volume. Each word was a breath. She felt disorientated, a little hysterical. 'What... what... wha...' she breathed as the nurse got nearer. 'I have been talking to myself... excuse me...'

'Oh, my dear,' said the nurse in English, putting her arms around Anna, who returned the embrace as firmly as she could as she tried to recognise the nurse's accent.

'You sound like Katherine Hepburn,' she told her, tears forming and flowing with her urgent breathing. 'The film star. *Sind Sie Amerikanerin? Are you American?*'

'*Ich bin Kanadierin*. I am Canadian,' said the nurse, wiping her own eye while continuing to hold Anna, who slowly whispered to her:

'I can speak English. Are the British soldiers here?'

'British and Canadian. Yes.'

'So is our punishment, our undeserved punishment, over at last?'

'Yes, my dear, it is.' The nurse gently released Anna, and wiped Anna's eyes and then her own with a flannel. 'But you have to take it easy. You have had typhus. You are very weak now and you need to rest to build up your strength. That's why you have been brought to this hospital. It's a former German military building just a little way from that dreadful place where you and the others have been kept in such terrible conditions. Brigadier Glyn Hughes—that's the man in charge—kicked out the Germans to make way for you and others like you. You've been asleep for a couple of days.'

'My friend Frida? Is she here?'

'Oh, I wouldn't know that, my darling. And don't bother your head with worries now. Our boys have captured Belsen from the Nazis. Everything will be all right. You are one of the lucky ones, sweetheart. Many hundreds, if not thousands, have died. And many of those who are not actually dead are not actually alive either.

'It's very tough for a nurse to watch helplessly as people die, masses of them, and we can do nothing. But you're going to be OK, sweetheart. And I must stop wearing you out with my talking. It's so good to see you awake again. But you have to rest now. I'll be back. And Brigadier Hughes himself is coming to visit the wards later. He wants to show the hospital to some British army officers. Let them see how we're taking care of you. But don't worry your head about that. Just rest.'

'I have been in a coma,' said Anna, straining to draw on her medical knowledge.

'The world has been in a coma, my sweetheart. You have just been asleep. Now put your head back on the pillow. You're not ready to start dancing just yet, my darling.'

The nurse gently touched Anna's head, stood up from where she had been sitting on Anna's bed, turned and walked away. Anna compliantly let her head fall back on the pillow. Her face was damp but she was able now to smile. And close her eyes. And, for another couple of hours, return to sleep.

Among the handful of British soldiers who later accompanied chief medical officer Brigadier Hugh Llewellyn Glyn Hughes on his visit that afternoon to the patients and staff in his charge, was Roderick Vane, a young captain from the town of Esher in Surrey. Like his fellow soldiers, Roderick Vane was still affected by the shock of the unimaginable sight that they had encountered upon entering the grounds of Bergen-Belsen.

It was a sight that the surrendering Germans had tried to hide from the British by setting up a typhus exclusion zone around the camp. A German officer with a white flag had approached the advancing British troops under the command of Colonel Bob Daniels to warn them of a severe outbreak of typhus at Bergen-Belsen and that they should consequently proceed on their victorious way without coming into contact with the contagion.

Daniels refused. Instead, he drove his tank into the camp complex and broke down the door of a perimeter hut used by the SS as an office, where he discovered the commandant, Josef von Kramer, desperately trying to destroy reams of paper. Kramer was apprehended; the British troops continued into the grounds of the camp. Someone shouted: 'My God! Look in that trench.'

The 'trench' was a vast open grave, with huge mounds of excavated earth piled above it on two sides. Inside, a rotting mass of three thousand corpses lay in a tumbled heap, like so many discarded sticks. Eerily, the putrefaction released a gas that made it appear as though the bodies were moving. Several of the battle-hardened British soldiers choked and wept at the gruesome sight and the pervasive smell.

Elsewhere in the camp were other bodies, dumped like refuse or strewn around other, smaller burial pits. Nearby, half-dead skeletal figures sat virtually motionless while a few starved and haggard survivors greeted their liberators, clutching at their uniforms and kissing their hands.

Up to the moment of entering Bergen-Belsen, Roderick Vane had always managed to control his emotions. School and the army had reinforced the effects of his privileged upbringing in the Home Counties. He prided himself on his physical and moral strength and his ability to cope with whatever life should throw at him.

But even active war service had not prepared him for what he saw and experienced that April day in 1945. Minutes after his eyes and his brain had adjusted to the deathly vista with which he was suddenly confronted, he had heard the voice of his commanding officer, Colonel Daniels, calling out names. And then he had heard his own name.

'Captain Vane.'

'Yes, sir.'

'Come with me. Arms at the ready.'

Roderick and half a dozen others followed Daniels to a corner of the camp where four young SS men, aged no more than twenty, were shooting at the bodies of prisoners lying dead, or close to death, on the ground. They were aiming at the genitals of both men and women. At the sight of Daniels and his men they stopped, stricken with fear. Without hesitation, Daniels shot dead three of the four and turned to Roderick.

'Vane, I'm out of cartridges. I suppose we'll have to let that one stand. Have him arrested for now.'

The surviving youth had dropped his gun and was raising his hands above his head. Podgy and raw-faced, he looked like any boy with or against whom Roderick had played rugby at school in England a handful of years earlier.

Roderick felt giddy. He had to steel himself to quell the nausea rising through him along with the thought that everything he had learned, the morality, the manners, the behaviour—the rules—had all been overturned. There was no solidity, nothing to depend upon.

The twitching body of a young woman lay at the podgy German boy's feet. As Roderick looked down at her, so did the boy, who then looked up at Roderick, just in time for their eyes to meet as Roderick steadied himself, aimed, and fired his handgun.

His callow, puffy victim fell on to the now motionless young woman, his arms outstretched in a sickening imitation of her final posture, the difference being that the bullet that killed him had been to the head.

Daniels, who had turned to go, stopped. 'Vane,' he said sternly. 'You disobeyed my order.'

'Yes, sir. I'm sorry.' His hand was shaking.

Colonel Daniels took away his gun.

'I'll tell you what I'm going to do, Vane,' said the Colonel, before pausing and then addressing Roderick in a matter-of-fact but quiet, warm voice: 'I'm going to commend you for following my lead and saving the hangman a job. Just make sure you never disobey an order again.'

'Yes, sir. Thank you, sir.' Roderick tried to appear composed.

Without a look back at the slaughter behind him, Colonel Daniels stood tall and addressed the small band of officers who had witnessed the scene. 'All right, men,' he barked. 'Fall in. Provisions are available. All of you get yourselves a strong, warming drink.'

Now, several days later, in the reassuring calm of the medical facility that Brigadier Hughes had set up in a former German army barracks a couple of kilometres from the concentration camp's perimeter, Roderick found himself thinking of home, and his parents. His father had similarly been in uniform at the climax of a world war, twenty-seven years earlier. Like Roderick, he too was in his early twenties and at the end of a period of army service. And, like Roderick, he had been engaged in hostilities, though of a much more dangerous intensity. He had told Roderick that the experience had completely reshaped his philosophy of life.

'Well, I am certainly unlikely to forget any of this,' Roderick told himself as they came into a room that was being used as a women's ward. The patients looked weak and most could barely sit up, but these were clearly survivors.

In comparison to the walking skeletons he had seen Glyn Hughes administering to earlier that day, delousing them and feeding them the 'Bengal Famine mixture' of rice, sugar and paprika, these young women were pictures of health. They had flesh on their bones and even a bit of colour in their cheeks.

'These girls will be placed in a displaced persons section next,' Hughes had said as they entered the ward. 'And pretty soon after that, some of them can be repatriated.'

'These are more as I remember girls to be,' Roderick whispered to a comrade. 'That one over by the corner, with big, dark eyes. She looks frail, more so than most of the others here but so pretty. And delicate. Like a helpless little bird.'

When Roderick stopped by her bed and asked her if she spoke English, he was taken aback when she answered, 'yes.' He had expected to be able to tell her how much he liked the look of her, protected from the normal restrictions of politeness and modesty by her lack of comprehension.

He had wanted to say, quite directly: 'It's ages since I had even a short conversation with a pretty girl, with a girl of any kind, let alone somebody so very beautiful. How on earth could anyone want to harm you?'

81

But she could understand English. So Roderick Vane, feeling himself blushing, smiled and simply asked her what her name was and, having been told it was Anna he said: 'I hope you get better soon. Good luck.' And then he turned away and caught up with Brigadier Hughes, who was talking to one of the Canadian nurses.

When Anna had first awoken in Glyn Hughes's field hospital, the sight of the Canadian nurse, strong and capable, hurrying towards her, acted upon her in the manner of a transfiguration. This was not a helpless dying mother approaching with her dead baby, or any other of the poor wretches among whom she had become accustomed to existing. These light and warm surroundings represented a new existence, an escape from the dense, unremitting darkness. The realisation that her head was resting on a pillow and that all around her was stillness and space, was an indication that she had awoken from the worst of nightmares.

But then she could not believe that she was free, that there would be no going back—from the enveloping softness of her bed, the whiteness of the sheets, and the calm, caring atmosphere—to barbarous captivity. Gradually, however, over a week or more, her acceptance of the new situation had grown, strengthened by two especially uplifting developments.

One had been the discovery, by her 'Katharine Hepburn' nurse, that Frida had survived and was being cared for just along the corridor of the very same building in which Anna was now recovering. Suddenly, she and her friend, with whom she had shared such painful experiences, had an incentive to raise themselves from their beds, to walk, to live.

The second boost to Anna's feelings had come in the form of the shy, young English captain who had become Anna's own regular visitor, initially simply to ask how she was feeling and smile encouragingly before being shooed away by the nurses. But he was too drawn to her to be so easily dismissed and soon took on the role of go-between for both Anna and Frida.

To Frida, whose English was not as good as Anna's, Roderick merely passed short messages. To Anna, little by little, he spoke more openly. He told her about his unit's advance towards Bergen-Belsen and how Colonel Daniels had rejected the typhus warning of the German officer with the white flag and charged into the camp. He spoke in general terms, not in detail, and avoided mentioning that he had shot dead a brutalised young member of the SS.

He told Anna about his life in England before the war and about his family, especially his father, the former soldier and prosperous owner of a family business founded by Roderick's grandfather towards the end of Queen Victoria's reign. He spoke warmly of his brother in the navy and his sister who was training to become a nurse, both of whom, together with Roderick and their parents, lived in comfort in a large villa in substantial grounds on the edge of a Surrey town.

Anna, too, tried to speak of her family but was unable to unscramble her confused and anxious thoughts. By contrast, her physical recovery was proceeding well and was some way in advance of Frida's. She was the first of the two friends to be able to walk, with the aid of a stick, her feet encased in what felt like luxurious slippers given to her by Nurse 'Hepburn'. And, once a doctor had given her permission, she was allowed, with the nurse's help, to leave her room and shuffle twenty yards along the well-polished, wooden corridor floor to a slightly larger ward where Frida was still confined to her bed.

Within a day or two of that first visit to Frida, Anna was allowed to progress unaided along the corridor, where sunshine through a fanlight exposed patches on the walls from which photographs of members of the Nazi hierarchy had been removed. Soon, Anna was able to allow herself to sense the beginnings of recovery, of renewal, of being able to describe her feelings and confide, without fear, in another person; to talk—and listen—to Frida who, though much weaker than Anna, looked forward eagerly to her friend's increasingly inspiring visits.

It was Frida who gave Anna the strength to tell Roderick, with whom she was clearly experiencing a tentative happiness, about Budapest, the ghetto, her friends and family—and to accept, as Frida herself had done, the probability that her parents had not survived.

While Roderick still regularly looked in to say hello to Frida, he now devoted his time to Anna. And, before long, sitting on Frida's bed, she was able to talk freely to her about Roderick, about how strong and thoughtful he was.

'He just held me,' Anna told her friend. 'For about ten minutes. Held me close. Not speaking, just holding. He didn't kiss me, didn't try to fondle me, didn't touch my face or my hair. He just kept his arms around me. I felt so warm. So protected. Being held like that. It was what I needed more than anything. He knew instinctively. It felt right being held by him in that way. I felt loved. Which I greatly needed to feel.'

It had been when trying to put into words the recollected images of her parents—her father in his white doctor's coat, her mother at her piano—that Anna's emotions had overcome her and Roderick had held her, wordlessly, close to him. And helped to restore her fluency, at least in her own language, enabling her now to express to Frida the tenderness of her feelings for Roderick and how he had 'just held me'.

By the middle of May, when Brigadier Hughes announced that Anna—but not yet Frida—would be able to leave within a matter of weeks, she and Roderick had grown so much closer than either could have imagined amid the horrors of a few weeks earlier. The sight of them wandering hand-in-hand along the hospital corridors had introduced a note of amusement and delight into the grim wards of this German army institution.

One evening, Nurse 'Hepburn' had come upon them kissing in a quiet corner of an otherwise empty room reserved for staff and British army officers.

Roderick had overcome his early inhibitions. 'I must tell you, my darling,' he revealed to Anna, 'that I was smitten the first time I saw you. And I actually wrote you a letter.'

'I never received a letter.'

'No. I destroyed it.'

'What did the letter say?'

'I was writing down my feelings. About you. How, when I first saw you, you reminded me of a little bird. And that my feelings for you went far beyond pity for what you had gone through. And the more I wrote, the less likely it was that I would send you the letter, or still less hand it to you. I kept it in my uniform pocket for three or four days and then I destroyed it because I didn't want any of my friends here to see it. They would have joshed me mercilessly.'

'*Joshed?*'

'Teased.'

'So what was in it?'

'I said that I was in love with you?'

'And were you? Are you? Are you in love with me, Roderick?' Anna's voice had dropped to a whisper.

'Oh, yes.'

Shortly after this exchange, Roderick brought news that the Bergen-Belsen camp area had been cleared. The dead had been buried—

many by SS guards, both male and female, under the direction of the liberating troops—and the living had been brought out. British army tanks and flame-throwers were on the point of destroying the buildings.

For the first time, Anna found the courage to ask: 'Have the prisoners of Auschwitz been rescued?'

'I'm sure they have, my dearest Anna. The Germans have been defeated,' Roderick assured her in a soft voice, holding her in his arms, stroking her face and her hair. 'The war is over.'

Anna placed her head against his chest and said, almost to herself, 'I don't feel able to try to find out what has happened to my parents. I'm not ready to be told that they are dead. I know in my heart that I will never see my father again but I still have hope that my mother will have survived.' She tried to continue but her words were lost as she held Roderick tightly and cried. And cried.

4

30 July 1945
Esher, Surrey
Anna Vane to Sarah Weisz

Dear sweet Mama,

I have no idea if you are alive or dead. Therefore, I am quite likely to be casting these words into the air with nowhere for them to come down. But I need so much to write down my thoughts. So much has happened in the short passage of time since I last saw you that I feel I need the rest of my life to recover from it all.

Though I am still a young woman, I do not feel young. I do not have that spirit of youth that I seemed to possess so recently. How could I, knowing that Daddy has surely disappeared forever? And not knowing whether I will ever see you again.

My dearest, obstinate Mama, why did you not listen to Daddy's warning and my desperate pleading and leave behind your apartment and your books and your blessed piano? We might have got away. Others did. I cry every day for Daddy, for the loss, the waste. Oh, Mama, I feel no resentment, no real anger towards you. Only love. For how could you, how could we, possibly have known of the torture and humiliation that was to come?

One day, with perhaps a cooler head and a more settled heart, I will write about all that has happened to me since Daddy's arrest but the most important things for you to know now are that I was in Bergen-Belsen at the end, and we were rescued by the British army. I am now in England. And I am married!

My husband is an officer in the British army—the unit that came to free us. He is my personal saviour. The gentlest, most loving man. And a Christian. Yes, Mama, a Christian! We are living in a smart and peaceful part of England, not far from London but very far from any Jews. I am giving myself completely and utterly to my husband's life and leaving behind my Jewish life. You will be scandalised, Mama, I know, but where did being Jewish get us? What use were our devotions, our prayers, our scrupulous attention to doing the right thing, the Jewish thing?

I suppose the very strong possibility that you will never read this letter, that it will get lost in a pile at the Displaced Persons office, helps me to be more frank. But I am determined. If we have children, why should I load this painful history upon them? I want them to be happy and confident. Not scared. If I do write down our story, yours, mine and Daddy's, I will keep it locked away in a drawer and perhaps eventually destroy it.

When Roderick—my husband—asked me if I would marry him, he also asked if our different religious backgrounds would prove to be an obstacle and if I would prefer it if he would consider converting to Judaism. My answer was a bitter laugh.

I am not thinking myself of becoming a Christian. Nothing in any religion could provide faith strong enough to explain what you and I have been through. But I might, if it is possible and if we have children, join the church that Roderick and his family belong to—you can hear the bells ringing from where we live.

Whatever happens, I am done with Judaism and it no doubt is done with me. I have not tried to contact Daddy's 'English' cousin Istvan and have no intention of doing so. I do not know the man and have nothing against him but I do not want to have any reminders of the past, neither the long-time-ago good nor the very recent bad.

Will you ever read these words? And if you do, will you forgive me? And will you come and find me and bless me and my English family and English life? Mama, I feel it was important to send these words to you and, though it may cause you pain to read them, I send with them, dearest sweet little Mama, my undying love. If I believed in prayer, I would pray, above all else, to be able to see you. To hear you play the piano, walk with you and talk with you and do the simple things with you that we once did, like baking cakes and sewing, and that I am now learning to do in a new home in a new land.

Do you remember how I hoped to become a doctor? That is another part of me that is gone. I have seen enough blood, enough suffering. I couldn't endure any more, not in the detached way that a doctor has to endure it.

All my love,
Anna

It proved easier than expected for Roderick to arrange for Anna to accompany him back to England. Amid the immediate post-war upheaval, the acceptance into the country of a persecuted, educated, English-speaking young woman so that she could marry a young army captain—commended as exemplary by his commanding officer—turned out to be a minor, straightforward matter.

Acceptance into the Vane family, too, was a relatively untroubled business. Roderick had written ahead to his parents to tell them that he had met and fallen in love with a beautiful and brilliant survivor of Nazi brutality who had almost certainly lost all of her family. Their reaction was one of eagerness to meet this impossibly ideal paragon as well as anxiety about how to handle somebody whose life had been so damaged.

Above all, they were happy for their eldest child whose judgment in all things they had come to trust. They believed Roderick to be a person who would never be duped or persuaded by anyone into making a reckless or ill-considered decision. They could be certain that he would never bring home—and indeed request a room be prepared for—somebody unsuitable.

Even allowing for a lover's exaggeration in describing his chosen mate as the 'most beautiful girl I have ever seen', Cedric and Margaret Vane took pleasurable note of such of Anna's reported attributes as her fluency in English, ability to play the piano and medical training. And as, in Cedric Vane's words, 'diluted Anglicans', they regarded Anna's being Jewish with curiosity rather than concern—though they did hope it would be possible for the marriage to take place in their local church.

After the years of oppression and privation, Anna could barely believe how smoothly Roderick was able to arrange things. He had even managed to get hold of a ring. 'We'll choose a better one together in England,' he promised. With the army's assistance, he got them both on to a Royal Navy troopship, HMT *Galahad*—a rehearsal for their honeymoon, he told her. And, now that he had shed his awkward shyness, she felt increasingly bolder with him.

'I love you, Captain Roderick Vane.' It was a phrase she liked using and, when she said it to him with a smile that spread across her face as they boarded the *Galahad*, Roderick felt as though he could put the past behind him and, like his father before him, take forward its valuable lessons.

This was not a sentiment that Anna shared. The events of the preceding years that had flowed, more or less continuously, from the moment of the portentous, whispered 'Goodnight' of the trilby-hatted man who had escorted her father from the Dembinszky Street apartment laid too heavily upon her mind. The rupturing removal of her parents had bruised her soul. And her need for Roderick to provide solace was still too desperate to have complete confidence in him. Trust would take a long time to come easily.

Having herself fallen into the category of 'displaced person', she understood that this was a term with a virtually unlimited application, under the ever-expanding umbrella of which she now stood with thousands of others in her primal desire to discover the separate fates of her parents. And there was another blemish to her new-found happiness.

'Isn't it strange,' she said to Roderick as they looked out over a benign, unruffled sea from the deck of the *Galahad*, 'that Frida wants so much to return to Budapest and I so much do not want to.'

'It's a shame that she is having to wait to be released. She was in a weaker state than you were.'

'Physically, yes. But she has a strong mind. She has a sister in America but does not want to join her. There are relatives in Budapest who managed to survive in the ghetto, unlike mine, I believe. They have already made contact. Everyone in my family was classified as missing according to the Jewish DP committee—which means dead, doesn't it?'

'Not necessarily, my sweetheart. The committee is very hard-pushed. Now that Belsen is an important DP camp, there are hundreds of refugees arriving daily from all over Germany. It is very difficult to trace individuals and families in these circumstances. They just write "missing" in the absence of any real knowledge. Frida was lucky. Her relatives must be very enterprising.'

'She can't wait to get back. I will miss her. Do you know we went to the same school for years and never really became friendly until we were both about to leave? We will go to Hungary to see her, won't we? When I am ready. I must find out what happened to my dear grandmother and my cousins. I can't even think about my aunts and uncles. I can't believe *everyone* has disappeared. I am so glad we are going to Britain. I never want to live in Hungary again. But I am determined to go back when I can. To visit. And I would like you to see where I came from, my captain!'

'Of course we shall, my sweet adorable Anna. As soon as the dust has settled we will take every step to find out what has happened to your family. But first, you must meet my family. They will love you. How could they not? And…'

'And?'

'And we have to get married—and quickly.'

'Ah, however much you have exaggerated my good qualities to your parents, I don't think they will approve of you marrying a woman who is foreign and Jewish. And wrecked.'

'Darling, you are not wrecked. You have been through the worst of tortures and pain. And you have survived. No, you're not wrecked. Far from it. You are stronger than I could ever be. As for my parents, I really think they want what is best for me. And you are best for me.'

'They may not see it that way.'

'Well, they will have to. I never wanted to get married in a church anyway. I thought about that quite a bit during the war. Quite a few of the other fellows were expecting to have big church weddings but some of us couldn't stomach the idea after so much slaughter. A quick, quiet job in a registry office will suit me. And the sooner, the better. But what about your family? What would they say if they knew you were marrying a man who isn't Jewish?'

'They would hate the idea.' Anna's reply was automatic; but then she paused and reflected. 'No, that's not true. Quite honestly, I think my father would be disappointed but mainly because he always thought Jewish intellectual conversation was the most stimulating thing in the world. But if he knew how happy you have made me—and of course that you are definitely capable of the most brilliant conversation—he would give his complete approval.

'My mother would be more upset. The fact is, they would find it hard to countenance simply because it is such an alien idea to them. Nobody in the family, nobody they know, has married "out of the *faith*"—a word

91

my father always scoffed at... My God, I can talk of him only in the past tense, a man who was so alive, so wonderful...'

'What if I took lessons in becoming Jewish? I've heard of people who have done this. I would be willing to learn about the Jewish faith.'

At this, Anna's sad sigh was transformed into a short, disbelieving laugh and she shook her head and smiled at Roderick, who responded by taking her into a happy, possessive embrace.

Everything about Anna's first encounter with England felt like a gentle caress. It was a few minutes past noon on an undramatic British summer's day when the *Galahad* docked off the coast at Lowestoft, where Roderick's parents were waiting.

The warmth and light of the sun and the mitigating coolness of a just-perceptible breeze combined to create a softness that seemed to be reflected in the reassuring smiles on the faces of the middle-aged couple walking with arms held out in a welcoming gesture. To Anna, their easy manner, calm, unhesitant greeting, and even Roderick's father Cedric's tweed jacket and his mother Margaret's apple-green scarf, all combined to announce 'England'.

Cedric Vane's own father had died while Cedric was still serving in the army. The old man had built up a business selling high-quality country and outdoor wear—traditional hats and rainproof coats, hacking jackets, corduroy trousers, robust walking shoes and a miscellany of well-turned hunting, hiking and farming items. Cedric had inherited the company, called 'Vane Natural Clothing', and expanded it across south-eastern England.

Cedric's wife Margaret, who was a dozen or so years younger than her husband, had grown up in a village just outside Esher, the Surrey town where Cedric's family had taken root. Until a recent illness, Margaret had been headmistress of the village school that she herself had attended some decades earlier. Now, having recovered, she was busily occupied with a range of 'good works' that saw her out of the house for much of most weeks sitting on this or that committee, collecting from the fortunate and distributing to the unfortunate.

Margaret became fond of Anna virtually from the moment they met at Lowestoft Harbour. When the two couples of different generations sat down together for lunch in a local restaurant, at a table with an impressive view of the North Sea, they were able to fall into an agreeably lively conversation within a short time.

Anna's vigorous intelligence and her graceful reaction to initially awkward enquiries about her recent past enabled Margaret and Cedric to talk more freely. Margaret, in particular, warmed to the poignancy of Anna's observation when, looking out through the restaurant window, Anna said: 'This is the same water that washes the coastline of Germany—it looks so much brighter on this side.'

The profound contrast with her former life that Anna was experiencing was dramatically reinforced by the first sight of the house in which Roderick's family lived. After the ghetto apartment—her last address in Budapest—let alone the prison huts of Auschwitz and Belsen, any domestic building would have felt palatial. But, by any standards, the Vanes' solid-bricked Victorian villa on the outskirts of Esher would be regarded as a grand residence.

It was surrounded not by neighbouring homes but by its own luxuriant gardens and offered luxury far beyond even the formative comforts of the Dembinszky Street apartment in which Anna's childhood had been spent.

Roderick's family home had six or seven bedrooms, an elegant drawing room, and a study and dining room, both oak-panelled. Overall, it exuded a tastefully restrained prosperity. Anna was welcomed into an airy guest bedroom, from the window of which she enjoyed her first view of a smoothly green English lawn.

'We were so fortunate to escape being damaged during the bombing,' Margaret told Anna as she showed her future daughter-in-law around the house and gardens. 'In 1940, the Luftwaffe bombed an aircraft factory not far from here. But Esher was largely spared. We knew people in London whose homes were destroyed.' Both women remained silent for a minute or so after this recollection had served as an unintentional reminder of the still-unknown plight of Anna's parents.

Margaret felt a flush of shame at the sheer good fortune that she had just evoked, and at mentioning the two families of her acquaintance whose homes, but not bodies, were wrecked by the Germans, unlike the individuals and families, including Anna's, in Europe, who had borne such ferocious savagery. The caring, older Englishwoman felt her eyes filling as she leaned across to the dry-eyed Hungarian girl and gently squeezed her hand.

Over the next month, Anna found herself participating on an equal footing with her prospective in-laws in planning her wedding, despite her inability to make any financial contribution. While Roderick and his father went out to maintain the revival of Vane Natural Clothing, she and Margaret had several remarkably harmonious discussions about all aspects of the forthcoming marriage, including the religious one.

'Roderick's love—and, indeed, your kindness—are religion enough for me,' Anna told her mother-in-law to be. 'These things are real, not made-up tales. We used to have beautiful Sabbath evenings at my home. My grandmothers, aunts, uncles and cousins would come every week and, though we could not believe unquestioningly in the Almighty and the stories of the Bible—what intelligent, curious person could?—we followed the prescribed tradition.

'My dear mother played the piano, my father talked and talked and talked, but with great wisdom, arguing and laughing with his brother and brother-in-law. Nothing could have been more Jewish, more loving. And what was the reward for all this Jewish love? Destruction. Which fell upon the heads of even the most devout believers, too. The ones who obeyed all the rules, who devoted their lives to their maker. What kind of God repays devotion with destruction?'

'I can understand you completely,' Margaret said in reply. 'I doubt, much more than I believe. But there is beauty in life—in love, as you yourself say—and I do feel grateful for it. I don't definitely know how or to whom I should be grateful, but I do want to celebrate it—especially at such a harsh time as this when a wonderful thing like my child's marriage—your marriage—emerges like a flower on a bombed street. And I especially want to celebrate it with family and friends. People we know and love, who share a background with us and who have similar hopes, ambitions and dreams.'

Anna smiled but made no reply.

She was greatly sustained by Margaret's sympathy and industry throughout this period. Her mother-in-law's active engagement with the wedding plans, and with life generally, acted as a soothing distraction from Anna's longing for news of her parents. But it could not remove it. Most nights, Anna would awake in the darkness crying and feeling lost and isolated, especially after one of her frequent dreams in which her mother, father or other members of her childhood Friday-night cast would appear in some strange new apparition, or when she felt herself conveyed back to the ghetto, Auschwitz or Bergen-Belsen.

And, as helpful and welcoming as Roderick's parents were, Anna could not shake off the sense of cultural difference between these kind, contented, gentle and deferential English dwellers on the green borders of a small country town, and the loud, thrusting and disputatious inhabitants of her pulsating native city; between these passive non-believing Christians and her active non-believing Jews.

Even her ever-closer bond with her beloved Roderick, partially based on their wartime link, could not yet make her feel at home in the Home Counties. He still could not convince her that his parents could be entirely happy with her coming into their family. But there was certainly progress in that direction. For one thing, he could make her laugh, by mimicking the provincial ways of some of the locals, and she could not imagine wanting to spend the rest of life with anyone other than Roderick.

No objection was ever voiced by Cedric or Margaret to the union of a delicate, undernourished, lucky-to-be-alive, penniless, Hungarian-Jewish girl with their precious eldest child, who had been both christened and confirmed in the Vanes' local church—with whose vicar Cedric and Margaret occasionally socialised, despite seldom attending services.

Neither was there any sense of compromise in the air when the two indisputably in-love parties became man and wife in a small ceremony in the local register office, followed by a garden party at the Vanes' villa. By then, Roderick's brother had returned from the navy and his sister was on leave from her nursing training. Although Cedric was unable to procure any champagne amid the postwar climate of austerity, there was a perfectly acceptable fizzy alternative, which flowed by the gallon, along with a handsome wedding cake made by Margaret.

And when the party was concluded by a blessing administered by the Vanes' friendly Anglican minister, Anna felt no twinge of betrayal. She did, however, have a vision of her father, sitting at his desk in the Dembinszky Street apartment, where she used to tell him about her school work.

He was laughing.

In late July 1945, two men were anxiously standing in a small, badly-lit office next to the drab arrivals centre of an airport a few miles south of London. They were waiting for a woman from Iraq to complete her interviews with the immigration authorities. The two men were Azi and

Yusuf Haroun; the woman was Rivke Haroun, Yusuf's mother, who was about to enter into a new existence.

Four years after her son Yusuf and new daughter-in-law Farah had made their way on an RAF flight from Habbaniya in Iraq to Whitchurch Airport in Bristol, Rivke was able to take a similar route, this time to Croydon Airport, thanks to Sami and then Fouad having maintained their useful connection with the British officers.

And, in Britain, once again it was Azi who led the greetings, having driven Yusuf from Cricklewood in the Riley, upon which Azi still lavished great care.

The meeting was memorable. To Rivke, Yusuf had filled out, his frame now no longer looked thin but was muscular; his skin was smoother, his expression more confident. To Yusuf, Rivke looked frail, her face sallow, her cheeks softened and lined.

She also appeared to him at first glance to be somewhat shrunken, her posture bent. But her eyes—those unmistakable, deep dark-brown pools of light he shared—still radiated the warmth of her happiness at the sight of her son.

And, as she hugged him, and laughed and cried at the same time, she called out: 'Yusuf! Yusuf! How good it is to see you. How is Farah? I can't wait to see her. I can't believe I am here. Azi, thank you. You are so kind. How are you?'

'Oh, Rivke,' Azi laughed back to her. 'Welcome, welcome to England. It was nothing. I have brought your son to meet you, that's all. Do you recognise him? He is now a partner in the business.'

'Oh, I am so proud. My God, what a moment this is,' she said, standing back to take in the sight of the son she had not seen for four years. 'My little Yusuf, you are now truly a fine, handsome man. Azi, how good to see you! It is so kind of you to drive your car all the way to meet me.' She pinched Azi's cheek. 'I haven't seen you for years, since you came back home for a visit long before all the terrible events that have befallen us all. I see you have become quite fat,' she said. 'You must be doing well, *bel ayn el raa'a.*'

'*Bel ayn el raa'a,*' echoed Azi. 'And if I am getting fat it is because of my dear wife Miriam's wonderful Iraqi cooking. Even on war rations. And because we are happy and can celebrate that the war is over and our children are home and we are all safe, thank God, including my brother Ben and his family.'

'Azi, I am so sorry. How awful that you and Miriam had to go through this war. And I heard that you fought the Germans. You were a British soldier, no?'

Azi's round face beamed. 'A soldier, yes. A fighter, no. I was in British army uniform but I did not see combat. Neither did Ben. And now it's over.'

'Ummi,' Yusuf put his arm around his mother and steered her towards where the Riley was parked. 'Come to the car…'

'Ah, the car!' Rivke interrupted, stopped and turned to Azi, holding her index finger aloft. 'I have heard about this famous car. Some car, I understand. I shall be like the Queen of England riding in such a car.'

'Such a car?' Azi shrugged as he quoted her words back to her. 'Such a *fuss*! I can tell you the king and queen travel in smarter machines than my humble Kestrel. On the other hand, it is gleaming at the moment. I polished it especially. It's not every day that somebody as important as Rivke Haroun rides in my car.'

Rivke chided Azi with a gentle slap on the arm as the three of them strode out, laughing together, towards their object of conversation, the Riley Kestrel, which was indeed shining.

'It is beautiful, Azi,' Rivke said with feeling.

'I am so happy to see you,' said Yusuf, hugging his mother tightly into his side.

'This *Farhud* was a terrible thing,' said Azi once they were in the Riley and on their way back to Azi's home in Stamford Hill, where Rivke, Yusuf and Farah were all going to sleep that night. 'I am so sorry that it happened to you.'

'To me it didn't happen anywhere near as badly as it did to so many others.'

'How is Izaak?' Yusuf asked.

'He is well, thank God. He is in his father's business and engaged to a pretty American girl—Jewish, but not Iraqi. She came to Baghdad to visit friends, one of whom must have been quite a matchmaker because one minute it's, "I'd like you to meet my friend," and the next, it's *ay, ay ay* and letters to America.

'She's from a good family I understand, and is apparently a brilliant scholar. Your friend has had rubies drop into his lap. But all of Izaak's family—and all of us—still have heavy hearts over poor Sarai. And of course Izaak's car was destroyed. He hasn't driven since but his father is buying him a new car for a wedding present. How about you, Yusuf? Do you have a car?'

'Not yet, but I have a friend called Simon who is teaching me to drive.'

'A friend called Simon, eh? Listen to my Iraqi boy with his English pals. You are a proper Englishman now, I suppose.'

'By Iraqis, I am English, Ummi, but by the *English*... And Simon is hardly a typical Englishman. He is called Simon Saul and his family is originally from India. I met him at the synagogue.'

'Yes, I am so glad that you go to synagogue over here. A beautiful one, too, I understand.'

'I mostly go because of Farah. She is very involved there.'

'What a wonderful girl. And Azi, what about you, how are your children?'

'They are well. Miriam looks after them, so they are well, *bel ayn el raa'a*. Who wouldn't be well with such a mother? They were not affected by the war. They were safe outside of London. They stayed in the homes of kind people. We never experienced bombing, really. But Ben—'

'I heard. Their house was hit. What a terrible shock.'

'Yes, it was. They were lucky. They were not there. But generally we did not have a great deal to fear in the war. Unlike you in the *Farhud*.'

'Well, we were also lucky. Though it did affect Baba badly.' She was looking at Yusuf. 'I think it hastened his death. He was never the same...' She turned quickly to Azi, talking to the back of his head from the edge of the rear seat, straining forward, almost touching the front seats where Yusuf sat alongside Azi. 'But tell me all the news. Your family, Azi. Miriam. The children? Did they really stay with strangers? In homes that were not Jewish, let alone Iraqi?'

'They were with kind families. Sometimes being Jewish is not the most important thing. Or Iraqi. They and Miriam are well.' Azi hastily turned the talk away from the evacuation of his children. 'You will see them soon. Ben's family will be there, too. Everyone is excited that you are coming.'

'Oh, well, I am so excited to be coming. And, Yusuf, so tell me, how is your lovely wife?' Even the garrulous Azi was unable to interrupt Rivke's flow.

'Farah has never been better.' Yusuf was smiling, partly to himself. 'She...' He broke off and held up his hands in a gesture that signalled that he had gone a bit too far. 'She is fine. In good health. She can't wait to see you.'

'What do you mean, she is in good health? I know she has had… difficulties. Tell me, do you have good news?' Rivke was too sharp and perceptive for her son.

'She will tell you herself,' said Yusuf. 'I shouldn't have said anything. Look, she wants to tell you herself.'

'Oh, please God!' Rivke was uncontainable. 'The poor girl has suffered. You both have. I have prayed for her. She deserves this.'

'You must wait and hear from her own lips, Ummi. I promised her. I will be in trouble. Please.' But he was grinning.

Leah Haroun, daughter of Yusuf and Farah, was born on 27 January 1946. Rivke, who was renting a flat nearby, went to the family's Eastern Carpet and Goods Emporium when Yusuf was not there and bought from Azi an exotically decorated metal amulet for the baby. This was intended as protection against the evil eye and resembled, as Rivke vividly recalled, a charm that Aunty Alfassa had given her back in Baghdad when Yusuf was born.

When Farah's parents were able to come to London, in time for the birth of their first grandchild, they too brought protection against the evil eye, in the form of a jewelled amulet sewn into a delicately embroidered baby dress.

While Rivke was dismissive of what she saw as superstition, at the same time she delighted in succumbing to what she described as 'the traditional customs of our people, our family, our who-we-are.'

Rivke, together with Farah's mother and father, was welcomed enthusiastically into a crowded Lauderdale Road Synagogue for the newborn girl to be blessed. In the foyer, two tables, covered by immaculate white table-cloths, bore trays of nuts, sweets and popcorn. Inside the sanctuary, the main prayer-hall, once people had taken their seats, the rabbi began the ceremony by calling upon the biblical matriarchs, Sarah, Rebecca, Rachel and, with joyful emphasis, *Leah*!

Normally, the men and women were kept apart inside the synagogue but, on this occasion, while Farah held the baby, Yusuf and the three grandparents stood together behind her.

Rivke turned to her son and whispered: 'This is what I have been waiting for. I have prayed to the Almighty many times.'

99

Yusuf, full of emotion, quietly replied, 'this is what we have all been waiting for.'

The rabbi read from the Song of Songs: 'Unique is she, my constant dove, my perfect one…'

And thus was Leah Salama Haroun entered into the community. Her mother Farah, mindful of her two earlier miscarriages, wrapped her daughter in love and determined to strive always to protect her and to ensure that she was healthy and happy.

That night, the family gathered around the table in Miriam and Azi's home for an Iraqi-Jewish *lailt el-settee*—a baby girl's birth celebration. Along with Azi, Miriam and their children, Joseph, David and Violette; Yusuf, Farah and baby Leah; the London-based Harouns, now bolstered by Rivke and temporarily by Farah's parents, enjoyed a collective spirit of celebration none of them had experienced since the marriage of Yusuf to Farah five years earlier. For Azi and Ben, the veteran Londoners who had lived through the Blitz, it was even longer.

With the war over, Azi and Miriam's children safely home, the family business already building and Rivke settling into her new life in London, for everyone celebrating one little girl's birth that winter's night in Stamford Hill, the joy was palpable.

'Miriam, I want to thank you and salute you.' Rivke was on her feet, with a glass in her hand directed, along with her words, at her hostess. 'I do not normally drink but, on such a day as this, the *lailt el-settee* for a beautiful grandchild, *bel ayn el raa'a*, and given the chance to taste champagne, and pre-war proper champagne at that…' At this point, she turned with a smile to her host: 'Azi, I am amazed at how you manage to possess the most unlikely things. No wonder you are a success and a credit to the Haroun name.

'But,' she continued, 'it's your most prized possession of all, your lovely wife, I want to speak about. Like the ideal Jewish wife, truly more precious than jewels, and on whose tongue is kindness, she also brings food from afar and has prepared this wonderful feast, with such heavenly *kebab baamia* meatballs, almost on her own—though I do not discount the valuable help from Joseph, David and Violette. As for me, she would not even let me into the kitchen!

'Miriam,' she said turning, amid laughter, towards the object of her praise. 'You have been such a support—a *rock*—to Farah, through some trying times. To Yusuf, too, of course, but especially to Farah, in ways that only a woman can be to another woman'—here, Farah's mother loudly applauded—'and now, here we are on this most wonderful day… If only Sami had lived to see it, and *Bobbe* Eli…'

For the first time in this momentous day, Rivke's control wavered and she broke off to regain her composure. But, as Yusuf rose to comfort her, she signalled for him to sit down and held her glass high and, with a fond smile, acknowledged 'the truly wonderful lady of this house, *Miriam*! God bless you.' After taking the barest of sips of champagne, Rivke remained on her feet and continued: 'But now let's all of us join in a toast to our dear sweet little Leah. May she and her beautiful mother inspire each other to be loving, dutiful Jewish women forever.'

A little over two years later, a second child was born to Farah Haroun. Both the pregnancy and the birth were more difficult than they had been with Leah, but Farah was well cared for at St Mary's Hospital in Paddington by an Iraqi-Jewish doctor called Zilka, who played bridge and drank coffee with Azi on the first Sunday of every month. However, after the birth of the child—a son, Eli Abraham Haroun, named in memory of Rivke's lovingly remembered father *Bobbe* Eli—Doctor Zilka cautioned Farah against any future attempts to conceive.

On the eighth day of Eli Haroun's life, a party was held at his parents' home to celebrate his circumcision, marking his entry into the Hebraic covenant with the Almighty. The big treat was that Yusuf's sister Rachel flew in from New York for the occasion with her husband, David, who was given the honour of holding the baby while the *mohel*, a rabbinical assistant who carried out circumcisions, performed the operation.

Rachel reassured Farah that it was a painless procedure with little blood and that her two sons had recovered from it happily and rapidly. However, as soon as the incision was made, the only anaesthetic being a smear of ceremonial wine from the *mohel's* finger-tip, the child roared out his shock and distress.

Farah responded with her own loud scream, running towards her child and then stopping suddenly, stunned by the sight of much more blood than her sister-in-law had led her to expect. By the end of that week, she still had not come to terms with the experience but had to presume that little Eli had.

By the time of Eli's arrival, the oriental carpet trade practised by his father was recovering notably from the dip experienced in the war years.

Yusuf and Farah had bought a large house in Brondesbury, with a separate flat attached in which Rivke had set up home.

Both Farah and Yusuf had now learned to drive and Yusuf bought a car, a black Morris Eight, which they shared. Yusuf sometimes drove it to the Eastern Carpet and Goods Emporium but, within a few weeks, it was used more frequently by Farah to go to the Lauderdale Road Synagogue. Sometimes, she left the children with Rivke while she attended a ladies' guild coffee morning and sometimes she took Rivke and the children to mingle with friends who also had young children or older relatives.

Rivke loved going to synagogue, especially since there were usually a number of women there of her age, several of whom could speak Arabic. She had very quickly found her feet in London and, although most of her time was spent in the company of her family and other, mainly Sephardi and Oriental Jews whom she met at Lauderdale Road, she made friends with her neighbours in Brondesbury and acclimatised painlessly to transport, shopping, radio and newspapers and most other features of British daily life, including the weather.

Eli proved to be a demanding, wearing child. While Leah was self-contained and could sit or lie for hours gently rocking and cooing to herself, her young brother developed a series of rashes on his face and limbs, along with a loud and querulous way of crying.

Farah was constantly concerned about his health and whether he was developing at a normal rate. She would compare his progress towards various milestones—teething, eating, standing, walking, talking—with that of the children of her friends at synagogue, or other mothers at the local nursery, always imagining that Eli was lagging behind the others and that this signified a serious disease or grave defect.

Leah Haroun's calm self-containment throughout childhood was a boon to her mother. It enabled her to concentrate most of her caring energies on Eli. This continued, more or less, through the children's infancies, schooldays and adolescence. The principal adjustment made by Farah was to make her protective impulses less physical, less overt. She tended to internalise her anxieties, and suffer accordingly.

Her one, constant outlet came in the regular nocturnal conversations, in the dark, with Yusuf as they lay side by side, having just gone to bed, their heads pressed back on the pillows, faces turned upwards to the ceiling. Sometimes, they held hands.

102

Yusuf's body would be slumped, exhausted after expending large amounts of nervous energy over a delayed order, a sub-standard rug, a truculent customer, or the sheer onerous excitement of participating in a successful commercial enterprise. Farah, by contrast, would be taut, her body full of tension, her mind full of fear and apprehension over her son, as she tried to articulate her distress to her husband.

'I am so upset about Eli.'

'Relax. Sleep now. There's nothing you can do by lying here awake—and keeping me awake.' Yusuf resented the agitation brought on by his wife almost at the very moment when he was slipping into sleep. After turning heavily between the sheets, he would continue. 'Besides, you can do far more for him if you are relaxed than by passing on your stress and worries to him.'

'I'm not passing them on to him. I'm not telling him how I feel, how I'm so upset and worried. I'm telling you. I can't help it, Yusuf. He has been bullied at school. The teachers are no help and he is unhappy, isolated. He doesn't have a real friend. You read the headmistress's report. It was terrible.' Farah sighed deeply, a gear-change as she moved from the uneven ground of the present to the mountain that was the great, unknown future. 'What is to become of him? What kind of career, what sort of job could he possibly do?'

'Farah, darling. Nobody is remotely ready for a particular kind of career at Eli's age. Even the future doctors and lawyers. Not that I see Eli as a doctor or lawyer. He's much too dreamy. It's only the odd, swotty accountant or banking type who knows already what he wants to do. And that's because they are already so irreversibly dusty and boring. You want your son to be a boring clerk?'

'I wouldn't mind a bit of boring, if it meant he could settle down with a nice, decent, Jewish girl. You know, your mother is beginning to worry about him.'

'Farah, please! Ummi adores Eli and they have a great relationship. A marvellous understanding. It's lovely to see them together. It lifts my heart.'

'I'm only saying... She said she's worried how he'll turn out. That Leah will grow up to break a thousand hearts and Eli will have his heart broken a thousand times. That's what your mother said. She's worried that people might take advantage of his sweet nature, his innocence.'

'Fine qualities in a child, no?'

'I'm just saying. Anyone can see. He's so vulnerable.'

'Please, Farah, I've worked a twelve-hour day. I was so looking forward to coming home to my family and relaxing... and *sleeping*.'

In truth, Eli was a vulnerable boy. He was certainly intelligent, and loved books from an early age. He also loved to listen to and write stories, so much so that Farah sometimes wondered if he invented the accounts he gave of incidents at school in which he appeared as the victim. But he had a gentle, honest nature and, on reflection, Farah always believed him.

He and his much more confident elder sister had a close and clearly loving relationship. There was very little rivalry or jealousy between them. Leah was protective towards Eli without any of her mother's nervousness and Eli almost always deferred to Leah. They were comfortable in each other's company and laughed a lot. Eli was also seemingly happy in his parents' company and, as Yusuf had maintained, enjoyed a special relationship with his grandmother, Rivke.

But Eli would occasionally withdraw into himself and, now and again, Farah came across him crying in his bedroom. He never gave an explanation for this and always seemed to recover rapidly after his mother's affectionate intervention.

Despite continuous attempts by Anna and Roderick to obtain information about Anna's parents, Sarah and Chaim—including sending letters to the last-known addresses of Anna's two possibly surviving aunts—it was not until January 1946, by which time she had long given up hope of ever seeing her father again, that Anna finally obtained official confirmation of his death, and that of her mother.

A letter from the London office of the United Nations Relief and Rehabilitation Administration began with a brief introductory paragraph of dry, impersonal sympathy, followed by two further concise paragraphs:

Dr Chaim Aaron Weisz. Date of birth: 1 November 1903. Birthplace: Budapest, Hungary. Date and place of death: 6 or 7 June 1944, Oswiecim (Auschwitz), Poland. Cause of death: 'work accident'.

Mrs Sarah Eva Weisz. Date of birth: 28 March 1906. Birthplace: Budapest, Hungary. Date and place of death: 15 November 1944, Oswiecim (Auschwitz), Poland, in 'hospital for terminally ill Jews'. Cause of death: unknown.

'Born in the same place; died in the same place,' Anna declared through her tears as Roderick held her tightly against his chest. 'At least I know now,' she added, closing her eyes and trying to defy the wave of grief. 'I really knew all the time that she was dead, that they both were. I thought that my father had been killed while he was still in Budapest. And then I was told that he had been in Auschwitz, too. All three of us had that memorable experience. Only I survived. Why should they have died?'

She was speaking and weeping now, warding off both despair and hysteria, gasping out her sentences. 'I always kept this little flame of hope burning, that one day I would see my mother again. It was unreal to me. Her presence was so strong. We never saw my father after he was taken from us in Budapest, but my mother and I remained together. We were together in Auschwitz and I didn't die so I kept believing it possible that she didn't die either. But Frida helped to prepare me for this moment, when we were in Bergen-Belsen. A moment I hoped would never come.

'How prepared can a daughter be? My dear, loving, wise, brilliant, inspiring father. My sweet, lovely, musical, harmless mother—keeping the religion, playing her piano and making people happy. She never harmed a soul. Two intelligent, good human beings. Slaughtered. Why? What for? Killed by frightened, stupid, unintelligent thugs. For nothing!'

In a defeated cry of lamentation, she finally gave way to her feelings, clinging ever tighter to Roderick, her only family now—her English oak—in need, dependence and love, soaking his shirt with an unstoppable salt-water flow.

She put the UNRRA letter in the large brown envelope containing her father's last, hurried handwritten note, which she had kept constantly close to her in Auschwitz and Belsen, and placed it back in its drawer in her dressing table in the bedroom of the cottage that had been Cedric's wedding present to her and Roderick, not half-a-mile from Cedric and Margaret's villa.

At night, Anna's English bed, in her Englishman's arms, seemed the most natural place for her. Initially more soothing than erotic, their physical connection intensified along with their growing familiarity. Anna asked herself the questions about love just as she had done when she'd first met Imre, three years earlier. But now, she answered them with affirmation.

It was Roderick who raised the prospect of starting a family of their own.

'Roderick, my dear, sweet man. First, you want to rush into marriage and now you want to have children "with indecent haste".' Anna greatly enjoyed parodying the English manners and expressions of Esher's more sedate citizens. 'Indecent haste' was one that she found particularly amusing. On the actual issue, she felt cautious, despite having entered so spiritedly into her new life. 'I don't know,' she said. 'I still feel as though I am settling in. I'm not sure that I am yet ready, my darling.'

'Well,' said Roderick, smiling and stroking her hair. 'Whenever you are ready, you can be sure that I shall be, too.'

After more than a year, with Anna becoming worried and Roderick frustrated, a distraction arose. A local shop became vacant and Margaret suggested that Anna take it over—she had shown a flair for interior design and had decorated and designed the inside of her cottage, and here was a chance to be paid for doing it. Roderick approved of his mother's suggestion, as did Cedric, who said he would help Anna with the initial stock.

Anna was hesitant but inwardly enthusiastic. There had been a time when anything other than a professional, ideally medical, career would have been unthinkable. Bergen-Belsen undid that kind of ambition and she now welcomed the chance to show initiative and meet more people. At the same time, she was apprehensive.

'Nonsense,' said Margaret. 'You have a good eye for colour and design. You'll be a great success. And I shall come and help you. I'll be your assistant!'

This swayed Anna. Having her capable, intelligent mother-in-law at her side sounded perfect. And so Anna's Designs opened in Esher in May 1947—and thrived. The novelty effect of having such a bright array of colours set amid a line of mostly dull, grey shop windows immediately attracted plenty of the keen and the curious in and around Esher. After the initial spurt, business settled into a steady pace, producing a wel-

106

come source of income to augment that which Roderick brought home from Vane Natural Clothing.

One morning, a tall, thin, elderly woman, with tanned and heavily lined features, entered the shop. She announced—as though she was addressing a public meeting rather than one person inside a shop—that she was looking for curtain material. And, she emphasised, it had to be of the highest quality. Furthermore, she required a substantial quantity, for the curtains were destined to grace what she called her 'traditional English, French windows.'

When Anna gave a smile at this, taking it to be a witticism, the woman looked slightly offended. And when Anna brought out a length of floral-patterned material and laid it before her customer with a few comments of commendation, she was met with a brisk question: 'Where are you from?'

'What do you mean, exactly?' Anna asked in turn, finding the enquiry an odd one.

'Well, my dear. I have not been in your shop before. I believe it must be quite new. I have lived in Esher fifty-odd years and I've never seen it. You seem to have a lot of stock but I'm not quite sure about this particular material. Do you have something a little less… colourful?'

'Yes, of course, Madam.'

As Anna brought down two more rolls of material from the shelves, the customer carried on talking: 'I just wondered where you popped up from,' she said. 'That was all. Simple question.'

'I live about ten minutes' walk from here.'

'There's no need for cheek. Why are you being so difficult? I asked you a perfectly reasonable question. Your accent, if I may say so, clearly indicates somewhere rather more than ten minutes' walk away. Can I please see the manager?'

Anna was struggling hard to maintain the deference expected of a shopkeeper. 'I am the manager,' she said, forcing her face into a smile. 'And I am from Hungary.'

'Good gracious! Well, I must tell you that here in England we expect and treat one another with good manners, especially when one is serving a customer.'

'I did not come here directly from Hungary,' said Anna, her heart pumping hard against her chest, her cheeks reddening. 'I came through Poland and Germany, stopping at a couple of very interesting places.' She felt herself losing control.

107

'Well, wherever they were, they obviously weren't able to show you how civilised life is conducted in England. I'm afraid that I am not interested in your route to this country, and I have decided to take my custom elsewhere. Good day.'

Anna kept her gaze directed to the floor throughout this little speech. And after the woman had left, while the bell behind the door was still jangling, she looked around the shop, her eyes stinging. The table, chairs, sofa, rolls of material, cushions, dye-charts, tablecloths, china ornaments—all of it—began to swirl in a vortex of colour. She stumbled through the curtains at the back that marked off the public space from the private, hastily stepped into the wash-room, and vomited into the toilet bowl.

Some months later, while out walking with her mother-in-law across the green behind the row of shops in which her interior-design business was situated, Anna recognised the woman who had been so offended by her poor knowledge of 'civilised life.' The woman was approaching with a man in tweeds leaning heavily on a walking-stick. Anna realised with satisfaction that all trace had disappeared of the subservience she had originally felt at that first sight of the woman entering her shop. She was therefore intrigued rather than embarrassed when Margaret addressed the woman.

'Good morning,' said Margaret, exuding the calm pleasure of a woman taking delight in familiar open-air surroundings.

'Good morning,' returned the woman.

'Fine day,' the woman's companion croaked, pressing down still more heavily on his walking-stick.

'Good morning,' Anna chimed in. 'Did you find appropriate curtains for your English French windows?'

'I beg your pardon?' The woman was puzzled, on this occasion, rather than affronted.

'Curtains,' Anna repeated, holding out an arm in the general direction of Anna's Designs. 'You came into my shop some time ago, looking for curtains for your French windows—traditionally English windows, you said.'

'I don't quite recall,' said the woman, sounding slightly detached from reality.

'You appeared to be fascinated by the fact that I am from Hungary.'

'Oh really? Are you? Well, you don't sound as though you are. Lovely weather, don't you think?'

And so they parted politely.

'How do you know that woman?' Anna asked Margaret, eager to learn more. But there was no more.

'Oh I don't know them at all really,' Margaret replied. 'We've occasionally bumped into each other on the green here. The old man is usually walking his dog. Though not today. I haven't seen them for ages. I wonder if the dog is still alive.'

'She,' said Anna, with a smile almost of triumph, 'was the rude old witch who was so insistent on reminding me of my rightful servile role as a foreigner.'

'Oh dear, really?'

Her reaction to seeing the 'rude old witch' strolling on the green, and Margaret's laughter when she identified her as such, confirmed Anna's confidence that she was becoming steadily more acclimatised to her Surrey surroundings. Over time, this was also significantly helped by Margaret becoming increasingly involved in the shop, allowing Anna to have more leisure time.

She made a number of friends, joined a local library—from which she borrowed and devoured a steady stream of books—grew familiar with the surrounding countryside and, with Roderick, went almost weekly to the Embassy Cinema in Esher. Since their first visit, in the summer of 1946, to see Cary Grant play Cole Porter in *Night and Day*, Anna had developed a compelling love of films. And if the Embassy wasn't showing what she wanted to see, she was happy to go any manageable distance to satisfy her need for celluloid entertainment.

But her cultural appetite and curiosity could not be satisfied by just a weekly dose of the movies. Before the opening of Anna's Designs, she and Roderick had frequently ventured into London to visit museums and galleries, attend concerts and see plays. They saw Ralph Richardson play *Cyrano de Bergerac* at the New Theatre and followed his career closely thereafter.

In 1946, too, on Anna's 21st birthday, a few weeks after that first cinema visit, Cedric paid for Anna and Roderick to stay at the Savoy Hotel, in London, where they drank champagne before going to hear the seventy-eight-year-old Frederic Lamond, a former pupil of Franz Liszt, play at the Albert Hall.

Virtually from the moment Lamond's fingers touched the keyboard, Anna had to wipe her eyes, so powerfully did the music evoke her mother's memory. She told Roderick afterwards that she could almost smell Sarah's presence.

There were a number of Hungarians in the audience, some of whom were also clearly moved by this connection to their homeland. Once the concert was over, as Anna left on Roderick's arm, she became unsettled at hearing snatches of her native language emerge from the general murmur of audience chatter. She had to take deep breaths to recover some composure.

Back in their room at the Savoy afterwards, Anna was overcome with emotion and threw herself into Roderick's embrace. All through the night, she wrapped herself passionately around her eager husband's body, fervently trying to drown the remembered sounds of Hungary and the aftermath of her departure from Budapest, while at the same time hearing in her head, and yielding to, the insistent chords of Franz Liszt.

By the time they shared breakfast at the Savoy the next morning, Anna had thrown off the effects of being emotionally ambushed by Lamond's breathtaking exploitation of the Albert Hall keyboard.

'If it had not been for you, Captain Vane,' she said, 'I think I would have run away from life instead of confronting it.' With her right arm stretched across the table and her hand over Roderick's, she used her left to pick up, drink and enjoy her first, post-war, concentrated orange juice. 'This is paradise,' she said.

Generally, Anna Vane enjoyed the second half of the 1940s. She loved her husband, her home, her adopted country, her town, her cottage and her garden. She was healthy, her business brought in a reasonable income while Roderick's involvement in the running of Vane Natural Clothing had helped to bring about a substantial increase in profits.

Nevertheless, she frequently wondered if any of her family had survived, especially her cousins Ibolya, Judit, Sandor and Miklos. But she would always close off these thoughts as briskly as possible, throwing herself into some physical activity—shifting cloth in the shop, cleaning or even painting her kitchen, planting or digging in her garden, or taking Margaret and Cedric's dog for a walk. Otherwise, such musings would inevitably lead her to think about her parents. And, indeed, once in a while Chaim or Sarah would enter her thoughts unbidden.

One Sunday morning in 1949, after she had entertained her in-laws for breakfast and Roderick had gone to buy a newspaper, Anna watched

Cedric and Margaret depart along her garden path, dressed in what they always, slightly satirically, called their Sunday Best.

As she stood alone at her kitchen table, gazing vacantly at her in-laws walking towards the church, an episode from her Dembinszky Street past came into her consciousness with a sudden, disarming clarity. It was a Friday evening; the gathered family had welcomed in the Sabbath, uttered the traditional blessings and eaten. Chaim was, typically, railing against the ignorant Satmar Chasidim of Budapest.

'To have a closed mind, is bad enough,' he said. 'But when that mind is also a very small one, there will be disastrous consequences.'

Chaim's brother David was nodding in agreement. But Sarah, who rarely intervened in the men's post-prandial Sabbath conversations, certainly not to voice an opinion, on this occasion challenged her husband.

'Chaim,' she said, 'you sometimes forget my heritage—and yours, too. At home, my father would tell us many wonderful, uplifting stories of our distinguished rabbinical ancestors. And, as you know, these were men—and some women—of intellect, of distinction.

'But there is more to leading a good life than intellect.' Sarah was in her stride now in Anna's hallucinated domestic tableau. 'Two of my extremely religious aunts once heard that my grandmother's neighbour, an old lady, was seriously ill and had no family,' Sarah had said, her eyes locked with Chaim's.

'They visited her every time they went to see my grandmother and arranged for other Chasidic ladies also to visit the neighbour so that no day would pass without the woman receiving food—kosher food—or being helped to keep herself and her tiny dark home clean. And, you know what? This neighbour, who was able to live a few more years on this earth because of those Chasidic women—she wasn't even Jewish.'

Everybody was listening now, held as though inside a shimmering bubble. A secure family group within which contrasting viewpoints could be expressed loudly and forcefully and entirely without antagonism.

'That is a wonderful story, Sarah. A good, Jewish story,' Chaim told her, before continuing for the benefit of all present, especially his daughter—or at least, that's how it felt to Anna. 'Wonderful,' he repeated solemnly. 'But, listen, while I might sometimes forget my manners, I remain aware of my heritage—our heritage.' Pausing, he held up a hand as if to prevent any interruption while he was collecting his thoughts.

And then he seemed to look directly at Anna, his face thoughtful, caring, almost confessional, in a way comfortingly familiar to her from their conversations about science, art, medicine and religion.

'It's true that I love argument, intellectual curiosity,' he said. 'I love sitting around this table in this room filled with candlelight and love, waiting to appreciate the beauty of music, played by my dear wife. And all these things, to me, are Jewish, as is the idea that the mind must be consciously stretched, by probing, asking questions, creating, looking for cures.

'And if my probing, my questions, cannot be stopped by answers that are not answers but merely rules and prohibitions, then I am glad. And I will keep going though I shall never be counted among the black-hatted holy ones.' He was looking lovingly at his wife now. 'Yes, darling Sarah, your forebears, some of them—and one or two of mine—were great men, and women. Thinkers, as well as the kindest of human beings. They have spawned you, me, *Jews*. Nobody loves being a Jew more than I do. As a Jew, you stand on the fringe of humanity and yet also within its essence. You are both observer and participant. But, I concede to you, my wise and talented woman, and salute your noble ancestors and their own great teachers.

'For, whether you wear a doctor's white coat or a Chasid's black one, whatever kind of Jew you are—an atheist or a believer, a psalmist or a singer of profane songs—whoever you are, your origins can be traced back to a religious text. So the holy ones are closer to the flame, to the mystery—even the blinkered fools here in Budapest. And, as I love you and all of our family here, I do not, I promise you, forget our heritage, yours and mine, and now our darling daughter's.'

Just a few years on, in a cottage on the edge of a Surrey town far from Budapest, that same daughter released her grip on a kitchen chair, closed her eyes and sighed as her reverie was interrupted by her husband returning with the newspaper. She turned to greet him and he put down the paper as they embraced.

'Are you all right, sweetheart?' Roderick asked. 'You look a bit upset.'

She replied by shaking her head, trying to ignore the moistening of her eyes and wishing that Roderick hadn't drawn attention to her emotional state. But she was increasingly able to cope with such moments and hugged her husband without speaking, feeling safe, as always, with her head against his chest.

'Anyhow, I've got something to tell you that'll cheer you up,' said Roderick, talking over the top of her head and kissing her hair. 'A special surprise for your birthday next month. I've reserved seats at the Albert Hall for the opening night of the Proms. Schubert's *Unfinished Symphony*. Tchaikovsky's *Romeo and Juliet*. Elgar. Gounod's *Faust*, and heaven knows what else.'

'Oh Roderick!' She pulled back from his chest and held him at arm's length.

'And that's not all. I've reserved the same room at the Savoy that we had three years ago.'

'Oh Roderick, you are wonderful.' Now the tears came. Tears of—almost—pure joy.

If anything, the 1949 concert and stay at the Savoy Hotel was even better than the first one in 1946—and of more consequence.

Belinda Sarah Vane was born on 27 April 1950 in Epsom Hospital, seven miles from her parents' home. Roderick arrived bearing flowers from his parents' lavish garden and gently stroked his wife's hair and kissed her.

'I think we found the best possible way to finish Schubert's unfinished symphony,' he said, smiling.

Anna, too, smiled but her gaze was fixed on the beautifully sniffling, twitching, seven-pound-seven-ounce bundle that she held to her breast with delicate, loving strength.

In the many and regular conversations that Farah Haroun and her mother-in-law Rivke had about Eli, Rivke always inclined to optimism. This was partly because her daughter-in-law's anxieties and need for reassurance were so great, and partly because of her own abundant love for her grandson. She could not believe that others could feel anything less than a slightly reduced version of her own adoration for such a special, talented and beautiful child.

It was not that she did not sense his vulnerability. This was apparent from the subtly contrasting ways in which she showed her affection towards Eli, on the one hand, and his sister Leah, on the other. Rivke could never admit, nor bring herself to believe, that she loved them unequally. But she felt naturally less protective of her granddaughter.

She knew that Leah was clear-eyed, sensible and took a practical view of life. Eli was vague and careless.

And while Rivke gave her time and material generosity as fully as she could to both children, and displayed a scrupulously fair, grandmotherly interest in their progress, she took every opportunity to bolster Eli individually. She would never talk down to him and, when he spoke, she would always take him seriously, granting him the same level of patience and respect as she would an adult.

He was clearly a creative and intelligent boy with an advanced vocabulary for his age, a quick wit and a loud, spontaneous laugh, but his introversion, absent-mindedness and poor concentration meant that his native intelligence and creativity rarely received the recognition they merited. Having shown promise in his earliest school years, he began to fall behind most of the other pupils in his class, which disturbed Yusuf. At home, he increasingly reacted to simple enquiries about his school-life, what food he would like, even his health, with loud, impatient outbursts, which disturbed Farah.

Eli was much more at ease with his grandmother than he was with his parents and her flat was a refuge for him. He would increasingly be found there as he grew into, and then through, adolescence. He loved the sweet smells that pervaded the room at the front of the building, overlooking the street, which Rivke called her 'parlour'. Off one corner, there was a small kitchen, inside which was her old table from Baghdad. Eli could never recall this table being clear; it always seemed to be covered with pots for making Turkish coffee; jars empty or half-filled with mango pickle or almond biscuits, and bowls of dried apricots and dates.

Dates were Rivke's most vivid link with the past. They reminded her of Sami and of long, hot days sitting in their courtyard in the shade of the palm trees. She had found a stall in Portobello market run by a genial Arab called Muhammad, where she could find many things that brought back the tastes and aromas of Baghdad.

Muhammad would keep a regular supply of dates for Rivke. She called them 'Zahdi', suggesting they were inferior examples of the fruit of the majestic Middle Eastern palm, but 'better than nothing'. Dates, she believed were a source of strength and vitality.

'If you eat dates,' she would constantly tell Eli, 'you will be big and strong, like your daddy. Did you know that he was a champion at football and boxing when he was at school?'

Eli was fascinated by the way in which his grandmother had virtually recreated her Iraqi home in her parlour, with its exotic hangings, rugs and pictures, the ottoman, Sami's old armchair with its fading, torn upholstery and scuffed wooden legs, and even her old sewing machine that she had barely used even in Baghdad.

'Do you wish you were back in Iraq, Grandma?' Eli once asked Rivke. 'Daddy says your room is like it was in Iraq? Don't you like Britain?'

'Eli, darling, I love Britain,' she said, placing her hands on Eli's cheeks. 'But it is important to remember who you are, who your parents were, where you came from. You are a lucky boy because you can say, "I am British, and Iraqi and Jewish."'

'But which is the most important?'

'The most important is: "I am Eli—Eli Haroun." Always be yourself, before anything else. And if you know who you are, as an individual, it is easier to take pride in being part of something else, like a family, or being Baghdadi, British, English, or Jewish. Come, I have made some lemonade for you. From real lemons. And we'll both have a nice juicy date to eat.'

Lauderdale Road Synagogue became the family's social fulcrum. Rivke joined her daughter-in-law in the ladies' guild and developed an interest in bridge, which her sister-in-law Yocheved had begun to teach her back in Baghdad. And Yusuf enjoyed taking Eli and Leah to the Sabbath services. It gave him a feeling of connection with his father and with his beloved grandfather *Bobbe* Eli, after whom he had named his son. He also felt comfortable with the familiar liturgy, as did Farah, who—like her mentor Miriam—had become a serious student of Hebrew in order to take an active interest in her children's religious education.

Even so, if they had examined their deepest feelings, rather than their habits and customs, only Rivke would have been able to claim a genuine spiritual attachment to Judaism. For her, this had been deepened over a period of months between 1949 and 1951, when a large influx of émigrés from Baghdad arrived in London, many of whom passed through the 'Gate to Heaven' into Lauderdale Road, enabling Rivke to renew several old acquaintances.

A time of great pride, and respite from academic anxiety, came with Eli's bar mitzvah lessons, preparing him, at the age of thirteen, for the religious ceremony that would launch him into adulthood—a most

115

unlikely transition but still sentimentally valued. Eli loved it, the music, the attention, the sheer exuberance.

Moreover, while his contemporaries' voices were breaking from a ringing treble to an unpredictable, up-and-down warble, Eli's manifested an unusual, consistent sweetness. And under the tutelage of the synagogue's cantor, Reverend Eliezer Abinun, Eli came to revel in the religious side of the procedure. He enjoyed learning his 'portion' of the law, the public reading of which, in the form of a melodious chant delivered from the *bimah*—the raised platform at the heart of the synagogue—would symbolically lift him from boyhood into manhood. He equally enjoyed the riotous mischief-making with his fellow bar mitzvah students during the breaks in study.

When it came to the ceremony itself, the unexpectedly flawless rendering that Eli gave, in his still sweet voice, unlocked the tension gripping his parents, his grandmother and even his sister, and released and swelled their emotions in a happy tide.

Everyone echoed Reverend Abinun's verdict that it was a wonderful, heartfelt performance, though Eli himself—privately indifferent to the words he was communicating about the way a burnt offering should be made—even at the high point of his word-perfect chanting, was thinking to himself: 'What am I doing? This has no meaning.'

'It was a false dawn,' Farah would say of the bar mitzvah as she and Yusuf looked back during the ensuing years. She would wave away Yusuf's evocation of their son's admirable performance that day on the *bimah* as evidence that he would eventually settle successfully into adult life.

'He still has no confidence,' Farah insisted. 'It was an isolated phenomenon. A one-off. I worry even more as he gets older. He is still doing badly at school. I dread those open evenings listening to those smug, patronising teachers. And he still has moods—he still gets depressed.'

'I know.' Yusuf gave a conciliatory sigh. 'And yet, he did so well up there on the *bimah*. His voice was so loud. He smiled as he sang. He made eye-contact with Reverend Abinun. He was the most brilliant bar mitzvah boy. He has so much to offer. He is intelligent. You can tell. He's so full of clever wisecracks. He's a good-looking boy—those big Haroun eyes just like his mother's, that shiny, dark-brown hair. I'm sure the girls at his school adore him.'

'Yes, they want to mother him.'

'And you can't deny that he's creative. Arty. He absolutely loves that camera we bought him.'

'I don't know,' sighed Farah. 'I think he's spending far too much time on his photography. It's such a lonely hobby. He gets me down so much, and the way he talks to me these days. It's so rude. I just want him out of the house when he's like that.' Farah's face was dark with misery.

'He doesn't mean it,' said Yusuf, holding his wife tightly. 'I still believe that, inside, he has what it takes to succeed. And he's our boy and we love him dearly. Listen…'

At that moment, they heard Rivke and Eli opening the front door and Eli laughing loudly at something as he stepped into the house.

As Eli's A-level school examinations approached, he spent whole evenings in his room, ostensibly revising. But when Yusuf went into his room to ask how he was getting on, his son would too often be lying on his bed looking at photographs he had taken and listening to music. In reply to Yusuf, Eli would usually say he was doing 'not too well'.

Yusuf wasn't dismayed by this; his friend Simon Saul had a son, Ramon, with whom Eli had become very friendly, and he was too obsessed with sport to concentrate on his A-levels. Ramon was in his school's cricket team and, like most boys of their age (though not Eli) was excited about the forthcoming football World Cup finals to be held in England. It seemed that nobody was giving proper attention to A-levels.

Yusuf was much more worried by the fact that Eli seemed reluctant to venture out into the summer air and appeared content to remain indoors in a darkened room with his record player booming out songs like 'Paint It Black' by the Rolling Stones over and over again. As for the future, while Farah dreaded a loss of face at Lauderdale Road if her only son failed to get into university, Yusuf was secretly quite hoping that Eli would avoid university and come into the family carpet business.

He had helped out at the warehouse in his school holidays and appeared to enjoy it. Azi and Ben liked having him around and Azi in particular shared Eli's somewhat sarcastic line in humour. 'They bring him out of himself,' Yusuf had told Farah.

But Eli surprised his parents, just as he had over his bar mitzvah, by landing a place at art college. Reading his son's art teacher's startlingly laudatory reference, Yusuf eased a strained atmosphere—following a mother-and-son argument about the possibility that Eli might forget his Baghdadi-Jewish heritage, stay out on Friday nights and eat non-kosher food—by asking, with exaggerated astonishment: 'Is this really you, your teacher is talking about? To read this, anyone would think he's describing Leonardo Da Vinci.'

As a result of this unexpected good news, Eli's eighteenth birthday party, which Farah had been dreading, was a truly celebratory event. Guests included Eli's best friend Ramon Saul, other friends from school, Farah's and Rivke's friends from Lauderdale Road, Yusuf's business friends, Azi and Miriam and family, and of course Leah, who was by now happily enjoying life 175 miles away at the University of York. Leah brought a couple of university friends in tow—both female, both Jewish—and manipulated her younger brother into speaking and even dancing with them.

Farah prepared several bowls of *kubba* stew, multi-coloured mounds of rice cooked in a variety of ways with an array of herbs and spices, dates, onions, chillis, courgettes, and home-made flat bread alongside pita and pickled mangoes and cucumbers. She ordered kosher wines and Iraqi sweets and, with the help of her daughter Leah, created and laid out a wealth of desserts incorporating fruit, nuts, saffron and rose-water, augmented by scores of date biscuits and almond balls.

Eli looked happier than he had for months and, standing with Leah between their parents, raised a glass of sweet kosher wine high in his left hand and gestured across the packed room at the people talking and laughing as they ate and drank away the fruits of Farah's labours. 'This is Haroun heaven,' he proclaimed.

His father responded by holding up the thimble-sized glass he was holding, loudly declaring it certainly was, and sinking the tiny glass's contents in one gulp. Farah suggested later to Yusuf that their son's state-ment was intended ironically, as a criticism, a distancing, like the wicked son in the Passover Haggadah.

Margaret Vane was delighted when her granddaughter was enrolled at the local village primary school at which she herself had been both pupil and teacher. And it was thrilling for her to accompany Anna as she took Belinda for her first day's attendance at an institution where hundreds of children had begun their education since Victorian times.

Margaret hadn't been back to the school since a concert, by pupils and staff, had been given in her honour a month or so after her retirement. Since then, a good deal of building had taken place to add new structures and improve older ones. While the central single-storey 1870s brick facade, behind which lay the school hall and head-teacher's office, looked much as it had done when Margaret last departed from it, there was now a shining new gymnasium and indoor play area, and a separate kitchen and dining room. In her day, the main school hall served as assembly area, gym and dining room in one—and had done for generations.

Parents and grandparents jockeyed to take photographs, the sun glinting on their cameras, and a hubbub of young voices swelled as the school's new arrivals waited shyly or excitedly with their mothers—and a few fathers—at the gate.

Anna tried to make the situation as matter-of-fact as possible. She wanted to still the nervousness that had overtaken her and prevent it from communicating itself to Belinda. As Margaret took photographs, Anna chatted to Belinda and held her hand a little too tightly.

Belinda was a bright, curious child, who responded well to her mother's determination to ensure that she received an excellent education. Shortly after she was born, Roderick had bought a piano for the cottage and Anna had given their daughter gentle and gradual musical tuition at its keyboard from the moment the child was able to sit upright on the piano stool.

Before starting at the primary school, Belinda had attended a nursery near Anna's former interior design business—which still bore her name and gave her an income, though she had long, and willingly, ceded ownership to Margaret. Anna had helped in the shop at weekends and sometimes during weekday mornings when Belinda was at the nursery.

Other children were encouraged to come to the cottage to play with Belinda, and this—along with the elementary lessons Anna gave her in a clutch of subjects both intellectual, such as French and poetry, and practical, such as cooking and sewing—kept her occupied most days from waking to sleeping.

Belinda was a gregarious girl and retained friends from nursery to primary school and onwards. Her closest companion was a girl called Christine Thornington, whose cascading blonde curls were in arresting contrast to Belinda's long, straight, almost black hair.

119

Quite early in their friendship, Christine asked Belinda: 'Why does your mummy have a funny voice?'

'What do you mean?' Belinda asked her.

'Well, she sounds different to my mummy and other mummies,' said the precocious Christine.

'I don't know what you're talking about,' Belinda said sternly, putting her young friend in her place.

But, one Saturday, when Anna was helping at the shop, she happened to telephone the cottage to speak to Roderick. In the course of the conversation, he handed over the phone to their daughter so that Anna could say hello. It was the first time mother and daughter had communicated by phone.

'Hello, my darling, how are you?' Anna came across warmly and clearly.

'Hello, is that you, Mummy?' Belinda was tentative.

'Yes, darling it is. Are you having a nice time with Daddy?'

'You sound strange, Mummy. Why do you sound strange?'

Anna was unable to answer because she was laughing so much but managed to compose herself to say farewell and ask Belinda to 'tell Daddy I'll be home soon.'

After the receiver was replaced, Belinda persisted: 'Daddy, why does Mummy's voice sound funny?'

'Oh, that's just the telephone. It makes people's voices sound a bit tinny.'

'No, it's different. Her voice is different to Christine's mummy's voice.'

It was then that Roderick explained about accents. Later, when Anna came home, she added to the explanation by careful demonstration, though to most people her English pronunciation carried only the barest edge of a Hungarian accent.

Nevertheless, on the following Monday, Belinda proudly told her friend Christine: 'My mummy has a 'garian accent because she comes from Hungry.'

'Hungry?' Christine retorted. 'Why is she hungry?'

'No. Don't be silly. She's not hungry. Hungry is a country.'

As Belinda Vane grew, and her conversations with her mother—including those on the telephone—multiplied, Belinda developed her own Home Counties accent, expressed in an assured, well-modulated voice, and any difference in her speech and that of her mother went unnoticed.

Belinda blossomed into a tall, dark-haired beauty with a surprisingly shy and restrained smile quite at odds with her sudden bursts of laughter and spontaneous singing. She excelled at the accomplishments learned or inherited from her mother, such as French conversation, playing the piano, sewing and drawing, but found her schoolteachers uninspiring.

Her indifference to most of her school lessons continued when she moved from the local junior school to a private preparatory establishment just outside the nearby town of Leatherhead. Here, she picked up a new vocabulary. 'Tiresome' and 'tedious' were frequently employed epithets, which at first amused her parents but later caused them to chide her.

'Belinda,' Anna demanded one evening after her daughter had described her starchy headmistress Miss Macmillan with what was fast becoming her favourite word. 'I must tell you that your constant use of the word "tiresome" is itself tiresome and I must also tell you now to stop. It is very unattractive.'

Roderick, by contrast, still found it amusing but kept that to himself and, far from allowing Belinda to see his amusement, supported his wife's reproach. 'You must listen to your mother, darling,' was a sentence frequently uttered by Roderick Vane in those days.

After a couple of years at the preparatory school, Belinda moved on to St Madeleine's, the all-girls senior establishment that was part of the same foundation. Fortuitously, Belinda's favourite teacher at the prep, Miss Ainsworth, moved up with her and became her first-form mistress at the new school. With her hair gathered into a bun, her round, wire-spectacles and equally round, permanently pink cheeks, Maud Ainsworth looked like an actress auditioning for the part of a schoolteacher, so true to the stereotype did she appear. She was still in her early twenties but had clearly long settled on the style of dress and general appearance for which she expected to be known throughout her entire life.

In her first year on St Madeleine's staff, Miss Ainsworth performed the commendable feat of scraping away the boredom that had begun to cling to Belinda like a barnacle.

This delighted Anna and Roderick, as did St Madeleine's in general, with its air of tradition and accomplishment. Set in extensive, verdant grounds, it exuded prosperity and excellence. It was equipped with a new theatre and high-quality music facilities—to which Belinda especially warmed.

Roderick and Anna both loved going to St Madeleine's to see Belinda sing in the choir, or play the piano in the school orchestra—and occasionally solo—or to keep up with their daughter's steady if not spectacular academic progress. They never failed to be impressed by the poised and confident pupils deputed to greet parents, answer enquiries or show them around the classrooms, laboratories, the gym, or backstage at the Mole Vault—the school theatre playfully named because of the school's location next to the River Mole as well as the fact that the auditorium was located in the basement of the main school building.

Generally speaking, Belinda's time at St Madeleine's went smoothly. There were just two moments at which Anna, in particular, was subjected to powerful and disturbing emotions. The first was quite early on in Belinda's time at secondary school when the headmistress wrote to Roderick and Anna to ask them to give their consent to Belinda's joining a confirmation class to be taken by the vicar of St Hilda's Church, which adjoined the school grounds.

Belinda herself was keen to join, mainly because her friend Christine Thornington, with whom she had passed through both primary and preparatory school to St Madeleine's, had already enrolled. Roderick thought it a harmless idea. He had himself been confirmed in the Vanes' local church, he explained, and it had made little spiritual impact at the time and none at all since.

'I'd rather you didn't,' Anna told her daughter.

'Why?' asked Belinda.

'I just don't want you to.'

This refusal without explanation inevitably made Belinda persist. 'But why not?' she asked angrily.

The chilling of the atmosphere prompted Roderick to intervene: 'Look, darling, your mother and I went through the war together. We saw enough things to make us feel that praying is pretty pointless.'

'What things?'

Anna swiftly interjected. 'People dying who should not have died. Good people killed by bad people.' She had retaken control of the argument and something in her voice made Belinda pause and think back to the few desultory conversations she and her mother had had when she was a small girl in which Anna had quickly passed on from the brief statement that her own 'mummy and daddy'—always the two of them linked together—had died during the war.

122

'Mum,' she said hesitantly. 'How did your parents die? Did a bomb fall on their house?'

'Something like that, yes. I'll tell you all about it, about them, one day.'

It was hard for Belinda to tell whether she herself wanted to avoid the subject or simply couldn't summon up the strength to press her mother on how her parents died but, for whatever reason, she felt the need to shift the conversation back to confirmation with Christine at St Hilda's.

'Anyway,' she said. 'This confirmation thing, it's just a bit of fun to go with Christine. I am not going to turn into some mad churchgoer.'

'Well, look, I'm not going to prevent you going if you really want to,' said Anna in a conciliatory tone, after taking a deep breath. 'You know how I—we, Daddy and I—feel but you must make your own decision, of course.'

Anna sighed in Roderick's dependable embrace that night and apologised for her harshness towards their daughter. 'You know I don't mean to be so discouraging. It just felt like a train carriage in which I was travelling was being disconnected from its engine. I'm sorry.'

'You don't need to explain and you certainly don't have to say sorry,' Roderick said, gently kissing his wife.

The next day, Belinda did make her own decision and did not enter the confirmation class.

Anna's second emotional peak during her daughter's time at St Madeleine's came around four years later when Belinda took part in a sixth-form production of Bertolt Brecht's play, *The Resistible Rise of Arturo Ui*.

Just before leaving to see it, Anna had been watching the television in the sitting room of the cottage. A news conference on the Vietnam War was being broadcast, at which the United States' senior commander in South Vietnam, General William Westmoreland, spoke out strongly against anti-war protesters in America. Their apparent support for the enemy, Westmoreland had argued, gave that enemy hope that he could 'win politically that which he could not win militarily.'

Anna had listened to this gloomily. The Vietnam War had greatly upset her, bringing home, as it did, the fallacious nature of the belief that the end of World War II would also end the savage inhumanity, wanton destruction and unjust deaths that had been revealed to a bruised international public in the mid-1940s.

Thus her eagerness to see Belinda perform on St Madeleine's impressive stage was tempered by an anxiety that Brecht's dark, satirical allegory of the satanic career of Adolf Hitler might undermine her sense of having overcome so much anguish.

In the event, she was so moved by the performance, the music, the imaginative direction by the school's head of English, Mrs Osborne; by Belinda's unexpectedly accomplished acting and, above all, by the over-whelming effect of watching Brecht's epilogue being delivered by this daughter who embodied the future that Anna had thought would be denied to her, that, at the close of the performance, Anna could not move from her seat.

Standing in front of a giant photograph of Hitler, his arm angled out in the 'Sieg Heil' salute, on a stage in a private English girls' school's production, Belinda Vane, three days before her seventeenth birthday, looking calmly down at the mesmerised audience, concluded the epi-logue in a clear, steady and deliberately quiet voice: 'Do not rejoice in his defeat. For, while the world has stood up and stopped the bastard, the bitch that bore him is in heat again.'

It brought a collective gasp from the audience and a long, profoundly deep exhalation from the young actress's mother.

Farah need not have worried about Eli straying too far or behaving too wildly. He dropped out of college after six weeks spent mostly closeted in his room with his records, his photographs, his books and his tears. Just before he left, he and a fellow student had to be physically separated after Eli had yelled at his adversary over some perceived slight, but the incident blew over and was never reported to Farah and Yusuf.

During his brief time at college, Eli made contact with his parents only once. They had gone to America to visit Yusuf's sister Rachel, at whose home the telephone rang at 3 a.m. for Eli to speak for fifteen minutes in a gloomy, repetitive monologue in which he said little more than that he needed to leave, to go home.

After this, by the time dawn had broken on the western edge of the Atlantic, Yusuf had contacted Rivke, and Farah had spoken to Leah. Leah offered to travel down and speak to her brother and urged her mother not to come rushing back.

But Farah was distraught and insisted that she and Yusuf cut short their stay. At the same time, at a distance from her son of more than three-thousand miles, in muffled conversation with Yusuf in Rachel's guest bedroom, Farah lamented Eli's failure to appreciate the benefits, present and future, offered by his being at college or the importance of paying due attention to his studies.

Their host, Yusuf's brother-in-law David, having seen his son smoothly through law school prior to easing him into a cushioned seat in David's own law firm, could not understand Farah's—and still more, Eli's—consternation.

'Stay,' David urged. 'There's no need to go home yet. The boy'll be fine with his grandma and sister there to make a fuss of him. He'll probably feel so smothered that he'll return to college in a coupla days. Stay. At least till the end of the week. We have exciting plans for you here. Listen, he's probably got romance problems. *Cherchez la femme*. He'll get over it. No problem He's a handsome Iraqi kid *bel ayn el raa'a*. And he's got a Haroun head on his shoulders.'

Privately, Yusuf thought this last observation might be part of the problem. In recent weeks, when Eli's moods had become so unpredictable and so contrasting, Yusuf had found himself musing, for the first time in many years, about his Uncle Reuben, over whose life and death such a thick veil seemed to have been drawn.

Yusuf could recall his own, powerful curiosity at the party in the family courtyard celebrating his bar mitzvah, when his father Sami made a speech in which he recited the names of several people who couldn't be there, the rhythm of which was broken when he mentioned 'my poor dear brother Reuben'. At this point, Sami had stopped and, for a few seconds, the only sound that could be heard was a slight rustling in the leaves of the two Haroun palm trees. Later, Yusuf had asked his sister Rachel about Uncle Reuben.

'He was Baba's brother. He was mad,' Rachel said, tapping her head with her index finger.

'Did he die from being mad?'

'I don't know. It was long, long ago.'

This seemed a satisfactory enough explanation not to spoil the rest of the evening's festivities and the name of Uncle Reuben quickly faded from his mind.

Years afterwards, in the inexplicably anxious phase experienced by Yusuf during the weeks preceding his wedding, he had reflected frequently about the mysterious Uncle Reuben. He sought out the solitary photograph of him in the family album, and Reuben's lugubrious expression and downward-drooping moustache seemed to symbolise the man, filling Yusuf with a vague fear. He shivered and closed the book abruptly before returning it to its special place on the bookshelf.

Now, still more years later, a day or two after returning from his and Farah's shortened New York holiday in order to settle Eli back into the family home, Yusuf went to see his mother in her flat. While she was in the kitchen laboriously preparing *silaan*—date syrup—he took down the Haroun album from its new pride of place in Rivke's Brondesbury parlour behind the sliding glass doors of her treasured new bookcase that Yusuf and Azi had obtained from the company's furniture supplier.

Yusuf turned back towards the window, beneath which was the sofa that had once been in the Baghdad house, the sofa that, now as then, was covered with an Afghan carpet. He sat down, carefully opened the album and sought out the picture of Uncle Reuben.

This time, Yusuf saw a man more frightened than frightening, and much younger-looking than he had remembered. Reuben's eyes looked hunted, suspicious of the photographer. Despite his moustache, there was something unusually soft about his features. His head was a little to one side and his shoulders were tilted back, as though he was wary of what was about to happen. His suit looked slightly too big for him and a little frayed. Perhaps it had been handed down.

As Yusuf stared at the portrait, a preserved moment in Reuben's short and curious life, he felt an overwhelming sadness, which was somehow intensified by the sweet, nostalgic aromas of date, apricot and almond issuing from Rivke's kitchen. As he sat with his mother drinking tea and eating biscuits that tasted of earlier days in the old house in Baghdad, Yusuf tentatively asked her what had caused Uncle Reuben to die.

'I can't say,' she replied.

'Does that mean you don't know, or that it is a secret?'

'It is more of a mystery than a secret. I never knew him but your father talked about Reuben a lot in the early days. He said Reuben was an exuberant child but then became quiet and withdrawn, after your grandfather died. And lazy. Baba told me that when they were working together in the shop, Reuben never showed willing. Baba always had to tell him what to do. Perhaps "lazy" is the wrong word. He was a kind man and kind people are never really lazy. "Inactive" is better.

'He did become excited when he met the young woman who was to become his wife. Baba used to laugh when he told me about the enormous fuss Reuben would make of her. Treat her like a queen. Buy her things that he couldn't afford. But she was, what do you say, "too hot to handle". It seems she made Reuben nervous. He occasionally showed signs of his old cheerful self but also used to get angry very quickly, even with Baba, the big brother he looked up to. He was moody, depressed.'

'But to *die*? Of depression?'

'It was a sad end.'

'But what caused it? Did he… bring it about himself?'

'I can't say what the cause was. It was a terrible thing to happen. That is all I can tell you. Except that he was not a normal man,' and then, warding off further enquiry: 'Let me make you some more tea.'

As his mother prepared tea, Yusuf picked up the photograph album from the coffee table where he had left it. Before restoring it to the bookcase, he leafed through it once more and, for the first time, noticed that Rivke had placed a new folder inside the album's back cover.

He took it out and discovered that it contained three pictures of himself and Farah. One was a grainy shot of them both standing in the old Haroun courtyard in Baghdad on their wedding day. The second was the Lettice Ramsey studio portrait taken on their day out with Uncle Azi in Cambridge. The third was taken by Eli outside the Brondesbury house as they were leaving for a function at Lauderdale Road Synagogue— Yusuf in his dinner jacket, Farah in a shimmering silver dress. Yusuf had completely forgotten both the occasion and the picture.

'What a beautiful photograph,' he whispered to himself and closed his eyes and then the book, anxious not to let Rivke see him so emotionally affected.

She called him from the kitchen 'What are you doing Yusuf?'

'Oh, just thinking about Leah and Eli.'

That Eli would come home, having barely explored the topics covered by his early classes, was not in question, although Yusuf did try to elicit from his son an explanation for his feelings and to encourage him to consider the many favourable aspects of his situation. But Eli's complete inability to articulate those feelings, and his obvious distress, convinced Yusuf to act with compassion, above all, and to take whatever practical steps he could to help his son.

He and Farah continued to hope, however, that Eli's depressed state was temporary and that he could be persuaded to persevere with what appeared to the outsider to be a not very demanding course of study. And while Yusuf's hope for his son to join him in the Eastern Carpet and Goods Emporium still burned at the back of his mind, this was not the moment to initiate the idea. He intended the emporium to offer Eli a stimulating career environment, not a retreat.

As ever, it was Rivke who provided the most welcoming shoulder for her grandson to cry on, though even she, after Eli's return, found their first conversation difficult. There was none of the customary laughter, Eli was subdued rather than lively, withdrawn rather than curious, and his eyes looked down or to one side rather than directly at his adored Grandma Rivke.

While Farah's response to the situation was to fall into a kind of contagious depression herself, and Yusuf's was to try to find the best possible psychoanalyst for Eli—enlisting the help not only of the family GP, Doctor Lewis, but also Farah's former and now retired obstetrician, Doctor Zilka—Rivke's solution was to pray for Eli.

'Maybe the prayers are working,' Farah said one weekend when Eli had gone away to Scotland for a few days with three friends and his camera. 'He phoned home without needing to be told,' she reported to Yusuf. 'And he said he is having a "really good time". For Eli, "really good" is the top of the scale. And he told me that Scotland was a "very inspiring" place and that he'd taken loads of photographs.'

On his return, Eli pursued his photography obsessively and signed up for an evening class at a local school. Within a week or two, however, he grew disillusioned with the teacher.

'He's an idiot,' he told his parents and sister at dinner one evening. 'He seems to think that wedding pictures are the pinnacle of possibilities for the camera.'

'Well, at least it's a reasonable way of making a living.'

Farah's reaction struck her son as entirely unsympathetic.

'Mum, can't you appreciate that photography, real, creative photography is an art? I doubt if Cartier-Bresson bothers to take wedding pictures.'

'There's no need to be rude,' countered his mother. 'I'm only think-ing of you. It seems a decent enough career. You could probably make a lot of money taking really artistic wedding photos—and bar mitzvahs.

There's a *simcha* just about every week at Lauderdale Road. You could get in there. Why not?'

But Eli did not even try to get in among the celebrating Lauderdale Road families and, at home, reverted to his withdrawn self. But he still went out with friends and continued to show willing when Yusuf took him to work at the emporium two or three times a week. And when he read about a new degree course in photography and film at Brighton Technical College, he applied and was buoyed by being granted an interview. He spent the weekend before the interview gathering together a portfolio of his photographs and went off to Victoria Station to catch the Brighton train propelled by his family's good luck wishes.

But his luck was not good and he was hit hard by the college's rejection. When he received the letter, he read out the phrase 'we wish you luck in finding a suitable alternative' in the mimicked voice of a spoilt, complacent, got-it-all child. And he took to drink, though he managed never to appear drunk in his own house.

After a few months of Eli's ebbing and flowing, bright days and dark, Yusuf persuaded his son to see the psychiatrist whom Dr Lewis and Dr Zilka had both recommended months earlier, an Iraqi Jew called Alfassa, who saw patients at his home in Holland Park, west London, and who occasionally showed his somewhat careworn face at the Sephardi and Oriental 'Gate to Heaven' on Lauderdale Road.

Dr Alan (born 'Abraham') Alfassa came highly recommended, not least perhaps, among London's contingent of Baghdadi Jews, because on some distant branch of his family tree he could claim kinship with the legendary Aunty Alfassa, old Jewish Baghdad's matchmaker and mystical healer.

'Clearly, I am carrying on the family business,' he would frequently remark.

When Eli returned home after his third session with the psychiatrist, the following exchange took place in the Haroun household in Brondesbury:

'I really don't see the point in going to the analyst,' said Eli.

'Why ever not, darling?' Farah was solicitous.

'Well, it's your money, or Dad's rather, but for every twenty-three thousand words I say, the analyst says one. Or more often just goes, "hmm".'

'But it's good that he is encouraging you to talk freely. That sounds very helpful to me,' said Farah.

'En-*couraging*,' Yusuf echoed, in an attempt to sound wise. 'He is giving you the courage to speak. To get things off your chest.'

'Honestly, Dad, I am not getting things off my chest. I am simply filling in time and space in what would otherwise be a tedious silence, with old Dr Alfassa sitting there mentally counting his money.'

'But even if you say the first thing that comes into your head, that's significant, Eli darling.' Farah's voice was almost pleading. 'A psychoanalyst can see past the immediate things we say.'

'It's not really the first thing that comes into my head, Mum. I make up things before I get there. Little stories. Rhymes, sometimes. Drivel. And he can't see that. I think he's useless.'

'You mean, you don't say anything spontaneously—anything that you haven't prepared in advance?' asked Yusuf, who was beginning to worry about his considerable investment in the curative skills of Dr Alfassa.

Eli blew out a tired breath. 'Well, not much.'

'But even the fact that you have bothered to prepare your words in advance is significant,' said Farah. 'Creating a distraction. Hiding from yourself. And hiding yourself from Dr Alfassa. He can interpret that. He is a clever man.'

'But even when I haven't prepared anything and do come out with something that is spontaneous,' Eli said, 'it's not truly spontaneous, in the sense of being unpremeditated. It doesn't just jump out from my subconscious. It's always made up on the spot. Quickly, but still made up. Just various words and images that don't link together and don't make a lot of sense. Just like a haphazard collection of different photographs. Or like in a dream.'

'A dream—ah!' Farah seemed intent on carrying out her own analysis. 'Dreams are important. They have meaning. And experts like Dr Alfassa are trained to interpret them.'

'Nobody can interpret dreams,' said Yusuf the plain-speaking man, the sceptic.

'Oh, and what about Freud?' Farah clearly had more faith in psychoanalysis than her husband did.

'What about him?'

'Look,' Eli interrupted. 'I didn't say I was telling him my real dreams. I just said I was making up little scenes and images, like in a film, and describing them.'

'Well, maybe you should tell him your actual dreams.' Farah was tenacious.

'Do you honestly think this man can cure me? Free me from these moods, these anxieties? Sometimes I feel too nervous to go out in the street. Sometimes I feel so angry.'

'Have you told Alfassa all this?' Farah saw an opening.

'Of course,' said Eli in a tone that verged on contemptuous.

'So what's *your* feeling, Eli,' asked Yusuf. 'Do you think this man can cure you?'

'I don't know,' Eli was shaking his head, looking downcast. 'I feel guilty because you are paying all that money and it may just be a waste of time.'

'You mustn't worry about that.' Yusuf was reassuring. 'Do you have another appointment booked?'

'What do you mean?' Eli looked up suddenly, his voice rising. 'He's fixed up a whole schedule of appointments!' And, after a pause: 'Oh, I'll go again next week.'

And then he walked off into his room. Farah went to follow him but Yusuf gently restrained her.

'I don't know if "cure" is the right word,' she said quietly.

'Maybe not,' Yusuf agreed. 'But if anyone can at least help him, Alan Alfassa can. And we are doing the wrong thing interrogating Eli. It's a confidential relationship. The worse thing is to pry and that's what we've been doing.'

'I'm just trying to do the best for my son,' said Farah. 'I just wish I could get into his head and make him feel safe, make him feel happy.'

'But it doesn't help. It may even set him back,' wondered Yusuf. 'He clearly isn't going to give us the complete picture. What he said was just a smokescreen. I don't think Alfassa can cure him but I do think he can help him. And, in the meantime, we are going to have to respect the privacy of what is said in Alan Alfassa's consulting room.'

Whether or not it was on account of the restraint that his parents were able to show, at least in front of him, in relation to the efficacy of those confidential sessions with Alfassa, Eli did settle down into a weekly routine. Every Monday at 7.30 p.m. saw the same assertive ring at the doorbell by Eli, the same tilt of Alan Alfassa's head as he opened the door, the same welcoming smile, the same quietly spoken phrase: 'Eli, hello, come in, let's go into my consulting room.' And, for Eli, the same solitary cigarette and pint of Young's afterwards at the pub on the corner of Alfassa's street.

At first, Eli would not lie back on the couch, which he regarded as a ludicrous theatrical prop. Instead, he perched on the edge of it, holding his back and shoulders very straight as if to demonstrate an impregnable composure and confidence. Gradually, however, he felt the need to surrender to what he perceived as pressure—though, if it existed, it was unspoken—emanating from Doctor Alfassa and lay back with a degree of relief.

At home, Eli seemed to be more at ease as the consultations progressed, though he went through a spell of morose resentment when his sister Leah spent a substantial portion of her final spring vacation with a fellow University of York student—and Londoner—called David Marks.

It was shortly after Leah had returned to York that Eli had his first violent outburst. He had spent most of a weekend shut away in his room and reacted with mounting impatience to his parents' urgings to make contact with friends; his closest friend Ramon Saul, was now studying at Durham University, but Eli still occasionally went out on Saturday nights to pubs or clubs with a couple of local boys he had known at school.

This, too, made Farah anxious as it became apparent that Eli was not only drinking but gambling at some of these places, and clearly losing money. And smoking—and it was about this that Farah felt compelled to remonstrate with him on the Monday morning after his hermit-like weekend.

'What is happening to you, Eli? You worry me so much, my darling. You have friends you can see regularly—and I am worried why you haven't seen them this weekend—but you seem to be just hanging around and drinking and smoking. It's so bad for you.'

'I know it's bad for me, Mum. I don't do it because it's bad for me. I am old enough to know that it is bad for me. Lots of things are bad for me. I live in London, there's lots of traffic. I could get knocked down by a car any time.'

'You're being silly. It's a false comparison. Smoking is equal to running in front of a moving car.'

'Will you leave me alone? Let me grow up, for God's sake.'

'If you met a nice girl, you wouldn't need to smoke and drink.'

Eli laughed loudly at this remark.

'Don't laugh at me.' Farah was annoyed. 'I mean it. You could take her to the cinema, or the theatre. And there are some nice kosher and vegetarian restaurants. Dad will help you with the money.'

'Leave me alone.' Eli repeated his plea more loudly and went back into his room. Farah went to follow him but hesitated and then stopped and went back into the kitchen as the soaring, juvenescent music of the Beach Boys resounded through Eli's closed door. Within a few minutes, this was augmented by the noise of cups and glasses being smashed against the wall.

Farah steeled herself and avoided confronting Eli. Instead, she cried over the telephone to Yusuf at the emporium and followed his advice to say nothing, but to leave a dustpan and brush outside Eli's room.

Eli picked up the hint and cleared away the shattered pieces from his floor, after which he apologised and went out, announcing that he was meeting a couple of friends and emphasising that neither of the friends smoked, 'so it will be easier for me not to.'

The incident wasn't mentioned and, over the next few weeks, life was quieter. Yusuf took Eli into work a few times but, while he started eagerly enough, he quickly ran out of steam and sulked when asked to perform any but the most menial task. He continued to take an interest in photography though the images he produced tended to be dark, languid or just obscure.

Around this time, Eli began to write poetry. One day, when he had gone with Yusuf to the emporium, Farah went to collect a tray and some glasses from his room and noticed on his bed a page torn from an exercise book with the dedication, 'to Esther', written across the top. Farah picked it up and read what were clearly the handwritten opening lines of a love poem, but one shrouded in darkness:

In my room, my walls thicken,
My windows thwart my view,
Every day I sicken,
Each night, I long for you.

Release me from my pain,
Take hold of me complete.
Cling fast and keep me sane,
Bring coolness to my heat

Oh, Esther, Esther, why…

And there it broke off. The paper was faded and slightly creased and Farah wondered if Eli had finished the poem and delivered it to the mysterious Esther. She knew that she should not ask Eli himself and put the sheet of paper back on the bed in the same place, just as she had discovered it. But she did copy the words into her personal notebook and impatiently waited to have a private moment in the evening to share her discovery with Yusuf.

She was presented with an opportunity when, shortly after arriving home with Yusuf, Eli declared that he was too tired to eat and took himself off to his room to sleep. Upon reading Farah's scribbled copy of Eli's nine brief but intense lines, Yusuf's initial reaction was to express his pleasure that his generally withdrawn son appeared to be in love. He admitted to Farah that, in her position, he too would have read the poem but not copied it and counselled her not to pry further.

'You don't have to tell me,' said Farah. 'I wouldn't dare.'

Eli's unvarying response to his family's requests to read his poems to them was already well known: 'One day, I'll show them to you, once I feel they are actually finished and don't need any more revising.' He did, however, share with his grandma Rivke a short, sweet verse about her love of dates, but he asked her, even for this, to swear to secrecy.

If anything, Eli was more sociable than normal during this period and went out quite frequently and happily. He seemed to crave company, especially that of his more humorous friends, such as Ramon Saul whenever he was down for the weekend from Durham.

'I have gone mad,' Eli would declare, grandly clutching his forehead with his right hand and then laughing loudly. 'It's official. On the authority of a descendant of an ancient Iraqi witch.'

But every so often at home he would yell or strike out angrily. One Saturday morning, when Farah had gone to synagogue with Rivke, a sweaty and unshaven Eli sat down heavily at the breakfast table and apologised to his father for a particularly wild outburst the preceding night in response to Farah delivering her familiar 'find-yourself-a-nice-Jewish-girl' chorus. He had punched the kitchen wall, causing his hand to bleed and making an indentation in the plaster.

'What is it that you are angry about?' Yusuf asked as calmly as he could. 'Who is it you are angry with?'

'I don't know,' Eli replied, looking at the floor. 'It was Mum last night and it wasn't fair because she meant well. I went right over the top.' And then, after a pause, 'it's probably me. I'm probably angry with myself.'

In January 1969, Leah, who, having long abandoned any ideas of taking up a profession after gaining her history degree, was now sharing a flat in Kilburn with a friend and enjoying working as a receptionist at a highly fashionable hairdressing salon in Bond Street, decided to spend her twenty-third birthday at home. Farah invited friends and family to celebrate. After they had all left and Yusuf and Farah were recovering in the kitchen, Leah and Eli were chatting together in the sitting room.

Suddenly, in response to a light, joking remark of Leah's, Eli yelled into her face: 'Don't call me stupid!' He carried on loudly, stating: 'I've had enough,' as his sister tried to assure him that she had not called him stupid and well knew that he was far from being stupid. Then Eli raised his hand and Leah feared he was going to hit her across the face. But he slapped, and then punched, a cushion on the sofa where they were both sitting. Immediately, he threw his head on Leah's shoulder and began to cry.

Once she had recovered from the shock, she consoled him and held him tightly, saying: 'I could never think you were stupid. I love and respect you. You must know that.'

The next evening, while Eli was concluding a session at Dr Alfassa's, Yusuf thought aloud to Farah: 'I think I'll phone Alfassa later. We all need some guidance. And the man is costing me a fortune. But is it fair to Eli for me to interfere—which is how he would see it?'

As he prevaricated, the phone rang. An almost too reassuring voice announced its owner: 'This is Alan Alfassa. Eli has just left. I have prescribed some medication but I think he needs a spell of residential care.'

From the time that she took part in *The Resistible Rise of Arturo Ui*, Belinda took her studies much more seriously than she had before. Under the twin influence of Maud Ainsworth—who had continued to take an interest in Belinda and encouraged her to read Shakespeare's poetry as well as his plays—and Mrs Osborne, her English teacher, Belinda developed a maturity of style in her written work along with a capacity to listen and understand.

She timed her bloom to perfection and gained a place at Newnham College, Cambridge, to read English. Anna and Roderick accompanied her on the first day of her first term, which, to Anna, vividly recalled the benign yet nervous atmosphere in which she had taken her first steps on English soil at Lowestoft. That day, she had been relieved and pleased at how accommodating Roderick's parents were to her. This day, in Cambridge, a skein of conflicting remembrances was smoothed out by the gentle October sunshine and the historical and literal perspective of the city's ancient institutions.

Belinda found herself settling into university life surprisingly quickly and comfortably, though when she joined a drama group, at which she expected to shine, she felt intimidated by the practised ease in verse-speaking, joke-telling, physical gesturing and the general air of thespian precociousness displayed by most of the other members.

Two terms in, Roderick took advantage of a business visit to Vane Natural Clothing's principal boot-maker just outside Northampton, to return home via Cambridge and take his daughter to tea. Their conversation, over a pot of Earl Grey and buns in Fitzbillies café, was not what Roderick had envisaged.

'How's it all going then?' Roderick asked.

Belinda was a little hesitant in her reply. 'Oh... all right... no, fine. Fine, I suppose... yes fine.'

'You don't sound very certain.'

'No, really, Pa, I'm fine.'

'Is there anything wrong? Something troubling you? Maybe I can help.' It suddenly struck Roderick how complacent he had been, basking in pride at his daughter's beauty, intelligence and achievements without really taking an active interest in what she was doing or thinking. And the only anxieties he had contemplated her having were of a routine, childish kind and therefore bound to be shed in adulthood.

'Honestly, I'm doing OK.'

'Just OK?' Whatever it was, even the slightest blemish in what he had always imagined was a life of complete brightness, he wanted to deal with it and bring her to a state of mind into which distress could not enter. However idealised his view of his daughter's existence had been, he now wanted to do all he could to make it a reality.

'More than OK,' she told him. 'Well. I'm doing well.' And then, after a slight pause: 'How could I not be doing well? I'm at one of the world's top universities in one of the world's most beautiful cities.'

'That's true but if something goes wrong in such circumstances, it can seem much worse than it is.'

'I'm sure that's the case but there's nothing wrong. Stop trying to probe me. I am great. I have friends. I'm physically fit—I've taken up tennis, by the way. I'm free. It's a good life. I didn't get a part in a play I auditioned for but that doesn't worry me. I didn't really want to do it. Just auditioned for the sake of it.'

'Well, there'll be plenty of other opportunities.'

'Yeah, that's right. It's not important. I'm relaxed about it. Just a bit tired, that's all.'

'Well, it's great that you've taken up tennis. I know now what to get you for your birthday. How are the studies going?'

'I'm working well, I think. Finding the tons of medieval literature we are having to read a bit of a grind but I'm not falling behind. And I'm looking forward to next year when we can start to specialise and come a bit more up to date.'

'*Grind* and *behind*. You're a natural poet. Literature's really up your street.' Roderick attempted to lighten the subject.

'Pa, honestly.'

'Sorry.'

'My only disappointment, really, is that it's a bit too much like St Madeleine's a lot of the time.'

'Is that such a bad thing? Your mother and I were always so impressed whenever we went along to the school. Your ma never tires of talking about *Arturo Ui*.'

'I know she does, bless her. It made quite a hit with her, I know. And yes, I know the school makes a fabulous impression on visitors and parents but that was the point. Everything seemed geared to looking good, sounding good—polished, poised, capable and all that.'

'But its results are outstanding.'

'Well, of course they are. It's a hothouse for clever girls and the exams were just part—the main part—of a ridiculously competitive culture.'

'But you loved your A-levels. You were in your element with all that Shakespeare and stuff.'

'That's true but, believe me, Maddy's was really *the* most competitive joint. I was OK because I could take care of myself. But other girls were casualties. More than half the pupils had anorexia or some sort of eating problem.'

'What?'

'It's true. And there's something of that up here, too. I've made some really nice friends but a lot of the girls here—*women*, I should say, and that's part of it—are ruthlessly competitive—academically, in various non-academic pursuits like sport and theatre, over clothes, looks, boyfriends...'

'Boyfriends, eh?'

'Ah, come on, Pa. Give me a break. Let's talk about what you've seen at the cinema, or concerts, or about Ma, Granny and Grandad, the garden, good old Esher, or anything outside of Newnham. That's not to say there's anything wrong. As I said, I'm lucky. I can take care of myself. And, as you can see,' she added, brushing sugar and crumbs from her lips, 'there's little danger of me getting anorexia.'

It wasn't just inter-generational embarrassment that led Belinda to turn the conversation away from the subject of boyfriends. She had, in fact, had a few. But none lasted more than a week or two. The longest relationship was with the president of the Cambridge Union, but although it took about four weeks to end they rarely saw each other more than twice a week as he was so busy.

Others included two members of the 'Hams In Cam Era' drama society and a philosophy third-year at King's who bought, sold, and heavily used, cannabis. The only one of these she told her parents about was the Union president, Timothy, whom she revealed she was quite seriously dating two days before a ragged night of mutual recrimination brought the relationship to a close.

However, the most disarming, if unlikely, setback suffered by Belinda had taken place before she had met Timothy. On a mild, sunny winter's day, she had been walking alone along King's Parade, stepping around the knots of tourists and smiling sometimes at a tourist or fellow student and sometimes to herself.

She was wearing new jeans and an exceptionally colourful Victorian blouse. She felt strength flowing through her body, a body that had grown longer and leaner in the preceding few months and which she had become accustomed to privately admiring in the long, ancient mirror in her room.

She took easy, confident strides, and guiltlessly experienced a sense of superiority as she surveyed the people of all ages around her on the street. Turning her eyes towards and then away from King's College Chapel, the powerful sunlight shaded by her dark glasses, she fully expected one or more of the tourists to approach her with a question about Cambridge and was ready to bestow on any such enquirer her knowledge and, more significantly, her presence.

This, she told herself, was her territory and her time. As she turned and walked in slow, measured steps across the market square, anyone watching Belinda Vane passing the food and clothes stalls at that moment of her utter contentment could have interpreted her distinctive, easy swagger as a kind of proclamation, a statement that she could go anywhere, do anything. Her mind was her passport, her body her chariot.

But, later that day, back in her college room reading a letter from her father, the sun's rays departing from her window, she seemed to be on a giddy descent. Now, she could think only of the transitory nature of that King's Parade moment, no sooner experienced than it was gone. And she was overcome by a strange feeling of impermanence, of time passing quickly. She was suddenly unable to revel in the bodily strength she had so recently and arrogantly flexed but which now was reduced in her mind to its essential, ineluctable brevity.

Now, weeks later, this feeling was still with her when she sat with her father over tea at Fitzbillies. It created a kind of screen between her and the person with whom she had always been most at ease.

After Roderick had confessed to a slight worry about Belinda in his subsequent report to his wife on returning home from Cambridge, Anna made a point of keeping in touch more regularly with her daughter, especially when, at the end of her first year, Belinda decided to stay in Cambridge for the long vacation to work as a cleaner and kitchen assistant at the nearby Fulbourn psychiatric hospital. Belinda took delight in telling her parents that Fulbourn Hospital had originally been named 'The County Pauper Lunatic Asylum for Cambridgeshire.'

She found her time at Fulbourn fulfilling and enjoyed a spirited social life with her fellow students employed there in similar menial capacities. There was a handful of students among the patients, too, including a classics scholar who wrote verse in his own blood on the walls of his private room. He would also make telephone calls to God. 'I wish I could see what number he's dialling,' Belinda joked when she told her parents about him. Whatever task she carried out, menial or not, showed her to be a keen worker, naturally sympathetic towards the patients and even, in part, identifying with one or two of them.

She had achieved satisfactory results in her first academic year and seemed to be on course to gain a good degree. She did come home for a couple of weekends during that summer and enjoyed catching up with friends, relaxing at the piano and helping her father in the garden. For the last two weeks of September, she joined some friends from Cambridge who were staying in a French farmhouse owned by the widowed mother of one of them. The day after her return, she went to the local bookshop in Esher and asked the manager to order three French novels for her.

Once the first term of her second year began, however, Belinda became increasingly difficult to contact at all regularly and Anna decided to visit her daughter one weekend in the lodgings she shared with a fellow English student called Helen, the quietly spoken child of a librarian and his wife who were devout Catholics living a relatively short drive away in Bedfordshire.

Helen was spending the weekend with her family when Anna arrived in Cambridge on the Saturday. Belinda seemed truly excited to see her mother and, within half an hour of Anna's arrival, daughter led mother on an exhausting round of sights, shops, cafés and a pub. Towards the end of the afternoon, the weather changed; the sky clouded over, it began to drizzle, and Anna declined a punt down the river.

Soon after they had returned, Belinda grew frantic because she appeared to have lost a notebook. 'It is my companion,' she shrieked, 'the single reason why I passed my first-year exams. I write something in it every day. Every valuable quote, every interesting or curious observation is in that book. Any worthwhile lecture note. Almost my every inner thought. I'll be devastated if I can't find it. I don't know what I'm going to do. Could I have dropped it somewhere? We've been to so many places today. I can't believe I've lost it. I always guard it with my life.'

After twenty minutes of disorganised, not to say crazed, searching through drawers and cupboards, under carpets and on the steps and pavement outside the house, the notebook still could not be found.

'I'm sorry, Ma,' Belinda announced somewhat melodramatically. 'I have to run a bath and have a soak and a smoke, or else I'm going to crack up.'

'OK, dear,' said Anna, trying not to show her deep disappointment at this revelation that her highly intelligent young daughter smoked. 'I'll tidy up all the ransacked contents of your wardrobe'—the comment was delivered with a smiling, not a critical face—'and maybe, as I'm doing that, the notebook will come to light. What colour is it?'

Belinda retreated into a private paradise of water and tobacco, the latter slowly burning within expertly rolled Rizla papers and gradually easing the young female smoker's frenzy. Around her, the smell of orange-scented bath soap leaked out of the bathroom, merging with the aromatic mixture of incense and patchouli that already pervaded the flat.

It didn't take long for Anna to restore her daughter's wardrobe and drawers to a semblance of order. She then embarked upon a more methodical search for the missing notebook, beginning in a built-in corner-cupboard crammed with old magazines, cardboard boxes, discarded carved wooden jewellery, the tennis racquet—still in pristine, unused condition—that Roderick had bought for her birthday six months earlier, and various other oddments.

Anna decided to be thorough and took out everything, eventually finding, right at the back of the cupboard, a shoebox clearly full of some-thing other than shoes. She removed the lid and discovered inside the box a small pharmacy containing packets and loose individual tablets among a variety of pills designed for a variety of requirements, from contraception to depression. Every bottle or box to which a prescription label was attached bore the name 'Miss B. Vane'.

As Anna sank into the flat's solitary armchair, holding the shoebox, the corner cupboard's detritus around her feet, Belinda burst cheerily out of the bathroom, dripping water and wrapped in a sarong bought earlier that day in the market, and cried out: 'I am such a fool. I've just remembered. I lent my notebook to Helen so she could copy some notes and quotes.'

Anna had no wish to darken her daughter's sunny mood and allowed her, as she saw the shoebox, to offer comfort in a phrase: 'Those are all basically just for insurance, Ma. I had no idea what to expect when I came up to Cambridge and so I thought I should be prepared. And even after a year I am still finding my feet. The doctor errs on the side of caution. And generosity. Please don't worry and please don't judge me. I am managing well. It still feels a bit like being back at Maddy's but I am capable of making my own way. I'm getting through a lot of reading and actually looking forward to the rest of the year.'

But Belinda didn't complete the rest of that second year. After spending a family Christmas at home, she decided not to return to Cambridge, other than to gather up her belongings from the flat, speak to her tutor and her director of studies and complete the formalities of severance.

Anna made no attempt to dissuade her and, in consequence, felt much closer to her daughter than she had for years. They hugged each other frequently, went for walks holding hands just as they had when Belinda was a little girl, and played the piano together.

Possibly because Anna refrained from interrogating her, Belinda felt more able to at least try to explain the reason for her decision to quit university.

'I feel as though there is enormous pressure inside me, especially inside my head,' she said. 'And I feel it's too hard to carry on trying to keep it in.'

Roderick, on the other hand, felt less able to understand. He had been so proud of Belinda getting into Cambridge and looked forward to her enjoying a distinguished career and a happy life. And, while he knew this would have given him enormous pleasure, more importantly, and more deservingly, he believed that Anna, too, would have derived so much from such an outcome.

He was much less patient than Anna in trying to get to the root of the problem. And the more conventional, the more logical, he became in his attempts, the less headway he made. Belinda found all his lines predictable and worse than unhelpful. 'You are throwing everything away,' he would say. 'Don't you realise what an opportunity you have?' Or: 'You love literature. What better surroundings in which to study it?' And, when his pleading became emotional, bordering on chastisement—'If you only had a quarter of your mother's fighting spirit'—in effect, without intending to, he pushed Belinda away.

Roderick himself suffered considerably through all this. He found it hard to concentrate at work, was short-tempered with his parents when they tried to offer suggestions and sympathy, and he couldn't sleep until he had unburdened his feelings of helplessness and inadequacy to Anna.

The two of them clung to each other as fervently as they had when they were young lovers, Anna somehow finding new reserves of inner strength.

'You must not be so hard on yourself,' she told him. 'You are my hero, remember. My rescuer, my knight in shining armour. How dare you call my hero weak and inadequate.'

Even when he did get to sleep, he was plagued by nightmares. He began to relive the episode in Bergen-Belsen when he shot the young German soldier in contravention of his commanding officer's orders. One morning, he awoke, drenched in sweat, from a horrific dream in which the young woman lying at the Nazi boy-soldier's feet was Belinda, calling to him: 'Don't shoot, Pa. Don't shoot!'

He sat upright in bed holding Anna's head to his chest as he had done countless times before and, in between heaving breaths, spoke to her in a quiet but imploring voice. 'I am in mental agony. Believe me, the war was much easier. I think that Belinda is, too, only in a far worse way. I have failed her.

'Look at us, Belinda and me, both absolute wrecks, and you, who have endured the truly agonising suffering, are the strong one. I love you both so much. We must find a way of helping Belinda. She needs some sort of expert treatment.'

'It's funny you should say that,' said Anna. 'Belinda herself has acknowledged that she needs help and has asked me if we will pay for her to have some form of residential therapy. I was going to ask you but I was slightly frightened of doing so. Not because of the money but because I was worried that you would regard it as confirming a failure. Admitting defeat. A big soldier like you.'

'Well, I was a soldier, and a good one, not some stiff-upper lipped type as you seem to imply. But you're right. We can win this. We can emulate your strength and determination. It's not as though she's gone mad, talking gibberish or making telephone calls to God, like that poor boy she told us about when she worked in the hospital.

'The only dramatic thing Belinda's done is drop out of university and even that's not so dramatic. Hundreds do it all the time—and go on to have happy and successful lives. Damn it, I never even went to university, and I have a good life with a lovely home and a wonderful wife and daughter.'

The Elms, in Sunbury, Surrey, near Kempton Park racecourse and Shepperton film studios, was surrounded by expansive lawns and impressive trees. Rare was the patient (or 'client' as they were sometimes called) who did not appreciate the opportunity to sit or wander in this greenery. There was even a magnificent willow tree.

And when, in the summer of 1970, Farah, Yusuf and Eli Haroun were escorted by the Elms's public co-ordinator around the grounds of an institution recommended by Alan Alfassa and described by Doctor Lewis as 'most prestigious', Farah was immediately taken with it. 'It looks wonderful,' she said.

'It's lovely,' agreed Yusuf. 'I can see why it's so expensive.'

The public co-ordinator, a highly groomed woman in her forties called Sandra Carter, smiled at Yusuf's quasi-humorous comment. Her smile, remarkably, remained in the same fixed position as her lips moved to speak: 'Ah, but we believe the Elms is worth every penny and more. The staff here are amongst the absolute avant-garde in psychological and psychiatric medicine. I know it's a cliché, Mr Haroun, but one really does get what one pays for.'

If there was any condescension in this statement, it was well hidden beneath that unfeasibly sustained smile, which, after its wearer had delivered that last cliché, became even brighter, possibly sparked by Sandra Carter's high wattage of self-satisfaction.

As far as Yusuf was concerned, the happiness of his son was above financial consideration and he was prepared to put himself in debt to his senior partners Azi and Ben, if necessary. Fortunately, the emporium was enjoying a boom. Oriental carpets were very much in vogue in newly fashion-conscious Britain, and the other goods that the Harouns could supply were also in demand, being regarded as all of a piece with the modish 'Oriental' style. More customers than ever before were coming through the doors of the showroom, where the atmosphere, Yusuf believed, still could not fail to enchant those who encountered it. Sandra Carter would have said the same about The Elms Psychiatric Clinic.

'So, how was it?' Leah asked her brother once they were alone after his return from the tour of the Elms.

'It's a swanky place, in a manicured green setting,' he told her. 'And if it can soothe my turbulent mind, well, what can I say? I guess I'm resigned, now. Actually, Mum's keen, and Dad seems happy to fork out, so I can hardly say no. To tell you the truth, I'm quite pleased to have a chance to get away from home for a bit and hopefully not feel under such pressure.'

'That's not fair. You know all their attention comes from love.'

'I suppose… but it still amounts to pressure. And, who knows, I might even have a bit more privacy there. I've got my own room. They showed us a couple of the rooms and if mine is anything like those, it'll be like staying in a bloody hotel.'

'Sounds pretty good. But make sure you come out in time for my wedding.'

'Your *what*? Why didn't they tell me?'

'Because Mum and Dad didn't know. I've only just told them. David asked me last night. He's bought a fabulous ring but it's having to be altered.'

'So *that's* what Mum's hysterical screech was about. You're getting married! I assumed it was something I'd done—or hadn't done. *Mazal Tov*, Sis. I guess I'll have to be polite to David now.'

'Yes, you are a bit brusque with him. Mind you, you're not exactly easy-going with most of my friends. David actually admires you. He thinks you are incredibly artistic and creative.'

'Perceptive man.'

'But you'd *better* be out by the time of the wedding. It won't be for months yet. Possibly not for a year or so. Don't let them keep you in that place for months, no matter how luxurious it is.'

'Amen to that, Sis. But, don't worry, I'm not going to let anyone keep me in the Elms for months. Dad would run out of money anyway. And you're *getting married*. So, you're going to be Mr and Mrs Marks BA York. God! Mum and Dad are now getting *two* financial headaches from their kids.'

Once the forms were signed, and the Alfassa and the Lewis signatures obtained, Farah drove Eli to Sunbury for his first day in residence, a Friday. 'This reminds me of your first day at school,' she told him, brushing away tears with the back of one hand while keeping the other on the steering wheel.

'I'm feeling a bit infantilised myself,' he said, looking straight ahead. 'Maybe that's part of the problem.'

'This isn't easy for me, either, Eli. But maybe you're right. Maybe I haven't let you grow up properly. Cut the umbilical chord. I've done too much for you instead of letting you do things for yourself. Let you make your own mistakes. As everyone keeps saying, that's part of life. But I worried so much about you. I never thought I would be able to have another baby after Leah. I had a hard time conceiving. You were so precious.'

'Hey, what's with the past tense?'

'Everything I've done for you has been done out of love.' She didn't pick up on his jokey tone, and now needed both hands to control the flow from her eyes. She swerved into a lay-by at the side of the road and braked hard.

'Mum! Be careful! For God's sake!'

The car came to a bumpy stop and Farah laid her head on the steering wheel and wept pitifully.

Eli self-consciously placed a consoling arm across her shoulders. 'I'm sorry, Mum. Please don't cry.'

She turned to him and hugged him so that he could resume the position of dependent child and she could show him that she loved him and, at least momentarily, iron out her sense of grievance, guilt and frustration.

By the time they arrived at the Elms, they both felt less apprehensive and were delighted with the room allotted to Eli, off a hotel-like corridor on the first floor with a fine view of the gardens.

'My God, let's swap! I could do with staying here for a while,' Farah exclaimed on their being shown into the room by the ornate Miss Carter, who later introduced them both to some of the nursing staff before gently ushering Farah away from where Eli was being led upstairs for his introductory assessment. Farah later described this as the moment when her only son was taken from her.

'I'll be fine,' Eli reassured her, and, though she uttered a silent prayer for him, she drove home in better condition than she had been on the journey south, stilled by the therapeutic aura of the Elms and enjoying a not inconsiderable feeling of relief.

'Pure luxury,' is how Farah described it later at home to Yusuf, Rivke and Leah. 'Oh my darling,' she said as she put her arms around her daughter, 'I am so happy for you. Maybe this will be a good year after all for both of my children.'

'And for you,' Yusuf added with a mock-weary smile.

'Please God, for all of us,' said Rivke in a conclusive cadence before Farah lit the Sabbath candles and the three women present covered their heads, made welcoming gestures with their hands and quietly uttered the traditional prayer of willing obedience to the divine command to illuminate the Sabbath's path.

Twenty-five miles away, Eli was lying on his bed having passed through the disorientation of his assessment, which took the form of asking him a number of questions about his family and medical history and a slightly more than cursory physical examination.

He had already unpacked and arranged his books on the shelves in his room, glad that the moment of farewell with his mother had passed undramatically. He was also feeling encouraged by the presence of several young patients around his age.

He was particularly encouraged by the sight of a young woman quietly reading. She was aged about twenty, smartly dressed in a black trouser-suit, and tall with dark hair and flashing eyes. Closing her book and rising from her armchair, she smiled faintly at Eli as she left the Elms' lounge area. He had a newspaper open on his lap but, though his eyes were directed at it, he wasn't taking in any of its words, so distracted had he been to note what the tall, dark and attractive girl had been reading. It was a collection of Shakespeare's sonnets.

The fact that the girl had been reading the sonnets offered Eli a useful way into conversation the following morning. He sat down opposite her at breakfast, served in a light, airy conservatory. She was reading again, but now it was *The Times*, not the sonnets.

'I saw that you were reading the sonnets last night. I would never have expected to see such a thing in a place like this.'

'What *did* you expect?' she said coolly, barely raising her eyes.

'I don't know. But certainly not poetry. Certainly not the greatest poetry ever written.'

'Oh, do you think so?' This time she did look up, and her smile was more engaged than it had been the evening before. 'I agree. I adore them. Do you have a favourite?'

'Well, it's corny to say so but, "Shall I compare thee to a summer's day?"'

'You certainly may,' she said with unanticipated humour and forthrightness, and they both laughed.

'My name's Eli,' he said.

'And I'm Belinda.'

Eli was desperate to impress her and not have her think that all he knew of the sonnets was the one most quoted. 'I am very fond of number twenty-seven,' he said.

'I'm not so good at remembering which is which number,' she smiled. 'How does that one go?'

'It begins, "Weary with toil, I haste me to my bed".'

147

'*Of course* I know that one,' she said in self-critical tone. 'Oh yes, isn't it wonderful? I love its ending,' and she appeared to be silently mouthing the lines until suddenly, but slowly, she uttered the last line aloud: '"For thee and for myself no quiet find".'

'Will you let me borrow the book while we're both in here?'

'Of course,' she said again, with a smile that, to Eli, conveyed pure beauty. He gave a short, modest laugh before announcing: 'I write poetry.'

'Oh really?' She seemed interested. 'May I read some?'

'God, no,' he said too quickly. He was startled and felt himself blush for having, in his own estimation, gone too far. 'I mean, not yet. When I know you a bit better maybe. I simply couldn't show you now. Especially in the same breath and context as Shakespeare.'

She liked the way he phrased 'breath and context'. She smiled again as she stood up from the breakfast table. 'I've booked to go for a swim and exercises at the spa,' she said. 'And then I have to spend a couple of hours with my consultant. But why don't we carry on our conversation later this afternoon?'

'That would be great,' he said. 'I'm tied up with my therapist this evening, and then I promised I would phone my parents.'

'See you in the drawing room about three, then?'

'Three is fine.'

Back in his room, Eli breathed deeply and tried to sort out his feelings. Having imagined that he would plunge into a kind of oblivion once incarcerated in the Elms, while clinging desperately to the hope that they had some expensive wonder drug that would be able to lift him out of his personal darkness, he found himself amazed that something so simple—in his own words, so clichéd—as meeting a girl had brought him to life.

'Bloody hell, she is so beautiful,' he said aloud. 'And intelligent. The sonnets. My God!' He laughed and reflected on how this combination of assets made her so much more attractive—'so erotic', he said to the empty room—than the 'pretty but empty dolls' he had been chasing over the past few years.

Seated on his bed, he whispered her name: 'Oh, Belinda, Belinda. What on earth are you doing in this place? You seem pretty damn perfect to me. What am I doing in this place?'

And then he sank into a silent interior monologue: 'Who am I kidding? I know why I'm here and Dad is spending so much money on me.

I'm really not well. I'm depressed. And angry. It's not fair. And, hold on. We've had no more than a few minutes' conversation. On which I'm building an epic romance. There's got to be something weird or cracked about her that she's not showing. Maybe sitting around reading sonnets is a classic sign of weirdness. An Ophelia complex. But who is Hamlet? Maybe it's love she needs. And of course I'm the man to supply it,' he laughed bitterly. 'If only. She probably thinks I'm a klutz, showing off that I've read Shakespeare's sonnets and telling her that I write poetry. How crass! What an idiot.'

When they met at three, they were both nervous, at once united and divided by personal awkwardness. It was Belinda who delivered the inevitable opening line: 'So, what are you in here for?'

'It's hard to say. I've been in therapy for several months,' Eli informed her. 'I don't know. I guess I haven't lived up to my parents' expectations. To my own expectations. I get keen on something—or someone—and then I lose all energy and I wonder at my previous enthusiasm, or even obsession.'

'I know what you mean. It's so much about energy. All my life, almost, I've always felt tired. I feel compelled not to show any weakness. Life is such hard work—like you, I have to live up to parental expectations. School lessons weren't enough for my mother. She taught me piano and sewing and cooking and stuff… Don't get me wrong, my mum's a brilliant teacher… I went to this terribly smart school where it was all about keeping up appearances… Don't get me wrong, I love my parents madly.'

'So do I,' said Eli with an emphasis that surprised him. 'But for some reason, it's hard. I'd like to have a proper conversation with them sometimes but never can. My mum seems to want everything to come right by waving a magic wand, or at least swallowing a pill or calling in help. Any conversations we do have either just fizzle out or break up quickly in a burst of impatience or hostility. Or just embarrassment.'

His present conversation, with Belinda, did not fizzle out but continued in animated fashion propelled by more conventional exchanges about literary, musical, theatrical and cinematic favourites. Belinda, who had arrived at the Elms two days earlier than Eli, told him a little about some of the other patients and the general routine. It had been quite a while in either of their lives since two hours had passed so quickly.

'It's been great talking to you,' said Eli, as Belinda stood up to go to a consultation.

She smiled what to him seemed a non-committal smile and then realised that she had brought the book of sonnets with her. 'I just remembered,' she said, handing it to him. 'You said you wanted to borrow this.'

Eli took it with him to his room and there he kissed it and began to read, constantly breaking off in a turmoil of hope.

They met again at dinner that evening and spoke about their families and their homes before parting with a formal handshake. While Belinda fell into an immediate, long and chemically induced sleep, Eli spent the night unable to settle, his body longing for her and his head filled with what seemed to him the most germane of sonnets, that with which he had connected to her, number twenty-seven. Though she had quoted to him the last line—'For thee and for myself no quiet find'—it was the preceding one, to which it was linked, that stirred him that night: 'Lo! thus, by day my limbs, by night my mind'.

As the sky lightened, Eli sat up and sighed. 'I must write her a letter,' he said.

5

12 July 1970
The Elms Psychiatric Clinic, near Sunbury-on-Thames, Surrey
Eli Haroun to Belinda Vane

Dear Belinda,

I have really enjoyed our conversations. It is far easier to share my feelings with you than with the doctors or the nursing staff. It's funny how I recognise so much of what you say you are going through when our two backgrounds could hardly be more different.

Your family sound so English while mine are so NOT English, though of course they have lived here for years, vote, pay taxes and all that stuff. Your parents are clearly of the stiff upper lip variety, cool, calm and collected. My parents are loud and demonstrative with a range of gestures and facial expressions, arguing loudly one minute and laughing the next.

Yet they are so narrow-minded. They follow every little detail of the Jewish religion and avoid outsiders. My dad works in a totally Iraqi-Jewish environment, even though his business (which he is trying to bully me into joining) takes him all over the world. My mum cooks only 'kosher Arabic' food and I doubt if she has ever tasted any other kind. But the most embarrassing revelation I have is that my mum and dad are FIRST COUSINS! Their marriage was arranged. Not only that but both of my grandparents' marriages were arranged, too. You probably think that's disgusting. But then, when you are a small, persecuted minority, you tend to protect yourselves and circle the family wagons.

We met only a couple of days ago, and this is a strange place to have met, but I feel that I know you, Belinda, despite coming from such a different world. And it is probably quite obvious to you (I've probably made it TOO obvious) that I am very fond of you—to say the least.

I am writing to you because I do not want to embarrass you with any inappropriate behaviour. And if you do not welcome my attentions and do not share my feelings, you can let me know in a short reply. And please let us stay friends. But if by some miracle you do feel the same, well…

Yours sincerely,
Eli

At first, Eli attempted to pad along the corridor leading from his room to Belinda's in order to push his letter under her door, rather than place it in an envelope and drop it into the patients' mail delivery basket. He was in his dressing gown and wore socks but no shoes, keeping as quiet as he could given that it was not yet 6 a.m. The silence made him dizzy. He could smell the polished floor and suddenly worried that he would slip and fall.

Her corridor was at a right-angle to his and he had just turned the corner and slowed down in his approach to the third door on the left— Belinda's!—when a sturdy, wholesome-looking female nurse entered the corridor and came towards him from the opposite direction. He noted how brisk and capable she looked and how fresh-faced in contrast to how he was feeling; how her hair, bonnet and uniform were all neatly in place; her black, laced-up shoes soft yet strong; her smile bright and business-like, more genuine than Sandra Carter's but much less beautiful than Belinda's.

'Where are you off to so early in the morning, my love?' Her strong, faintly Irish voice, just above a whisper, and her assured, authoritative manner, unbalanced him. He felt that he was sinking under a great weight of frustration, disappointment and guilt.

'I just wanted to deliver something.' A croak rather than a whisper. He felt himself reddening.

'A letter? Would you like me to post it for you if you don't want to give it in for posting at the reception? To your family, is it?'

'No, it's, er, no thank you. It needs an envelope.'

'As you like, my love. Have you got your medication?' She was speaking a little louder and Eli was worried she might wake Belinda.

'Yes, yes, fine, thank you. I'll go back to my room. Get an envelope later maybe.' He spoke as softly as he could, and turned away as quickly as he could.

153

Back in his room, he lay face down on the bed, still clutching the letter, and sank into an enfolding sleep. He awoke at nine to the sounds of chirpy staff members entering into—as Eli expressed it—the prevailing spirit of madness, along with snatches of conversation, coughs and a brief shock of hysterical laughter among the patients scuttling into breakfast.

Eli stood up. 'Breakfast!' he said to himself and then looked at his unshaven face and narrowed eyes, from the inner corners of which an inverted 'v' spread down his face either side of his nose. Turning away, he left his room and went to a balcony that abutted on to his corridor and from which he could just see the conservatory where patients and staff alike were eating.

And there she was, in clear view at a table near a window on the side nearest to the balcony on which he was standing. He tried to make out her expression to see if perhaps she was looking for him—or possibly for someone else. The sight of her both thrilled and unnerved him and he stepped back into the corridor and hurried back into his room.

He picked up the letter from where it had fallen, face down on the carpeted floor and rapidly read through it once more, before making his way, this time less conspicuously, along the corridor towards Belinda's room. He bent down and pushed his hopeful words through the small gap at the base of her door before returning to his room for a shower.

By the time he had shaved and showered and stepped out of his bathroom, he was in danger of missing breakfast, so he quickly pulled out a pair of jeans and a T-shirt from the wardrobe and crossed the room to the chest of drawers to grab a clean pair of socks.

As he did so, he noticed a folded sheet of paper on his mat with the word 'Eli' written neatly across it in a bold, feminine hand.

He sat on the bed to try to ease the sudden pounding in his head. His hands were clammy and he could feel a weight rising from his chest into his throat as he knelt down and picked up the paper, carefully opened it, and read.

Dear Eli,

I was so pleased to receive your sweet letter. I have also enjoyed our conversations. Your parents sound much more interesting than mine!

I spend a lot of time, here and at home and when I was at Cambridge, feeling so sorry for myself. I don't think you would feel so fond

154

of me if you knew what a misery I can be and into what black moods I descend.

But I must tell you, dear Eli, that talking to you lifts my spirits. My answer to you lies in the last two lines of Sonnet 30—the 'Proust' one—'remembrance of things past' and all that. You've got the book. Look at those two final lines.

B

He was uplifted by her single-initial signature. The letter 'B' suddenly carried a significance for him. He threw himself across the bed and reached for the book on his bedside table, flicking manically through it for Sonnet 30, beginning: 'When to the sessions of sweet silent thought...' and, after sorrowing over the author's sad state of mind, ending: 'But if the while I think on thee, dear friend, All losses are restor'd and sorrows end.'

Eli almost fell over in his rush to reach her room. He knocked but she was not there. He decided to read her note and Sonnet 30 over breakfast, which would be possibly the most wonderful meal he had ever eaten, however stale and humble the food. He rushed down eagerly to the conservatory.

In the event, he helped himself to cereal and, having unthinkingly poured an excess amount of milk over it, left it half-eaten. He felt some-how hollow but not able to eat. As he had done the previous morning, he smelt and eyed enviously the plates of eggs with bacon and sausages being devoured by the two patients at a nearby table—latecomers who, like himself, had arrived only just in time for breakfast. When filling in the application form with him, Farah had automatically stipulated a vegetarian diet, kosher food not being available. Had she known that Eli quite often ate non-kosher food when out with friends, she would have attributed it to his mental disorder.

Eli bit off a corner of toast and then could wait no longer. He pushed back his chair and strode upstairs to his room to compose himself as he brushed his teeth, combed his hair and dabbed cologne on his cheeks. Picking up the book of sonnets, he took a deep breath and made his way to Belinda's room. The nervousness that gripped him as he arrived at her door and tapped on it evaporated when she greeted him with that smile of hers.

'Eli,' she said, her voice slightly betraying her own nerves.

'Belinda, hi.'

'Come in.'

'I've brought the sonnets back.'

'Oh you could have held on to them for longer.'

'Well…' His irritation with himself for his own timidity was tempered by his intuition that she was feeling similarly inhibited. But she smiled, took his hand and spoke.

'That was such a lovely letter you sent me, Eli. It was moving and, as the man wrote, restoring.'

He felt there was enough poetry in the moment not to aim for the lyrical and said simply: 'I really like you, Belinda. Very much.' And he stroked her face with his free hand.

'A perfect fit,' Eli thought, as their mouths met gently and then more searchingly as their arms and bodies embraced. They moved apart gently, enabling each to look into the other's face. 'I'm supposed to be sick, crazy, screwed up,' said Eli. 'So how come, I feel so wonderful.'

'I'm so glad I met you,' she said, and they joined in a second kiss, less speculative, more exploratory than the first.

The next day, they discussed religion. They were lying on Belinda's bed, their heads close together on the pillow but not touching, sharing a calmness that neither had experienced in a long time.

'So, your parents sound like really religious people,' Belinda said. 'Is that usual for Iraqi Jews? I've never met one before.'

'Well, I don't think of my parents as *really* religious but, in their level of observance, I suppose they are fairly typical Iraqi Jews.'

'There were a couple of Jewish girls in my year at school,' Belinda said. 'But I didn't really know them that well. And there was a really nice girl called Jane Becker who arrived at Newnham as I started my second year. We went to a couple of lectures together and to the pub and I once borrowed her bike to cycle out to Grantchester. I thought we really hit it off—but, then, I didn't stick around long enough.'

'Well,' he said. 'I bet her family doesn't come from Iraq and that her parents aren't first cousins.'

'You're really hung up on that, aren't you?'

'Not really. It was standard practice in Haroun-land and so far as I know we haven't produced anybody with three heads or a tail. Except…' He suddenly broke off and looked ruminative.

'Except?' Belinda's expression was a mixture of curiosity and amusement.

'Except, back in Baghdad there was an uncle I never knew. Uncle Reuben. Great-uncle really. He couldn't wait to get out of the family's grip and get married. Which he did but I think it was unhappy. Nobody liked his wife and I think that upset him—she was a cousin but a very distant one. I think the problem was that she had too much personality—not good in an Iraqi-Jewish bride in those days. Anyway, poor Uncle Reuben died and his widow very soon vanished from the scene.'

'Did they think she killed him?'

'God, no. Reuben was clearly the one they thought was unstable. His name used to crop up every so often during my childhood and always in a secretive kind of way. Certainly he was different in some way. I know that he had a spell in hospital. But not for normal, "physical" reasons. That's the phrase my dad—and my mum—used. They both used the same phrase so it must have been handed down through the Haroun line. The most I've got my dad to say is that Reuben wasn't quite manly enough for marriage. So maybe it was just that he was queer—which in that community would have been down to mental illness.

'I've seen Reuben's photograph. He looked like a wise but sad professor. He's been swept under the carpet, like he's the black sheep of the family. I think my dad thinks I may have inherited some mental thing from him. It's certainly not homosexuality… But intermarrying with cousins doesn't happen any more, not in our generation. My sister is marrying some nice Jewish boy she met at university and it's much the same across the board with my cousins and Iraqi friends.

'As I said,' Eli continued, 'I don't think of my mum and dad as really, properly religious. They keep to all the rules and do all the rituals but I'm sure they never think about faith and belief. They certainly never discuss it. Actually, a lot of Jews who go to synagogue don't really believe in God. Unlike my grandma, who is a sincere believer and a wonderful advert for the religious life.'

Eli smiled at his recollection of Rivke and then added: 'My parents would certainly describe themselves as religiously observant, my mum especially. But, in my book, it's really a cultural thing. When I was a kid, I remember once saying that I didn't believe in God and my mum just said, "don't be silly", and that was it.

'They are both intelligent people—though they hardly ever read books and my mum is a complete philistine where art and music are concerned. And I never hear anything spiritual from them. Yet they would never think of themselves as secular and if you were to suggest that their attitude and behaviour were similar to those of an atheist—or an agnostic Jew who nevertheless loves the traditions and happily accepts them as his inheritance—they would reject it out of hand.'

'And what about you, Eli, what do you believe in?'

'No, enough! What about you, Belinda? I've been chuntering on about my family. What about yours?'

'What do you want to know?'

'Well, are you a good Christian girl? Are your folks churchgoers?'

'No. My grandparents go occasionally but I don't think my mother and father are interested in religion. We never talk about it. In fact, the only time they made any kind of religious decision concerning me was anti. They didn't want me to join a confirmation class at school, though that might have been because I was only doing it for social reasons and maybe they thought I wasn't taking the religion seriously enough. I'm pretty sure they were married by the local vicar.'

'And you?'

'Well, we had religious assemblies always when I was at school and I learnt all the biblical stuff and we were encouraged to debate and question it at my secondary school. I found that quite interesting, particularly in the sixth form when it was led by our history and philosophy teacher. She used to say: "Doubt about something you don't want to doubt is always the best stimulus to creativity." I used that in my Cambridge entrance exam. I maintain that's what got me in,' she smiled. 'I used to think I should have gone back and thanked Miss Phillips.'

'I often wish I had studied philosophy.' Eli said suddenly, allowing his eyes to take on a pensive expression.

'Me too,' Belinda said, another tiny link in the chain they were forging.

But then Eli broke it. 'Ah but if I got all twisted and confused with art, philosophy would probably have made me completely crack up. Sorry, I interrupted.'

'No it's all right. Religion hasn't played a big part in my life. And my ma and pa seem quite indifferent. I'm not sure what they really think. They got quite het up about that confirmation business, specially my ma. It's strange, really, because she loves religious music—Bach, Mozart's *Requiem*, all that. But I think it's just for aesthetic reasons. She loves beautiful things—music, painting. She's quite deep, my ma. She doesn't like speaking about her own mum and dad who died in the war. She would have still been quite young—it must have been awful. But of course so many people died. I don't like to press her because she obviously gets upset, or irritable. She said once that her father knew a lot about medicine. I asked her if he was a doctor but she didn't want to say any more.

'I can't see my parents doing all those things your parents do. Although, I think my ma would quite like lighting candles like you said your mum does on Friday nights. As I said, she's very aesthetic, my mother. I can just see her lighting the candles, closing her eyes and sniffing the perfumed aroma. She'd be in her element, I reckon.'

They both laughed and then Belinda continued more seriously. 'I do pray sometimes, though. When I'm at the end of my tether. It's simply an act of desperation on my part. It's that Miss Phillips thing again—doubting but desperately not wanting to doubt. But, if I'm honest, I can't believe in some mystical creator. I believe in the clear, hard evidence of science.'

'Yeah, me too,' agreed Eli. 'Ever since I was thirteen and had a bar mitzvah.'

'Oh, right.'

'I had this really sweet old bar mitzvah teacher, Mr Abinun. We called him "Rabbi" but I don't think he actually was a rabbi. I remember that he was musical and used to sing—liturgical stuff. I really wanted to believe in God for Mr Abinun's sake and I felt that I had more or less convinced myself, partly because, throughout that time, I was feeling so good, which was very unusual for me. But when I was singing my bar mitzvah piece—it's called a *portion*, a slab of stuff from the law, the Torah, and you stand up in synagogue and sing, or chant it in Hebrew...'

'Sounds terrifying.'

'It can be but I actually quite enjoyed it. And anyway, you could have coped. You were a young actress and musician and performed in front of audiences at school you told me.'

'True.'

'Anyway, as I was up there doing my stuff I started to feel a bit uneasy. Not about the performance—I had that under control. But about the purpose of it. I couldn't see the point. I looked down at all those men in their little hats and I felt… scornful. How could they be adults and yet so gullible and conformist, so unquestioning, I thought, still singing— or rather, chanting—away merrily. Mr Abinun taught me that a Jew should always question things but most of the people there, even if they paid lip service to that idea, would stop short when it came to questioning all the outrageous and miraculous stuff in the Bible.'

'That's one really good thing about my parents,' said Belinda. 'They really don't conform. They certainly do conventional things but it always feels like it's their true choice. They don't just follow like sheep.'

'But it sounds as though they nevertheless have a comfortable, very typically English existence.'

'Actually my mother is Hungarian.'

'Really? Do you speak Hungarian then?'

'Not a word. Neither does she. Well, obviously she must be able to remember some Hungarian but I've never heard her speak a word. I think she still has a trace of an accent but it's very faint. She was born there but now she is truly more English than the English.' For no apparent reason, Belinda began to feel uncomfortable at this point. Anxiety invaded her new, unfamiliar contentment. 'Eli, do you think we'll be in trouble if we're discovered together in one or other of our rooms,' she said, lifting her head from the pillow. 'Could we get kicked out?'

'You're joking,' replied a still-relaxed Eli. 'When our families are paying them all this money?'

She smiled and kissed his cheek but remained in a half-upright position.

'God,' said Eli, looking into Belinda's eyes. 'It is *so* good to talk to you. You obviously understand. So different from talking to the therapists. And especially my parents. I feel that we're completely on the same wavelength.'

'Is this a whirlwind romance?' she asked.

'Depends what you mean,' he answered. 'I don't think it's one of those holiday romances where you get seduced by the away-from-it-all atmosphere and it all fades away when you get back to reality, even though', he continued, smiling, 'the Elms does feel like a wonderful holiday resort at this moment. But, as far as I'm concerned,' he said, feeling a surge of what had to be love because he had never felt anything like it before, 'this is as powerful as any whirlwind.'

'Oh darling,' she responded, kissing his cheek again.

'Actually,' he said, 'I've written an old-fashioned little poem about falling in love.'

'Read it to me. Please.'

'Oh, no. I'm too inhibited.'

'How can you be after what you just said? Didn't you mean it?'

'Of course I meant it.'

'So read me your love poem. Old-fashioned or not.'

'Oh, I don't know.'

'Read me your *poem*.'

'I don't need to. It's short and I know it off by heart. It's meant to be an old lover advising a young lover.'

'Go on then!'

And he did:

'If you fall in love too easily,
And give yourself too willingly,
You will be hurt and so will she,
For instant love fades instantly.

But neither very cautious be,
And miss the opportunity,
To take that leap into the sea,
And soak yourself in liberty.'

'I love it.'

'I love you.'

And when she whispered to Eli that she was on the pill, wondering anxiously if he would fall straight into a sad imagining that he was but one in a line of lovers or if he would simply reject her for being what his upbringing had doubtless taught him was a loose woman, she was met instead by a lingering kiss.

Emboldened, she whispered again into his ear but this time a little more loudly: 'My love is at least as strong as yours—as you said: powerful as any whirlwind.'

And, that afternoon, with the July sun warming them through a window in the bedroom of a psychiatric clinic, two fragile individuals discovered how passion, however temporarily, could chase away unhappiness.

Belinda was the first to leave. By the time she was discharged at the end of July, the bond between Eli and herself was, they both agreed, unbreakable. He was due home the following Monday, 3 August, and was eagerly awaited. There was no doubting the improvement in him. It had been apparent on Farah's first visit three days after she had taken him to the Elms, and when Yusuf came with her the next weekend he was so emotionally overcome to see his son so cheerful, open and relaxed that, after a few minutes, he had to excuse himself and hurry into a lavatory cubicle to deal with the tears that had sprung into his eyes.

But Eli wasn't completely open with his parents. He and Belinda agreed they were not ready to be introduced to their respective families. Even by July's end, when it was certainly apparent to patients and staff within the Elms that they had a romance in their midst, Anna, Roderick, Farah and Yusuf remained unaware of the flames that had been lit in their children's hearts. One Sunday afternoon, the Vanes and the Harouns had entered the Elms drawing room almost simultaneously and sat within a few feet of each other, yet still were untouched by the heat of this proximity.

On 3 August, it was Yusuf who came to collect Eli, accompanied, to Eli's delight, by Rivke. Farah remained at home, cooking. After the formal farewells to some of the Elms staff, including a beaming Sandra Carter, Yusuf unlocked the car and Rivke wrapped her arms around her grandson. Cupping his face in her hands, she told him loudly: 'I have missed you.' As they got into the car, she opened a large biscuit tin on the back seat. Inside this, she had prepared a picnic of Iraqi bread, hard-boiled eggs, almonds, apricots, halva, fruit juice and, inevitably, dates. 'It's a long drive,' she said to Eli. 'You'll be hungry.'

Food was also on Farah's mind. She spent most of the day planning a welcome-home dinner in Eli's honour and had asked Leah and David, as well as Rivke, to be there. But Eli did not show the expected gratitude for his mother's efforts.

'I've already had tons to eat, courtesy of Grandma,' he told her when she revealed her intentions about an hour or so after he had returned.

'But I'm talking about this evening. A special dinner,' Farah said, anxiously. 'I'm cooking your favourite—lamb and couscous with a fresh, chopped salad.'

'I don't think I'll be hungry,' he said. 'Besides, I've arranged to go out this afternoon and I won't be back in time for dinner.'

'Eli, this is your first day home after nearly a month. I've been so looking forward to seeing you. Everyone is looking forward to seeing you. I can't understand. Why do you have to go out the minute you get back home? Where are you going, anyway? Who are you going to see?'

'Just friends.'

'Just friends? You're prepared to annoy and let down your family on such a day for "just friends". What friends? Who is it who is so important?'

'Look, lay off, Mum. I've just got out of an institution and already you're starting on me.'

At this point, Yusuf entered the room. 'What's happening?' he asked quite placidly.

'He's going out! He doesn't appreciate how hard I have been working for this dinner. For him!'

Behind Eli's back, Yusuf raised his eyebrows and patted the air with the palms of his hands, a gesture that said: 'Be careful. Be calm.'

Eli closed his eyes and spoke without opening them: 'I've been shut up in an institution for almost four weeks and I need some freedom and independence.'

Farah was hurt. 'I suppose that's your therapist talking. *Institution*. It was not exactly a prison, was it? A luxury hotel, more like.'

'Just leave me alone. Please. I won't be back that late and I'll eat then. Start without me. I'll be back in time to see everybody. I've already seen Grandma; she fed me like I was a man dying of starvation.'

'That's fine,' said Yusuf. 'We'll keep a plate for you. It'll be delicious and you'll appreciate it even more a bit later—and that means appreciating your mother who made it so lovingly for you.'

'I know,' said Eli. 'I'm sorry, Mum, but I made this arrangement.'

'Who with? When did you arrange it?'

'In the Elms. Look, it's arranged now and I'm not cancelling it. I told you, I need to walk free.'

Farah breathed a sigh of acceptance. 'Well,' she said, trying to over-come her disappointment by looking at her son with love and gently squeezing his hand. 'It's nice that you were able to phone out from there to people other than your parents.'

Eli released his hand, smiled a 'thanks-Mum' smile and went to the bathroom to freshen his face and hands before changing his clothes and dashing off to the station.

Meeting for the first time outside the confines of the Elms made both Eli and Belinda feel slightly apprehensive, like two birds thrown out of the nest. They met at Regent's Park and both arrived almost half an hour early.

As if to recreate a contained environment, they made straight for the zoo, where they strolled around chattering, laughing, holding each other tightly, and happily gazing at the animals. They sat on a bench, watching people walking past before getting up to walk themselves. By now, they were once again talking freely.

'I don't want to make you feel like one of those monkeys in its cage, Eli,' said Belinda. 'But I really feel we already have a strong bond. And it feels like love to me.'

'And to me,' breathed Eli. 'I have wanted to be in love, have anticipated being in love, for ages, and occasionally imagined I was in love. But I know this is different.'

Belinda looked worried. 'Well you are a poet. With an imagination. How do you know you are not imagining it now? How is it different this time?'

'Oh, Belinda, how can you doubt it? This is real. For me, it's real. I don't know what I would do if you didn't feel the same.'

'I do feel the same, but should we worry about these feelings emerging in what was an artificial situation? In a psychiatric clinic, shut away from the real world. I still feel the same, but we are like birds—lovebirds—just out of the nest. It's early days yet.'

As Eli's eyes saddened, Belinda smiled and grabbed his hand. 'It's real for me, too. Come on, tell me about your other women—my rivals.'

Eli laughed uncertainly and then spoke: 'I used to write poems about love and desperately wanted to have someone who I could direct them towards. Even my mum is always telling me—and not approvingly—that I have a "romantic imagination". There was this mysterious-looking girl with a dark complexion and shiny black hair who I saw once at someone's engagement party at the synagogue my family belongs to in Maida Vale.'

'Ah, the dark lady of the sonnets.'

'She was just a dream, a vision, a face. And a name—Esther. I never actually spoke to her. Just looked. I used to wonder if love was something we carry around inside, a kind of potential connection, and then aim it at someone we see who fits our mental picture of a lover. Or whether real love is something that enters your heart when the right one comes along. Is it the need or is it the girl? That was basically my compulsive philosophical conundrum. And now I've solved it. It's the girl. It's you! You're the real thing. I'd have fallen in love with you even if I wasn't remotely looking to fall in love. So, it's not the need, it's the girl.'

'It's both, you fool.' Belinda smiled and linked her arm into his.

By the time Eli arrived home, he was light-headed. He gave his mother a hug before heartily devouring the plateful of his favourite food that she had kept for him and drinking a toast to his sister and future brother-in-law.

'And welcome home, Eli,' his grandmother added loudly.

'I think your mother's a little tipsy,' Farah whispered to Yusuf. And she undoubtedly was, partly from the wine but mostly from seeing her grandson look so happy. She was not to know that Eli's happiness was compromised by his feeling unable to tell his family that the source of it was not some idealised Esther-like figure but a real, flesh-and-blood, gentile girl.

Things were different in Esher. When Belinda arrived home, Roderick was out working late at the office with his father. Anna, observing the look of joyful contentment on her daughter's face, asked her if she'd had a good time out with her 'friend from Cambridge'.

'Yes, thank you, Ma,' Belinda replied breathlessly. 'It wasn't a friend from Cambridge. Ma… I've found someone.'

That Eli had been a fellow patient at the Elms took the edge off Anna's pleasure at the fact that Belinda had found a man who made her happy. She tried not to show it when she gave her daughter a hug but the anxiety she had been experiencing for some time over Belinda's welfare seemed to solidify with this news. That night, in bed, she shared her concern with Roderick. 'What if he is a depressive? What if he is dangerous? In any event, he must be extremely needy. It'll be too much for her.'

'When I met you, my darling,' said Roderick in a voice at once both reproving and reassuring, 'it would hardly have been possible to imagine anyone more "needy" than you were.'

'I know but I had you to take care of me. It's too much for Belinda. She needs looking after. She needs a young Roderick.'

'I think you may be worrying unduly. Let's at least meet him. And, if he genuinely makes her happy, isn't that all we could ask for?'

The next day, when they were alone together, Anna asked Belinda to tell her all about Eli. And, after initially softening to the idea of her daughter's relationship with a young man who was apparently very gentle, intelligent and cultured, who loved music and wrote poetry, she inwardly and irrationally shuddered with alarm at a revelation that Belinda expressed with a kind of casual enthusiasm.

'He is Jewish.' And when her mother suddenly closed her eyes: 'Ma, you don't exactly look keen. I can't believe that you might be prejudiced. After all, you are Hungarian. Imagine how horrible it would be if someone was prejudiced against you for that.'

'Yes, I know. It has happened,' Anna said vacantly.

'His family sound really interesting.' Belinda wanted to press home the point. 'His parents come from Iraq. They are very religious.'

Anna resolved not to let her inner turmoil show and carried on the conversation, relieved when Belinda moved on to enthuse about her own and Eli's shared love of Shakespeare's sonnets.

'The Bard brought us together,' said Belinda, laughing.

'How wonderful,' Anna said with forced encouragement, trying almost too hard to eradicate the impression she feared her earlier reaction had given.

Later that day, after Belinda had left to meet Eli in London, Anna went to her bedroom and sat silently on the bed. She couldn't have explained her feelings at that moment to anyone else, even Roderick. She couldn't explain them even to herself.

Without knowing exactly why, she went to her dressing table and took from the back of the bottom drawer the thick envelope in which she had stored away both the letter from the United Nations Relief and Rehabilitation Administration office detailing her parents' deaths and the scribbled note from her father that she had carried with her into Auschwitz, Bergen-Belsen and across the sea into Britain.

She read them to herself, though she knew them by heart. And then she put her hands over her eyes, her mind a dark absence, before standing abruptly and putting the two documents back into the envelope and carefully restoring it to its secret corner of the drawer.

Meanwhile, in a café somewhere in central London, her daughter and her boyfriend were romantically committing themselves to each other.

'I am totally yours,' said Eli. 'Head, heart and loins.'

'I'm having to pinch myself, this is so amazing,' said Belinda. And then, laying a hand on his arm, 'I'm dying to introduce you to my parents. They're both mad about art and music and books. My mum loves it that we got together over the sonnets. You'll love them. And, my darling Eli, they'll love you.'

She was more curious than concerned when this shaft of joyful enthusiasm on her part was met with a darkening of Eli's face. He suddenly dropped his gaze as if to look into the cup of coffee in front of him.

'I wish I could say the same,' he said.

'Darling, what do you mean? You look so sad. What is it?'

'I've told you how bloody strict my parents are. I haven't yet summoned up the courage to tell them about you. They've been here long enough to accept that their children don't have to marry relatives, or Iraqi Jews, but—forget about marry, just to go out with a girl who isn't Jewish is more or less a sin in their book.'

He took hold of her hand before continuing. 'Look, Belinda, this is not a proposal, but the way I feel I can't ever imagine wanting to marry, or just be with, anyone else but you. But if I did marry someone who wasn't Jewish, they'd probably cast me out. I'm not talking about being thrown out of home but, in effect, banished. They might well never want to see me again.

'If we did get married, they certainly wouldn't come to the wedding. And if we had children I'm not even sure they would be prepared to see their own grandchildren. But, as far as I'm concerned, I'd be happy to be cast out for your sake. I do love my family, my mum, dad, sister and, I have to confess, especially my grandma, but you are the most important person to me. That might sound mad after we've known each other only a short time but that's how it is. So I was wrong earlier; this is a proposal. Belinda Vane, please marry me.'

'My darling, it doesn't sound mad at all,' said Belinda. 'Because I feel exactly the same about you. The answer's yes. And surely your family can understand about falling in love? Your parents must have been in love when they met.'

'Strangely enough, I think they were in love when they were engaged—betrothed is the more appropriate word—but that was just a lucky coincidence. The marriage was arranged. They had known each other since they were kids.'

'Aren't you going to tell them? Are we going to run away?'

'No. Of course I'm going to tell them. I'm not ashamed. I'm proud, I'm happy. But I am scared. I'm certainly not looking forward to it. They'll try to stop me seeing you.'

'They can't.'

'No they can't. Even if they lock me up, they won't stop me seeing you.'

'But will they all feel the same—your mother, your father, your sister? What about your lovely grandma?'

'She will be saddened. She is, after all, the most traditional. But she won't be angry with me. My mum and dad will be furious. I like to think I'll get some sympathy from my sister but her head is full of her wedding that's coming up in a few months—I think I told you, to a non-Iraqi Jew she met at university.'

'Do you think you'll be able to tell them tonight?'

'I'll try. I must.'

As it turned out, it wasn't only Eli who received a less than satisfactory parental response to the lovers' declaration of devotion. Both Anna and Roderick met Belinda's account—which left out the marriage proposal—somewhat coolly. Anna wanted to display a united front with her husband and did not try to generate an enthusiasm she did not feel this time, while Roderick expressed no more than token curiosity about Eli.

'Haroun? That's an unusual name,' Roderick said in as gentle a tone as he could muster, knowing how strained his wife was feeling. 'Is he Arabian?'

'He's an Iraqi Jew, Pa. Didn't Ma tell you anything?'

'Yes, but not everything,' he replied slightly distracted by this revelation and wondering why Anna hadn't mentioned this significant fact to him. Perhaps, he mused, as Anna took up the conversation with their daughter, she hadn't mentioned it precisely because of its significance.

To Roderick, it was of no real consequence. If anything, he felt rather comforted by Belinda's having fallen for a Jew. It somehow strengthened the bond between father and daughter. At the same time, he knew that his wife, despite her protestations to the contrary, had not buried her past. How could she?

At that moment, her tone towards Belinda was one of friendly concern.

'Sounds nice,' she said of Belinda's day in town with Eli.

'I'm very sure of him, Ma.'

'And *I'm* sure that is indeed how you feel *at the moment*.' Anna stressed those last three words. 'And Eli does sound a lovely, sensitive boy. But, without trying to sound like some disapproving old person, I must warn you not to rush headlong into this. I don't want you to get hurt.

'Eli has come along at a time when you happen to be a little vulnerable. And you're still so young, sweetheart. You may have had some dates at Cambridge that you're keeping to yourself but, so far as Daddy and I know, the only other boyfriend you've had was that snooty fellow who was president of the union. And that hardly turned out brilliantly.'

'What are you saying, Ma?'

'Simply that you must not rush into things and not at this stage put all your eggs into—what is that phrase?—a box, *a basket*. Well, you know what I mean. It is important to take things carefully in these initial months following your treatment at the Elms.'

'Believe me, the best treatment I got at the Elms was not from the medical staff, as good as they were. I am more than thrilled that I went there because I feel so much better. And I feel so much better because of Eli. Listen, Ma, I am not rushing into things and I will take things, as you say, carefully. I just know that however carefully I take things, Eli will be the one.'

'All right, sweetheart. Let us see. Just give it some time, that's all.'

Roderick emerged from his thoughts to remind Belinda that, 'we both love you very much and want only the best for you. This young man may be it, he may not. Time will tell.'

'Well, you two hardly waited for years,' Belinda's exasperation was showing and she stood up and went to the kitchen to boil the kettle for tea. She needed to end the conversation, prudently deciding not to tell her mother and father about the storm expected imminently in the Haroun household. And indeed, that storm was not long in coming.

'To think I spent all that money to get you back on the rails and you end up going off the rails even further.' Yusuf's anger was compounded by a sense of acute disappointment that his son's stay at the Elms should have led to what he saw as a severe transgression. And, because it had been his decision to pay for Alfassa and for the Elms, Yusuf felt angry and disappointed with himself.

'Dad, I've never been so "on the rails", as you put it, in my life.' Eli was growing more determined and defiant the more the pressure was applied.

'Eli, you've never been fully on the rails,' screamed Farah, whose anger, unlike her husband's, was undiluted, resentful, volcanic.

'Oh, thanks a lot, Mum.' This latest barb reinforced Eli's sense of righteousness.

'That was a stupid remark, Farah,' Yusuf said before quickly turning to their son. 'Your mother didn't mean it. It came out wrong. She just wants you to know what you are doing to your family. You'll have to get over this infatuation.'

'I'm in love, Dad. Love! Have you forgotten how you told me how much in love you were with Mum?'

'How could you do this to us?' Farah said at the top of her voice.

Yusuf waved a placating hand and tried to keep calm as he answered Eli. 'Yes, son,' he said as steadily as he could. 'That's true. We were very much in love. We still are in love. And that's the point. Our love had a deep foundation. We were secure in our love because we came together naturally within a community. All the ingredients were there for a permanent relationship.'

'Don't you realise that you are breaking off hundreds, *thousands*, of years of tradition?' Farah's attempt at pleading, her hands dejectedly rubbing her temples, still came out as raw anger.

'I didn't deliberately set out to fall in love,' said Eli in a raised voice, questioning in his own mind whether that was actually true.

'But you could have stopped yourself,' said Yusuf, trying to sound both paternal and reasonable. 'You could have told this young lady that you could not see her as anything other than an acquaintance, or even a friend.'

'I knew we shouldn't have sent him away to that place,' Farah said, her entire body quivering.

'Mum, when I came home from the Elms you were beside yourself with joy saying what a wonderful effect my stay there had had.'

'Well, obviously I was wrong.'

'No, *I* was wrong in thinking I was in there because you cared for me. It's not exactly a great confidence booster having to go into a nuthouse because you can't cope properly outside. And then hearing from your mother that it was a waste of time.' This was Eli's parting shot before going to his room and slamming the door behind him.

Leah arrived at the house an hour or so later to find her parents in the kitchen, her mother sitting on the edge of a chair like a tightly-wound coil, her father pacing back and forth. In the background, the amplified sound of Jimi Hendrix's guitar was blasting out from Eli's stereo.

When Farah explained the cause of the high-tension atmosphere, Leah immediately berated her parents, employing one of the household's most favoured rhetorical techniques: sarcasm.

'Oh good idea, folks. Your delicate son has just returned home from a stay in a psychiatric institution and is for once happy and in a relationship and you of course know exactly what to do—demolish all that good stuff. Make him feel bad. Make him feel guilty. Make him unhappy. Set him back a few years. For God's sake, what is the matter with you?'

'Now don't get high and mighty, Leah,' her mother said, uncoiling from her chair. 'We only want the best—for both of you.'

'And anyway, what's the big deal?' Leah wasn't going to be placated so easily. 'It's just a girlfriend, probably his first serious one.'

'Leah's right.' Yusuf's sadness was now becoming compounded by remorse. 'We were a bit too harsh on him.'

Farah pressed on, talking to Leah. 'She's not "just a girlfriend". He's going to meet her parents tomorrow.'

'So what?'

Yusuf butted in: 'She might be a lovely girl. She's intelligent. Went to Oxford, Eli says.'

'Cambridge.' Farah corrects him.

'Oxford, Cambridge, never mind,' said Yusuf. 'My point is that she might well be prepared to convert and one day we could have plenty of Jewish grandchildren including from Leah, please God.'

'For goodness' sake.' Leah's mouth and eyes simultaneously opened wide. 'They've only been going out five minutes.'

Suddenly, Farah looked weary. 'He insists that she is "the one",' she said quietly and a little hoarsely. 'He is probably going to ask her father for his daughter's hand tomorrow.' Sarcasm, again. The family weapon. 'They are a terribly English family,' Farah added, trying to make Leah appreciate the unbridgeable distance between the Harouns and the

171

Vanes, 'quite well-off it seems and they live in the country somewhere not that far from the Elms.'

'Why not ask him to bring her home? Why not meet her?' said Leah, and then, after a pause: 'It might help to repair the damage you've done.'

And, later, Farah and Yusuf did relent a little and suggested to Eli that he should bring Belinda home.

'She said she would like to meet you,' Eli said, relieved not to be sucked any further into a bitter conflict with his parents. 'But I'm not going to bring her if you are going to be rude to her.'

'We promise not to be rude, don't we darling,' said Farah, turning to her husband for confirmation.

'Of course,' said Yusuf.

But when, on first encounter, Belinda's beauty, intelligence and politeness were obvious, more than matching Eli's description, this did not make Farah feel any easier about her son's attachment to this melodiously well-spoken English girl. If anything, it made things worse. Secretly, she had hoped for someone much less desirable, more superficial and less likely to have the staying power to withstand Yusuf's and her own disapproval. Someone, in short, for whom, given time, Eli's love would wither.

As for Yusuf, it took him some time to summon up the courage to tell Rivke of her favourite grandson's liaison. And when he did, her immediate reaction was: 'Let me talk to him. Bring him to supper here tonight.'

And so, after a typically sumptuous Iraqi spread, at the heart of which was a delicately cooked *kebba baamia*—chopped lamb meatballs with okra, flavoured with mint and lemon—Rivke, her son, daughter-in-law and grandson drank glasses of tea, also flavoured with mint and lemon, and ventured into the subject they had avoided throughout the meal.

Rivke smiled warmly at her grandson and addressed him directly in a sympathetic tone: 'She must be very special, this girl.'

'Belinda,' Eli quietly insisted, determined that the object of his devotion should not be rendered anonymous. 'And yes, Grandma, she is very special.'

'And not Jewish.'

'Yes and neither is she Iraqi. In that sense, things have advanced, even for the Harouns. Even Leah's very Jewish fiancé would have been

172

frowned upon in the past, back in Baghdad. But we're living in London. We can't carry on being suspicious of people "outside the clan". We've moved on.'

'Well, we are always moving on,' said Rivke, conscious of the fact that Yusuf and Farah were nervously awaiting her words, expecting wisdom to flow from her mouth. 'Which is why we need a strong and constant thread of tradition to hold us together, to keep us from splintering into thousands of pieces. To hold on to our spiritual identity, our cultural identity, in the face of many threats.

'You are a sensitive boy, Eli, and I know that you are sensitive to this feeling of identity. You know that you have a great historical and religious inheritance handed down to you, to us, from ancient times, an inheritance that you will want to hand down to your children.

'You are sensitive also to the pain that we have suffered, personally and collectively. You know about the terrible *Farhud* that threatened to destroy our community. But it didn't. Thank God that you, your parents and your sister were not there to witness those events. You were not even born. But then you did come along, you and Leah, to show our enemies that the Jewish light cannot be snuffed out.'

Rivke took a sip of tea before continuing. The others sat in silence without a thought of interrupting. 'I know you feel things deeply, Eli,' she said. 'It is sometimes hard for you. But, thanks to your parents, you have been to this wonderful modern clinic that has helped. Your great-uncle Reuben also was a deep, sensitive man, and he suffered for being sensitive. But you have been in good hands, caring hands.'

She took a breath and, for a moment looked away from Eli's face before resuming. 'Nobody understood how Reuben was feeling,' she said. 'Not even the doctors. Now, people, the doctors, especially here in England, they understand. They can help. And this does not mean there is something wrong with being sensitive or that you should ever stop being sensitive. I know it is not easy; it can bring unhappiness at times. You can feel bad things more strongly than others do, but you can also feel good things more strongly. It is a gift. You must remember that.

'You know,' she said, smiling and nodding at Eli, 'I have always dreamt of you as a handsome bridegroom, just like your father. And of your wedding being as wonderful as that of your mother and father. And *that*, believe me, was wonderful. Its memory is a part of the life of everybody who was there. Even your dear late grandfather, God rest his soul, was dancing. I never saw him happier. Such joy, you can't imagine. That is what I want for you.'

'Thank you, Grandma,' said Eli, putting his hand on hers and kissing her cheek. 'I do love all of my family. And its traditions. Like this beautiful meal we have just eaten. But for me,' he said, standing up, 'there is more.' And, with tears in his eyes, he left the room.

After Eli had gone, with his adored grandmother's words circling inside his brain, Yusuf put an arm around Farah, who was weeping softly in time with her breathing. Rivke's breathing, too, was audible. Following Eli's dramatic exit, none of them had risen from the table even though minutes had passed and the sound of his footsteps along the pavement outside had faded.

Rivke was the first to speak. 'You know, he is a fine boy and I think he is right. We have kept ourselves inward for too many generations, cousins marrying cousins. I say this even though I believe that you two are a perfect match and that I myself was devoted to Baba. But our outlook is too narrow. We know too little of the world. And it's not always so healthy. A couple of your distant aunts never married because they were, you know, a little bit weak in the head, poor creatures. I am very pleased that Leah is going to marry outside the family.'

'But not outside the family of Judaism.' Yusuf's sudden interjection sounded a discordant note across his mother's table, still laden with tea glasses and discarded fruit, date biscuits and baklava.

'Yes that is true,' Rivke answered before continuing, her voice softening in keeping with the evening light from the window. 'And, you know, I think that Eli is just as much in love with this girl as Leah is with David. I believe that he will teach her about our Iraqi ways and our Judaism. We can only see what time will bring.'

This last phrase had been echoed, almost word for word, in Esher when Belinda's parents were reflecting to each other on Eli's visit to their home. Roderick's first encounter with Eli had impressed him. Clearly, this was a well-mannered young man, fine-looking, smartly dressed and knowledgeable about art, books and music.

Eli's interest in music had also found favour with Anna. Although Eli had bracketed contemporary popular music with the great classical composers in his stated enthusiasms—one of which, female jazz and blues singers, he shared with Belinda—he was clearly a music-lover. Anna couldn't have borne the thought of her only child involving herself with someone who did not love music.

But she remained reluctant to deliver wholehearted approval. Similarly, Roderick was concerned that Eli was only the first boyfriend of Belinda's he had ever seen and that she was still, in his mind, 'very tender'. He also recognised and understood Anna's hesitancy and had no wish to countermand her desire to wait and see.

Anna seized on Roderick's word, 'tender', agreeing that it was an appropriate term for their daughter, not simply in the sense of young and impressionable, which was what Roderick had meant by it but, rather, because Belinda was of a tender sensibility and needed a protector more than she needed a loving companion, especially one of a similar disposition.

Inwardly, however, Anna was experiencing a burning guilt because her growing sensation of old wounds reopening derived directly from her daughter's happiness. Yes, Anna could tell herself, Belinda was falling recklessly into the arms of somebody who was as vulnerable as she was, if not more so. Yes, she was still young and relatively unworldly.

But yes, too, she was in love. And who wouldn't want one's daughter to be in love? And with a handsome and cultured young man. She yearned to sing her delight from the innermost part of her heart. But her heart was gripped by a shadowy yet terrifying fear.

'What am I frightened of, Roderick?' she asked in the middle of a sleepless night. The fact was that her fear was of the sort that drives nightmares: the vague, unnerving fear of being exposed, laid bare.

Meanwhile, the lovers themselves, fully aware of the fragility of their respective mental states, delighted in the support they were able to give each other. 'If ever I need shoring up,' wrote Eli in one of the many self-consciously poetic notes that passed between them, 'who better to turn to than my mistress?'

Each blossomed in the other's company. They sat together in cafés, parks or hotel bars engaged in unstoppable conversations both stimulating and affectionate. They went to the cinema, laughed a lot, walked and swam and played tennis. They shared a particular fondness for Indian food, enhanced no doubt by the fact their first meal out together had been at a little Indian restaurant in Maida Vale. They never tired of each other. Never lost the mutual lift to the spirit they experienced whenever and wherever they met.

Yusuf, who was happy to give Eli a job at the carpet emporium even though he knew that Eli was spending the money he earned on Belinda, had to admit to himself that it was heartwarming to see his son working so willingly and efficiently, drawing praise from Azi and Ben. He tried hard to suppress his resentment that the person most clearly responsible for Eli's new energy and enthusiasm was the classic gentile temptress of tribal folklore.

As for Belinda, she too was earning money, helping out two days a week in Anna's Designs—long since sold to a prominent wallpaper manufacturer but retaining the name—and two days with Roderick at Vane Natural Clothing. Both families would have been shocked had they realised that their British daughter and Iraqi son were saving money in order to get married and find a place to live together—and not necessarily in that order.

While Yusuf enjoyed Eli's company on the way to and from work, seldom mentioning Belinda's name, Farah became increasingly distraught the happier her son appeared to be. Eli began to feel sorry for his parents until one day his announcement that Belinda was coming to the house for dinner the next week, uninvited by Farah or Yusuf, sparked off a tempestuous response.

They all knew that a family dinner would represent a step towards validation of the relationship. Against all the odds, Eli wanted to try to make it happen. He tried flattery.

'I've told her what a brilliant cook you are,' he said to his mother in hopeful ingenuousness.

'Yes,' Farah said bitterly. 'It would be a real change for her to eat kosher food after being used to pork chops or whatever they eat down in the country.'

'There's no need to be like that, Mum. And, as it happens, Belinda is interested in learning about kosher food.'

'Oh, is she? No, I'm sorry, Eli. I'm not having her come here. It's too much. You had no right to invite her.'

'I have every right. I am an adult.'

'Oh, you think so?'

'I am an adult and this is my home. I can do the cooking.'

But he didn't cook and Belinda didn't come to dinner at the Harouns. They did, however, continue to see her when Eli brought her back to have coffee or prior to going out somewhere in town. She was always friendly and Eli was always manifestly proud of her. Leah befriended her and became her brother's ally in the continuing conflict with their parents.

Belinda also made sure that Eli made the occasional appearance at her home, where Anna was pleased to extend his knowledge about the classical composers he liked, and introduce him to the work of others. On one occasion, Belinda and Eli managed to draw Anna and Roderick into their laughter at a joke that Eli had been told by Uncle Azi.

Then, three months after his discharge from the Elms, and upset at the unhappiness he was causing his parents, Eli succumbed to their urging to go on a date with a 'perfect' young Iraqi-Jewish girl whose mother was a member of the Lauderdale Road Synagogue ladies' guild. Her father— whose business interests were of formidable breadth, encompassing property, textiles, diamonds, art, travel and a variety of more minor pursuits—was something of a beacon within Iraqi-Jewish circles on account of his active involvement in a number of Jewish charities.

Eli made this decision after he had attended Alan Alfassa's consulting room for a pre-arranged three-month review. Eli had gleefully told Alfassa about Belinda and they spoke for a while about love.

'Do you want to marry this girl?' Alfassa asked him.

'Oh yes,' said Eli emphatically.

'But you don't want to hurt your parents?' Alfassa seemed to be scrutinising Eli in a much more direct way than he had in the past.

'I don't and there are constant rows at home. But they'll just have to come round in the end.'

'That's almost certainly what they would say about you.'

'I suppose so. They don't give up. They have even tried to set up a date for me with an Iraqi-Jewish girl.'

'I think it would be a good idea for you to take them up on it.'

'You are joking!'

'It would help prove to them the strength of your feelings for Belinda—and to yourself.'

'I don't need to prove them to myself.'

'If you knew how many people I've heard express such certainty only to have it shatter in later years, you'd be astonished.'

'I can't imagine the future without Belinda.'

'The truth is, Eli, you cannot imagine the future, full stop. No one can. Or, at least, you can imagine, but you cannot foresee. People change. If you can change together, that's good. But it is not inevitable that you will. And then love dies with marriage. Actually, a lot of arranged marriages work well,' Alfassa added, 'because older, wiser heads have worked out that the two young people are well suited. If you can show your parents that this girl they have found for you does not match up to Belinda—does not feel right—then they may be forced to start acknowledging that there is genuine feeling and immovable solidity in your relationship with Belinda.

'If not, and the blind date stirs something in you, in however small a way, you will have learned a life lesson and you'll have to acknowledge that they know what they are talking about in relation to suitability for marriage, as opposed to a fling. After all, they are very suited to each other themselves, are they not?'

'I suppose so.'

'And, if it doesn't work out with the girl on the date, she'll get over it. It won't exactly be the end of a long and beautiful relationship. And don't forget you're on trial, too, as far as she is concerned.

'So remember,' Alfassa said, 'I've seen it all. The madly intense crush, which dries up with marriage, and the carefully arranged marriage that really works. And,' he added as Eli was leaving, 'there is of course a third scenario. This is when both parties, having thoroughly wallowed in each other's company for a serious amount of time and taken on board advice from their families, have absolutely no doubt on both counts—love and compatibility. In which case, you can take her in your arms and run down the aisle. But,' he said with a wink, 'you go on that date first. Your relationship with your parents is important, too.'

As he made his way home, Eli wondered how much Alan Alfassa's opinion was influenced by his being married to a non-Jewish woman. And wondered, too, how happy that marriage was.

The remark came out of the blue: 'Why do you make Eli feel so unwelcome?' Anna and Belinda were alone in the cottage, in the bright, rectangular living room, with its two sets of windows—one facing south over the front garden, the other looking on to the open, western side of the house where there was a gravel path running from the back of the garage to the rear garden.

It was a balmy, late-November afternoon, one of those in which the autumn seems reluctant to depart and winter is merely a hint. Roderick was on his way home from Vane Natural Clothing's main retail store in Horsham in Sussex. The living room was warmed by a gently burning log fire contesting with the hot, red sunset glowing through a casement window.

Anna was seated at the piano, which faced sideways into the centre of the room from the middle of its northern wall. She had just finished playing one of her mother's favourite Chopin pieces as a means of calming herself. Belinda had waited for her to emerge from the singularly peaceful resonance that always transported her for the first few seconds after the conclusion of her playing, before putting forward her critical question.

After three months of an increasingly intimate and strong, loving relationship with Eli, Belinda no longer felt she needed her mother's approval—though she dearly wished for it—and was thus confident enough to probe her directly.

Anna was looking up over the top of the piano, to where a print of Felix Vallotton's *La Dame au piano* hung, a painting that approximated to the scene below it in the Vanes' drawing room. She was letting Belinda's sudden, testing question settle into her mind

'I do hope Eli doesn't feel unwelcome,' she said after another few contemplative seconds. 'You know you can bring him here whenever you like.' Despite the welcoming sentiment, Anna, having turned to face her daughter, sounded more affronted than accommodating. 'Has he said he feels unwelcome?'

'No, Ma, but you never show real enthusiasm. Even when you are talking to him in a friendly way, your tone is always a little cool. Not like your usual self. Not, for example, with anything like the enthusiasm you just showed on the piano.'

'Oh, I always get carried away with those Chopin pieces. It's a way of helping me to stop thinking about my mother dying too young. Keeping her memory alive.'

'Why don't you talk to me about it instead? You never do.'

'I'm fine now, darling. Please don't worry. And, as for Eli, he's a fine young man. I like him.'

'But?'

Anna took a breath. 'Well... your father and I both feel you might be taking things a bit too fast. You have both only recently come away from treatment. You are still vulnerable. You need to take things slowly.' Anna turned her head to the side, away from Belinda, as she continued. 'And yet… the two of you. You are all over each other. Touching and kissing all the time…' She stood up. 'Sorry, darling, excuse me, I have to go to the bathroom.'

As Anna closed the bathroom door behind her, she heard Belinda call out: 'It's called love, Ma.'

This was enough to trigger Anna's tears. To conceal them, she splashed her face with cold water from the bathroom tap, took a couple of deep breaths and looked accusingly at her still-wet face in the mirror. 'What is the matter with me?' she said under her breath to her own image and then heard a second voice calling out. Roderick was home. She listened as he greeted Belinda.

'Hello, sweetheart. How are things?'

'They would be a whole lot better if I wasn't staying in tonight.'

'What do you mean? What's wrong?'

'Never mind,' said Belinda, jutting out her chin theatrically. 'Just a small fly in the ointment of my happiness. I'm going to my room to read.' She sighed as she undressed, dreamily puzzling why her parents seemed so reluctant to accept Eli. Then, after a shower, as she lay back on her bed, holding open the copy of *Le Grand Meaulnes* that Eli had given her, her thoughts turned sympathetically to him as she read Alain-Fournier's words in the English translation: 'Then he breathed deeply, like someone who has long endured a heavy heart and who was at last going to divulge his secret.'

While Belinda was reading and resting contentedly, believing Eli to be with friends, he was in fact seated in a large, vegetarian restaurant in Leicester Square. There, he was awaiting the arrival of Ruthie Menachem, elder daughter of the Lauderdale Road Jewish community's most bounteous giver to charities. Eli waited uncomfortably. Having turned the matter over and over in his mind, he was still wondering whether he should have told Belinda that, purely as an act of appeasement towards his parents, he was going on a blind date.

When a young, raven-haired, olive-skinned woman approached his table, looking slightly anxious, Eli stood up, uncertain of whether or not to offer his hand.

'Hello,' she said, smiling. 'Ruthie,' and proffered her right hand for him to shake.

He was instantly relieved, having just experienced a further stab of anxiety wondering if his date was religious and therefore not to be touched. 'Eli,' he said, copying her single-word mode of greeting and introduction. 'I was worried you might be religious. Orthodox.'

'No, I'm a modern girl,' Ruthie said with a self-conscious giggle, as she sat down opposite Eli. 'We are kosher at home, and I never eat non-kosher food, but I'm not at all fanatical.'

'That's good. My parents are pretty observant and keep a kosher home, but they're not that strict. My dad has been known to work on the odd Saturday.'

Ruthie shrugged, her face indicating that this minor transgression was all right by her.

'So,' Eli resumed. 'We didn't need to come to a strictly vegetarian restaurant. We could have had pasta or fish in the Italian down the street.'

'Yes, but I like it here. I've been a few times before.'

Eli wondered if the earlier times had also been dates and surprised himself by resenting the possibility that the waiter might see him as just the latest of Ruthie Menachem's suitors.

She was, he thought, a handsome rather than a beautiful girl, tall, big-boned and rather square-jawed with strong, dark eyes. Her hair was so black it shimmered and looked almost blue under the restaurant lights. She was friendly but unexciting, and loquacious rather than articulate. She had a very easy and pleasant laugh, however, and a refreshingly irreverent attitude to the Lauderdale Road hierarchy. And it didn't take long for Eli to find himself enjoying being in her company.

He even thought of asking her if she wanted to go to a nearby bar for a drink after their abstemious vegetarian dinner but settled for coffee at their table. When it came, they both drank slowly, and carried on talking about films (which Ruthie far preferred to reading books), music—and their families. Which is how he found out that Ruthie's younger sister—'smaller than me, with equally dark hair, but prettier, always popular with the boys'—was called Esther.

This bombshell, reminding Eli of his former idealised vision of love, now almost accessible, threw him off balance. 'I think I might once have been at the same party as your sister,' he said, feeling dazed, and inwardly recalling Alan Alfassa's remark about the possibility of the blind date 'stirring something' in him.

After a polite and chaste farewell, in which both he and Ruthie expressed thanks but made no mention of a possible further meeting, Eli made his way home slowly, in order to postpone for as long as possible the barrage of questions with which Farah, in particular, would greet him.

It had rained while they had been in the restaurant, and in the freshness of the now drying air and the wet pavements reflecting the lights of the West End, he began to experience a sense of calm resolution. This, he told himself, was a sign of maturity, enabling him to recognise a division between what he could now see as a distant, adolescent longing for Esther and an adult and perfect closeness with Belinda. His self-conscious smile lasted most of the journey from Leicester Square to Brondesbury Park.

At the confrontation later that evening, after Eli reported well of Ruthie, Yusuf and Farah tried to persuade him to invite her out again.

'I hear she has a nice sister, who is also single,' Farah persisted in the face of Eli's stated disinclination to see Ruthie again.

'You are doing well at work,' said Yusuf. 'I am proud of you. It's not too soon to think of your future, of finding a nice, suitable wife.'

'We can help you,' Farah was almost pleading.

'With finance,' added Yusuf.

'Will you please try, my darling boy?' Now Farah was pleading. 'If not with Ruthie, then with someone else. There are so many eligible girls at Lauderdale Road alone. You will make your family so happy—us, your grandma…'

'And what about my happiness?' Eli's calm was weakening.

'The right girl will make you happy.'

'I know. I have found her.'

'You cannot be happy with a Christian girl. It won't work. Believe me, I know better than you do.'

'What makes you think that?'

Farah's eyes widened. She was in no mood to debate the issue with her son. 'I forbid you to marry that girl,' she said suddenly, shaking, on the edge of weeping. 'Stop seeing her at once!'

'Listen, Eli,' said Yusuf, interrupting the sharpening mother-and-son exchange. 'I have promised you financial help—to set up home. But not if you continue to defy us like this. If you choose to stay with this girl.'

'Belinda!' Now Eli was shouting. 'She has a name.'

'If you choose to stay with Belinda,' his father resumed, 'and you do not marry a Jewish girl, then financially you will be on your own.'

'So be it.'

Peace was eventually restored by the arrival of Rivke, who, after learning of the outcome of the interrogation concerning the blind date with Ruthie Menachem, invited her grandson to spend the night under her roof.

It was a night when sleep was impossible for any one of the quartet of parents in their respective beds in north-east Surrey and north-west London.

In the latter, Yusuf tried to placate Farah. 'I think he is really in love,' he told his wife.

'But I don't want him to get hurt,' she replied. 'He hasn't even tried to find a Jewish girlfriend.'

'I know, and I also don't want him to be hurt. But he seems much calmer these days. He has been a good boy at the showroom. Really keen. Maybe my mother is right and this girl will be prepared to convert. She seems very capable.'

'I think he will drift away. From Judaism and from us.'

'I'm worried about that, too, and that it will be our fault for not listening to him but instead driving him away.'

'That's the last thing I want to do. But another "last" I don't want is to be the last of the Jewish Harouns.'

They were both able to smile at Farah's phrasing and—after Yusuf gently reminded his wife that they also had a daughter engaged to a Jewish man—to rest for a while in each other's arms.

But in the Esher cottage there was no rest for Belinda's parents as Roderick patiently urged Anna to examine her seemingly unshakable objections to Belinda's choice of boyfriend. Eventually, she sat up, switched on her bedside lamp and eased herself from the bed. Roderick, intrigued, asked what she was doing as she rummaged in one of the drawers of her dressing table.

'You remember the letter from the United Nations Relief agency, giving details of the deaths of my parents,' she said, pulling out a large brown envelope from the drawer.

'Of course. I've often wondered whether you'd hung on to it. I assumed you probably had but I never felt it was right to ask.'

'Oh, yes. I have kept it. And that's not all I have here.' She held up a foolscap notepad, several pages of which were densely covered with her careful, precise handwriting. 'I began to write about my parents and my early life. It was my intention to continue, and talk about Auschwitz and Belsen but I just can't. I haven't touched it for years.

'And this,' she said, turning on the main bedroom light, and handing Roderick a crumpled piece of paper carefully preserved in a transparent plastic holder, 'is the note my father managed to get to me after he was taken. I have kept it all this time. I can still see the face of the boy on the bicycle who brought it to me, as clear as if it had been yesterday.' She had to take a few breaths before continuing. 'And now, this fine, handsome young Jewish boy...' she said, her voice breaking. 'Of course she loves him. Of course he doesn't mean to... has no idea. This lovely, sensitive young man... has brought back all the pain.'

Roderick held her as she released, in convulsive cries, the anguish she had been holding back since Belinda's revelation that Eli was Jewish and Belinda's unknowingly ironic questioning of her response as racially prejudiced.

'I still can't believe how lucky I am, how lucky we are,' she said as she began to recover her self-control, 'to have this wonderful, precious daughter. I cannot carry on like this. I must apologise to her and explain. How cruel I have been. And selfish.'

She went over immediately to her writing desk and tore a couple of pages from her notebook. She wrote her daughter's name at the top of a page, stopped, and said, to herself as much as to her husband: '*Do not hesitate.* Those were my father's words in that last note of his; there they are, in Hungarian. *Ne Habozzon.*' And then she resumed writing.

6

My beloved Belinda,

Please forgive me for having clipped the wings of your happiness by failing to acknowledge—and stopping your father from acknowledging—the clearest, most obvious thing in the world: that you and Eli are very, very deeply in love. Your happiness is what I want more than anything in the world and I won't stand in the way of it any longer.

There is a tragic but also absurd irony behind my behaviour towards you these past few months. I have refused to respond to your father's entreaties to try to meet, or even phone, Eli's parents. For one thing, I am quite sure that they want nothing to do with us—except perhaps to offer some threat or bribe to keep you away from their son. For another thing, I don't think that I could remain polite towards them and their tribal rejectionism.

Just like your father and I, and anybody who sees the two of you together, Eli's parents also cannot fail to realise how much their son is in love with you and they will want his happiness just as much as Dad and I want yours. But it is of the utmost importance to them, a matter of family survival even, to see their son marry in a synagogue—and the irony is that THEY CAN.

You see, my darling, I have tried to spare you the details of my past history beyond telling you that I was captured in the war and that your father and I met soon afterwards, that I lived as a child in Hungary, that my parents died when I was very young and that I have no family.

This is not the entire truth and now that you have grown into a beautiful, intelligent and understanding young woman it is time to tell you the real story.

185

You see, my father, my mother—your grandparents—and I were all captured by the Nazis and put into the concentration camps. All of us were in Auschwitz, in Poland, and I was also in Bergen-Belsen, in Germany.

I didn't tell you how my parents—your grandparents—died because I didn't want to upset you. I didn't want to tell you they were Jewish because I didn't want to burden you.

I did tell you that your grandfather was a clever man and that you might have inherited your love of music from your grandmother but I hid the fact that we were Jewish.

I always kept it vague in case you asked questions but my mother, Sarah, was an exceptionally talented pianist; my father—your grandfather Chaim—was a doctor. They came and seized him one evening without warning and we never saw him again. I discovered later that he was sent to Auschwitz. Your grandmother and I were taken there but did not see him. There we were separated, and I ended up several months later in Belsen, from where the British army, in the shape of your adorable father, liberated me.

While I survived, my parents did not. When I feel ready to describe my experiences from the night of my father's arrest until your father came along, I will, and also tell you something of my childhood in Budapest. But the important thing now is for you to tell Eli, and for him to tell his family, that according to even the most Orthodox of rabbis, your mother is 100 per cent Jewish and that means that you, Belinda my angel, are also Jewish.

I can't carry on writing at this moment. I am shaking. I feel too emotional and the quicker I get it to you, the quicker you can take steps to achieve your dream. There will be much to talk about when you have absorbed all this.

Be happy, my loved one. My blessing upon your love.

Please forgive me for deceiving you all this time.

Your loving mother

The next day was the most emotional in Belinda Vane's young life. The evening found her, along with her parents, at the Elms for a hastily arranged family session with a woman called Deborah Foreman, who had been Belinda's supervising therapist during her stay there. Belinda had taken up Deborah's suggestion that she should keep in touch and had phoned her three or four times since her discharge to report on developments. To Belinda's gratified surprise, her erstwhile rigidly neutral and non-committal therapist had expressed pleasure and encouragement in relation to Belinda's relationship with Eli.

It was also one of the most joyous days of Belinda's life. It had started with the disorientating experience of slowly reading her mother's letter, the content and consequences of which took some time for her to absorb. When she did, she immediately broke her self-imposed rule of never telephoning Eli at home. It was still relatively early in the morning and she knew that he wasn't going in to work that day until late afternoon to help with the half-yearly stocktaking so she rang the Brondesbury house. Fortunately, it was Eli who answered.

'Tell me,' she asked him, 'how many Jews did you meet at the Elms?'

Eli responded with a little laugh and said: 'Apart from three or four of the medical staff, I would say there were none. I certainly don't recall any other Jewish patients there. What's this about?'

'I'll tell you in a minute. First, I have another question for you. How many Jews would you say live in our road in Esher?'

'Haven't a clue. Belinda, what are you talking about?'

'It's very hard for me to explain. I have to see you today.'

'We've already arranged to meet.'

'I know but I can't wait until lunchtime.'

'My darling, are you going to keep me in suspense? What is this all about?'

'The answers to my questions are, there was one other Jew in the Elms and there are at least two Jewish residents in my road.'

'Really? So?'

She took a deep breath. 'You remember I told you that my mother was Hungarian?'

There was a brief pause at both ends of the telephone line.

'Oh my God,' said Eli, half-anticipating what was about to be revealed.

'Yes,' announced Belinda. 'Anna Vane, née Weisz, born in Budapest to Sarah and Chaim Weisz, both of whom died in Auschwitz…' At this, she dissolved in tears and could hear Eli gasping at the other end of the line.

Within a couple of hours, they were urgently embracing alongside the exit to the platform at Waterloo station at which Belinda's train had just arrived. Eli had dashed from his house without making any contact with his parents, both of whom were out when Belinda called. He needed to hear this news from Belinda's own mouth. It was too much to take in, or even believe, without some physical confirmation.

'Oh my darling Belinda, I don't know what to say.' Later, he would beg her for details and insist that they buy a bottle of champagne—for now, he was just trying to look into her eyes but she had squeezed them shut.

'You don't have to say anything,' she said, opening her eyes at last. And neither of them did speak for a while as he wrapped his arms around her in consummate joy.

For Belinda, this was the third cathartic embrace of the day. After Anna had given her time to read and absorb the contents of the letter, the two women had held each other long, tightly and wordlessly, their voices combining in a piercing cry, like that of a newborn child. Next, she had thrown her arms around Roderick, abandoning her habitual way of addressing him as 'Pa' and reverting to her childhood style, repeating: 'Daddy, Daddy.' And then: 'What a good and strong man you are. I love you both so much.'

By the time Belinda reached the Elms to meet her parents and Deborah Foreman, her mass of emotions had reduced into a kind of guilty happiness. During the family session, she and Roderick sat either side of Anna, each of them holding one of her hands. While Deborah was speaking—so much more fully than Belinda had thought her capable, so silent had she been for such long periods during their one-to-one consultations—Belinda and Roderick kept protective eyes on Anna, whose own eyes produced a constant trickle that she allowed to flow untouched.

The most dramatic moment came when Anna took off the cardigan she was wearing, rolled up her sleeve and showed her daughter the tattoo on her forearm, the permanent mark of her degradation by the Nazis. The letter 'A' followed by five numerals, which looked as though it had been written with a fading ballpoint pen. The skin around it was a little rough and blotchy as though Anna had tried to scrape it off or cover it up.

'How on earth have you concealed that from me?' Belinda, shocked, put her hands up to her face and then took hold of her mother's hand more firmly than before.

'By being very careful,' Anna replied. 'Too careful. For too many years.'

'But you bathed me when I was a child. Took me swimming.'

'When I bathed you I always wore my towelling dressing gown. It got a little wet but that didn't matter. I had all sorts of stories ready in case you ever saw this… this mark of shame. I would have said I'd had to remember a telephone number and quickly written it on my arm because there was no paper, that sort of thing. I was paranoid.'

In the course of the conversation, Deborah Foreman revealed that her own father had lost two brothers and several cousins to the Nazi death machine, and Belinda came away with an entirely new view of her former dispenser of pills.

When Eli imparted the news that evening in Brondesbury, his father's initial elation was quickly mitigated by Farah's scepticism.

'Are you sure?' she asked, disbelievingly. 'It might be a ruse, a way of hooking you.'

'My God, I hope not,' said Yusuf. 'But that would be so extreme. It would be the end as far as I'm concerned. I have to admit, it does sound too good to be true.'

'*Honestly*,' Eli was becoming exasperated while trying hard to understand and sympathise with his parents' feelings. 'Who could possibly make up a story like that? And it's hardly too *good* to be true, Dad. Belinda's mother's experiences are not exactly happy.'

'I'm sorry, son. You know what I mean.'

'Eli,' said Farah, suddenly grabbing her son by the shoulders. 'I pray that it is true and then we must invite Belinda's parents to come to dinner as soon as we can.'

'You know,' said Eli the next day to Belinda, 'I've always loved all that Baghdadi-Jewish culture but I'm feeling disenchanted by my parents' version of it right now. We are all exactly the same people that we were a week ago. Essentially, nothing has changed. So why is it suddenly all right because of some technical biological detail? Not even biological but because of some old racist religious policy.'

They were having a muted celebration in the tiny Indian restaurant in Maida Vale. Eli was intent on not allowing his parents to imagine that they were forgiven for their exclusivist attitudes whereas Belinda was more tolerant towards them. When he had asked her if she felt Jewish, laughing as she was about to put a forkful of decidedly unkosher *dhansak* into her mouth, she had answered, with a caught-in-the-act smile, 'well, just you try and stop me having a full-blown Jewish wedding.'

But, before all that, there were plenty of formalities to tackle. And, over the course of the following Saturday evening when Roderick, Anna and Belinda went to dinner in Brondesbury to share a lavish table of Iraqi-Jewish cuisine with Yusuf and Farah Haroun, their children Leah and Eli, Yusuf's mother, Rivke Haroun, and Leah's fiancé David Marks, these were explained to the Vanes.

It turned out to be an evening of the most improbable delights. For the first time since Eli's eighteenth birthday party, Yusuf and Farah had opened up the double-doors that divided their already large dining room and a smaller sitting room to form one enormous area, creating space for a couple of polished inlaid tables bearing various pre-dinner drinks and snacks, including delicate little *kebba* meatballs, some mixed with beetroot, others with okra; as well as dishes filled with almonds, walnuts, figs and dates.

After the formal introductions and the politely exchanged observations about the Harouns' house, the Vanes' journey, Leah and David's wedding plans and the unseasonably mild weather, the initial awkwardness melted away, mainly because of the sheer glow of love emanating from Eli and Belinda.

If any nervousness lingered once they were all seated, it was dispelled by Rivke unaffectedly stroking Anna's arm and remarking to her: 'My dear, you and your daughter are an exceptionally beautiful pair of women,' adding, in order to lighten the proceedings: 'You know, you could almost be Iraqi,' at which everybody laughed, no one more heartily than Eli.

Roderick was placed alongside David Marks who, having enjoyed a course in military history as part of his university degree, was excited to be sitting next to a man who had seen action in the war. Accordingly, David probed Roderick with questions. Farah was on Roderick's other side and, although her having constantly to stand up to attend to some aspect of the meal prevented any lengthy conversation, she enjoyed responding to Roderick's genuinely interested questions about her dazzling culinary skills.

Rivke volunteered as dispassionate an account of the *Farhud* as she could manage and, moving on to more agreeable and colourful recollections of life in Baghdad, paved the way for Anna to talk about her parents and friends in her early life in Budapest. It was a liberating experience for her and it was all she could do not to direct her words exclusively at Belinda—which would not have been necessary, for her daughter was entirely captivated by Anna's story, and listened with a mixture of admiration and adoration.

It was a strangely comforting feeling for Anna to be able to talk freely about her parents to a group of virtual strangers. She had anticipated a highly strained evening but it was turning out to be the opposite. 'I really loved Friday nights,' she heard herself saying, before describing the family gatherings around her parents' table in Dembinszky Street, how her father humorously poured scorn upon the Orthodox Jews of Hungary, how her two grandmothers were treated like queens and given the best chairs with cushions, how she loved to play tricks upon her cousins, and how her mother would feign reluctance when urged to play the piano.

'You play the piano, too, Mrs Vane. I've heard you.' After three glasses of wine, Eli was speaking a little too loudly. 'She plays brilliantly,' he announced to the room.

'You must play for us,' said Farah. 'Our piano is never played these days. Both of the children had lessons but neither of them took it seriously. It would be lovely to hear it again after all these years.'

191

'Oh, really, I couldn't,' said Anna, and when she again declined as others, including Belinda, pressed her, she said: 'My goodness, I sound like my mother.'

'Of course you do,' said Rivke. 'Your mother lives on in you, just as her mother lived on in her.'

And so Anna, also becalmed by wine—in her case, just one small glass—moved to the unused, out-of-tune piano in the corner of the dining room and played, with controlled emotion, the *Heroic Polonaise*, and became again the small girl in her school in Budapest, over forty years earlier, playing the same music on a different piano, but one also left forgotten in the corner of a room.

And, once more, she could see the look of utter astonishment on the face of her friend Eva Kaller. Where was Eva now? Was she even alive? Anna was brought back to the present moment at the conclusion of the piece when the silent attention of her audience was broken by loud applause.

After this, to everybody's overwhelming surprise, Farah stood up and announced that she wanted to say something. The murmurs died down and eight faces were directed at their hostess, each of them indicating acute curiosity.

'This has been a very special evening,' she said. 'I have learnt a lot. It has been a great pleasure to welcome Anna and Roderick, Belinda's parents, here and, as I say, it has been very special. And may I say now that I want Eli to ensure that it does not end here but to make it his business to find a special ring for his very… special… *Jewish… fiancée*—if I may use that word. So please, everyone else, raise your glasses and toast: Eli and Belinda!'

Even allowing for the fact that Farah had drunk three-and-a-half glasses of sparkling wine—probably more than she had consumed in the preceding twelve months—this was a remarkable speech. Here she was, publicly urging her son to pledge himself to a young woman of whom she had been speaking in base, contemptuous terms a matter of mere days earlier. And, in the opinion of both of the young lovers, making an admission of guilt and asking for forgiveness.

'Mum, I'm in shock,' Eli said, hugging Farah.

The next morning, when Anna telephoned to thank Farah for her spectacular hospitality, Farah continued in much the same vein, offering to

192

hold an informal engagement party at the Brondesbury house. And, when Anna again thanked her and insisted that she and Roderick take care of the wedding, Farah promptly offered to be responsible for the food.

'If it's anything like we had last night I'm sure we'll be very happy with that.'

'I'll make myself available to help with whatever you need.'

'That's very kind. It has been a long time since I had anything to do with a kosher celebration.'

'You can leave that to me,' Farah said. 'Yusuf and I will help with the required formalities. As I mentioned yesterday, the children need to go to the Jewish rabbinical court to obtain permission to get married in the proper Jewish way. This court is called the Beth Din in Hebrew—please stop me if I'm telling you something you already know—and our rabbi at Lauderdale Road will vouch for Eli's character and confirm that he is Jewish.

'This can also be done by Leah's fiancé David's uncle, Tony Pomerance, who is himself a rabbi—he will be marrying David and Leah. I think they mentioned last night that they all wanted to be married by the same rabbi—and maybe even have a double wedding. That's why I think it will be a good idea to do the formalities through Rabbi Pomerance's Beth Din, which is different from the one we Baghdadi Jews answer to. Eli can also take along the *ketubah*—the Hebrew wedding certificate that Yusuf gave me at our wedding.'

'I know what a *ketubah* is.'

'Oh, yes, of course. I'm sorry.' And then, in her unconscious excitement, 'do you still have your… your mother's *ketubah?*'

Fully ten seconds passed before Anna answered with the quiet firmness that a patient adult uses to a child who has asked a foolish question: 'No.'

'Well, don't worry, Yusuf and I will vouch for Belinda. And for you. We will get the rabbi at Lauderdale Road, our synagogue, to write to the other Beth Din. Oh, and Eli and Belinda should really start attending synagogue. It will certainly be necessary for a period before the actual date once that is agreed upon. Yusuf and I will be happy to accompany them to Lauderdale Road.'

'That is very kind. Thank you. But you will need to take that up with Eli and Belinda themselves.'

This conversation was immediately followed by another. Belinda snatched the telephone as soon as Anna had stopped talking to Farah so that she could talk to Eli, which she did for the next thirty minutes.

'There's something that Eli has in common with Pa,' Belinda told her mother when she had eventually put down the telephone.

'Oh, what's that?'

'He wants to get married as soon as it's humanly possible. He thinks we should go to the Beth Din as soon as we can after the letter from the Harouns' rabbi arrives.'

'And I sense that you similarly have something in common with me,' Anna said.

'What do you mean? I have a million things in common with you.'

'I know, sweetheart, but when Daddy said he wanted to get married quickly I was one hundred per cent in favour. And I think you are, too.'

The Reverend Solomon Eshvinoff was born to be a clerk. Pale, bookish and short-sighted, he was unmistakably an indoor man. His clothes matched the greyness of his hair, though most of the time this was covered by a black, velvet *koppel*. The dull sparseness of his beard was offset by a surprisingly black, pencil moustache that sat neatly, like a new hat, above his upper lip. His nose was of a length and protuberant sharpness that caused it to appear to have been created specifically to support the wire-rimmed spectacles that permanently straddled it.

Reverend Eshvinoff was a devout man and was therefore more than pleased to occupy the post to which he believed himself to be ideally suited, that of clerk to the judges of a Jewish religious court. Indeed, his pleasure at being paid to work for the Beth Din of one of Britain's main Orthodox Jewish movements was such that it bordered on complacency and he could not help but present to the world a somewhat self-congratulatory air.

This was the man with whom Eli and Belinda were granted an appointment when they made their application to get married, in the words of the official regulations, 'in accordance with Jewish religious tradition and practice.' Eli brought with him his birth and bar mitzvah certificates, his parents' *ketubah*, and a letter confirming his status from the rabbi of Lauderdale Road Synagogue. Belinda brought her birth certificate and a letter from that same rabbi.

The clerk's office was cramped, musty and had one small window that let in very little light. This clearly did not bother Reverend Eshvinoff as he carefully perused Eli's documents first, tracing his index finger along each line, nodding and occasionally allowing a sound—'hmm' or 'yee-es'—to emerge through his closed mouth.

Reverend Eshvinoff was nothing if not thorough. He took pride in his work and took care not to let standards slip. 'We are probably the strictest Beth Din in the world,' he often remarked to those who came before him. This, he believed, was a good thing. And here he was, at the heart of a very important legal authority, personally entrusted with the responsibility of making official pronouncements and even issuing life-changing verdicts.

In short, Reverend Eshvinoff was a man who derived great satisfaction from his role as gatekeeper to a body of indisputably wise men authorised to marry, convert, divorce, adjudicate, condemn or otherwise pronounce judgment. 'Sometimes people have clearly come to the wrong place altogether,' was another of his regular utterances. 'They don't have any idea.' But his keynote phrase was: 'It's important that we maintain the highest of standards.'

'Well, that seems to be in order,' he said to Eli, handing back his documents. 'But I will need to speak to you both further about the important preparations you need to make in order to undertake a Jewish marriage. So please wait until I have finished with your fiancée. May I see your papers, miss?' he asked, turning to Belinda. 'You don't appear to have much with you. Do you have your parents' *ketubah*?' he asked, looking sceptically at the Lauderdale Road rabbi's letter of commendation.

'No, they don't have one,' said Belinda brightly. 'They didn't marry in a synagogue.'

'I see,' said Reverend Eshvinoff. 'I'm afraid,' he continued, holding up Belinda's birth certificate and the rabbinical reference in his two separate hands, 'this is not enough to enable me to grant you permission to have a Jewish wedding ceremony. You haven't even brought your parents' official secular marriage certificate. I know neither that they are married nor that they are Jewish.'

'My father is not Jewish,' Belinda felt her face reddening. 'My mother is.'

'Ah, but can you prove it?'

195

Now, Belinda, buoyed by Eli's enthusiastic support, delivered her trump card: 'My mother was in Auschwitz. My grandparents were murdered by the Nazis.'

'Her mother was also in Belsen.' Eli sought to press the case.

'I am very sorry to hear that,' said Reverend Eshvinoff, addressing Belinda without deviating from his standard bureaucratic tone, 'but your fiancé's rabbi makes no mention of that. He says very little. He merely states that, "I have it on the entirely trustworthy authority of respected congregants that this young lady and her mother are persons of good character, that her mother is Jewish and that the young lady herself is more than capable of running a kosher, Jewish home."

'I have to tell you that this is nowhere near good enough. Are you, incidentally, capable of running a truly Jewish, kosher home? Have you had any Jewish education at all?'

'Yes, no, I am sure I can learn.'

At this, Reverend Eshvinoff involuntarily snorted and then quickly continued. 'You have my deepest sympathies, young lady, for your family tragedy,' he said, fixing Belinda with a stare that made her feel she was being pinned to the wall by his sharp nose, 'but I'm afraid that doesn't prove anything. There were other, gentile prisoners in Auschwitz. Gypsies and Polish Catholics, for example. After all, you admit you don't have any Jewish education or knowledge and, if I may say so, there is nothing particularly Jewish about your appearance. I am sorry, I cannot accept this application,' he said shaking his head and standing up.

'Can you believe that vile bastard?' Now it was Eli who was shaking his head as he and Belinda walked out of the Beth Din office into the street dazed from their peremptory interview.

'I'm honestly not sure I want a big wedding if that's the kind of person in charge of it,' said Belinda in a shocked, dejected tone. 'I feel kind of violated. I came to arrange the happiest day of my life and I'm made to feel like a liar.'

'Come on,' said Eli. 'Let me take you home.'

'Yes, come and have lunch, and maybe a strong drink.'

Anna was pleased to see them both arrive together. 'Eli can stay for lunch, can't he, Ma?' Belinda asked as soon as they walked through the front door.

196

'Of course, and Dad's home, too, so we can all eat together. But come into the kitchen and tell me, how did it go today?'

Lunch had to wait while Anna, standing at one end of the kitchen table, absorbed—and reacted to—the couple's report of the interview that had taken place a couple of hours earlier. 'What kind of pig is this,' Anna said, her fury mounting. She called Roderick from his study and told him what had happened. 'I shall go and see this man, this Eshvi whatever. Who does he think he is? Is this what a survivor of Auschwitz and Belsen can expect from a fellow-Jew in London?'

Roderick was reminded of his first sight of her, of her big brown eyes shining out across the makeshift hospital ward set up within breathing distance of the foul air of Bergen-Belsen. Those eyes had mesmerised him. But he had never before seen them ablaze, as they were now.

She telephoned the Beth Din office and demanded an urgent appointment, which she was granted for the following afternoon. 'Tomorrow, Eli and Belinda,' she said in a voice of steely determination, 'you will both come with me to see this servile Hebrew. We will see him at three.' Whatever remained of Anna's bottled-up emotions was released in her venom directed at Reverend Eshvinoff—which came out laced with the faintest, but clearly discernible, Hungarian accent.

The next day, at the Beth Din, when Reverend Eshvinoff ushered them into his office, greeting them with a brisk 'Good afternoon' and gesturing them towards three seats facing his desk, Anna remained standing. 'So you are Mrs Vane, Belinda's mother, I take it. Please be seated,' said Eshvinoff, having consulted the thin file before him.

Anna ignored his invitation to sit down and, before he could speak again, held up her palm and entered upon the speech she had been planning in her mind since the previous day. She began with a deferred response to his greeting: 'Good afternoon.' And continued, looking pointedly into Eshvinoff's eyes. 'I notice that you offer your hand to my daughter's fiancé but not to my daughter or to me. Nevertheless, I offer you my hand.'

As Reverend Eshvinoff opened his mouth to respond, Anna remained standing, rolled up her sleeve and thrust her arm towards him so that he could see her tattoo from Auschwitz. He was unable to speak and had turned even paler than his normal hue. He automatically declined to shake Anna's hand. She withdrew it slowly and carefully rolled down her sleeve, all the time fixing him with a stare.

'And in here,' she said, taking an envelope from her handbag, 'is the written authority that you need to give your *permission*'—the word was uttered with devastating contempt—'to my daughter to marry this man. These are two very, very valuable documents. Kindly photocopy them, taking great care, and give me back the originals.'

She then produced from the envelope the letter from the United Nations Relief and Rehabilitation Administration officially confirming the deaths of her parents in Auschwitz and, in its plastic cover along with a certified English translation, the last scribbled note from her father that she had carried and concealed for more than thirty years.

'My father's name,' she told the cowed official seated opposite her, 'was Chaim Aaron Weisz. *Doctor* Chaim Aaron Weisz. You doubtless set great store by purity. Well you must preserve the purity of this piece of paper,' she added, indicating her father's note. 'If you fail to do so, may your heart be tainted—even more than it is now—forever.' And, as she continued to stare, Eshvinoff's face became transformed, in her eyes, into that of a trilby-hatted man staring at her, whispering 'goodnight' before taking Anna's father away.

Only then did Anna sit down.

Belinda and Eli quickly put their first encounter with Reverend Eshvinoff behind them, though the second meeting, at which Anna reduced the man to a frightened animal, was one that they would continue to cherish for years. As they would their nuptials.

For several weeks beforehand, the atmosphere at the homes of both the bride's and the groom's families was transformed into that of a wedding-planning cottage-industry. In Esher, it began tentatively, until the mooted double wedding with Leah and David was finally abandoned after David had a skiing accident that put him in hospital for a fortnight and left him limping badly for weeks thereafter. Once that decision had been taken, Roderick and Anna dropped all remaining inhibitions and sprang into action.

'It's lucky we've had a good year.' Roderick said, referring to the profits of Vane Natural Clothing as he contemplated the cost of it all.

In the spirit of romance, Roderick and Anna decided to hold the reception—which was to be a jubilant affair of varied cultural influences—at the Savoy hotel, where they would stay overnight in the very room in which, almost a quarter-of-a-century earlier, the bride—their

198

daughter—had been conceived in the afterglow of Schubert, Tchaikovsky and Elgar at the Royal Albert Hall.

David Marks's uncle, Rabbi Anthony Pomerance, the man who would marry Eli and Belinda, was a genial, rotund Scotsman who had been the minister of a sedate, outer London, Orthodox synagogue for almost three decades. On the first meeting in his office to discuss the marriage, in notable contrast to Reverend Eshvinoff, he stood up from his desk and almost bounced, like the large ball he resembled, over to the young couple in repetitive greeting—'*Mazal Tov, Mazal Tov!*' He then shook hands with Eli and Roderick conveying equal warmth to both, nodded with a smile to Anna and Belinda, and drew Yusuf and Farah into a collective hug as if they were old friends, though they had met him only two or three times.

Rabbi Pomerance seemed as flexible and reasonable as Reverend Eshvinoff had been rigid and bigoted. 'I must confess,' he said laughing, 'I am a little disappointed that I've lost the opportunity of officiating for the first time in my career at a double wedding, thanks to my nephew failing to distinguish himself on the slopes in the manner in which he does in the courts.'

Roderick was quite taken aback when the Rabbi then whispered to him in a broad Glaswegian accent: 'Never mind. It'll be one for the price of two, eh?'

The main point of discussion at that initial meeting was Eli's wish to design the *ketubah*. 'What a wonderful idea,' Rabbi Pomerance beamed. 'So long as it's kosher, my boy. Are you an artist?'

'I like to think so,' answered the young groom.

And so Eli set to work, with a mixture of enthusiasm, amusement and scepticism, drawing up a document addressed to Belinda, promising, in return for becoming his wife 'according to the laws of Moses and Israel', to 'honour, support and feed' her and ensure that she would receive 'the necessities of life and conjugal needs according to the universal custom.' He based the design on a *ketubah* from Renaissance Italy and incorporated a phrase from Shakespeare's Sonnet 27—which had supplanted 'Shall I compare thee to a summer's day?' as Eli's favourite.

The Shakespearean theme received its apotheosis in the exquisite, seventeenth-century-style English wedding dress that Margaret commissioned for her granddaughter from an aristocratic dressmaker who lived in Esher, using yards of white silk from the stock of Anna's Designs.

And, as well as working on the *ketubah*, Eli decided to compose a sonnet, to be read aloud at the wedding.

Although Roderick and Anna took on responsibility for the overall planning for the big day, they did accept Yusuf's offer to pay for the ceremony—which would be conducted at the Savoy by Rabbi Pomerance, augmented by Rabbi Lobatto, a participating guest from the Lauderdale Road Synagogue—and for the musicians at the reception, a mixture of Iraqi performers and the Savoy's resident small orchestra.

While Eli was working at home on the *ketubah*, his speech and his sonnet, Belinda went for fittings to her dressmaker, Miss Ursula Scott, and wondered at the detailed creativity of this supremely skilful woman as, week by week, the dress took on more of its seventeenth-century shape.

Belinda also prepared, and constantly rehearsed, her own wedding speech, which began with, 'Eli, your love has enriched me', and concluded with '… my mother, my father—and husband—I never knew I could experience such unlimited love.'

After almost six months of all this activity, the day eventually came and the parties stood under the wedding canopy in a room set aside and decorated at the Savoy. There were intrigued murmurs among those present who understood Hebrew when Rabbi Pomerance, reciting the *ketubah* that the groom was about to give to the bride, declaimed the words, '*machshevotai mipa'atei mishkani elayich orgot hen aliyat regel*'—the Hebrew for 'my thoughts, from far where I abide, intend a zealous pilgrimage to thee'—and still more murmurs, mainly of appreciation, when the rabbi read out the *ketubah* in English and explained that the bridegroom had borrowed those words from Shakespeare.

Rivke, drunk on nostalgia for Baghdad's 'last *simcha*', watched through a mist of time as Eli, exactly as Yusuf had done a third of a century before, stamped on the traditional glass.

Rabbi Pomerance explained this was, 'according to some to momen-*tarrrily* mitigate the unfettered joy of the occasion lest the bride and groom ignore and fall foul of worldly hardship or, according to others, was to mourn the destruction of the Temple, or, according to still others, was simply to bring a bit of sobriety to the proceedings. But that won't make me, as a Scot, refrain from toasting our happy couple with a glass of whisky.'

Yusuf tried hard, but failed, to resist a tinge of sadness as he, too, remembered his own wedding at which he had stood alongside his father

Sami. But this did not undermine his joy, all these years later, at the sight of not just his sensible, dutiful daughter but also his unstable, rebellious son singing the words of Psalm 137: 'If I forget thee, O Jerusalem, may my right hand forget its cunning.'

After Belinda faultlessly delivered her speech towards the end of the opulent wedding banquet curated by Farah Haroun, Eli was on his feet. He began by describing the wonder of the day as beyond measure adding, to laughter, that, 'to see my old friend, best man, and world-champion scruff, Ramon Saul, looking like James Bond in a perfectly fitting, elegant dinner-jacket and a black bow—not clip-on but a real tie-it-yourself job—is itself possibly the eighth wonder of the world.'

He then thanked Ramon for his friendship, support and patience, acknowledging how much he had needed it and, now propelled by emotion, thanking his best man for having described him as 'one of nature's artists'. Eli then put aside his prepared speech and addressed his bride directly, praising her intelligence, kindness and sweetness, rounding off with the declaration that, 'while her dress is seventeenth-century, her beauty is eternal.'

He resumed less dreamily: 'Belinda and I have come along a rocky road to reach this happy ending, though that is nothing compared to the hardships and pain endured by some members of our families, united here tonight, and I want to reflect on that in a sonnet—Belinda's and my favourite art form—that I have written for the occasion.'

And then he gave his attentive listeners what was, as a happily tipsy Cedric Vane remarked at the time, 'almost certainly the first reading of an original sonnet by its author in the entire, magnificent history of the Savoy Hotel':

'Of music and marriage and love I would sing,
Or my mistress's sweetness of breath,
But that would forget too many a thing,
Like hatred, starvation and death.
All had their part to play in the chance
That brings us together today;
We must heed the loss before we can dance,
We, some of us, must stand and pray.
We shall then, all of us, be ready to bless
My sole and unparalleled choice—
My bride, my love, my Hebrew princess

So English of bearing and voice.
After the storm, we feel the sun's gaze;
May it warm us for all of our days.'

Between them, the Iraqi band, the Savoy musicians and their vocal-
ists brought the guests to their feet with an exuberant range of style and
content. The Middle Eastern and European aspects of the menu blended
perfectly. And the Savoy's River Room glowed continuously from the
sunshine of the afternoon to the evening's electric dazzle.

Within a week of returning from a Roman honeymoon, both Belinda
and Eli had spoken to their therapists. Eli rang Alan Alfassa to thank
him for his help in the past and to report, long after the event, how his
attending the blind date arranged by his parents had served to confirm
his total devotion to Belinda. In Belinda's case, it was Deborah Foreman
who phoned her, to ask about the wedding and how Belinda's mother
had adjusted to the changed circumstances of her life.

'Pretty well, I would say,' Belinda replied. 'There's no obstacle Anna
Vane can't overcome. And she and my pa are pleased to see their daughter so happy. All these changes are actually really exciting. Eli and I *love*
our flat.'

And, indeed, they had comfortably adapted to living in an upper-sto-
rey conversion of a substantial terraced house in Chalk Farm, north
of Camden Town, and took great pleasure in the novelty of shopping,
cooking and cleaning together in their own household.

Early on in their tenancy, they gave a dinner party around their large
kitchen table. The choice of guests was perhaps unlikely given the striking
contrasts—physically and philosophically—between them. Eli invited
his best man, Ramon Saul with his younger sister Nina. Belinda invited
her long-time friend from her schooldays, Christine Thornington, who
had missed the wedding because she was away on holiday. Christine
came to Chalk Farm with her boyfriend Charles Appleyard, a solicitor.

It was a bold move to mix the dark-skinned Indian Jews, the Sauls,
who were fervent Labour party supporters (Nina was a volunteer at her
local constituency office), with the pale-skinned, fair-haired Conserva-
tive-voting couple across the table from them.

While Ramon and Nina were secular Jews, Christine had, since meeting
the churchgoing Charles, begun to revive her childhood Christianity.

Moreover, Ramon was a guitar-playing collector of rock'n'roll records, while Christine played the cello and had little or no interest in anything other than classical music—and hymns. Charles thought there was too much foreign immigration into the United Kingdom, Nina thought there was too little. And, if all that wasn't enough, Ramon—and to some extent Nina—followed the fortunes of Arsenal Football Club, while Charles loathed football and Christine's sole outdoor pursuit was horse riding.

'We're going to have to be referees,' Belinda warned Eli once they had realised the implications of bringing these disparate pairs together.

In the event, it was heated but stimulating, with spirited argument over the prime ministerial qualities of Harold Wilson, trade unions, the football World Cup, town-living versus country-living, the cinema, the theatre, weddings and even religion. But such was the good-humoured aura of the host and hostess and the success of their adaptation of a couple of Farah's recipes that the atmosphere turned neither sour nor flat but was full of laughter and enthusiasm.

After dinner, Christine reminded Belinda how, back at St Madeleine's, the two of them, along with a clutch of other choir members, would raise the school roof with full-blooded versions of their favourite hymns, 'Dear Lord and Father of Mankind' and 'Praise My Soul, the King of Heaven'. Belinda was surprised to find how warm this memory of her young, 'pre-Jewish' state remained, and needed little persuasion to lustily re-enact, with Christine, their erstwhile, schoolgirl devotion, bringing on applause and accompaniment from the others.

Even so, it was after this dinner party that Eli called Alan Alfassa and made an appointment to see him.

'I can't just throw off my parachute,' was how he explained this to Belinda. 'I am so ridiculously happy to be your husband,' he told her, 'that I keep worrying that something will happen to spoil my happiness. Having been so depressed for so long, I can't believe in the reality of this intense joy.'

Belinda's response was to pull him on to their bed, remove both her clothes and his, and show him that nothing was likely to spoil it any time soon. As they rolled and laughed and hugged, Eli uttered the words 'I love you' a hundred times.

But he kept his appointment with Dr Alfassa and found there were still anxieties to be aired. He had been disturbed when, at the height of the table arguments with Ramon, Nina, Christine and Charles, his opinions had been dismissed, once as 'ridiculous' and once as 'mad'. The others had laughed on both occasions, and so had Eli, as he put on an affronted act with an 'I'll-show-you-"ridiculous"-young-lady,' attitude to Nina, and a mock-sarcastic 'thank you very much, I'm sure' to Charles.

'My laughter was partly in the spirit of the occasion,' Eli told Alfassa, 'but was also to cover my feelings of being irritated and even a bit hurt. I'm far happier than I have ever been in my life but still feel that I'm not going to be able to carry on coping. I'm so annoyed with myself about this. I feel it's so self-indulgent when I am living with such a beautiful, intelligent and loving woman. And in that particular case, it would be right to say I am mad—mad about her. Oh, I don't know… I feel so fragile and I suppose somewhere deep down I can't believe that someone as wonderful as Belinda can actually love somebody like me.

'On the way here, a pretty girl passed me on the pavement from the opposite direction and she had a big smirk on her face. And I couldn't help feeling that it was directed at me. That I am in some way laughable. Whenever I hear people in twos, threes, whatever, laughing loudly in the street, I always think they are laughing at me and therefore I am a figure of fun, a laughable wretch. And if that's how I feel when I am in such a great situation, well… what is wrong with me?'

Although Alfassa said very little throughout the session, Eli felt more relaxed when he left, having unloaded some fears that he had not articulated before. 'I feel much better,' he told Belinda when she asked how it had gone.

'Good,' said Belinda. 'But don't forget, I know how to care for you, and I'll do it without payment.'

'I know, my love, but I don't want you to see me in a weak state.'

'You're not in a weak state. You are my strength. My rock. There aren't many who could fill that role. And, anyway, I want to see you in whatever state you are in. Don't you want to see me when I am weak? Crying out in childbirth, for example. Perhaps you don't want to see me naked, stripped of all my coverings.'

They both laughed at this and held each other tightly and very soon gloried once more in their physical nakedness and their love.

'When shall we have our first child?' Belinda whispered on the pillow.

'Let us be selfish and enjoy each other's exclusive company for a while first,' Eli replied.

'Fine by me,' said Belinda.

It would be three years before their first child would arrive, three years in which they were constantly together, never spending a single night apart. Three years in which they travelled to a dozen countries.

These did not include Israel, despite Belinda's urging from the moment the wedding ring was on her finger. 'How hilarious,' Eli remarked, 'that you are persuading me to go to Israel, not even a year since my mother, wearing her bigot's hat, was trying to warn me off you, scared that you would contaminate our Jewish purity. Now look at you with your Israeli maps, your Hebrew books and your kosher Iraqi cuisine. You're much more Jewish than I am. But, yes, let's go one day. But let's have children first, so that we can take them.'

While Eli continued contentedly working with his father by day, writing poetry most evenings and taking photographs at the weekend, Belinda landed a job as a junior editor at a large publishing house in central London, bringing home fat, unbound manuscripts, which piled up alongside Eli's notebooks and photo albums in the corner of their bedroom.

The two of them pursued interests together—swimming, tennis, Italian lessons—and separately. Belinda took up the piano again, and singing, and yoga; Eli attended art classes and took clarinet lessons. They read poetry to each other in bed, Eli extending beyond love poems to Belinda so as to try out his own experimental work on her. He also read to her from John Donne, Robert Frost, Marvell, Keats, Coleridge, the Israeli poet Yehuda Amichai, and of course 'the immortal sonnets of Shakespeare'.

Eli also took many photographs of Belinda, carefully collecting them in an album and hanging one, framed, on the kitchen wall—an off-guard, black and white image of her in repose, a strand of dark hair floating across her cheek, a suggestion of a smile around her eyes and mouth.

They entertained royally, friends in the kitchen, family in the living room—having carried the table through from the kitchen. They also ate out, sentimentally at the Maida Vale Indian restaurant, locally at Marine Ices, or more adventurously at the Pizza House in Goodge Street or Le Cellier du Midi in Hampstead, where they also sometimes drank with friends at the Holly Bush or the Spaniards Inn. Together they established a Sunday-morning ritual of going to one of a handful of local cafés to read the newspapers over coffee and croissants.

205

There were also regular visits to their parents, Friday nights in Brondesbury and Saturday or Sunday lunchtimes in Esher. Eli would also call in on his grandmother Rivke during weekday evenings for mint tea and date cake. Leah and David married three months after Eli and Belinda's wedding, setting up home in Hampstead Garden Suburb, and the two couples saw each other at least two or three times a month.

Eli thrived at the emporium and was part of the reason for the firm's growth in prosperity. In the spring of 1976, Azi and Ben opened a new retail outlet, a smart shop in Kentish Town and made Eli its manager. He was now living and working within a mile's radius, and was able to convert a small conservatory at the rear of the shop premises into a gallery where he sold framed copies of his photographic work and, in the course of time, even the odd drawing he had done at his art class. When he sold the first of these, the entire proceeds went on a bottle of celebratory champagne.

In May 1977, Belinda gave birth to a daughter, Sarah, named after Anna's mother. As the little flat became even more cluttered, Eli's camera proliferated a wealth of images of Sarah—mostly alone, but also with her mother, her father, grandparents, great-grandparents, aunt, uncle and various combinations of these including, just a couple of months later, a cousin. This was Hannah, the first-born child of Leah and David.

Eli and Belinda's second daughter, Emily, arrived in June 1979. That same month, Rivke was taken to hospital with a trapped gallstone. She was home a mere three days after being operated on, with the nurse who delivered her by wheelchair to Yusuf's waiting car describing Rivke as 'a tough and determined lady'.

On the journey home, Rivke told Yusuf that, while in hospital, she'd had vivid, disturbing dreams, of wandering in the alleys of old Baghdad, and young boys in bare feet running past her as she tried to stop them to help her buy lemonade for Eli—'but they just kept running'.

Eli became very anxious about his grandmother and questioned his father about her at the earliest opportunity after Yusuf and Farah had eased her back into her own bed.

'I am so pleased to be home, with my family,' she cried, crying and clinging to her son and daughter-in-law in her gratitude. 'So pleased to be out of that place. Such noise. Such nightmares. I went in and I wasn't ill, and now I come out and I am ill. All those germs.'

'Is she going to be all right, Dad?' Eli was like a boy begging his father to chase away his night-time fears.

'Yes, I'm sure she is, but it'll take a little time,' said Yusuf, ruffling his son's hair as he used to when Eli was a boy. 'We'll take good care of her. You would think she'd have little strength after the operation but she hasn't stopped complaining since I went to pick her up from the hospital. So there can't be too much wrong.'

It was an eventful summer. At the Haroun carpet emporium, Azi and Ben both decided to reduce their hours and arranged a schedule in which one would work while the other took time off, the two of them coming in together only on Friday afternoons to review that week's business and prepare for the next.

The day-to-day management was now handed over to Yusuf, assisted by Ben's son Adam. Yusuf still hoped that Eli might eventually become a partner but recognised that Adam was far more committed to the company, and of more use to it, even though he was several years younger than Eli. Azi's children, meanwhile, were pursuing successful professional careers.

Once again, Leah followed Belinda's lead and her second child, a boy named Sami, was born in July. Around the same time, Belinda and Eli, with the financial assistance of Roderick and Yusuf, bought a ground-floor flat in Muswell Hill, another Victorian house conversion.

The move, a short distance to the north-east, was completed by the end of the month. In August, Ramon Saul became engaged to none other than Ruthie Menachem, Eli's one-off blind date. Eli naturally agreed to repay Ramon by performing the best-man duties at the wedding, planned for the following spring.

Deborah Foreman continued to call Belinda two or three times a year during the early years of her marriage.

Then, the day after Sarah's third birthday party, Belinda called Deborah for the first time. 'Can we talk?' Belinda asked.

'Depends,' said Deborah.

'On what?'

'On whether or not you want therapy.'

'I thought we were friends.'

'We are. But we also have a professional relationship and the two are entirely separate. I would say the phone is basically for the friendship.'

'I don't know if I want therapy. I want to talk to see if I do. I agree that would be better discussed face-to-face but am I going to have to *shlep*—you can hear how Jewish I'm becoming—down to Sunbury? Are you going to charge me?'

'Is that what you're worried about—becoming more Jewish?'

'No! And I didn't even mention that I was particularly worried.'

'Look, Belinda. You don't have to *shlep* to Sunbury, to the Elms. You can come to my home in Belsize Park. And I won't charge you. But if the discussion reveals a requirement for therapy, then the sessions thereafter will be chargeable as normal.'

'Hmm. I suppose that's fair.'

And so, the following Tuesday morning, Belinda went to see Deborah Foreman at her home in Belsize Park, not far from where Deborah's hero Sigmund Freud had lived during his years in London.

'Let's sit in the conservatory rather than the consulting room,' said Deborah, with a welcoming smile. 'Tea, coffee, walnut cake?'

'Now that's what I call therapy,' said Belinda. 'Tea, milk no sugar, and yes please a slice of walnut cake.'

'Take a seat in the shaded part of the conservatory. I'll be with you in a couple of minutes.'

Belinda called out after her: 'Eli has a conservatory in the family shop he is now managing. He's turned it into an art gallery.'

'So,' said Deborah, once the two women were comfortably seated either side of a coffee table on which were tea and cake. 'You wanted to talk.'

'Yes,' said Belinda. 'Both of us. I want *both* of us to talk, not just me. A friendly conversation. I don't want you to do that psychoanalytical-blotting-paper thing where you just sit there, absorbing, occasionally nodding but saying nothing. As you've said, it is not a therapy session. I would actually like to have your advice. That means both of us will be talking.'

'I'll do what I can.'

As she waited for Belinda to continue, Deborah smiled and placed her hands on the arms of her chair, trying, not altogether successfully, not to look like the professional therapist.

'Well, it's nothing serious,' said Belinda. 'I have a great life, a great marriage, great husband, great kids. I couldn't imagine anything better.'

'Fabulous.'

'Yes I know it is, but… it's very hard to pinpoint. It was Sarah's birthday party on Sunday. We held it in the garden and it was quite a success, I think. Eli was everywhere, organising games, playing music, telling silly jokes and stories. The children lapped it up. And he still had the energy to tell Sarah a bedtime story later. That's a real mutual admiration society, those two. A love-in.'

'Sounds brilliant.'

'Yes it does. It was. But in the course of the afternoon, when I was serving cakes and sandwiches and a couple of other mums were helping me, there was a crashing sound from inside the house, followed by Eli swearing very loudly. The children seemed not to notice and the mothers didn't hear anything, or perhaps they pretended not to hear.

'Anyway, once Eli and I had got our kids to bed and gone into the sitting room to recover, I asked him what that crashing sound was. He told me he had dropped the record player. It wasn't even damaged but he was very upset about this. He said he was "so useless". He told me he'd been dropping things all day long and this was the last straw; he was just incapable of functioning efficiently. I told him he had done brilliantly. Which he had—the children all loved him. And he turned to me, almost in tears, and yelled: "Don't patronise me," in my face. And then he stomped off to bed. I was so shocked.'

'I understand that you were upset,' said Deborah coolly. 'And I don't want to sound unsympathetic, but this is not an especially remarkable incident. He was clearly exhausted after all his efforts at the party. Did you make it up between you?'

'Immediately,' replied Belinda. 'I followed him to the bedroom no more than five minutes later. "I'm so, so sorry," he said and held me in his arms.' Belinda then seemed to stare into her cup of tea before taking a sip and continuing: 'But that's not him. He's not like that. At least, I didn't think he was. I thought—we both thought—that we were able to give each other all the support either of us required. And, yes, that we *would* go through the rest of our lives not fighting but totally loving each other for ever and ever amen.'

Belinda paused, took a breath and then another mouthful of tea and cake. Deborah's instinct was to remain silent and wait for Belinda to speak again but she knew that Belinda wanted her to say something.

'He's being very hard on himself,' Deborah ventured.

'He talks about bright blue skies having clouds suddenly floating across them, and I tell him he's wrong,' said Belinda, replacing her cup in its saucer. '"That's not us," I tell him. "In our skies, there are only sunbeams and rainbows".'

And, after a pause—in which Deborah remained instinctively silent—and a sip of tea, Belinda continued: 'But actually, I don't think he is wrong. I have to confess that I feel a bit the same. Why can't I just enjoy this wonderful gift of love without, inside my head, waiting for it to come crashing down? For goodness' sake, I couldn't ask for more than I've got. Two beautiful children, my own wonderful parents, and I know that Eli, the absolute love of my life, feels the same. It sounds stupid that we neither of us have the wherewithal to deal with happiness. Sounds perverse, doesn't it? Can you understand how hard it can be to hold in a delicate balance the sheer joy and the fear that it is going to end?'

'Are you still going to yoga classes?'

'Occasionally, nowhere near as frequently as I did before the girls came along. But why do you ask? What a strange question.'

'No it's not. You are going to ask me if I think therapy would help you—and by the way, any more therapy has to be with somebody else. Any advice I happen to offer is just as a friend—but before anything else you need to learn to relax and yoga is good for that. If you each know that the other loves you unconditionally then you should be able to take anything that he says or does—and that you say or do to him—without being hurt.

'This man does not want to hurt you. Look how quickly you made up. You need to develop a more secure stance, a thicker skin. Think of the other, not yourself. Think, above all, of the children. And how unquestioning that love is. If that should change, *then* maybe it will be time to seek therapy. I don't think that's going to happen.'

'Gosh. When you were my therapist in the Elms, you barely spoke. You used to give me pills.'

'You've got something much more effective than pills. And I'm officially not your therapist now. But I am your friend. Would you like some more tea?'

Belinda loved the old Baghdadi aura that pervaded the Haroun household in Brondesbury. She was amazed at how the normally edgy Farah could lose herself completely in the preparation of elaborate dishes, magically acquiring composure and patience in a small world of distinctive aromas, tastes and textures.

This was where Farah herself felt most at ease, among the fleshy apricots and apple jam, quince with chopped almonds and cardamom seeds, chicken soup with chickpeas, or aubergine stuffed with lamb, rice, mint, and spices. Belinda watched and listened eagerly. Such was daily life in a traditional Iraqi-Jewish household, so richly layered to Belinda's eyes. Farah's devotion to her task somehow lifted it above the mundane.

Something similar happened when Rivke told her practised and venerable tales of Baghdad and long, detailed anecdotes about this or that member of the Haroun clan. Urged on by her menfolk Yusuf and Eli as they sank into her armchairs drinking scented tea or coffee, Rivke seemed able to draw a moral lesson from every tale.

Whether she was standing alongside Farah listening to her explain each aspect of her cooking, or seated spellbound with her daughters nibbling at almonds and dates as they listened to Rivke reminiscing, Belinda was transfixed. Belinda's sister-in-law Leah referred to Rivke, without irony, as 'the sage'. Even the forceful Farah deferred to her.

One morning, when Belinda and Eli had followed a night of languid, loving intimacy by asking themselves yet again the cloud-in-the-sky question of how they could be endowed with such fortuitous happiness and not simply take and enjoy it without fearing its end, Belinda decided, on a whim, to consult Rivke. After all, Rivke appeared to have such a strong connection to her family, her religion and her traditions, that she would regard such anxieties as sheer indulgence and know how to dispel them.

'I look around at the world, at my family, at Eli, the girls, and I find myself constantly worrying,' Belinda told Rivke. 'And I think of my mother, all that she has been through, and I feel guilty. Nothing remotely like that has ever happened to me and I worry and get depressed, and she seems so calm. And what about you? You retain your faith even though you had such bad experiences towards the end of your time in Baghdad,' Belinda observed. 'Didn't the *Farhud* cause you to question your faith, and even your belief in God?'

'Why would it?' Rivke replied, simply.

'Well, did you not wonder why a loving God could allow such things to happen? I have never been able to talk to my mother properly about her experiences in the camps and losing her parents in such an unimaginably cruel way, but I am sure that she could never accept the idea of a God who allows such things to happen.'

'It is we—human beings—who allow such things to happen, my darling,' said Rivke, stroking Belinda's hand. 'And if we never felt pain or outrage when they happen, how would we live our lives? What would constitute joy or pleasure or love, with nothing to measure them against, nothing to contrast them with?

'And,' Rivke continued, 'if there is no God, and these bad things happen anyway, then we have to accept each catastrophe, every evil act, as something that is just part of our reality, something *ordinary*. A meaningless, cruel life. But the existence of a creator, a shining light, instils in us a sense of justice, an ability to balance good and evil, and to recognise that, whatever our differences, our similarities are much stronger because we are all human. And if we can look to our parents and our teachers to show us the way towards the light, then we have something to live for.'

Rivke paused briefly before continuing. 'I must tell you that I think your dear mother and father are exceptionally good people, and I can see in your face when you are with them that you have a special, deep feeling towards them. A feeling that is not something matter-of-fact but much greater. It is because they are your parents that you feel for them in a special way—and they for you. This is love, and its power and its mystery comes from God. If there was no God and this was just a matter-of-fact existence, then our parents would be just another two people. And they are not.'

'I believe such love to be genuine,' said Belinda. 'But it can as easily be biology as something called God. I so wish I had your kind of faith but I have a need for evidence.'

'All around you is evidence,' Rivke retorted. 'Not proof, because nobody can prove that God exists just as nobody can prove that he does not exist. Anybody who claims to be able to prove *either*, like a scientist proves that water will freeze at a certain temperature, is a fool.'

'But my education, my knowledge, my observations,' said Belinda in an urgent tone, 'tell me that whatever we do, whoever we are, our lives are surrounded, past and future, by oblivion. Where is God?'

'I don't *know*, darling, but I *think* he is present in everything we do. Your existence and my existence are evidence of his existence. Listen, the possibility or probability of God's existence is exactly the same as it is for his non-existence. You know, there is a verse in the Bible in which God lays out the contrasts of life and of death, telling us we have a choice, but exhorting us to "choose life", which to me is very wonderful. And that is what I am doing, even as death comes nearer to choosing me.'

At this point, Rivke stood up and went into her kitchen, returning with two glasses of tea flavoured with lemon and honey, which she set down alongside a plate of date biscuits with a grand gesture commanding Belinda to drink, as though the tea was an elixir. And, as Belinda took a sip, and a nibble from a biscuit, Rivke returned to her theme.

'You know,' she said. 'During the *Farhud*, a wonderful Muslim neighbour of ours, Mrs Habash, bravely stood up against the mob, condemning the thugs to their faces and doing her best to protect the Jews who were being attacked. Very few were so brave. Most just stood by or even urged on the attackers. Some young men quite near to our district joined in.

'Mrs Habash was kicked to the ground and was fortunate not to have been killed. Now, not only do I believe that such actions as hers are godlike, but that our natural reaction to such actions—to be moved to tears—is also something that hints at the existence of God.

'Someone else I remember from our old country,' Rivke continued, 'is a man who used to walk the streets selling pickles. *Abul 'am bah* we called him. He was a little man with a face all shrivelled and brown like a nut. People would say that he had been around pickles for so long that he had become pickled himself.

'But the thing about him was that he had a wooden leg. And yet that didn't stop him scurrying through the streets calling out to people that there were "delicious, tasty, lovely and cheap" pickles for sale and that the women in the houses should "hurry, hurry, hurry" to come and get them.

'He had lost his leg trying to rescue his son, who had fallen on to the railway track as a train was approaching. His son was killed and our *abul 'am bah* had to have his leg amputated. Those who heard his cries of pain and lamentation said he sounded just as he did when he called out "hurry, hurry, hurry" to the housewives of Baghdad. He was back on the streets working a few days after his operation, and always smiling. When I saw him smiling and heard him shouting out "delicious, tasty, lovely and cheap", it always made me happy.'

Rivke then moved forward in her chair. 'There are two possibilities,' she suddenly declared, like a teacher to a pupil. 'God exists,' she said, holding out her right hand, 'or he does not,' holding out her left. 'Choose one.'

Belinda experienced the distinctly irreligious feeling of being shown a conjuring trick by a stage magician. But then she was immediately entranced by her grandmother-in-law's gentle sincerity, and the warmth of her expression.

'For me—and I am a realist not an idle dreamer,' said Rivke, in a voice that seemed to distil decades of experience, 'the one to choose is: "God exists".' She held up her right hand triumphantly before carrying on. 'How much better it is than the other choice—of darkness and pointlessness.

'And, you know what? I think you have made that choice, Belinda. The same as me. You and my wonderful grandson are full of life, and love. It is a gift. And, for me, our beautiful Jewish prayers and customs give meaning to my life. I believe that, in choosing each other, you and Eli have made the same choice as I have. The right choice. Giving yourself to love, to life, rather than wasting time in fear and darkness. You want evidence? You have it in your darling Sarah and Emily, *bel ayn el raa'a.*'

Belinda laughed. 'Eli is always saying that—and he is someone who thinks religion is mere superstition and that superstition is complete rubbish. But it doesn't stop him making incantations to keep away the evil eye, however satirically he claims to be saying it.'

'Hah! He's a lovely boy, all the same. Drink your tea, darling. And have another biscuit. I know you like them.'

'*Bel ayn el raa'a!*' said Belinda.

In August 1981, Farah Haroun held a professionally catered party in the garden of her house to celebrate the eightieth birthday of her mother-in-law. Rivke sat regally at the head of a table, with Yusuf and Farah either side of her. While there was a lot of activity in and out of the house, with laughter and fond remembrance, Rivke remained seated throughout. Rather than mingle among her guests, as she had done so many times in her life, her guests came to her, young and old moving over to the table to speak and listen to the matriarch of the Harouns.

'Do you think she's enjoying herself?' Eli, at a nearby table, asked Belinda anxiously as he mentally absorbed the sadness of seeing his beloved grandmother so uncharacteristically still in her chair and noticing, for the first time, true signs of age upon her as she smiled pleasantly but somewhat passively to the family members and friends surrounding her with congratulations.

'It looks as though she has taken some drug,' Eli whispered to his wife.

'I think she looks completely relaxed and peaceful,' said Belinda.

'That's as maybe, but peaceful is not her. She's a livewire who doesn't normally sit down until she has made sure that everyone has enough to eat or drink.'

'She's smiling happily. I don't think she looks drugged.'

'Maybe, but I have never really seen her looking old before. Look how flat and lifeless her hair is in the sunshine,' he said, reducing still more the volume of his voice. 'Such a dull and aged shade of grey. Like dust. How lined her face seems to have become overnight. How disengaged her eyes are. God, I hope she's all right.'

'Why don't we go over and speak to her and see? Look, she's laughing. Her eyes aren't disengaged. I don't think there's much wrong with her.'

'Oh, darling, I hope you're right.'

At that moment, Farah disappeared into the house and re-emerged with a birthday cake that she had spent a large part of the previous day preparing. The finished item glowed magnificently in the reflected light of eight flames—to represent eighty—flickering over the top layer of almond and vanilla icing. And then Rivke did stand, in order to blow out the candles, which she did in one mighty breath, laughing as a variety of voices sang 'Happy Birthday'.

Eli, too, laughed—in relief. 'I don't want her to be ready to go before I'm ready,' he said to Belinda while holding her hand. 'Come on, let's go over and add our congratulations.'

However, while Rivke's eyes were clear and her mind alert, she was markedly frailer than she had been at her seventy-ninth birthday party the year before. This did not prevent her continuously smiling at the party guests and hugging her grandson in the same way as when she had needed to bend down to do so. Now it was Eli who had to bend to her; he was the one nine or ten inches taller.

This was Rivke's last birthday party at home. The following year, she was in hospital and too weak to celebrate, having been operated on following a fall at her flat. Her condition rendered her open to infection and, when she duly succumbed to bronchitis, her stay in the Royal Free Hospital, Hampstead, was extended.

She was allowed home in October and Yusuf, Farah, Leah, Eli and Belinda ensured she was constantly cared for. In December, she appeared to rally and, with Farah's help, baked a batch of pistachio and almond biscuits. As the family later sat around her dining table eating the biscuits and drinking tea, Rivke patted and pinched Eli's cheek and, with regained vocal strength and enthusiasm, uttered '*mashallah*', just as she had when he was at the same stage of life as his two daughters were now.

When she told Eli, 'I want you to have the Haroun photograph album after I've gone,' he replied: 'That's wonderful, Grandma, but let's hope it will be a long time yet.'

But it was not to be a long time. Rivke Haroun died in December 1982, aged eighty-one. She was buried, on a bright, clear, piercingly cold afternoon, at the Spanish and Portuguese Jewish Cemetery in Hoop Lane, between Finchley Road and Hampstead Garden Suburb in north London, two-and-a-half thousand miles from her birthplace.

More than two hundred people attended her funeral. Anna and Roderick brought Roderick's mother Margaret (Cedric was too frail to attend and would himself die less than a year later) and Ramon Saul brought his father, Simon. They heard Rabbi Norman Lobatto, of the 'Gate to Heaven' synagogue, apply the words of the Book of Proverbs to Rivke Haroun, for she 'undeniably was a virtuous woman valuable "beyond the price of rubies", who did "gird her loins with strength" and of whom it could undoubtedly be said: "She openeth her mouth with wisdom; and in her tongue is the law of kindness".'

Other mourners included Yusuf's old friend and cousin Izaak, who had come from his home in Israel, where he had been living for more than thirty years. He recalled to Yusuf how kind Rivke had been to him and his family after his sister Sarai's death in the *Farhud*.

Yusuf's sisters Rachel, with her husband David, and Nura, by then divorced, came from America. Nura and Rachel wept over their absence from their mother's later years and held each other throughout Rabbi Lobatto's consoling words and Yusuf's reciting of the mourner's Kaddish.

Several of the 'Ladies from Lauderdale'—as Eli called Rivke's friends with whom she had played cards and discussed books and food and families—were quite overcome in their distress.

Azi, now stooped and slow-moving, and his brother Ben supported Eli, their distraught young colleague and cousin, from the prayer hall to the graveside. Azi's wife Miriam put an arm around Farah, who was crying for her heartbroken husband and son, and the two women stood together with Leah, Belinda and Anna, all wrapped in layers of clothing against the cold wind.

Azi and Miriam's children—the Oxford graduates and lawyers Joseph and Daniel, and the Cambridge graduate Violette, now a journalist—were also there, looking both solemn and assured. Farah was cheered by seeing Joseph. 'Do you remember, when you were a little boy, and you came with your father to meet us from the plane in Bristol? Then we saw you off to go to your evacuation somewhere in Wales. You looked so miserable. I was so sorry for you.'

'Actually, I came to like it,' said Joseph. 'There were some American GIs stationed nearby and they used to give us chewing gum. I grew up quickly in the war. Maybe you remember, the war ended just as I was due to join the RAF. I was truly disappointed. I wouldn't have minded a career in the air force but I did get to do national service, and then came Oxford.'

When Rabbi Lobatto repeated in English the Hebrew plea for Rivke as her coffin was lowered into the grave—'May she come to her place in peace'—former British Royal Artillery Captain Roderick Vane's mind went back suddenly to April 1945, when the British Jewish army chaplain, Reverend Leslie Hardman, had used a poignant adaptation of the same phrase, in conducting a mass burial service in Bergen-Belsen. 'They shall rest peacefully upon their lying place,' Reverend Hardman had said, his words directed not only at the Bergen-Belsen victims, or the annihilated millions but to every individual among them. Roderick shivered, and his eyes automatically sought out his wife, Anna. She turned to him and smiled; a shaft of warmth in the pitiless cold.

In the weeks following Rivke's funeral, Eli slipped back into unpredictability. He continued to shower love upon Belinda and their daughters but, in between, would slump into dark moods, either curling up in bed and missing work, or going in but reacting with sudden impatience to customers.

Inevitably, Azi and Ben brought in somebody, a former college friend of Adam's, to cover for Eli both at the emporium and the Kentish Town shop. At home, too, Eli occasionally snapped, invariably seeking afterwards to make amends with remorseful words and actions—buying flowers for Belinda or chocolate for Sarah and Emily.

Belinda leant on Deborah Foreman's friendship—no longer augmented by a separate, professional relationship—and urged Eli and his father to talk about Rivke, to recall and celebrate her remarkably spirited and colourful life. And, gradually, the Muswell Hill flat regained its happy atmosphere.

In 1986, over the months of June and July, Eli and Belinda hired a cottage on the Devon coast for a three-week holiday with their daughters, Sarah and Emily. It was a joyous interlude, a time when Sarah described her parents as 'moonstruck hippies' after she and Emily walked in on them one afternoon to see them dancing frenziedly to an old rock'n'roll record. It was not unusual for Eli to take hold of Belinda and get her to dance, anything from an Irving Berlin waltz to Jimi Hendrix but, on that Devon holiday, the girls were both astonished and delighted at their parents' energies. Eli wanted to take them all swimming—or at least paddling—at midnight, and succeeded on a couple of the warmest and calmest occasions.

Eli and Belinda read poetry after dinner—their own and other people's—and Eli had them all composing spontaneous rhymes. He took uncountable numbers of photographs. Belinda wore a straw hat the whole time and bought a piccolo in the local market—which she taught her daughters to play. The adults walked everywhere hand-in-hand. Years later, describing the holiday to her grandmother Anna, Emily would recall it as 'the happiest time of my life'.

Upon their return from that holiday in Devon in the summer of 1986, Belinda and Eli decided to buy a house and give themselves and the children more room. They sold their flat, having found a stately but rundown Victorian house towards the bottom of Muswell Hill, close to Alexandra Park. Once in, they embarked enthusiastically upon radical renovation and redecoration, with Sarah and Emily employed as more-than-willing assistants covering their clothing in paint and bringing a lot of girlish laughter to the task.

The renovation of the new house took the place of a summer holiday in 1987 and by the following summer—with the help of cash gifts from both sets of parents—the work was more or less completed. Eli and Belinda rewarded themselves and the children by taking the long-mooted trip to Israel.

'Wait till you see Jerusalem,' Ramon Saul told Eli. 'The world's most beautiful city.'

'My parents say Haifa is lovely,' said Eli. 'And Tel Aviv—I am looking forward to seeing Tel Aviv. It sounds good. We are staying at the Dan Hotel, right near the beach. Sarah and Emily will love it.'

'Where are you staying in Jerusalem?'

'In the King David. My mother insists.'

'Wonderful. You'll have a fabulous time. In Jerusalem especially. Even you will get a spiritual kick out of it, believe me. I've never been to Haifa, but Tel Aviv?' Ramon made a noise like a lamb bleating. 'It's crowded, it's rushed, it's noisy. Everyone's rude or mad or both. The kids can enjoy the beach but, believe me, Jerusalem will be unforgettable.'

'I believe you,' Eli said, laughing.

In the event, while Belinda was entranced by the ancient city's atmosphere, and Sarah and Emily were spellbound wherever they were throughout the entire fourteen days of the most exotic experience of their young lives—especially by the startling sight, in restaurants, of young soldiers with rifles sitting at tables close to theirs—Eli found Jerusalem oppressive.

'Too many religious backwoodsmen and commissars sending out disapproving glances, when they bother to look at you at all,' he told Ramon Saul upon his return. 'I *loved* Tel Aviv. I didn't find the people rude, or mad. To me, they were just full of life. I loved sitting in cafés on Dizengoff Street watching the constant procession of proud, young Israelis.

'I can understand people finding the swaggering soldiers and strollers of Tel Aviv a bit too superior for their own good but I think the girls especially are magnificent. Yes, they are arrogant, but they're entitled to feel imperious carrying on their shoulders the future of a country of such painful antecedence. I love them. Not just for their beauty but for their *vitality*. It's that *holy* arrogance of the *frummers* in Jerusalem, loftily condemning you if you so much as water the plant on your window sill on the Sabbath that I can't stand.'

The view that Belinda conveyed to Deborah Foreman was somewhat different. 'Eli couldn't wait to get away from Jerusalem,' she said. 'But I was… transported. I don't want to make it sound as though I had some kind of epiphany or out-of-body religious experience. I didn't. But I loved it.

'Eli was spooked by the very religious people but they didn't bother me. It's hard to explain but being there with my lovely husband and children felt like being at the heart of something. Not something fanciful or especially spiritual but something real.

'This was the moment, for me, even more than our wedding had been, when I fully and finally assimilated my mother's revelations in the letter she wrote to me about her incredible past. I finally felt its embrace. I don't mean that going to Jerusalem felt like coming home, at least not in the sense that it was where I wanted to be, to live. But there was a kind of coming home in my head and Jerusalem provided the context, the backcloth, to that, and somehow enabled it.'

'It helped you to feel Jewish?' Deborah asked.

'Yes, I suppose so. But it was more than that—and indeed less than that, it was a simple settling into myself.'

'Did it upset you that Eli felt differently about Jerusalem?'

'Not in the slightest. We had a fabulous holiday, all of us, from start to finish. It was really sweet in Tel Aviv meeting the family of Eli's dad's cousin Izaak. He has a furniture business, a lovely American-born wife, who is a lecturer at Hebrew University, and two stunningly beautiful daughters, both younger than me.

'They each have shining black hair and those famous Haroun eyes like deep, dark pools. One is doing a PhD at the university—not her mother's subject, science, but history, I think she said—and the other is in the army. What a girl that one is, funny, engaging, a true force of life. She was home for the weekend when we were there. Sarah and Emily adored her. Irit, her name is.'

'So,' Deborah smiled. 'It was a great success.'

'It was, it was. It's just that...' Belinda paused and Deborah remained silent, waiting for her to speak.

After a few seconds, Belinda did speak. 'Oh, I don't know. Eli was so disorganised,' she said. 'I had to make all the plans, get the tickets, sort out the maps. Which was fine. I don't resent that one little bit. In fact, we laughed about it. And I know I am perfectly capable. It's just that, inside, I have no faith in my ability to be depended upon. I keep judging myself. I am such a bloody pessimist with absolutely nothing to be pessimistic about.'

'Parents and lovers always have a certain amount of pessimism,' Deborah said in a tone of pedagogic reassurance. 'It's built into the role. They worry about the ones they love, worry that something bad might befall them.'

'I know,' Belinda said, nodding. 'But that's in the realm of horror and speculation. But mine relates to the mundane, day-to-day world. I have a yearning inside me to embrace life—as Irit, Izaak's lovely daughter in the Israeli army, does even though she might face real, physical danger—but I feel I'm not well-enough equipped. I just can't relax. It's partly because everyone seems to think I am such an able, resourceful person. That's my role. Fine, I can do it, but it's a real effort. An act. I feel I'm a fraud.'

'Let me tell you something,' said Deborah. 'When it comes to our reputations, at some level we all feel—and are—fraudulent.'

Some time in 1988, Eli submitted to Belinda's constant promptings to try and get his poetry published. Normally, he would laugh at the idea, reminding her that most of it was directed at her and therefore private. But, this time, he put together a book of verse and photographs and Belinda took it to an editor at the publishing house for which she was now working three days a week.

Eli took the title, *A Journey in My Head*, from, predictably, Shakespeare's Sonnet 27: 'But then begins a journey in my head,/To work my mind, when body's work's expired.' The editor, a classically educated and considerate man who Belinda thought would be an ideal person to approach, responded warmly to the book but was unsure whether the pictures and the words formed an effective combination, and referred Belinda to a small independent imprint run by a man called Tom Herler. 'I think Tom'll get this,' the editor told Belinda. 'It's up his street. Though don't expect pots of cash.'

Tom Herler's office was above a shop in Kentish Town, walking distance from the Haroun shop-cum-gallery, the management of which was now shared between Eli, Adam and Adam's friend Marcus. The three of them also rotated duties at the emporium.

The name of Tom's modest imprint was Kentish Press and his sense of community inclined him towards publishing the work of a local author even before he had looked at it. But then, once he had read Eli's poetry and examined a selection of his photographs, Tom was genuinely enthused and readily agreed to publish it. He did so in tandem with an art-book publisher who was used to dealing with photography.

A launch party was held in the Owl Bookshop in Kentish Town and attracted a small crowd, boosted by a contingent of relatives and friends including an emotional Farah and Yusuf, a supportive Leah and David, a curious Anna and Roderick with an elderly but upright Margaret, and a proud Belinda, Sarah and Emily—all three of whom acted as waitresses dispensing cheap wine and sandwiches made by

Tom Herler. Some prints of Eli's photographs were on display on a couple of bookshelves cleared for the purpose. Eli was pleased, and indeed flattered, by the way this had been done by the bookshop staff under the direction of Tom's co-publisher who had organised the printing of the images.

But Eli was much less comfortable with having to read some of the poems from the book to the assembled company. He found it difficult to find four—the number Tom had asked for—once he had ruled out many of the more intimate verses addressed directly to Belinda, along with some others he felt to be a bit below the general standard.

'That was excruciating,' was Eli's verdict on the event afterwards when alone at home with Belinda. 'Principally because of having to read out the poems. I don't think I could do that again. But it was lovely to see Sarah and Emily buzzing about and Emily taking books off the shelves to look at. I thought she looked quite interested in some of them.'

'Yes, the ones with the pictures.'

'Well, that's all right—my book is also a picture book. God, I was so self-conscious reading aloud those poems meant just for your eyes and ears. I'm not sure I should have agreed to this project.'

'Of course you should. Your work is so good.'

'Tom was trying to get me to read that little ode I wrote to your pubic hair. Can you believe it? He is such an old hippy. I had no idea it was in the book. I just handed him a bunch of poems and when we went through them, we made a selection. I definitely told him not to include the pubic hair one and now I discover he has. And he wanted me to read it aloud—with my mum standing just a couple of feet away. Not to mention you being there next to me. That was never going to happen. Can you imagine?'

'Well, I would have blushed but would also have been bursting with pride and taken pleasure in no doubt being the object of widespread envy among the females in your audience.'

'I would have burst with embarrassment.'

Eli's misgivings remained with him over the next few weeks. They were reinforced when Tom Herler reported modest sale figures for *A Journey In My Head* for the first three-month period. This sparked a rash of 'you-see-it-wasn't-worth-the-angst' comments by Eli to Belinda.

It took Eli a further six months to take up his poetry pen again. This was to write a short verse in memory of Belinda's grandmother, Margaret

Vane—who died quietly in her sleep in the spring of 1990—and, inevitably, his own beloved Grandma.

Your grandmother
Picked bluebells in the wood
For her mother.
Can there be a more perfect
Gesture of love?

My grandmother
Brought sweetness to my world
Like no other.
Can there be such grandmothers
As these again?

Margaret's death led Belinda to see much more of Deborah Foreman though Deborah wouldn't hear of putting their meetings back on a professional footing. A large part of Belinda's need to seek out Deborah's counsel stemmed from Eli's apparent inability to provide a shoulder, metaphorical or literal, to cry on in the way that she had witnessed her father doing for her mother over the years; or, indeed, to offer more caring time for their daughters as Belinda mourned Margaret's death with her parents.

Instead, it was Eli who was the weakest one in the house, just when strength was what was required of him. This was something that he recognised and about which he often despaired.

'I am utterly dependent,' he lamented to Belinda one midnight on the pillow. 'I am dependent on my family for a job, on my dad for money and especially on you for anything about the home or the children. And I resent it. I can't make any decisions for myself. I have no initiative...'

'Of course you have initiative. You are a brilliant, creative man...'

'Half the time, I am completely immobilised...'

'Oh Eli, don't be ridiculous, you're not...'

This cross-cutting exchange was brought to an end when Eli flung his hand upwards in a spontaneous gesture of rebuttal as he loudly began to insist on his dependent status and his hand unintentionally struck Belinda's face.

Belinda screamed aloud in shock and pain, as Eli, immediately contrite, tearfully apologised.

'I am so, so sorry,' he pleaded, attempting to touch her, to hug her, as she turned away. 'That *hurt*,' she yelled, getting out of bed and making her way to the bathroom, where she put on the light and examined her face in the mirror.

Eli tried to follow her but she locked herself in. He spoke to her through the bathroom door, pleading with her to come out, repeatedly telling her he was sorry, that he loved her and would never intentionally hurt her.

'I know,' Belinda said, unlocking the door. They were both crying now.

'Let me see,' he said, and kissed her bruised cheek. Slowly and gently, she returned his embrace, kissing him and stroking his hair as he clung to her, still weeping his apology.

Holding each other, they returned to bed. And, as on so many occasions before, their lovemaking had a healing quality.

7

18 July 1990
Alexandra Park, London
Belinda Haroun to Eli Haroun

My darling,

I love you so much and I am so afraid for you. I have thought long and hard and believe now that the best way to show my love—probably at this point the only way—is to stop burdening you with a responsibility you simply cannot handle.

You are so terribly weighed down by life and this causes me great distress. I am so unhappy when I see your face so dark and depressed in the mornings and when you retreat early to bed at night because of one of your moods.

I am sure that the children are also unhappy to see their daddy so often miserable at home. Although you have not been into work too much lately, when you have gone and when we all come to see you there or pick you up from there to go out to a film or play or to the Chinese restaurant, it is so different. You are so different.

So I think it best to allow you to live apart from us, perhaps in Rivke's old flat that you have so lovingly redecorated. I must let you go to give you a chance of regaining your self-belief. Nobody will understand that this is an act of love, but it is. It is surely impossible for two people to have been as much in love as we have been. But we cannot continue to live together as we are. We both need to be cared for but without losing our sense of self, our individuality, especially you, my darling. And I think that is best done by being detached from each other's private darkness.

If, at least for a time, we sleep under separate roofs, we will be able to be more helpful to the children and in our different ways give them more attention. We can remain the incomparably close friends—and even lovers—that we have been, tell each other our troubles and listen and advise and laugh, if we—and especially you—can draw on some inner, independent strength.

We need freedom. Freedom from helplessly witnessing the torment of the one we love. I think being a mother has made me a little stronger but fatherhood has overpowered you. You need some distance from it. And so I offer it to you. My gift. This does not mean you should not see the children whenever, wherever and however you want. And then one day, in a month, a year or perhaps when the children have grown and left home, we will be fully together again, stronger.

With love,
Your soulmate,
Belinda

Eli was unable to overcome his regret at having struck Belinda, even though she repeatedly reassured him that she knew it had been an unintentional blow.

'My face got in the way of your frustrated gesture, that was all it was—an accident,' she told him. 'You were gesticulating—a bit wildly, but you are an expressive, passionate man—and I happened to be a bit too close. You could equally have hit the wall. And, anyway, the incident was totally eclipsed by spending all the hours of the night in far, far more meaningful physical contact. It also sorted out your frustration, I thought.'

But Eli would not accept any kind of reassurance. 'I believe it was unintentional,' he said. 'But my mother—who seems to be something of a fan of Sigmund Freud—would probably say that I meant it subconsciously. As no doubt would Deborah Foreman and quite possibly Alan Alfassa, too.'

Eli spent an increasing amount of time on his own, reading or walking. He began to cry off work and asked his father if, for a week or so, instead of coming in to the carpet warehouse, he could paint Rivke's old flat, which Yusuf was very happy for him to do.

Yusuf and Farah had often spoken of letting Rivke's old flat but had never got around to doing so. Much more than the main house, the flat was redolent of Baghdadi traditions and, despite Yusuf's often-stated fear that it was in danger of becoming a shrine, it remained largely untouched since Rivke's death, retaining her furniture—apart from Sami's old armchair, which Yusuf had taken for himself—her kitchen implements and a couple of pictures from Iraq that still hung in the same positions on her wall.

All the photographs that she used to have on display had been removed by Yusuf and Farah, who had put them away in a drawer, except for two—one showing Rivke seated at her eightieth birthday party and the other a black and white image of Eli and Leah as young children awkwardly dressed up in smart clothes prior to some special occasion. Now, these two images stood in cold regimentation on top of Yusuf and Farah's unplayed piano alongside Eli's bar mitzvah portrait, in which he was seated, rigid-faced, a thin black and white prayer shawl around his neck like a superfluous scarf; and Leah's graduation picture, a moment of laughter held in perpetuity.

Farah had been disappointed that Rivke's copy of Eli's bar mitzvah picture had occupied a central position in her parlour portrait gallery, while that of Leah's graduation was—as Farah saw it—relegated to a corner of the kitchen.

But there was no such pettiness attached to the family's most prized pictorial object—the Haroun photograph album had been restored to its pride of place in Rivke's bookcase. The folder containing the three photographs of Yusuf and Farah, the most recent of which had been taken by Eli himself, was still neatly tucked inside the back cover of the album.

Eli had not been inside his grandmother's old flat on more than half a dozen occasions in over three years and it felt odd now to enter it with brushes, pots of paint, a ladder and various other decorating appurtenances.

On his first day, he suddenly remembered that his grandmother had wanted him to have the Haroun family album and he went over to the bookcase and removed it. He took it into the kitchen. Having placed it on the table, Eli was unable to resist looking through the decades of portraits even though he had not even started to cover the floors and furniture of Rivke's parlour with the old sheets he had brought along which, to him, in that place and time, seemed like burial shrouds.

As Eli began to turn the pages of the album at random, the first image that struck him was one he couldn't remember noticing before. It showed Azi and Ben as young boys of around nine and eleven. Both had the same thick bush of black hair and both wore long, tunic-like white shirts over their trousers. Both, too, were staring at the camera but with distinctly contrasting expressions. The young Ben—in the lineaments of whose face Eli discerned a startling blueprint for Ben's son Adam—was standing holding a stick placed nonchalantly upon a large wooden hoop that stood as high as his waist and which he might have been about to whip into motion.

The face of the boy who was to become the man betrayed little emotion beyond a hint of idle wonder at the photographic process that was causing him to stand unnaturally still and pause in the middle of some active, boyish pursuit. Or were the hoop and the stick merely studio props used by an enterprising photographer to gain the attention of an energetic child?

And while Ben's pose, though probably calculated to convey a sense of motion, was one of complete stillness, Azi's attitude exuded physical activity. His face bore a caught-in-the-act expression. He looked as if he was trying to conceal from view an object that he was holding in both hands. It looked like a pomegranate though Eli could not be certain, any more or less than any viewer of this remarkably captured scene would be.

The object, whether pomegranate or some other magical sphere, was partly in shadow. Azi's body was twisted so that his left shoulder was the most forcibly presented part of his anatomy. His lower body was turned sideways with both knees bent as if he was about to run away. The heel of one foot was raised, the toes pressing into the ground.

Somehow, the anonymous photographer had managed to freeze—or, perhaps more astonishingly, create—a vivid boyhood moment. Every element of the picture was sharply focused, from the oval formed by Azi's lips around his wide-open mouth, the evenness of Ben's grip upon his stick, and the shiny curve that was the only fully visible part of the pomegranate-like object shielded by Azi, right down to the crumblings and abrasions of the brick wall in front of which Azi and Ben were standing.

The photograph had a strong effect on Eli, whose painting task was deferred for more than an hour as he sat at his grandmother's old kitchen table, leafing through the album, marvelling at the suspended animation within it and reflecting how strange it was that the camera work he was contemplating, of a necessarily rudimentary, even pioneering character, seemed of so much finer an artistry than that of contemporary photography, including his own.

Sitting back, he held up the portrait of his great-uncle Reuben and tried to look into Reuben's mind through the enigmatic expression of his eyes. Eli sighed and addressed the image aloud: 'Oh, poor Reuben, how unfair life was to you.' He closed the book gently and placed it on the kitchen shelf before returning to Rivke's parlour, setting up his ladder and carefully arranging his shrouds.

When he came home in the evening and Belinda asked how the day had gone, he told her how distracted he had been by the family album, and how the photographs it contained had shown that the Harouns all seemed to have 'such sad eyes'.

Everyone who saw it praised Eli's painting and redecoration of Rivke's flat.

'You can make a second career for yourself,' Farah said, not entirely lightly. 'Your work is much more artistic than the average decorator's. It's high-class. You should seek out some trendy clients.'

Yusuf, who had come to the flat at the end of each day to inspect his son's work and check on his progress, told Eli: 'We've missed you at work but clearly your time off has not been wasted.'

Belinda assured him that 'Grandma Rivke would have been delighted. And I've always said you and my mum would make a great interior design team.'

Eli returned to work at the emporium but abandoned the shop and gallery to Marcus. Most mornings, Yusuf rang the Alexandra Park house, cheerfully announcing to Belinda, who invariably was the one who answered the telephone: 'Good morning. This is Eli Haroun's alarm call.' But even this did not improve Eli's spasmodic attendance. When he did appear, he worked efficiently enough but rarely with the enthusiasm he had shown in the past.

During Eli's first week back, Belinda twice drove across north London to pick him up from the Haroun emporium at the end of the working day. On both occasions, she took Sarah and Emily. Having collected Eli, they went straight to their local Chinese restaurant in Crouch End. And, on both occasions, Eli was in ebullient mood, hugging Belinda, showing great interest in his daughters and joking with the waiters. Yet, in private, he repeatedly apologised to Belinda for having hit her.

'Please, my darling. Please stop,' Belinda told him. 'This obsessive apologising, this bloody self-flagellation, is infinitely worse than the little accidental bruising you gave me.'

Eli's moods continued to oscillate. Almost every morning he would wake up around dawn in a state of despair and then slump into the bed sheets for about two hours, his brain a dark chamber of negativity, until he would slip into unconsciousness and then, when awakened by the children or his father's 'alarm call', be too fatigued and depressed to get up in time to go to the showroom. At night, he clung to Belinda but increasingly to seek comfort or solace rather than love or the satisfaction of desire.

One evening after Eli had spent the day at home, he and Belinda went out to the Chinese restaurant and Eli apologised, not this time for striking Belinda but for his general apathy, and said he was determined to return to active work. When they arrived home, he phoned his father and told him he would be coming into the emporium in the morning. The following day, Eli kept his promise to return to work, where he was given a friendly welcome.

'I'm so happy to see you, Eli,' said his father. 'I have to go to the Kentish Town shop at lunchtime. Why don't you come with me and see what those rascals have been up to while you've been away?'

Eli nodded, without showing any enthusiasm.

At the same time as Yusuf and Eli were making their mostly silent way to Kentish Town, Belinda was having lunch with Deborah, close by in Camden Town. But this was far from being a silent get-together.

'It's the unpredictability that I find so wearing,' Belinda told her psychotherapeutic friend. 'I wake up every morning feeling tired and depressed. If it weren't for my girls…

'It's as though Eli keeps hiding in a form of disguise, slipping out of character. One minute, he is laughing and loving, his normal sing-ing-and-dancing self, the next he retreats into some dark place of his own. I am nervous of approaching him, of asking him how I can help, which is ridiculous.

'He was always so open with me. We were totally open with each other. For the first time in both our lives both of us could be totally open with another person. I want to take away the burden that he is carrying. He loves all of us—Sarah, Emily, me—and we love him, but he can't cope with us somehow as a family. What can I do?'

'Have you thought of anything specific you want to say to him, to suggest to him?' Deborah remained non-committal.

Belinda exhaled before speaking. 'Well, I think maybe the best way I can show my love is not to impose upon him the burden that a conven-tional, responsible family life seems to be.'

'How would you do that?'

'Suggest that we live apart until he can throw off his demons and come to see how he needs to be in a loving home environment where he can just be himself. Not somebody doing his duty. The rest will flow from that. He thinks he is too dependent. He needs to see that there is nothing wrong in being dependent as part of a mutual dependency.'

'What would you do? Sell the house?' Deborah asked, completely taken by surprise. 'Would it not be counter-productive if he goes off to some depressing, squalid bedsit? Or do you think that would be precisely the circumstances to force him to appreciate how much he is missing, how much he needs you—and the children?'

'There is no question of my barring him from seeing the children. It is vital that he sees them as often as he wants. They will certainly want to go on seeing him.'

'But where? Are you offering to move out?'

'He has just done a fantastic job of decorating his late grandmother's flat. It's a lovely place with lots of warm memories. The children are very familiar with it. It adjoins his parents' house, part of the original building, which they own. I'm sure they would let him live there rent-free.'

'Have you put this possibility to him? Hinted at it perhaps?'

'I cannot speak to him. I feel I am treading on eggshells all the time. I never know how he is going to react. And the last thing I want is to make him more unhappy. This is what makes me sad. We never used to have any secrets, any inhibitions.'

'If you cannot communicate by speaking, then why not write him a letter?'

'A letter?'

'Yes. It has the advantage of your being able to set out your thoughts calmly and clearly, which he will then be forced to understand.'

'You don't mean post it?'

'No, no, just leave it on his desk or bedside table or somewhere he cannot fail to see it.'

'I don't know. It seems artificial. It seems an admission that our romantic claims of total, free-and-easy, intimate communication are just silly dreams.'

'Look. Why don't you draft something and then bring it to me to look at and you can then decide whether or not you want to send it, or, rather, leave it out for him?'

'I'll try.'

And so, when Eli next responded to Yusuf's 'alarm call' and went to the emporium, Belinda took out a sheet of paper and began to write: 'My darling, I love you so much and I am so afraid for you…'

Two days after composing the letter, Belinda was at Deborah's flat discussing the content of the letter and the wisdom, or not, of giving it to Eli.

Having made no comment on the letter beyond telling Belinda that it sounded as though it came from the heart, Deborah was careful not to pronounce on the issue of whether or not to deliver it to Eli but to wait until Belinda made the decision for herself.

Eventually, Belinda decided to postpone the decision for a week. She arranged to come back to Deborah's flat after seven days and seek Deborah's blessing on whatever she had decided to do. She folded the letter into her handbag and took it home. When she arrived, she found an envelope on her dressing table with her name written on it. She opened it; inside was a handwritten note from Eli.

8

20 July 1990
Alexandra Park, London
Eli Haroun to Belinda Haroun,
Sarah Haroun and Emily Haroun

I cannot go on. My precious Belinda, I struck your beautiful face. I cannot forgive myself. I am getting worse. The despair I feel when I wake each morning is becoming unbearable. I don't know what I would do if I didn't have the remedy of seeing your face on the pillow next to mine. But it is not fair to you. What a hopeless case I have become. I am unable to give you the life you deserve. I am unable to inspire my wonderful, adorable daughters.

Sarah and Emily, what must you two think seeing your father weeping one minute, and dancing and singing with Mummy the next, and then the blackness and despair descends again, even after such happiness. Round and round in circles.

You would all be relieved and better off without me.

After all the years of my parents forcing God upon me, now that I need Him, I cannot believe in Him. I wish I had their apparently unquestioning belief. I have to guide and help myself. And I can't. Make my own decision. And I can't. I wish I could conjure up God.

Please always remember as long as you live, even though I am weak and have let you down, I love all three of you so much more than I could possibly have imagined loving anybody.

Eli. Daddy.

Belinda's immediate reaction upon reading Eli's note was to tear up her unsent letter to him. Her next was to panic. Where was he? What was he doing? She called out his name, loudly and repeatedly as she raced through the house and into the garden.

She came back into the bedroom and read his note again. Her head rang with questions: 'Has he gone away? Did he anticipate my suggestion? Or know about it? How could he have known about it? I didn't mention it to anyone. Or did I? No. Only to Deborah. Would she have said something? Surely not, no, that's ridiculous. Did he simply have the same idea about living apart for a bit? Oh, Eli. I don't want to live apart. I want to be with you always. Don't you realise you give me strength just as much as I give you strength? It's a two-way thing, you fool.'

By now she was crying and trying to hold the telephone in her shaking hand. She tried Eli's parents, misdialling twice in her frenzy. When she eventually got through to their number, there was no answer. 'Did he go to work today?' Belinda was talking aloud now, as if to another person. And then she resumed her interior monologue: 'He was in bed when I left this morning. I wonder if Yusuf made his alarm call. He probably came round and drove him in as he has for the past two days. Yes. Yes.' She tried the showroom but the line was engaged.

She tried Ramon. 'Oh hi, Belinda. How are you?'

'I'm fine, I'm fine. Have you seen Eli?'

'When, today?'

'Yes, yes. This afternoon. Today.'

'Isn't he at work?'

'I don't know. The phone is engaged. OK. Sorry to bother you. Bye.'

Next, Belinda tried Leah's phone. David answered: 'Hello, Belinda. If you want Leah, I'm afraid you've just missed her. She left for her yoga class about five minutes ago.'

She tried the emporium again. And again. It was still engaged.

'Damn it, I'm going to find him.' She put her coat back on and ran out to the car just as Emily was coming through the gate. She looked confused.

'Mum? Where are you going?'

'Oh, darling. I thought you were doing some rehearsal tonight at school.'

'I did. It's finished.'

'And what about Sarah?'

'Grandma picked her up. She's having supper there.'

'Oh, of course. I forgot. I haven't made you anything to eat. Let's go in and see what's in the fridge.'

Once inside, Belinda picked up the phone in the hall. 'You look, darling. I just need to make a quick call.' She dialled the carpet showroom. Still engaged. She slammed down the phone. 'Darling, I have to go.'

'Why? Where? What about supper?'

'Later. I won't be long. Is there nothing in the fridge?'

'There's cake.'

'Oh no, you're not eating that… no, wait, it's OK. OK, have some cake, why not for once? Have some cake and watch the television and I'll be back as soon as I can.'

'From where?'

'I just have to run an urgent errand. For Daddy.' She quickly turned her head away so that Emily would not see her crying and called over her shoulder, 'bye, darling. I love you,' before racing down the garden path and along the road to where she had parked the car.

Having fumbled with the keys, Belinda managed to open the car and sink into the driving seat, breathing rapidly. She was unable to move out into the steady flow of traffic and swore loudly at a driver whose car was passing and innocently preventing her from driving away from the kerb.

Fifteen minutes later she reached the main road off which the Eastern Carpet and Goods Emporium was situated—half the time it normally took her—exceeding the speed limit for most of the journey, swerving around cars in queues of traffic and racing through at least two red lights, her head and heart pounding. About two hundred yards from where she needed to turn she could see a flashing blue light reflected in a window.

'Shit, I've been seen speeding,' she howled. 'Oh, I don't care! I just want to see my darling Eli!'

As she approached the lane, it was apparent that the police lights were not flashing on account of her speeding. The lane to the emporium was cordoned off. 'I'm afraid you can't go down there, miss,' said a peaked-capped police officer in a cockney baritone voice of cold authority. 'There's been a nasty accident.'

Ten days later, Belinda was seated in Deborah Foreman's conservatory in Belsize Park, asking unanswerable questions.

'Why did it happen, Deborah? I didn't even know there was access to the roof—why should I have known? What made him do it? You know, I was angry when I first heard. How could he have left me, left us, like that… But, then… My poor, darling Eli. What was going on in his head? My God!'

Deborah pushed her box of tissues in Belinda's direction.

'My ma has been a great support,' Belinda said after issuing a deep sigh. 'The trouble is I am too inhibited to cry in front of her and speak about my pain to her. I can't help thinking that part of her thinks that what she has had to deal with dwarfs my suffering.'

'Why should it?' Deborah asked abruptly. 'Do you really believe that is what she thinks? Do you see your mother as that kind of victim?'

Belinda used two more tissues before speaking again. 'No. She is the most wonderful person. Maybe my inhibition is because I don't want to load her with any more pain.'

'Don't you think your mother wants you to express your anguish? Let out your pain?'

'For God's sake, Deborah. You should have seen how much I wept at the funeral. I used up a hundred years' worth of tears. You know, when I composed that letter to Eli, the one we discussed, I thought it was so clever of me, so practical, such a reasonable solution to a painful problem. Move out into your dead grandmother's flat. For your own good.' She gave a brief, sarcastic laugh. 'An act of love! I actually felt pleased with myself that I could be so… *sane*. Now I see it as completely, stupidly, inhumanly, selfishly *insane*. I am so ashamed. Thank God he never saw it.'

'What was the funeral like?' Deborah asked after a few moments in which Belinda drew a few deep breaths.

'It was beautiful,' Belinda said, crying between breaths, her face crushed. 'The kind and lovely Rabbi Lobatto decreed that the death was "a tragic accident, a fall from an inadequately fenced roof, perhaps brought on by illness," which was why the burial was allowed to be in consecrated ground. His father was an assistant rabbi at my wedding. He was Rabbi *Norman* Lobatto, I think. The one at the funeral, his son, was *Ezra* Lobatto.'

Deborah held Belinda's hand and neither woman spoke, until Belinda broke the silence: 'What painful, dark thoughts had taken over his mind? The poor, poor soul. He thought I would be relieved! That the children would grow up better without him.' Again, she paused. 'They are having bereavement counselling. They seem to be coping. The house is quieter now. Filled with sadness. And marked by love. But quieter. Certainly much quieter.'

She turned and faced Deborah, with suddenly dry, bright eyes. 'Please tell me that life will be easier in time,' she said.

Eli Haroun was buried at the outer edge of the Spanish and Portuguese section of Hoop Lane Cemetery, not far from his grandmother Rivke, close to where the West London Synagogue Ashkenazi (central and eastern European) Jewish burial ground was marked out. And Belinda had indeed wept copiously at his funeral though Farah had seemed to be even more distraught. She could not stand at the graveside and had to be supported by Yusuf and Leah.

At the beginning of the period of mourning for Eli—the *shiva*—held at Farah and Yusuf's home, Farah took herself off into her bedroom, from where her visceral wailing could be heard downstairs in the room where the prayers were being conducted by Rabbi Ezra Lobatto.

Yusuf supported her as much as he was able but his son's death had also taken a grievous toll on him. For the first few days, they could not talk about Eli. Then, they were invited to Roderick and Anna's home. They had never forgotten the calm, dignified way in which Anna had spoken to them, at their first meeting, about the loss of her parents and her experiences in Bergen-Belsen. It had moved and inspired them. Though enervated by grief, they attempted to draw on that inspiration now.

It took them a little time. When Anna opened her front door to them and put her arms around Farah, and Roderick shook Yusuf's hand firmly as he steered him into the living room of the cottage, Farah broke down and stopped weeping only when she became aware of having dampened Anna's dress with her tears.

'Oh, I'm so sorry, look at me. I've made you wet. I'm sorry.'

'It's nothing, Farah. Come, sit down. I'll make some tea for us.' Anna took Farah's jacket and indicated an armchair.

'Or would you prefer a drop of whisky?' Roderick's question was directed at Yusuf but he turned his glance towards Farah, with an inclusive gesture.

'No, tea's fine,' said Yusuf. Farah shook her head. 'Is Belinda here?' she asked anxiously.

'No,' said Roderick. 'She's looking after the children.'

'How are they... how are they coping?' asked Yusuf.

'They're doing well. They have been seeing a bereavement counsellor. A very nice lady who specialises in helping children.'

Farah suppressed a sob and Yusuf hurriedly passed her a tissue. Anna then reappeared carrying a large tray with a teapot, cups and saucers, milk, sugar, spoons and a large central plate piled high with tea-cakes.

Yusuf broke the silence. 'It's so hard,' he said simply.

'I know.' Roderick managed to combine verbal economy with a naturally sympathetic tone.

'I feel a little ashamed that my feelings all seem to be directed towards myself,' said Yusuf. 'But I can't help it. I keep thinking about how much I miss Eli and feel guilty for not appreciating him enough, appreciating what a loving, creative boy he was. I keep thinking, if I had been a more understanding father, this wouldn't have happened.'

'It's natural to feel like that, I'm sure,' said Anna, with a renewed and sharp sense of her own, much earlier loss. 'There is so much that I wanted to say to my mother that has had to remain unsaid. I wanted to reassure her that I loved her. I felt that she believed I loved my father more. I was certainly more in tune with him but I adored them both equally, both separately and, especially, as a couple. They were so in love.'

'Eli was so young. Such a waste.' Farah was looking down as she spoke, at the cup of tea and the plate bearing two tea-cakes that Anna had placed before her on the large coffee table. Then Farah raised her eyes towards her husband. 'I've much more cause to feel guilty than you have, Yusuf.'

'No you haven't. I think maybe both of us could have been more understanding.'

'Maybe so,' Farah conceded. 'But would it have prevented... After all, he was so happy with Belinda and he still... I don't know? I just can't understand it.' Turning to Anna, she asked: 'How is Belinda?'

'Quite well, considering the situation. She is a strong young woman. She has to be, for the girls. If anything, she seems to have gained strength in proportion to Sarah and Emily's needs.'

'Those poor girls,' Farah sighed. 'We couldn't have wished for sweeter, cleverer grandchildren.'

'And children,' added Anna. 'They were a life force together those two, Eli and Belinda. That's what makes this so difficult.'

'I agree that guilt is a natural reaction,' said Roderick after the others had fallen silent. 'But it is unproductive. We all have to help Belinda, Sarah and Emily but also support each other now. And honour Eli's memory. He was a wonderful man.'

'Roderick's right,' said Farah, trying to create an air of determination. 'We have to help one another.'

'You haven't touched your cake, Farah. Have some,' Anna urged. 'It's lovely with a cup of tea.'

'Eat—always the Jewish solution,' Farah said, smiling for the first time in well over two weeks.

Anna could not help but bridle inwardly at the phrase, 'Jewish solution', but the atmosphere had eased and they passed a couple of relatively agreeable hours, even managing to move on to other subjects.

Meanwhile, Belinda shored up her children's lives by day and cried herself to sleep at night. She returned to work and they to school as soon as they felt ready. All three females were united in wanting to restore life's momentum. Sarah said it: 'It's what Daddy would want.'

A few weeks later, Yusuf and Farah went to the synagogue on Yom Kippur. As the service approached its conclusion—'avenge before our eyes the blood of thy servants that hath been shed'—Farah collapsed and had to be carried out. An ambulance was called and she was admitted to hospital not having eaten for a great many more than the twenty-five hours constituting the Day of Atonement fast—and not having ceased thinking about her late, lost son for much longer than that.

She never recovered. Yusuf found himself at Hoop Lane Cemetery in profound mourning for the second time in a little over two months. He was told that Farah had suffered sudden cardiac arrest, probably the result of self-imposed starvation. Yusuf believed the cause was much more obvious. It was grief.

In the spring of 1991, Leah and David and their children moved into Yusuf's house and he moved into Rivke's old flat. In the summer of that year, a tombstone-setting ceremony was held at Eli's grave in Hoop Lane, at which Belinda recited Shakespeare's Sonnet 27. Afterwards, distressed, she accepted her parents' offer to go home with them to Esher and stay overnight.

She continued to work hard at the publishing house and tried to be less reliant on Deborah, feeling disappointed and guilty that their relationship had in essence returned to its former patient-therapist status but without the fees. Anna and Roderick helped by regularly looking after Sarah and Emily, who stayed with them during half-term. Belinda tentatively began to rebuild her social life with the odd meal or coffee with Leah or Jasmine, a work colleague.

In September, she put the Alexandra Park house up for sale. When the estate agent arrived with the first two prospective buyers, Belinda turned them away and told the agent that she had changed her mind. Over the next three years, Belinda spent her time trying to be both calm and active at the same time. She kept a diary—in which Eli's name seemed to appear on almost every other page—became more engaged with her work, helped an increasingly frail Yusuf with his accounts, and saw a lot of her parents.

'I have kept my promise at last.'

One Sunday afternoon in February 1995, with his wife, daughter and granddaughters gathered around him in the drawing room of the Esher cottage, Roderick Vane's face betrayed both affection and a sense of achievement as he started to reveal to Anna what his gift to her would be on her seventieth birthday that April.

Belinda and her girls, who were in on the secret, were smiling in anticipation as Roderick tried to appear composed while, on the inside, experiencing a turbulent mixture of nervousness, apprehension, pride and excitement.

'What do you mean?' Anna asked, wrinkling her brow in an expression of intelligent curiosity. 'What promise?'

'For your birthday, darling.'

'I don't recall you making a promise for my birthday.'

'I didn't make it for this coming birthday, or for any other birthday in particular. But I did make the promise. A long time ago.'

'How long ago?'

'Fifty years ago, in 1945. It wasn't tied to your birthday or any other special date but I felt that your seventieth is a perfect time to honour it.'

Anna looked at her smiling daughter and granddaughters. 'Are you all in on this mystery, you crafty lot? Is anyone going to tell me what this is all about?'

'I have booked a trip for all of us—a ten-day trip that includes your birthday,' said Roderick. 'To Budapest.'

'Oh, Roderick,' Anna said, placing one hand on her chest, her mouth open as if to pronounce a second 'Oh'.

'Are you all right, Grandma?' Emily asked, stepping forward and helping Anna on to the sofa.

'I don't know what to say,' Anna said as she sat up, perching on the edge of the sofa, before looking across fondly at her husband, daughter and granddaughters and repeating herself: 'You crafty lot! Roderick, I thought I said I wanted a really quiet seventieth birthday. But, how wonderful of you. It's going to be hard...'

'I know it is, but—'

'—it will be very special.' Anna interrupted Roderick as he took her hand. 'It is, I think... necessary. Are we really going? All of us?'

'Yes, all five of us. It will be special,' he agreed. 'And I have already begun a little research—with the help of our brilliant daughter. I have been in touch with the brand new Jewish community centre in Budapest. I spoke to a nice young woman who told me, in perfect English, that we will just miss their Purim festivities, which are apparently something extraordinary.'

'*Purim* festivities,' Anna exclaimed. 'That's what they do in Budapest these days? My God, I feel quite disorientated. Purim. It's just a word to me now. This was a time when we dressed up at school to celebrate some ancient Jewish victory over a tyrant. I'm not sure whether that now feels very appropriate or very inappropriate. It's one or the other. Or perhaps both.'

'I have even made an appointment to go and see somebody there,' said Roderick. 'They are also putting us in touch with another office—I think at the main synagogue—where they keep all kinds of official records, about the community, survivors and so on.'

Anna flung her arms around Roderick, and Belinda and her daughters joined in the noisy embrace.

Two months later, on the morning of 22 April 1995, their plane took off from Heathrow airport. It was the day before Anna's birthday, which, as she never tired of telling her English neighbours in Esher, was on St George's Day.

Anna, Roderick, Belinda and the girls stayed in the Kempinski Hotel Corvinus, near Dohany Street Synagogue and not far from Anna's old school. Once they had settled in and changed, they set out for Dembinszky Street. Anna walked along the street with her arms around Sarah and Emily.

'I am going to show you where I spent my childhood,' she told them. 'And where your great-grandma played the piano every day and your great-grandpa practised medicine and taught me so much. I expect to see a few ghosts,' she added, squeezing her granddaughters tightly. 'And so I rely on you two to protect me.'

When they arrived at the block, they halted on the pavement outside, Anna looking up and shaking her head. 'So much has changed,' she said, as Roderick took a couple of photographs.

'Shall we knock on the door of your old apartment?' he asked.

Once more, Anna shook her head. 'No,' she said quietly. 'I don't feel strong enough for that.' And, after a pause: 'Let's go. Let's sample some Hungarian coffee.'

On the evening of Anna's birthday, 23 April, they ate a celebratory meal at the newly-opened Shiraz Restaurant. Roderick had developed a taste for Middle-Eastern food, having been introduced to it by Farah in sumptuous fashion all those years earlier in London. And when they found the Shiraz, which served Persian dishes, Anna insisted they go there since the menu sounded so similar to Haroun-style Iraqi food.

At Szalbocs Street, they made their way to the site of the former Jewish hospital and, as she stood outside it, Anna shook her head more vigorously than before as if drying her tears in the breeze. The building was still there, no longer a hospital but the faculty of health and sciences of Semmelweis University.

'I'd forgotten that great tree in the courtyard,' she said with feeling, shaking her head again as she stared at the giant old plane tree, which at that moment represented Anna's childhood. 'This,' she announced to her daughter and granddaughters, 'is where I was born, where I was admitted with diphtheria when I was a small child, where your very clever grandpa—and, to you two girls, great-grandpa—Chaim worked and taught me a lot about medicine, and where I met my first boyfriend to whom, until now, I never gave a thought once I had met'—holding Roderick's hand and smiling at Belinda—'your father and'—pointing towards Sarah and Emily—'your grandfather, Grandpa, standing right here with his camera.'

Roderick's camera played a substantial part in that Budapest holiday, from which they would come home to England with almost three hundred photographic images to reinforce the vivid memories that leapt over the decades of Anna's history.

'We shall rival the famous Haroun family album,' Anna said as yet another shot was taken.

At first, Anna refused to speak Hungarian but, once she began to understand what the people she encountered in the streets and the shops were saying, she consciously embarked upon a process of mental excavation to rediscover something of her native language. It was a process that was rapidly accelerated once her trivial conversations relating to restaurant menus and requests for directions were superseded by more meaningful connections.

Anna had made two or three attempts to make contact with Frida after arriving and then settling in Britain. She and Roderick both tried hard, through military connections, to invite her to their wedding. But the trail always went cold in Hungary. This time, however, not only were the Hungarian authorities more willing to help but Roderick and particularly Belinda were more forceful and determined.

As a result of Roderick's initial approach to the Budapest Jewish community centre and Belinda's energetic research many weeks before the departure for Budapest, sometimes involving long, expensive telephone calls, they had gained access to a list of residents called Goldberg in the Hungarian capital. It was not a long list and no one was called Frida. But Belinda was not deterred and started to get in touch with the Goldbergs of Budapest, one-by-one. And her tenacity eventually paid off.

One of her calls was answered by a Rabbi Goldberg, who spoke English. He told Belinda he had a distant cousin, with whom he had unfortunately lost touch, whose mother, he thought, had been in both

Auschwitz and Bergen-Belsen. He could not recall his cousin's mother's name, but, as he was sure that this cousin did not speak English, agreed to try to find her himself.

'You realise,' he emphasised to Belinda, 'that I have no way of knowing whether or not my distant cousin's mother is your mother's old friend—and even if it turns out that she is your Frida, she may no longer be alive. I don't know but I will certainly try to find out.'

This exchange took place on 15 April, precisely a week before the family's departure. On the day before they were due to leave, Rabbi Goldberg reported back to Belinda. 'My dear lady,' he said, somewhat formally as though he was addressing her from his pulpit. 'I have news.'

And then, more warmly: 'And not only news but a telephone number. Two telephone numbers! One is that of my cousin—my second cousin as I explained—but she does not speak English. The other number is of her mother, Frida Kremer—who does speak some English and, you will like to know, was born Frida Goldberg and, with her mother, was taken into Auschwitz in October 1944. She is very much looking forward to hearing from you, and especially your mother, and insists that you visit her as soon as you can once you have arrived in Budapest.'

Belinda had time for one quick call to Frida before leaving to join Sarah and Emily to stay at her parents' house overnight. From this call, Belinda discovered that Frida was herself leaving with her husband for a couple of days away at Lake Balaton.

In broken English, Frida extended an invitation to Belinda, her parents and daughters for the day after Frida's return. 'I know it sounds crazy,' she said to Belinda, 'but, even after all these years, it is painful for me to wait for these two days to see my beautiful friend Anna. And you, my dear; you must be a beautiful and happy person to be the daughter of two such wonderful people as Anna and Roderick.'

The third day of Anna's birthday holiday was one of extreme but contrasting emotions. In the morning, they attended the offices of the Great Synagogue in Dohanyi Street. Here, in the course of a meeting of almost two hours over photocopied sheets from the community archives and burial records, Anna learned that her Uncle David, Aunt Rachel and their two sons—her cousins Sandor and Miklos—had all been murdered in Auschwitz, as had her Uncle Mordy, and her friend Eva Kaller along with her entire family. Anna's grandmother—her mother's mother Hana—survived the war but died in her ghetto apartment in

1946. There was no record of Aunt Ruth or Anna's other cousins, Ibolya and Judit—nor of her old boyfriend Imre Handler.

Later, in the afternoon, at the community centre, Anna was informed that Aunt Ruth, aged 100, was living in an old people's home just outside the city and that her cousin Judit was also alive. When she telephoned Judit, she learned that Judit's sister Ibolya had been in Bergen-Belsen during the period that Anna was there but had died before the camp was liberated.

The unmarried and childless Judit told her: 'We tried to trace you but gave up. We knew you and your parents had been sent to Auschwitz and I suppose we didn't want to hear of yet more deaths.'

Then, in the evening, came the reunion with Frida.

Frida's husband opened the door of their apartment. 'Good evening, I am Nandor Kremer,' he said, greeting the visitors with old-world politeness. As he waved them in, an inside door across the exotically carpeted lobby was opened and an elegant, matronly woman stepped out.

Though dramatically fatter than when Anna and Roderick had last seen her—how could she not have been?—Frida was instantly recognisable. Her hair was now white, and piled extravagantly high upon her head, but her dark, intelligent eyes transmitted recognition and delight. Her still perfectly shaped mouth opened just enough to allow a deep sigh to emerge as a prelude to a sonorous exclamation of a single word: 'Anna!'

For many ticking seconds, no further words followed Frida's cry as she and Anna fell into each other's arms, simultaneously yielding control and offering support.

At dinner, Nandor, a retired engineer, described in halting English the history and intricacies of Budapest's Chain Bridge while Frida summarised her career as a museum curator. Roderick and Anna rehearsed their tourist itinerary and the two teenage girls politely answered questions about their school life and Sarah's stated intention to study law at university.

They all ate their way through nourishing portions of braised goose liver, followed by sausages with potatoes, onions and cabbage. The two teenage girls excused themselves from the further indulgence of almond cake with lemon tea but remained at the table as the talk moved inexorably towards the past.

'Do you know about how your grandmama and I were friends?' Frida asked Sarah and Emily, while flicking her gaze at Belinda and Anna for acknowledgement of the weight of this question—and for their approval of her asking it.

'Because you were prisoners in Belsen, the Nazi concentration camp, which was where my grandparents met,' said Sarah, adding, in the same assured, adult tone: 'So there was something good that came out of that evil place.'

'Yes, my darling, you are so right,' said Frida, turning to Anna to remark in Hungarian: 'How sweet she is, a sweet clever child.'

Anna's reply was also in Hungarian: 'Not so much a child—a wise young woman.'

Frida turned again to Sarah and produced a smile that encompassed Emily, too. 'And,' she said to both girls, 'we have not seen each other again until this night—the best of all our nights, because you two girls are here with your mother.'

As they continued to eat, drink and talk—in English with asides in Hungarian—Anna was reminded of the first meal at Farah and Yusuf's home. Now, as then, she felt her apprehension melt surprisingly quickly. She experienced the same sense of release, of talking freely, of inner celebration.

Though, when the memory of Bergen-Belsen was gently introduced in the shape of the young, shy Roderick acting as 'postman' to both Anna and Frida, Anna's now elderly husband could not prevent his own mind throwing up the persistent image of the Nazi youth whom he had killed and the face of that boy's female victim on the ground beneath him.

Sarah and Emily were both relieved to see and hear their grandmother laugh at the mention of her days in the makeshift hospital where she first met Roderick. The girls themselves, together with Belinda, laughed, too, as they recalled, for Frida and Nandor, some of Eli's endearing actions and words.

Frida spoke proudly of her two sons, passing round photographs of the medical scientist in Israel and the theatre director in New York, as well as her daughter—the university teacher and distant cousin whom Rabbi Goldberg had contacted on Belinda's behalf—and her various grandsons and granddaughters. She and Nandor promised to visit England, not only to see Roderick and Anna but also, in Nandor's case, to see the Clifton Suspension Bridge in Bristol and, in Frida's, the British Museum in London.

'I am fan of Isambard Kingdom Brunel,' Nandor said, beaming.

'I cannot get used to such lavish beauty and knowledge that we can see after all that was taken from us,' said Frida, seeming to understand and speak more English by the minute.

'We certainly witnessed the worst of mankind,' said Anna.

'But,' said Frida, 'we had the strength, the will—'

'The luck!' Anna interrupted her friend.

'And, yes, of course, the luck. But you and I had the ability to look forward to a time beyond. A time when we would talk about the things that we suffered and the things that we saw.'

'We saw more than enough for one lifetime. And what is a lifetime? So many lives were cut short.'

'And some were ended when they had barely begun. But there was nothing we could do about it then and nothing we can do about it now.'

'Talking now,' said Anna, 'I feel a great release. I can now think of Belsen not as the place of my suffering but as the place where our friendship deepened and where I met the love of my life. I have no need to torture myself, or try to replicate the shock, or feel guilty, or try to comprehend the barbarity, the evil. Or to feel any regret about my behaviour or any of my actions—or my reactions to the horrors that we have witnessed.'

'This is just as I feel.' Frida endorsed Anna's words. 'Our strength as human beings shows in our survival. Our lives after war are a kind of defiance. Just living instead of dying shows a spirit—*Fékezhetetlen*.'

'Indomitable!' Anna translated.

'Do you remember,' Roderick asked, 'the service that the British clergyman, Reverend Leslie Hardman, held in the camp on the first Friday evening after liberation? "The children of Israel liveth," he said. I've never forgotten that.'

Anna and Frida arranged to go out together for coffee and pastries, just the two of them, while Anna's family was still in Budapest. Then, as the visitors were making ready to leave, Anna said quietly to Frida: 'We always said we would talk about the woman with the dead baby.'

'I think we just did,' said Frida.

The two women remained in correspondence with each other over the following months but their next meeting, which took place in the summer of 1996, a year after their reunion in Budapest, was neither in London to visit the British Museum, nor in Bristol to see Clifton Suspension Bridge.

It arose out of a comment made by Frida in a letter to Anna on 2 January 1996. 'Dearest Anna,' Frida wrote, 'I wish you and your lovely family a happy new year. I always find the opening of the year difficult because it is a time when I feel the wheels of history turning. All the events of the world and all the periods of my life merge. Everybody seems so breakable. Everything seems so contingent. And of course these feelings bring back our experiences. I don't know if you have similar thoughts but now that we have renewed our friendship I believe that I can gain the strength to cease becoming so *tébolyodott*—unhinged— and, even at this late stage, begin to live properly.'

In her reply, Anna described her own feelings differently. 'As I mentioned when we had coffee and cakes together in April, I have tried several times to write down my story. I did make a start almost as soon as I reached England all those years ago, strengthened by the happiness given to me by Roderick and his family. But I somehow couldn't keep it going and so I put my scribblings away in a drawer. I think at first that this was part of my determination to put it all behind me, particularly once my parents' deaths were confirmed.

'Then, once Belinda had met Eli, her future husband, I tried again. It was a kind of therapy. But, as their romance blossomed, and they married, and had Sarah and Emily, all of that was therapy enough. I was capable of feeling great joy.

'So I put my notes away again. I did not destroy them, I still have them but now they are a kind of souvenir, the end of a chapter not the beginning of a book. But of course what you and I went through will always be a part of me and I do feel a little guilt that I may have simply shelved it and may need instead to exorcise—*kiűz*—it. So I have a suggestion to help us both.'

Anna's suggestion was fulfilled six months later when she and Roderick, Frida and Nandor, met in Hanover, in northern Germany and from there went to visit the site of the Bergen-Belsen concentration camp.

The two couples walked over the site, both holding hands and not speaking. There was no sign, nothing to indicate the location of the women's camp in which Anna and Frida had been incarcerated. There were some unmarked graves and a large memorial, a symbol. After a while, Anna and Frida told the two men that they wanted to explore the area alone together. Nandor and Roderick went into the museum by the entrance to the site and then to look for a place where they could have coffee. The women were gone for nearly two hours.

'It was like being in a dream,' was how Anna described her return to Bergen-Belsen to Belinda once she was back in Britain. 'The place is barely recognisable. It is now covered with trees and grass. Hardly a trace of the buildings remains and there are now just clean and solemn memorial structures. The sun was shining; it was a beautiful day. But Frida and I both felt that there was still something poisonous in the air. We struggled at first to get our bearings but gradually we worked out—or believed we worked out—the layout, where the huts and other buildings had been in our time.'

After a pause, Anna went on: 'Frida and I specifically searched out the spot where, one day, a skeletal woman on the point of death handed her very young child to me. She dropped dead at my feet as I was holding her baby...' Anna closed her eyes and paused again before speaking.

'What did you do?' Belinda asked. 'How could you care for a child in that place?'

'We placed him—it was a boy—in his mother's arms. He had been dead for probably a couple of days and his poor, delirious mother hadn't realised.'

'Oh, Ma,' Belinda cried in a surge of sympathy.

Anna, encircled in her daughter's arms, continued in a cracked voice: 'We believe we found the spot, now grown over. All the time, as the breeze blew through the trees I felt that I could hear voices. It was as if I was only half-awake. But afterwards, thank God, Frida and I had each other. We stood for ages where we imagined we had laid the mother and baby, unburied, above ground, but together. Frida and I hugged and cried. It was quite emotional.'

'"Quite emotional" sounds very English.'

'Oh no. It was very emotional. And Hungarian. And Jewish.'

After the Bergen-Belsen visit, and in the light of Anna's continuing recollections to Belinda of her early life, a cloud seemed to lift from the

Vane and Haroun families. In the autumn of that same year of 1996, Frida and Nandor did make their sight-seeing trip to England and it was a happy time without the unstated pain and regret that was just below the surface in their reunion at Frida's Budapest apartment.

Yusuf was persuaded to come out of his shell and meet the visitors from Budapest over an exquisite dinner, with a lot of laughter and music, at the Vanes' Esher cottage.

Later, in December, almost six-and-a-half years after Eli's death—Belinda agreed to be introduced to a divorced male friend of Leah's, a lawyer called Jonathan Henry. He took her to a matinee performance of *Guys and Dolls* at the National Theatre and then for dinner at an Italian restaurant in Soho.

To her surprise, Belinda found the show exhilarating—she couldn't wait to buy a recording and play it to Anna—and Jonathan's company perfectly agreeable, which was more than she had anticipated. They continued to see each other once or twice a week for a number of months until one evening the following April, when they met after work in a bar in West Hampstead near Jonathan's flat, and he mentioned that he had booked a table at a local Indian restaurant.

They chatted happily about their working day—Jonathan had been in court and Belinda had spent the afternoon with an irascible novelist—and it wasn't until they began walking towards the restaurant that Belinda was seized with a sense of foreboding. They turned from the side-road where Jonathan had parked his car into a main road and it took Belinda a few seconds to realise they were in Maida Vale.

'There,' said Jonathan, with an outstretched arm. 'It's that little place over there. It's really good.'

It was their restaurant, hers and Eli's, the one where they had been for their first evening out. She stopped, abruptly, on the pavement. 'I'm sorry,' she told Jonathan. 'I'm not feeling well.'

'What's the matter?' he asked, concerned and slightly affronted.

'I'm really, really, honestly, sorry...' And, as if on cue, a taxi was approaching from the Marble Arch direction and she ran forward with her arm held up high to hail it.

'But, Belinda, you don't have to get a taxi. I'll take you home.'

'No, please, Jonathan. Please don't worry. It's well out of your way. I'll be fine.'

'I'll call you tomorrow.'

'Yes, fine, of course. I'm really sorry. I'll explain.'

Even after six years, Belinda was clearly not ready to consider a close relationship with another man. When she arrived home, she soaked herself in a hot, scented bath and took herself to bed with the photo album of the 1986 family holiday in Devon, on the cover of which was a picture of her and Eli laughing—she in her straw hat and he in a nautical, blue and white, horizontally striped T-shirt.

Over the next few years, Belinda went on the occasional dinner or theatre date with one of a handful of men introduced to her by Leah, Jasmine or somebody encountered through her work—and remained on friendly terms with Jonathan—but never felt the full force of significant attraction.

'Eli is too much in my system,' she told Deborah, who had become such a close friend that Belinda found it strange to recall that she had once been her therapist. 'The years have gone so quickly and I still feel unable to contemplate love. It's not that I am brooding on the past and what might have been but, after the shattering of what seemed to be our paradise, I am still somewhat wary. That's not to say I am unhappy. In fact, in some ways, I feel surprisingly happy—as a mother, daughter, friend and, increasingly, calm human being. I am more concerned about becoming smug than being lonely.'

She was also preoccupied with the growing up of her daughters, whose similar, feet-on-the-ground temperaments continually amazed and thrilled her, given the anxieties she and Eli had experienced in their own roads to adulthood and beyond.

The main serious difference between the two girls lay in their career paths. Sarah marked one out early on, studying law at King's College, London, while Emily came through three years reading history at Cambridge without any definite professional inclinations.

When Eli died, Belinda had feared that Sarah and Emily would find life fraught with unfair and insurmountable misfortune. Yet not only did they both show great powers of resilience but, like their grandmother Anna—and, Belinda recalled, their Haroun great-grandmother Rivke—their attitude to life, rooted in patient calmness and compounded of humour and intelligence, was often inspiring to those around them.

One person clearly attracted to these qualities in Sarah was the son of two Jewish professional musicians, a young graduate of the Royal

College of Music. Richard Lewis was an accomplished pianist whom Sarah met when he was playing jazz at a party held by a fellow King's law student. Like Eli, Richard loved poetry; unlike Eli, his sunny disposition was rarely darkened by clouds. Belinda was delighted when he and Sarah announced their intention to marry.

Although her emotional response to this news was partly driven by the realisation that Eli's absence at the wedding would be overwhelming, and that there would be no sonnet written to their daughter's happiness, Belinda was by now at ease over the loss of her husband. As she expressed it to Deborah, in a nerve-calming conversation on the eve of Sarah's wedding: 'all of us, including my dear father-in-law Yusuf, who absolutely dotes on his grandchildren, can now think of Eli, above all, as a provider of happy memories.'

It was for this reason that Belinda's experience of her elder daughter's wedding—a much more modest affair than her own had been—was her happiest in eleven years.

A few weeks later, Belinda disclosed to Leah that she was thinking of marking the thirteenth anniversary of Eli's death, which would fall just under two years later in the summer of 2003, in some special way.

'Your dad tells me that thirteen is a significant number in Judaism,' Belinda explained. 'I have been in touch with the rabbi and the authorities at Hoop Lane about having a ceremony at the cemetery. I'm not quite sure what form this will take but it will be as meaningful as we can make it. Even my atheist mum is excited by the idea. Sarah is already getting her teeth into it.'

And, indeed, after discussing suitable prayers with the ever-sympathetic Rabbi Ezra Lobatto, Sarah Lewis née Haroun tackled the burial committee, for she had devised a radical core that would give the ceremony meaning.

Eli's grave was at the end of a row at the Hoop Lane cemetery a yard or so from the path. Sarah's plan was to dig a small trench in the area between the path and the grave and in it bury a strongbox containing a number of documents that reflected Eli's life and the loving connections between him and his family. Some burial-committee members were reluctant to allow this at first but Sarah showed great determination.

'I think she is trying to emulate her grandmother,' said Belinda.

'She is going to be a great lawyer,' said Roderick.

'And mother,' added Richard proudly.

So it was that, in July 2003—precisely one hundred and twenty-five years after Moss Haroun opened a small shop in Baghdad, and a hundred years after Chaim Weisz was born in Budapest—a plaque was placed flat on the ground alongside the grave of Eli Abraham Haroun, husband of Belinda and father of Sarah and Emily, in Hoop Lane Cemetery in Golders Green, north London, marking the place where the documents were buried, bearing the words, in white lettering on a black granite background:

> In memory of Eli Haroun
> (31 March 1948 – 20 July 1990; Adar II 20, 5708 – Tammuz 27, 5750)
> From his girls, 'Love Upon Love'

'Love Upon Love' was a reference to a collection of Eli's poetry, printed and photocopied, which was buried, within the box, beneath the plaque. These were unpublished poems that Eli wrote in a notebook. Most were dedicated simply 'To Belinda' but on the cover of the notebook—a replica of which lay with the copied poems—Eli had written:

> To my girl
> Who bore my girls
> Beauty on beauty
> Love upon love

Also placed in the box was a copy of the photograph of Farah and Yusuf that Eli had taken and Rivke had placed inside the Haroun album; a laminated copy of Shakespeare's Sonnet 27 along with a copy of *A Journey in My Head*; and, also laminated, a letter to Eli, dated the same day as the memorial plaque and written by his elder daughter.

9

20 July 2003
Golders Green, London
Sarah Haroun Lewis to Eli Haroun

Dear Daddy,

All these years, Mum thought that Emily and I believed your death was an accident. We always knew that it could not have been. But she wanted to protect us, bless her, until this month. It is exactly thirteen years since you left us and here I am, a first-class honours graduate, a qualified lawyer, and pregnant with your first grandchild. So Mum decided to show us, after thirteen years—half of my life—your last letter. She always planned to do so one day. After all, it was addressed to all of us.

I want you to know, Daddy, how proud I am of you. And that I miss you and do not blame you for leaving us. I know that you meant it as an act of kindness. We all miss you—Mum, Emily and myself. And this little person growing inside me, be it a boy or a girl, will be told all about you and be proud of you, too.

He or she will learn about how you used to tell us stories that kept us awake way past bedtime instead of sending us to sleep. How you loved to dance and how you could always make us laugh, especially Mum.

I am so proud of the way that you defied Grandpa and Grandma Haroun because you loved Mum so much (I wouldn't have been here if you hadn't! Nor would the little person waiting and growing inside me) but you also understood how they meant well, how they loved their tradition and only wanted the best for you. And they soon realised that Mum was the best and were always the kindest of grandparents to Emily and me.

How lucky we were to grow up in a house so filled with love, and in such a loving family made up of such brave, defiant and extraordinary people. What a magnificent couple Grandma and Grandpa Vane are. What an amazingly poignant and romantic

255

way it was that they met. How dashing a soldier Grandpa Roderick was. Since learning how it happened I have milked them for the details. And Mum loves to tell us how Grandma brandished her tattoo at the man at the Beth Din and made him shrink into a tiny mouse-like creature. Again, what courage Grandma showed to survive the camps and to deal with the loss of her parents. And what an exceptional parents-in-law/son-in-law relationship you had with her and the lovely Roderick.

And then what about all those Baghdadi tales (and food) flowing from the Harouns, especially those stories that your Grandma Rivke used to tell you and that you in turn told us?

What wondrous stuff we are made of!

Though I still miss you so much and always will, it was in more ways than one that you gave me life. And now I am pregnant. I have been married for two years to my lovely man, Richard, who is a pianist (like great-grandmother Sarah). Now I will give life. And I am strong—and so is Emily (who by the way, is in love—with an Iranian-Jewish boy! She couldn't find an Iraqi Jew?). I feel so happy. We and our children-to-be are so lucky. Nobody could have better parents—and grandparents—than you and Mum.

My darling Daddy, you were wrong about being unable to inspire Emily and me. Nobody could have inspired us more than you did. With your sensitivity and intelligence. With your generosity. With your refusal to be dull. Above all, with your boundless love.

Your everlastingly adoring daughter,
Sarah

Acknowledgements

A number of people helped to make this book come about. Hospitality and generosity came in abundance from the Cambridge contingent— Stephen Brown, Anne Garvey and Caiti Grove; Sandra Smith; Simon Baron-Cohen; Richard Serjeantson and Daryl Burchell. Tony Rocca and Mira Shamash were not only supportive but gave me a copy of Mira's mother Violette Shamash's book, *Memories of Eden*, a fabulous treasury of the components and atmosphere of old Baghdadi-Jewish life, to which I am grateful for so much, specifically including the tale of Eliyahu, a victim to whom, it was said, thieves returned their spoils. Miriam and Rafael Halahmy gave valuable assistance and were especially informative about Iraqi-Arabic terms. In Budapest, Irisz Gonda carried out assiduous research. Amos Witztum was a patient, encouraging reader and helped with Hebrew. Also encouraging was Moris (Mousa) Farhi who read a very early manuscript. And, last but not least, all at Quartet, particularly my wise and worldly publisher Naim Attallah, and James Pulford, an editor of true literary sensibility.